Jacky Gillott was born in 1939 and began her writing career on the *Sheffield Telegraph* in Yorkshire. Since then she has worked in the arts, news and current affairs divisions of the BBC, was the first woman reporter on ITN's News at Ten programme, has contributed to *The Sunday Times*, *Punch*, *The Listener*, *Nova* and *Cosmopolitan* and regularly reviews novels for *The Times*. She is currently involved with the BBC Radio 4 programme, Kaleidoscope, and lives in Somerset. One of this country's leading novelists, Jacky Gillott is the author of *War Baby*, *A True Romance* and *Crying Out Loud*. Her most recent book, *Providence Place*, is her account of the many animals at her West Country home.

Also by Jacky Gillott

A True Romance
Crying Out Loud
Salvage
War Baby

Non-fiction
Providence Place
For Better For Worse

Jacky Gillott

The Head Case

A PANTHER BOOK

GRANADA
London Toronto Sydney New York

Published by Granada Publishing Limited
in 1980

ISBN 0 586 05088 4

First published in Great Britain by
Hodder and Stoughton 1979
Copyright © Jacky Gillott 1979

Granada Publishing Limited
Frogmore, St Albans, Herts AL2 2NF
and
3 Upper James Street, London W1R 4BP
866 United Nations Plaza, New York, NY 10017, USA
117 York Street, Sydney, NSW 2000, Australia
100 Skyway Avenue, Rexdale, Ontario, M9W 3A6, Canada
PO Box 84165, Greenside, 2034 Johannesburg, South Africa
61 Beach Road, Auckland, New Zealand

Set, printed and bound in Great Britain by
Cox & Wyman Ltd, Reading
Set in Intertype Plantin

Granada ®
Granada Publishing ®

For J.F.

Enter Tamino, pursued by serpent
                    (opening of *Die Zauberflöte*)

While you here do snoring lie,
Open-eyed conspiracy
His time doth take.
If of life you have a care,
Shake off slumber and beware.
Awake! Awake!
                    (Ariel's song to Gonzalo, *The Tempest*)

Part One

LUGHNASA

I

Six months after the death of Edmund Pike (late proprietor of the Sunnybank Guest House), his widow Bella woke early, rose promptly, breathed deeply and took a fresh grip of herself.

'White rabbits!' she cried as she tied the belt of her pink dressing-gown with unaccustomed firmness – it was, as she had suddenly realized, the first day of August. It was also, though she did *not* realize it, the feast day of Lughnasa, the day when propitiations for a good harvest would once have been offered. Her ignorance of this obscure and long-forgotten fact was so widely shared that it could not have been anything more than coincidence which made her feel, on waking, that this day was different: that this day marked the unofficial end of her mourning period. That this day, new energies should charge her marrow. She must be *doing*.

The curtains, already half-parted to admit the brilliant early-morning light, were flung more eagerly open, and Bella Pike inhaled a yet deeper breath of the good salt air that had been considered, by eighteenth-century visitors to the town, a tonic to rival the spa waters of other fashionably healthy resorts.

Although the sea could not – except by climbing to the attic floor and manoeuvring the head carefully – be seen from Sunnybank, something in the sharpness of the light, in the ringing clarity of sounds that rose from Tidmouth's steep and cobbled streets, intimated immediately that this was a seaside town.

Bella lifted the drape with one finger and gazed with new-found pleasure at the mottled slope of the roofs sliding down to the harbour. Clamorous gulls wheeled, a distant white, above the unseen fishing boats. The catch was coming in. Such as it was. Today, the fishing boats were mainly used for trips by holiday-makers who found an hour at sea was as much as they could endure without becoming either bored or ill.

Silently, Bella Pike prepared a list of things to do ... *Dear Edmund!*

Swiftly she dressed. How thin she had become! No ... *slim*. A new dress. A new hairstyle. Oh, many, many prospects! Mrs Pike became quite excited and ate a proper breakfast for a change. After washing up her plates and egg cup, she applied a lively lipstick to her mouth and, taking out her collecting boxes from a cupboard under the stairs, arranged them on window sills around the house.

On that first, bright day of August Bella Pike arranged for a course of driving lessons, called in at St Teresa's to check on the time of services, fixed a hair appointment, selected a Jack Russell puppy from the most recent litter of Mrs Chedzoy's bitch, put her name down for pottery classes in the autumn, and arranged for a man to come and alter the signboard.

By four o'clock the following afternoon, it read:

SUNNYBANK
Rooms to let
Reasonable terms
Prop: Mrs Bella Pike

Although she didn't specify, Mrs Pike hoped – quite reasonably – that she might have teachers as her tenants. Reasonably, because there was an unusual profusion of schools and other educational establishments in the vicinity, varying from progressive public schools where the pupils were encouraged to insult the staff to the sort of place where young women of rather vague ambition could be taught to type, cook to a *cordon bleu* standard, arrange a few twigs with great delicacy, and keep their own horses.

Teachers, it seemed to Bella Pike, belonged to a respectable profession. And in addition to their seriousness of purpose, they might well go away for long stretches in the holidays, either leaving her a retainer or permitting her the opportunity to double-let.

She had gone so far as to kneel in the cool of St Teresa's and actually pray for this outcome to her efforts, as well as lighting a candle for dear Edmund. Although her lapse had been of exceptional long-standing, perhaps because she had – without knowing it – observed more than one god on that August morning, her petitions were met with remarkable promptness.

It wasn't long before she was ringing her daughter Daphne to tell her of her good fortune.

* * *

Reggie, too, had felt the first day of August to be propitious.

His interview had taken place on that day.

A month had elapsed since. His opinions had suffered terrible swings of confidence since. But on that day he had felt this could be a completely new start. An end to the enervating limbo. The limbo had persisted since leaving Dorothy. This was partly Reggie's own fault. By renting a room only just around the corner from his wife (ex-wife) in the totally perverse hope of glimpsing Dorothy drive her wire chariot from the supermarket or wave down the Uxbridge bus in the manner of one who planned to ambush it, he still felt dumbly captive.

So on the first day of August, in response to an advertisement in *The Times Educational Supplement*, he had made the journey down to Tidmouth and found himself confronting the headmaster of Turtledown. A greying, but boyish-faced man, Garsington was head of the kind of prep. school Reggie thought he most abhorred. In fact it was the kind of school Dorothy most abhorred. This in itself had lent him the divine glee he needed to convince Garsington (and more astonishingly, himself) that he would be ideally cut out for the teaching post advertised. Garsington was half-way to conviction without Reggie's help. 'The education world has a dangerously self-narrowing effect, I'm afraid,' he had smiled, and then expanded on his policy of introducing members of the outside world into his staff. 'How useful and excellent,' he had confided, 'the experience of a man like yourself, Mr Morris, could be.' And Reggie, euphoric, nodded in vigorous endorsement.

Standing now outside Casterwich station, looking without much commitment for a taxi that would take him to Tidmouth he could think of nobody less suitable than himself for teaching small, fee-paying boys whatever subjects he had claimed to be conversant with. He shuddered over the ardent interest in literature and pre-history he had expressed to Garsington. The man couldn't have known much himself to be so quickly persuaded, and that was a comfort. A mathematician, Garsington, thank God. No mutual territory at all.

Reggie sighed, consulted his watch for lack of anything better to do and flushed a surprising scarlet.

He must have been mad!

*   *   *

Mad is not a word Reggie uses lightly: incorrectly, but not lightly. The upset of the past few months have made him feel intermittently unhinged. To retire early, to leave your wife, these are alarming steps for a man of small imaginative capacities in his mid-fifties. For a man whose life has been spent inside offices, committees, structures of every sort, whose habits in all respects but one (the fundamental one) have been conspicuously regular, such unshacklings are bound to intimate a temporary lunacy. Even the tiger, loosed from his cage, will think twice about bounding abroad.

However, Reggie did not wake up one morning and walk out. The process has been more gradual than he sometimes thinks.

*   *   *

After a lifetime in 'Monuments', the re-organization within the Department of the Environment had left him disgruntled. He had sulked and huffed for at least three years. He felt he had been overlooked, or, as he put it to Dorothy, 'undervalued'.

Dorothy had regarded him stonily and blown smoke rings through his threats to retire.

His anger had taken a more specific turn after finding a target in the Roman villa.

Involved in motorway planning for the Kent area, the Department had met fierce objections from 'Rescue' when their bulldozers rolled towards an exceptionally complex settlement. Adjusting direction a little, they had then encountered a particularly fine villa lying on the outskirts of the main settlement. By this time the Department had lost time, patience and money, and Reggie, undisguisedly jubilant, had taken the side of the 'Rescue' diggers. Discovering a precedent in which the Department itself had made a grant for a dig in Somerset 'to prevent further vandalism of the site', he used it to embarrass his superiors. 'Vandalism on a grand scale!' he had been heard to shout along the corridor on the floor above him.

Undoubtedly the Civil Service could have found ways of containing Reggie in its muter recesses, but the vision of destruction he now exultantly harboured drove him to take an ever greater interest in, first of all, the Roman remains, then in the idea of remains generally. Beneath the Roman settlement was found evidence of an earlier Iron Age dwelling and beneath that, who knows? Evidence of successive waves of destruction, each episode more far-reaching than the last (with the motorway representing a manic peak in civilized barbarity) wrought such a frenzy in Reggie that he resigned before a post with little opportunity for mischief could be devised for him.

Three months frittered away at home while Dorothy barged about on her own crusades had made Reggie conclude that what had been wrong all the time was his marriage. The vision of destruction was modified. He was no longer the destroyer but the destroyed. He became morbid. He dwelt on lost opportunities . . . His youth, which had never been fully experienced because of the war years . . . He had not even been sent abroad on active service, something that became, retrospectively, a further cause of resentment, although at the time he had privately been most thankful to kick his heels at Peover Hall in Cheshire . . . He thought of the women he had never had, of the places he had never seen, of the promotions that had failed to come his way. 'The trouble is,' Dorothy had remarked one day whilst rushing out of the house with anti-apartheid posters clasped to her bosom, 'you're such an unimaginative man!'

An unimaginative man!

Of all the barbs that had been exchanged over the years, this one, for some reason not immediately fathomable, this one rankled the most.

And what, thought Reggie, as a Post Office van pulled away from the pavement in front of him, to be replaced by another vehicle, and *what* had imagination got to do with it!

As he perfectly well knew, it had something to do with his being here on the pavement outside Casterwich station, about to embark on a new career as a schoolmaster in a part of the country quite foreign to him.

'Taxi?' inquired the driver of the cream Cortina.

'Thank you,' said Reggie, and began hauling his bags about in a useless sort of way.

Ha! It had taken imagination to make the break. It had taken imagination to persuade Garsington of his keen interest in the subjects advertised.

'Where to?' asked the driver who had removed Reggie's luggage from its owner's inconsequent grasp and stacked it neatly away.

'Er . . .' Reggie swallowed. 'Well, now,' he confessed, 'I don't have an *exact* address.'

Ezra (for that, as the taxi driver quickly made known, was his name) sorted Reggie out in no time. In the time, that is, it took to drive the nine miles from Casterwich to Tidmouth. The oddity of a man taking a job which was due to start in three days' time and neglecting to find anywhere to live did not trouble Ezra. He was a man of solutions. 'I know the very place,' he called out cheerfully as they climbed between the steep, burnt downs.

'That's excellent,' murmured Reggie, aghast at the emptiness of the countryside. It was all very well in paintings and things, but it made him nervous to think that people actually thrived in such space. They passed through two villages without any shops at all. He couldn't believe in any of it. Couldn't believe he was about to be a part of it himself. Which was why he hadn't brought himself to fix up lodgings: the entire undertaking was quite unreal.

Ezra was explaining his complicated relationship by marriage to the landlady he had in mind. Reggie followed none of it. Fortunately Ezra seemed to find his grunts and dislocated cries of 'Really!' perfectly friendly.

'Next year,' Garsington had said, 'some living-quarters should fall vacant within the school . . .' Next year, Reggie had thought dizzily . . . this year, next year, sometime . . . never.

Never. And here he was amongst the sunburnt fields.

To his great relief they gave way to some reassuringly suburban houses, a garage, little gardens dried out by the freakish summer, a general store, a newsagent's. At the top of the hill Ezra's gears groaned, and Reggie suddenly looked down and beyond to a great expanse of blue, marked by a thin and darker division of sea from sky. The taxi trundled downhill, sinking as it were into the sea. On his previous visit Reggie hadn't come into Tidmouth itself at all. He shrank back against the cream upholstery and tried to enjoy what was, by any standard, a pleasant view, but the unreality of it made him apprehensive. It was like a thousand postcards. He closed his eyes for a while to steady himself, and heard Ezra's rounded accent tumbling on.

'What did I tell you?'

Somehow, they had stopped. Somehow Ezra had already exchanged words with a woman already waiting within the porch doorway. Reggie was struck by the unlikely possibility of Ezra's having been in radio contact. The thought evaporated as Ezra returned to the Cortina and pressed his face to Reggie's window. He made an eager winding motion, urging Reggie to lower the window further. 'No need to waste any more of your day,' he beamed, his face elaborately mazed with happy lines. 'Out you get.'

The woman, too, was smiling.

Sunnybank, read Reggie.

It was a forgivable misnomer. The house stood on the shadowed side of the street. Indeed, by virtue of a curve on the hill the substantial, yellow-brick Edwardian building faced northwest and received only the blaze of the setting sun, a fact which had always kept the tariff reasonable. Plus, of course, the minor disadvantage that it was fully ten minutes from the sea and an arduous uphill climb back from the beach. (Many a vexed parent had sworn, as he stopped half-way up Chandler Street to lift a grizzling child on to his back, that next year they would find something more convenient. But the resolve had repeatedly been undermined by the competitive prices and the excellence of Mrs Pike's cuisine.)

'Perhaps . . . first . . .' Reggie stepped out and looked about him.

'He wants to see the amenities, B. love!' called Ezra.

'Of course he does,' cried Mrs Pike. A woman of strong and reliable intuition, she had felt her heart go out instantly to this middle-aged man standing desolately amidst a collection of luggage that Ezra, even now, was assembling in his own formidable grasp. 'Of *course* he does!' she repeated and indicated to the gentleman that he should step inside. Somewhere, at the back of the house, a dog yapped.

It was very clean and neat. The hall mirror shone. A faint smell of polish was being overwhelmed by the homely aroma of stew. Reggie's starved appetite began to strain downwards to the excellent scent as he followed Mrs Pike's trim form up the carpeted stairs. The brass stair-rods gleamed like imperial regalia.

By the time they reached the front room on the first floor, Mrs Pike had made a very full account of her widowhood, her inability to cope single-handed with a large turnover of holiday-makers, her swift letting of the attic floor to the two lady teachers. It had seemed such a climb for them, but the view (and the terms, she supposed) were a factor. Ezra kept up an affirmatory chorus in the rear.

'Best cook for miles around . . . You don't know what a cream tea is till you've tried B.'s . . . And hot-pot!'

'He was north-country really, Edmund, but he loved this coast.' Mrs Pike flung open the door on a spacious, bay-windowed room.

'Eating, that was Eddie's hobby,' reflected Ezra from the landing.

'The air, the views,' continued Mrs Pike while Reggie gazed around the comfortable, unstylish sitting-room.

'Of course, it needs a few possessions,' she said, to give the gentleman time to take things in, and then explained to Ezra how she'd moved herself downstairs.

The armchairs were of the squashy sort and had floral linen loose covers; the carpet was a strong, blurred accumulation of red, brown and yellow. A square, oak table (with leaves) stood in the bay window and bore signs of use. A 'fifties, kidney-shaped coffee table stood before a green tiled fireplace in which a gas fire had been installed. Either side of this leaned a glass-fronted cabinet and a bookcase which supported a small television set.

'Black and white,' said Mrs Pike, keeping pace with his glance. 'I'd have popped a few flowers in if I'd known.'

Over the fireplace, against a maroon and white Regency striped wallpaper, hung a David Shepherd print of an elephant charging. A different paper – beige with raised white floral medallions – covered the transverse walls. Here, partially obscured by the fluted and tasselled shade of a tall standard lamp, hung a study of Venice in some lustrous material whose sheen moved with the light.

'Linen's provided.'

Mrs Pike began to retreat to the next room along the corridor. It was a rather dark bedroom with an enormous wooden-framed bed and two heavy wardrobes. Beyond the window, sun shone on houses and villas cladding a hillside that Reggie guessed must end in limestone cliff. His juices yearned towards the kitchen below.

Bathroom (to be shared), kitchenette (a converted end of the bathroom, dark but adequate), breakfast, and an evening meal at six-thirty. Gas and electricity included. A price was named.

'Marvellous value,' remarked Ezra.

The facts barely penetrated Reggie's consciousness. A relieved sense that this would do perfectly well and that no further effort was required of him moved his acceptance. A few more bookshelves, perhaps; something *he* could do . . . 'Something *I* could do,' interrupted Ezra. A sea view would have been nice, thought Reggie, but this was that little bit closer to the school. Yes, this would do splendidly. 'Ideal,' he said aloud and took in Mrs Pike properly for the first time. She was saying how very pleased she was to have teachers in the house. 'Turtle-down isn't it?' she queried. 'Very nice, very select.' She smiled brightly and Reggie saw a well-preserved woman of fifty or thereabouts, with blonde hair – not brassy – a fresh and cheerful lipstick, and glasses that seemed neither to enlarge nor reduce her eyes in any exceptional way. She wore a short-sleeved tomato linen dress with white piping. Not a sombre woman, but not coarse either.

'I expect you'd like a little time to think,' she said kindly.

'Oh I've thought!' Reggie sounded over-eager.

'That's *right*!' Ezra congratulated him on his decision as he made to bring up the luggage.

'Yes, I think it will suit me very well.'

'That *is* nice.' Mrs Pike smiled warmly. 'Oh, that *is* nice, Mr Montis!' (She seemed to have absorbed a considerable amount of information about him from Ezra on their tour of the amenities.) 'I hope you'll be very comfortable.'

Bella Pike saw a man lost, in need of tactful looking after. Without any conscious design she felt it would be better, somehow, to have a man in the house.

A high-pitched barking began as they trooped after Ezra.

'Oh, shush now, Bundle!' called Mrs Pike fondly. 'It's only Mr Montis.' And as soon as they reached the foot of the staircase she disappeared to the back of the hall returning with the wire-haired puppy. 'I hope you like dogs,' she said, offering it up by way of introduction.

'I'm very fond of them,' said Reggie, who had no strong feelings one way or the other about dogs. Obligingly he scratched behind Bundle's ear and the puppy barked wildly.

'She'll get used to you in no time, I'm sure. She's such a baby still.' Mrs Pike cuddled the rough-haired animal briefly before putting her firmly back in the wonderfully redolent kitchen.

Ezra was tramping heavily upstairs.

'I'm watching the wallpaper,' he called. 'Eh, lummy, Mr Montis, what you got in here . . . a body?'

'Mostly books, I'm afraid.' Reggie activated himself. 'I'll give you a hand.' He wondered if the stew were for supper or, fearful thought, for the lunch that wasn't included.

'Nearly twelve already!' Mrs Pike caught sight of the grandfather clock in the hall. 'Now why don't you, just for today, until you've sorted yourself out a bit, Mr Montis – why don't you let me give you a spot of dinner?'

Dinner? Reggie took her meaning, gulped ecstatically, and leaned over the banister. 'That would be most kind of you Mrs Pike. *Most* kind!'

* * *

'She must have been a remarkable woman!' exclaimed Mrs Pike on hearing the accomplishments of Mrs Montis. 'North London Ladies Singles Champion! She must have been quite somebody!'

'Oh, she still is.' Reggie swallowed hastily. 'I never thought to see a dumpling again, wonderful! No, she still is.' He caught Mrs Pike's puzzled eye and realized that she had, by some process of sympathetic identification, assumed that he too was widowed. 'The tennis was some time ago. We met at the Harrow Lawn Tennis Club. No, my wife and I . . . our marriage . . . we've agreed . . .' he sought an unshocking phrase '. . . agreed to go our separate ways now the children have left home.' It was a rush. 'It seemed . . .'

'Oh I *am* sorry.'

He might just as well have been widowed, to judge by the depth of condolence in Mrs Pike's expression. 'I hope you didn't think I was prying.'

Bella found it hard to adjust to a generation in which divorce was not necessarily the outcome of sin or cruelty on the part of one guilty spouse. Promptly, she concluded that Mrs Montis was the injuring party; she sounded a forceful sort.

Reggie suffered a momentary glimpse of his forceful wife. Tall, burning-headed, good-looking, possessed (still) of a remarkably shapely pair of legs and an accusing manner, Dorothy was a difficult woman to forget. Her manner had once been her great charm. Once they had accused things together in joyous union. They had become prominent in their locality for their vigorous espousal of reform in education and welfare – larger family allowances, lower council rents, smaller classes, a wider application of preventive medicine. He had felt bold, a maverick in his department, with Dorothy's hot breath behind him. It was only gradually, his energy flagging as Dorothy turned from one issue to another, that Reggie had seen her drive was increasingly directed towards female issues: her pre-school nursery campaign, then her cervical screening campaign, her single-parent family campaign. When she began marching for equal pay he discovered that, although he had no intellectual quarrel with her aim, he had less and less time to march alongside her thrusting shoulder, and slowly, by degrees, he had sensed that the fiery slant of her anger was pouring upon him.

'I'm sorry?' he said, the dumpling swallowed.

'I hope you didn't think I was prying.'

'Not at all, of course not, no. Well there we are . . . now the children have left home as I say . . .'

'Children? How many?' Mrs Pike's voice trailed unpressingly as she quietly placed a second helping of her excellent stew on Reggie's plate. Button onions and carrots glistened among the savoury juices.

Reggie explained he had one of each.

'A boy and a girl?' said Mrs Pike.

'That's right.'

How shy he is, thought Bella Pike. 'You must miss them,' she murmured, dabbing gently at her mouth with a Sunnybank Guest House serviette.

'Indeed, yes,' lied Reggie.

The truth was – as he'd had plenty of occasion to think since leaving the family home – that Dorothy's strong personality had somehow come between him and his children. He felt rather cut off from them. He wasn't sure he knew them terribly well. Once they were old enough to find their parents imperfect, neither Gilbert nor Antonia had had much further communication with them. There had been a brief phase in which they had – independently – tried to outdo their mother's crusading nature by demanding the legalization of all drug use and the lowering of the age of sexual consent to thirteen (for both homosexual and heterosexual children), but that had relapsed into a tired form of silence followed by absence.

'The boy – Gilbert, that is, not a boy exactly – twenty-two – the boy's studying medicine. My daughter, a year younger, has just completed a sociology degree. She has no job as yet.' He laid down his knife and fork neatly.

A host of responses leapt into Bella's mind. The dreadful situation facing young people today, the interesting careers Mr Montis's children had planned for themselves, the financial strain of keeping your children in further education . . . Finally she chose to remark on the evident cleverness of Antonia and Gilbert. 'They've obviously got their brains from somewhere,' she said, eyeing the top of Reggie's head.

Instinctively, Reggie raised a hand to his skull. 'Oh, not a lot on offer there!'

'I don't believe it!' Mrs Pike overrode the self-deprecation. 'You've got a real scholar's face.'

At this Reggie laughed more naturally. 'Yes,' he agreed. 'Grey and dusty.'

'Oh *really*, Mr Montis. *I* don't know.'

In case she had sounded too familiar, Mrs Pike rose to see how things progressed in the oven. It was to avoid familiarity that she had served dinner in the dining-room rather than the kitchen. Now that she departed thence to check the state of her pudding, Reggie was confronted with a view of himself in a mirror with pink-tinted side panels that had been obscured by Mrs Pike's seated form. Because it hung out from the wall at a slight angle it revealed all too plainly how he was thinning on the crown. Grey and dusty was about it, thought Reggie ruefully, and tried to shift his gaze to a framed print of (he thought) Bellini's *Pietà*, but the image proved less absorbing than his own.

What a very dull-looking man he had become, one of a crowd of identical men. Not that he'd ever been exactly godlike, but he had to own he'd once possessed a pleasant enough face, with a keen expression and well-defined features. Also, he'd been told, a charming smile. He smiled. The grimace was the sour and cynical badge of all middle-aged men. Charm had completely withdrawn behind a worried frown and spectacles.

Reggie was, it has to be said, being unnecessarily harsh.

His sheepish glare returned once more to the wounded Christ draped on the woman's lap. He discovered a personal element there. He was a diminished man. Literally. He felt as though he'd physically shrunk over the years, whereas Dorothy – who'd always had an inch and a half in height over him anyway – had become straighter-backed, more lioness-headed. Altogether *bigger*.

'I've had others inquiring, but well, you know, I thought I could afford to be a bit *choosy*.'

Mrs Pike, chattering as if she'd never been absent, swung through the door. Reggie pretended to be examining the smears on his glasses. He began polishing them on a corner of the tablecloth. His expression brightened as a crisply-topped meringue pie was set before him.

'I like to see a man enjoy his food.' Mrs Pike stood back and cut a generous slice. 'It's miserable, feeding women. They're always trying to lose weight.'

'It looks delicious.'

'Cream's to your right.'

'Oh, cream!' He tried to pour some out, but it was clotted.

'Go on! Take a good spoonful.'

'You make me feel quite greedy.'

'Nothing wrong with that once in a while. If you've been living away from home I don't suppose you've eaten properly in weeks.'

'To be perfectly honest, my wife . . .' He hesitated, not wishing to be disloyal, but he could see Mrs Pike awaiting the end of his sentence. 'Well, she wasn't awfully interested in cooking.'

This was sufficient of an understatement not to be unkind. The final chapter of their lives together had come when Dorothy declared she was no longer prepared to do anything of an exploited nature in the house. This seemed to include cooking, washing up, ironing his clothes and, finally, making his side of the bed. After some weeks of struggling to do his own chores and watching Dorothy eat her own individually deep-frozen and re-heated faggots or shepherd's pie, Reggie had quietly announced that the situation had reached a pitch of intolerable absurdity.

'On the contrary!' Dorothy had countered, dumping a pile of undarned socks on his lap, 'it is only just ceasing to be intolerably absurd. If you want a nanny-cum-housekeeper, then hire one.'

She had looked particularly handsome – her short, tawny hair leaping electrically from her brow, her clear blue eyes indomitable – but he had resisted the appeal of her noble stance.

'I think I had better go,' he'd said, and left the room without further argument, his heart beating painfully.

Some of the pain of this recollection still lingering at his mouth, Reggie realized that Mrs Pike was urging him to enjoy his pudding right to the last scrap. He jumped visibly as Bundle released a battery of yaps at the back door. A young voice could be heard in the kitchen, making soothing noises, and the yapping subsided to a whimper.

'That'll be my grand-daughter.' Mrs Pike half rose and called out, 'That you, Phoebe darling?'

'Can I take the dog out, Gran?'

Phoebe, a small child of about five, with a striking burst of golden hair forming a nimbus around her pretty face, came into the hotel dining-room, ignoring Reggie.

'Not until you've said hello to Mr Montis.'

'Hello, Mr Montis.' The child acknowledged him blankly. 'Now can I?'

'Have you had your dinner?'

'We had it early. Mum's gone in the lorry with Dad.'

'You'll have tea with me then, will you, darling?' called Mrs Pike as the child retreated, the long, ringleted curls spreading so far and wide across her small back, that Bundle, clutched beneath one arm, was lost to view.

'OK.' Phoebe turned and studied Reggie more lengthily. She had a cool poise quite extraordinary in so young a child. 'Are you the lodger Gran was looking for?'

Reggie spluttered as genially as he was able beneath the cold blue stare. 'Well, I'm not sure I am *precisely* the one your grandmother was looking for.'

'You monkey!' reproved Mrs Pike affectionately.

'She said she was looking for a single, middle-aged man. Preferably a schoolteacher.'

'Well,' cried Reggie, treating this infant's precosity as a joke, 'then I suppose I might be that very man!'

'Back by four,' called Mrs Pike as the child vanished

apparently unperturbed by being so accurately reported. Her lack of discomfiture eased Reggie's embarrassment.

'What a charming young creature,' he was able to croak.

'Poor little thing, yes,' murmured Mrs Pike, both implying that some allowance had to be made for the child and inhibiting any inquiry into why that might be. Tackling the last of her own lemon meringue pie delicately, she observed that the boys of Turtledown House were very well mannered indeed.

Again, the unspoken suggestion seemed to be that Phoebe's manners were less than perfect. There followed quite a lengthy discussion on manners, from which Reggie learnt that Mrs Pike held old-fashioned views on the subject and, although this couldn't be altogether reconciled with her grandchild's demeanour, Reggie was most relieved to know Mrs Pike's belief that the proper conduct of her lodgers should be met on her part with an absolute respect for their privacy.

This point made tactfully clear, his relief burgeoned in a more joyful sensation altogether when, on automatically gathering the empty dishes, he felt her restraining hand on his arm and heard her horrified but sombre voice exclaim, 'Mr Montis! Mr *Montis*! That will never do!'

Reggie escaped, his heart lighter than he had known it for weeks.

2

Freedom!

Although he has, less than a minute previously, listened carefully to the water restrictions which Mrs Pike explains are in operation, and faithfully vowed to limit his use of the precious substance, Reggie feels a general and heady lifting of restriction. He strides down Chandler Street swinging his blackthorn stick, wearing a newly purchased tweed cap and feeling liberated.

He had not felt liberated in Hounslow – and not just because he remained within Dorothy's physical orbit. There was no possibility of experiencing a deeper freedom, a freedom within the soul (as Reggie occasionally thought of it) when he was bothered by the petty, daily needs of servicing his own person. By the need to cook small boring meals (he had begun ambitiously, but found the time spent preparing beforehand and cleaning up afterwards quite dimmed his pleasure in the eating interval). By the need to sit glumly in the launderette at least once a week, and generally more, since he forgot things or dropped them somewhere between his bedsitter and the Quickspin; by the need to hunt down little portions of food for one in the supermarket, tiny tins, two ounces of cheese, miniature pots of jam and marmalade. Apart from the humiliating sense of being reduced by this form of shopping, Reggie loathed the actual search, the bewildered poking and stooping and wandering and fumbling through special offers that were imposed on the lonely basket-holders. Trolley-pushers surged confidently past, making one cower against the shelves.

He had begun to notice other men suffering the same shame as himself. They looked shiftily at one another without any bond of comradeship developing. They simply shuffled further downshelf and spent a long time reading the small print on their purchases as if trying to work out in economic terms the loss they endured when buying in small quantities. The phrase self-service had taken on a punitive ring. *Condemned to thirty years' self-service.*

Reggie had become convinced that all the television eyes were trained quite specifically on the aimless course of lonely men, while the apparent aimlessness of those men who trailed behind active wives (snatching, dropping, snatching, dropping) had become a matter of envy to him. They were not without purpose, but lordly. Men of leisure. Freemen.

Now, a good meal undergoing digestion inside him, his shelter assured, the dread of the new job temporarily receding, Reggie walks with the spring of a man on holiday. Every so often a V or a more irregularly shaped view of the sea appears between roofs and alleys, a glittering green segment more solid and gem-like than water.

Everything that presented itself to his vision gave him special delight. The two pale frigates he could see beyond, on the bluer horizon – they must be heading westwards to the naval dockyard at Portland Bill – even the holiday-makers who were still about, distinguishable from the fustian residents by their espadrilles and shorts, added to his carefree spirit. On the lower curve of Chandler Street, as it flattened out towards the sea front, he spotted a small museum which boasted (rather unreliably, he suspected) an incomparable collection of fossils. For the moment, he put aside the temptation to stop and dawdle over the collection, but it amounted to another pleasing future prospect. If he could have whistled, he would have done so.

Nearer to the promenade, an accumulation of tea-rooms jostled for space before giving way to an attractive row of Georgian cottages facing the sea. They bulged and leaned in a canopied line on a pavement raised above the promenade, each a different ice-cream colour – strawberry, vanilla, mint, and a deep, double, dairy cream. They toppled pleasantly against one another for about a quarter of a mile before coming to an abrupt halt beside the Fun Hall, a clanging arcade of fruit machines and non-stop bingo, where the numbers were being called by a discreetly yawning girl. A student, Reggie guessed.

Here a flight of steps led down to the pebbly beach and a few families sat beside their windbreaks, wearing jerseys over their swimsuits and watching their young brave the weed-fringed water. Ahead, a small stone harbour reached out to sea, and Reggie idled there a while, studying a map of the district and reading the blackboards which advertised mackerel-fishing trips and water ski-ing. The single-masted boats, shabbily picturesque, offered a restful gossiping ground for gulls.

As he wandered on, a man in a slippery skin-diving suit saluted him vaguely and Reggie, assuming he'd been mistaken for someone else, returned the greeting with a startled air, then, warming to the notion that Tidmouth was an unusually friendly place, challenged a few selected passers-by with a bold 'Good afternoon!' It was most effective. The readiness of their responses hugely increased his benevolence.

Aglow as he was with fellow-feeling, Reggie was intrigued by the emptier, stone-strewn shore to the west of the harbour. Obviously not favoured by the holiday-makers, Granny's Gate, as it was described on the map, was fascinating to Reggie and, clearly, to a few, indistinct couples further along the shore, as a fossil site. As one slithered over the stones and past the last of the beach chalets, it was easy to see why Granny's Gate was avoided. The cliff face that rose out of the lower greensand, and continued as far as the eye could see, was a sinister black slab marked by horizontal striations of blue lias clays compressed into wafery layers. Here and there, the horizontal piling had been overswept by slips of clay which gave the cliffs the appearance of slag heaps, grey, unlovely slopes of ejected rubbish. Whole logs protruded from these steep falls as if in the slow act of being swallowed, and indeed, as Reggie understood it, this sucking action of the lias was the very thing that made it so remarkable, for it absorbed and digested at billion-year intervals the sea creatures later regurgitated as ammonites and belemnities and left in careless profusion upon the shore.

*   *   *

Reggie can hardly believe his eyes. Hopping from one boulder to another, he seems to dance on fossils imprisoned in stone.

Some of the larger smooth blue boulders are thickly starred with ammonites. He longs for a hammer to tap them free. He thinks of the sacred stone that is said to scream. The rounded spirals of ammonites are like so many mouths screaming.

Ammon, Amun. He thinks of the principal of the Theban gods, usurper of the sun symbol, destroyer of Re the sun god before him. Ammonites are said to take their name from the triumphant Theban.

*   *   *

So many swirling suns. Reggie gazed at the giddy graveyard beneath his feet and danced upon it. He sang to himself in tuneless joy until his attention was caught by a persistent, trickling sound that came from the cliffs. They were weeping. Thin, ceaseless tears dribbling from the gloomy fissures, as if the whole dark cliff grieved over its own nature. Reggie wanted to stroke it, then withdrew his hand with a sense of foolishness. He glanced around. Nobody was watching. The tiny figures in the distance were slowly peering at the ground as they walked.

Silly chump!

He sprang seawards and stood for a moment, tugged by the wind, gazing back down the beach with satisfaction. His new-found home!

Tidmouth itself, he realized from this viewpoint, was contained within a fissure of the hills. On either side of it lay dry, open, yellow countryside, but the town, wedged in a cleft of the hillside, gave the impression of a place whose houses, sliding eagerly down towards the wider space at sea level, were crushed and jumbled by their race. Reggie was unable to pick out a single clear row of houses anywhere. He liked the irregular outcome of their fight for space.

The little town and its adjacent downland were contained in the curved embrace of Tidmouth Bay. Its two encircling arms were ill-matched limbs. The oolitic lias which formed the black and wrinkled arm of Granny's Gate was in quite startling opposition to the geology that determined Tidmouth's easterly arm. There, some two miles across the bay from where he stood, the cliffs rose far higher in fabulous white fan formations, their layers erupted and crushed by a mighty glacial force. Absorbing the full brilliance of the clear afternoon light, the folds of distant cliff-face glared so purely white that the shadows defining their ancient shapings were barely visible.

Thus was the town clasped within one white, one black arm, a conjunction so freakish and intriguing that it had always occupied geologists. Seeing it for himself, Reggie understood their passionate curiosity. Nor, he thought, did the wonders end here. He had read that the coastline further to the east continued to change its character in a quite unparalleled way, its colour altering every jagged half mile or so from red to white, and black again, where the shale which the early Celts had used to fashion their jewellery was to be found.

The prospect of the walks he would have, the objects he might find, intoxicated him. Here in this primordial landscape he would start again. Not just a change of place – a break with time itself!

He closed his eyes and heard the gulls whoop encouragement, heard the waves crash gloriously upon the fossil-ornamented shore, and felt again childishly, deliciously free.

He also felt the mild, but not disagreeable strain of indigestion. As he wandered back towards the harbour, he nursed the sensation pleasurably.

It is only a short leap in his day-dreaming from indigestion to Dorothy.

She seems less distressing. Reggie is able to think about her more clearly, without quite the same hot, confusing access of malice. Perhaps he has been over-ready to blame.

The truth is, his disillusion lies over a wider range of things than Dorothy. They simply crystallize in her.

It is all so much more complicated. *So* complicated, Reggie sometimes thinks, that his mind is incapable of locating and holding all the different strands that feature in his furious despair. Or *accidie* . . . the better word, perhaps. So he makes do with Dorothy and knows at the bottom of his heart that this isn't wholly just.

Even so *An unimaginative man!*

Reggie snorted to himself and picked up a stone to throw

into the sea. Satisfyingly, it leaped three times across the surface of the water without his even trying to make it jump.

All he knows is that progress isn't a clear development towards a finer world, but that each step forward, whatever indisputable benefits it brings, equally sacrifices something irrecoverable. Something of quality.

Norman Herrington, the secretary of 'Rescue', worked in the British Museum. One day Reggie had met him there. Admiring the delicate craftsmanship of the Bronze Age artefacts, they had hung together over the cases and then as they moved on to another case labelled 'Iron Age A', the sight of those later crude blades and pins of the Hallstatt type had shocked Reggie into a state of mind he'd always before considered defeatist; the whining after things past, the insistence that what was lost was superior in standard of skill or morality or whatever other yardstick people chose for measuring their present discontents. No matter that as the two men passed down the hall they came upon the fine La Tène work fashioned some two hundred years before the birth of Christ – a bronze collar, heavily bossed and inlaid with opaque glass, torcs, great ropes of gold, superbly chased shields and bucklers – Reggie had acquired a sense of loss. He was forced to admit, looking in those cases, that much of what he and Dorothy had fought to achieve was accompanied by loss. Oh, specific problems had been cured, yes, but sometimes (it seemed as he retraced his steps past the graceful rapiers of earlier centuries) a higher standard of living, of health, of education had not brought the new Jerusalem one jot nearer. Instead, by a perverse process he couldn't fully understand, its arrival had increased the amount of coarseness and cruelty and stupidity abroad.

That, says Dorothy, is the reactionary viewpoint. It is the failure of middle age speaking. She has a number of terms for it. All that is called for, she says, are revised goals and methods, a continual programme of modification.

She made him panic. She must be blind. As she headed tirelessly towards the future, he became convinced that she would, with each new act, compound the ugly tangle all round them. It was as though some minor error, some wrong assumption, some little misdirection, barely noticeable in their original charting, had slowly, with time, been aggravated to such a major fault that their entire political planning and thinking was grossly off-course. He was confused by it. Tired, disappointed.

Leaving Granny's Gate behind him, sauntering past the harbour, he wonders coolly whether his departure had been prompted by fear rather than by conviction.

Has he thrown himself off a ship heading for the rocks and left proud Dorothy at the helm? No, it was a common or garden case of incompatibility which should have been acknowledged sooner. They were both free to follow their own course at last. Good thing for everyone concerned. An *excellent* thing.

His spirits recovered their buoyancy. Why, even his constipation might be cured now that he was removed from the source of nervous tension. This last thought, however, was sufficient to make him stop off in the Spar grocer's at the bottom of Chandler Street, where he bought a large box of All Bran and a coffee-flavoured walnut whip.

*   *   *

Why had he supposed the two lady teachers upstairs to be elderly? Dimly, he recalled Mrs Pike's murmuring about the climb to the top floor . . . a print of seized-up joints had obviously been slotted into the computer.

The two girls were already seated in the dining-room, dipping their heads over their soup. They sat against the wall, beneath the '*Pietà*'. The one facing him looked up. Quickly, Reggie introduced himself. The girl had an unusually handsome head, dark, close-cropped curly hair, straight brows and a very level, rather searching gaze. Her nose and cheeks were deeply freckled by the sun and gave her a glowingly healthy air. She was quite without any artificial colour.

'Anna Cox,' she smiled, a little guardedly. 'And Stephanie.'

Stephanie turned. Swallowing her soup she nodded gravely.

'Stephanie?'

'Cox,' replied Stephanie.

'Oh I see,' responded Reggie, thinking they didn't look like

33

sisters. Stephanie had long silvery fair hair and a pale, trans-
lucent skin touched with a faint violet tint around the eyes, the
sort of skin that looked as though it might bruise easily. 'So
you're at Turtledown,' she said in a small, sweet voice and
smiled. Her eyes had that misty blueness he associated with
myopia. There was a tender fullness to her mouth, a feature
that Reggie found most kissable. He suffered a small, involuntary inward leap.

'That's right. And you? Both more experienced teachers than
I, no doubt. I'm a very new boy.'

They laughed kindly at his self-effacement and explained
that they taught at St Nathan's comprehensive 'PE,' said Anna
of herself. Their term started tomorrow, Tuesday.

Any chance of further exchange was interrupted by Phoebe,
who squeezed round the door, carefully carrying Reggie's soup.

'Thank you, my dear.' Reggie sat down and removed his
napkin from its ring. 'Did you have a nice walk this afternoon?'
His tone was ludicrously avuncular. He felt a need to ingratiate
himself with the child.

'I saw you,' said Phoebe, setting down the plate and removing a slopped crescent of soup with her thumb. 'At Granny's
Gate.'

'Ah, Granny's Gate. That's right.' It made him feel mildly
uncomfortable to know he had been watched. Though
'watched' was a silly term. 'I didn't see *you*,' he went on,
twinkling furiously.

'No,' she said. 'I saw you collecting pebbles.' This observation was made accusingly. As though he'd been spotted thiev-
ing. The Misses Cox, he noted, were busy with their spoons.

A hatch beside the frosted-glass door to the kitchen was
pushed upward and a tray with two pots of tea and hot-water
jugs placed in view. Phoebe went to manoeuvre the tray off the
shelf and Reggie, thinking this dangerous for a small child,
leapt to help her.

'I can do it myself,' she said, tossing a ripple of hair over one
shoulder. He sank down. 'You're very capable,' he complimented her as she balanced the tray cautiously on his table
and lifted off the teapot. Phoebe ignored him. Her lower lip was

34

clenched between her teeth. Reggie tried again. 'I suppose you'll be starting school this term?'

'I've been at school for *years*,' she sighed witheringly.

'Ah,' Reggie accepted this childish exaggeration calmly. 'That explains it.' She probably spent too much time with adults.

The pastry encasing the bacon and mushroom flan dissolved deliciously; the accompanying baked potato was smothered with butter; the blackcurrant ice that followed compared well with any sorbet he'd ever tasted, and the roll, which he'd tried to avoid eating but couldn't finally resist, had the damp, yeasty warmth of home-made bread. Reggie sighed aloud with pleasure at the conclusion of his meal.

'Everything satisfactory, I hope?' Mrs Pike appeared in the doorway and invited congratulation.

'Terrific!'

'Smashing!' said the Misses Cox.

'Splendid!' endorsed Reggie. 'Truly splendid. And may I say, Mrs Pike, how very touched I was by the flowers.' He'd discovered a bright jugful of dahlias on the coffee table when he'd returned from his walk.

'My pleasure,' said Mrs Pike. 'Makes it a bit more like home, doesn't it?' And then, as if sensing this wasn't a terribly tactful thing to say, she rushed into the observation that she couldn't help noticing they shared an interest, Mr Montis and herself.

'Apart from an interest in your excellent cooking, you mean?'

'Oh Mr Montis, *really* ... still, it's very nice of you. No, pottery I meant. I couldn't help noticing. Only I've always been interested in pottery. In fact I'm – silly at my age, I suppose – I'm starting classes soon.'

Briefly, Reggie looked puzzled. 'Oh,' he exclaimed. 'My bits of pot! I hope you don't think they look awfully untidy, but I promised to sort them for a friend. That's why they're all in different trays.' He tried to explain about Norman's find and helping him out. 'But I mustn't be boring,' he concluded. 'Like all enthusiasts, I can be very boring.'

'Oh, it's not at all boring, is it?' Mrs Pike appealed to the

35

Misses Cox, who were sliding towards the door and murmuring something about going out.

'Not a bit,' smiled Stephanie, her vague and gentle eyes resting on Reggie in a way that made him glance down. Mrs Pike excused herself to go and fetch the new keys she'd had cut for him, and there was a little shuffling silence. 'We'll go on,' said Anna.

'I hope the dog doesn't bark too much when you come in,' cried Mrs Pike, returning. 'Your key, Mr Montis. Goodbye dears, have a nice time.'

Reggie attempted to leave.

'No, I don't find the subject at all boring,' repeated Mrs Pike. 'But I mustn't keep you.'

'Ought to get my books in order,' explained Reggie. He wasn't used to discussing his hobby. Dorothy had found it tedious. 'Anti-life,' she had remarked. 'Dead things.'

There was the sound of a heavy lorry drawing up outside.

'That'll be my daughter come to fetch Phoebe.'

A cuckoo sprang from a clock in the next room seven times. At the same moment, the phone rang.

'Whatever next!' gasped Mrs Pike, darting in several directions at once. Reggie slipped quietly upstairs as Bundle's yapping added to the turmoil. Something made him stop off in the bathroom. He examined the array of bath oils and talcum powder. *Bois de Santal*. Sandalwood, that was it. Unscrewing the top of the oil jar, he sniffed. Lovely. There were a few, dark pubic hairs in the bath.

His room was filtered with a coppery light that made the dahlias appear especially luminescent. Reggie sighed contentedly and began emptying his books from the cases. Once they were in order, he searched out a site for his gramophone, but finding nowhere either wide or steady enough for the unwieldy machine, he left it temporarily under the oak table on which he laid out his trays of shards.

Stupid, to bring the gramophone really. It was the old model the children had used until they'd complained about the hi-fi all their friends had and how nobody would come to their house any longer on account of it. Anyway, of what use was a gramophone to a man with one LP? To a man with no musical ear whatever, more particularly?

He couldn't think now why he'd bothered to remove *The Magic Flute* from Dorothy's collection of records, except that it had been his most recent present to her and he'd wanted, a trifle spitefully, to retrieve it. Not because he liked it — he'd never even heard it — but because she had explained so carefully to him exactly what she wanted: the Karl Böhm recording. She had written down the number with an air of impatience, as if to emphasize Reggie's own lack of imagination, his complete inability to go and choose the best recording for himself. Her attitude had been so insulting, it pleased him to snatch the record back.

Irritated even now by her charges of insensitivity, he hunted out the LP, removed a lump of fluff from the needle, and put the record on. The overture began.

Attracted by the majestic sunset outside, Reggie squeezed into the bay window and stared out. The whole sky above Tidmouth seemed ablaze. He was struck by the rarity of gazing into so great an expanse of sky unbroken by towers and chimneys. He stared until his eyes hurt.

Noises below made his gaze fall. Phoebe ran out ahead of a plumpish woman on very high wedge shoes with criss-cross straps up her legs. Both turned at the gate to wave, before clambering into the cab of a battered lorry loaded with corrugated iron. He could just see the driver's lap and a waving hand. Mrs Pike's daughter Daphne hitched up the fallen strap of her yellow sundress and waved a final flourish. Phoebe, beside her, stared straight up at Reggie and he felt his face burn with a deeper flush than that of the sinking sun alone.

He'd been too absorbed to listen to the music. But perhaps he had not entirely shut it out. Without giving it any close attention, he felt himself suffused with an unfamiliar joy. Could that be Mozart's subtle doing?

As the three ladies sang competitively over Tamino's fainted body, Reggie listened a good deal more closely.

3

Mrs Straker flapped at the clouds of tobacco smoke billowing across the staffroom and thrust herself between her colleagues with boisterous cries of 'Mind your backs!' as she bore Reggie's coffee to him.

It was milky and had a nasty, spotted surface. Reggie thanked the art teacher profusely for her trouble and she wriggled herself on to the arm of his chair, restraining his efforts to rise with a firm hand on the top of his spine. 'If you stand up you'll only soak six pairs of trousers,' she pointed out, indicating the tight-packed collection of teachers poised at various angles of discomfort over their coffee cups. 'There now!' and she settled herself more comfortably, wedging her generous backside against Reggie's shoulder. His cup arm shook. 'What do *you* think of it all?' She sipped gustily and he found it difficult, jammed as he was against Mrs Straker's hindquarters, to turn and reply.

'*I* think,' she answered herself defiantly, 'it's a bloody good idea.'

The surrounding buzz was transposed to a lower, more contentious key.

'Don't be so stuffy,' challenged Mrs Straker, alert to the changed note. 'It bucked you up no end having me here.'

'You, my dear Eleanor, more than adequately represent your sex.' Amis, the English master, ogled the art mistress with friendly disapproval, and she laughed at him, setting up a series of movements that made Reggie's cup clatter in its saucer.

'Do watch out, Eleanor, my sweet.' Amis handled his own cup delicately. 'Is Mrs Straker disturbing you, Montis? She has such an exuberant way with her.' He giggled a little.

After less than two full days at his post, Reggie didn't feel qualified to enter the routine banter, and merely gave a small, untroubled smile. He repeated Mrs Straker's original question.

'What do you think of the plan?' he asked in a general fashion, his eyes travelling round the circle formed by Dufferdill (history), Ogilvy (maths), Kean (French), Sopworth (geography), Father Starkey (classics) and Popplewell, whose scarlet track suit and whistle defined his function easily enough. He it was who responded first.

'Make my job bloody difficult,' he sniffed, wrinkling his leathery face. Popplewell was an ex-army instructor with a brutal haircut. The hair was only permitted to begin its modest growth about two inches above his large ears.

'About time we branched out,' asserted Kean, whose manner corresponded with his name. He clasped his knees and took a bright-eyed view of Garsington's announcement that the school would be obliged to include a few girls as from the next term. 'All wrong for boys to be herded together, in my opinion.' He brushed a lock of fair hair from his eyes. Amis sighed vastly.

'What about my showers? What about my scrum?' This, from Popplewell.

'*What* about them?' Mrs Straker, above his head, sounded a touch lascivious, thought Reggie. He attempted to press away the beginnings of a headache. There was a spot of pain behind his right eye, brought on, he supposed, by lack of sleep. For two nights running he'd been disturbed, late, by the sound of a hair dryer in the girls' room upstairs, and on the two successive mornings he'd woken wretchedly early after taut and alarming dreams about teaching. The clamour went fruitlessly on all round him.

'It's only a question of adapting here and there.' Father Starkey attempted to soothe Popplewell.

'They're not coming on my pitches. It'll be bloody rounders and skipping next.'

'Can't stand small girls,' Dufferdill contributed testily, his moustaches drooping. 'Always demanding to be noticed. I leave home when my grand-daughters come to stay. Always wanting to be bounced up and down and tickled.'

'So are big girls,' put in Amis, carefully not looking at Eleanor. It didn't avail him; a tremor reverberated through Reggie's shoulder.

'Don't know what the bloody country's coming to.'

'Oh, don't let it take on the scale of a national disaster, Popsy,' urged Amis. 'Do let's keep a sense of proportion.'

'That's enough of the Popsy.' The games master did a quick knees-bend before standing upright. His tennis shoes sparkled white.

'If it helps the school – the financial aspect, I mean,' murmured Ogilvy, but he, too, sounded glum. His long, bumpy nose leaned against his face like a tombstone. Scratching his low forehead he muttered that other methods might have been tried first.

'Oh, you are a miserable lot!' cried Mrs Straker gaily. 'One tug at the old tradition and you sprawl all over the show, whimpering.'

'It's all very well for you,' said Sopworth, adding darkly, 'it can affect my expeditions.'

'I don't see why it should,' countered Kean. 'It's not as though you're going up the Orinoco.'

'There's still a question of amenities, even on South Down,' retorted Sopworth.

Reggie smiled but said nothing. Sopworth had a black, resentful air that didn't encourage jesting. He looked like a man borne onward by successive waves of disappointment. Reggie wanted to keep on terms with Sopworth. They might have some decent geological chats together.

Mrs Straker yawned loudly.

'We know your view of the matter, dear.' Dufferdill looked at her over his bifocals. 'No need to express yourself quite so extravagantly.'

'Oh, pardon *me*!' She laughed. '*You* don't mind, do you, Mr Montis?' She nudged him in the back of the neck.

'I'm not in any position to mind. I don't know what it's like teaching small boys yet.'

'It's hell,' pronounced Dufferdill cheerfully. 'But they do go home for eighteen weeks of the year.'

'So will the girls,' retorted Kean.

'*While* they're here,' Dufferdill went on unheeding, 'I've no doubt they'll add years to me with their wretched, piping demands. *Years*. Please sir this, please sir that . . . Will they call us "sir", do you suppose? Is all that going to end? Girls are non-O.Q.'

'Non what?' said Mrs Straker.

'Officer quality,' explained Ogilvy patiently.

'Well, they won't call Eleanor sir.'

'Don't be frivolous, Amis,' reproved Dufferdill. 'Seriously, are we to be called by our *names* now?' His horror was striking. 'All my adult life I've been protected from the absurdity of my name by "sir". I am grateful to it. I am indebted to "sir". I will not relinquish it now.'

'They still call you Daffodil behind your back,' observed Sopworth with a grim gleam of pleasure.

'I know *that*, but I'm not supposed to, and that's what matters. There's no need for me to know.'

'They call me Starkers. Or, on occasion, Bonkers, short for stark, staring bonkers,' mused Father Starkey fondly. 'Think yourself lucky, Duffer.'

'I wonder what they'll call *you*?' Ogilvy pondered the possibilities of Reggie's name.

'Can't do much with Montis,' the owner of the name apologized.

'Monty? Mon ... Mon ... Mon-tesaurus, Montezuma?' Ogilvy thought hard, but disappointment quickly overwhelmed his features again. He made a final effort. 'Sherry. A-montillado. Get it? No, not a lot you can do with it.'

'Never mind,' beamed Father Starkey. 'We'll think of something.'

Thus occupied, they happily passed the seconds that remained until the bell rang, when Reggie was obliged to leave this civilized company and confront 2B with human history from its earliest beginnings.

* * *

'Making out all right, eh?'

Dufferdill stood in the sunlight, eyes screwed up behind his bifocals, nose in the air like a pointer. He tucked a pile of books more securely under his left arm. 'It's early days, of course, yet,' he commented before Reggie could frame an equally meaningless rejoinder. 'The little buggers loathe everything prior to 1066. Mind you, I'm not gripped by it myself. Nineteenth century, my period. Pity we never reach it before they leave. How about a drink? Oh, it's all right,' as Reggie fished about in his pockets, exchanging his brief-case from one hand to the other. 'It's all right. I've checked. You've no duties this lunch hour. Dump your stuff.'

'Well, fine,' Reggie grinned broadly. 'Thanks for the invitation.'

'You know all about the water restrictions, I suppose? So we're obliged to drink alcohol. One way of helping your country. Call me Duffer; they all do.'

'Duffer, thanks.'

They sprang into Duffer's tiny yellow Fiat and roared down the drive, scattering skate-boarders and marbles contestants to either side.

'Can't do a day's teaching on a parched stomach,' observed Dufferdill, steering Reggie across the public bar of the Gallows Tree. 'Can't give your best.'

With commendable speed, considering the numbers crowding the bar, he extricated two pints of draught ale and elbowed himself backwards out of the throng. 'Mind you,' he went on, observing no break whatever in his conversation, 'only took up this lunch place after the Changes.'

'The Changes?' inquired Reggie.

'Mrs Horstelwanger and Mrs Straker.' Dufferdill lowered his moustaches into the foam.

'May the good Lord forgive you,' remarked Father Starkey, joining them.

'Why *then*, exactly?' persisted Reggie, making acknowledgement of the Father.

'Oh, before then, the matron and *such-like* ate separately. Now it's all one big happy family. And why, pray, must the good Lord trouble himself on my account today?'

'Well, if I were asked to put an *exact* date on it,' murmured Father Starkey, his big, square face struggling towards solemnity, 'I would have to say your patronage of the Gallows

Tree did not correspond precisely with the Changes, but pre-dated them, ever so slightly.'

'Oh maybe, maybe,' Dufferdill conceded vaguely. 'It's not a matter for scholarship. Now then, Montis, how are you shaping up? We fellow historians! Not, as I say, that I care for your end of the business. Pre-history equals no-history. I refuse to teach it. What was it Tacitus said, eh, Starkey? "One must remember we are dealing with barbarians." Well, so we are bloody well dealing with barbarians.'

Reggie was unable to follow clearly, a difficulty that in-creased as the lunch hour wore on. Was Dufferdill referring to the Celts or the junior boys? He wasn't sure that Dufferdill was sure. If he meant the boys, then fine! Barbarians they probably were. About the Celts he thought he should appear more par-tisan, although Dufferdill had unwittingly manoeuvred him into taking up a false position, since it was the advent of the Celts that had virtually ended the Bronze Age in Britain, and this, as we know, was a source of some grief to Reggie. He flung his mind forward nearly a thousand years, to those Celts whom Tacitus had described. The new, improved Celts. The fearless horsemen, the shapely craftsmen who were to suffer their own defeats under the drilled efficiency of Rome. Another loss. He managed to adapt his sympathies. 'I can't,' he protested, 'let you put them down as dismissively as that.'

'Oh-ho!' roared Dufferdill joyously. 'We've got a solar lab-oratory johnny here, have we? A megalithic yard chap? How about that, Ned?'

Father Starkey (who responded to 'Ned') seemed oblivious of his colleague's new, historical confusion. Three thousand years at least stretched back between Tacitus and the megalith builders. The priest raised his glass and beamed.

'If you're going to try and tell *me*,' cautioned Dufferdill thickly, 'that those chaps did thingummy fractions and measured planet movements and so on, like that fool, Professor . . .' He waved his tankard wildly.

'Thom?' volunteered Reggie meekly. 'Alexander Thom.' He couldn't decide whether the senior history master's grasp of facts was exceedingly weak or whether he himself, as a new and junior rival, was being put to a test.

'That's the bloke,' concluded Dufferdill. 'Thom. Wishful thinking, all that.'

Reggie assumed that his colleague was just drunkenly confused. 'Oh, I don't know,' he plunged in courageously. 'There's plenty of evidence to suggest the – er – earlier peoples were pretty sophisticated. No, later, there was a lapse of some kind. As Iron Age culture developed, something was lost. Initially, anyway.'

'They got a damn sight better at making things,' said Dufferdill contentiously, already going some way to contradicting his previous position. He plainly sought and provoked argument. As if reading Reggie's thoughts, Father Starkey winked at him. 'Duffer enjoys his lunch-time scrap,' he said.

Weakly Reggie smiled back, still anxious to establish his own credentials if he were being put through an examination of Dufferdill's surreal devising. 'Eventually they became more accomplished,' he acknowledged, mindful of the lovely La Tène bowls and torcs, 'but the first Celtic iron work is so crude that it argues a profound change of attitude between themselves and the people they supplanted. When I say something was lost – and I'm thinking around the ninth century BC – I mean some particular spirit, some perspective vanished in the cultural changes that took place.'

'Aha!' pronounced Father Starkey importantly.

'Don't go on!' Dufferdill's restraining hand wavered. 'You'll be telling us next about the halcyon past. How you yearn for the bygone! I can feel it coming. Can you feel it, Ned?'

The priest just laughed.

'If I could be allowed one wish,' dared Reggie longingly, 'it would be to know *why*. What happened? Why did the Bronze Age form of burial stop? All the barrows, the mounds . . . suddenly, they stop. When those immigrants came from Europe with their iron-working secrets, what ideas did they bring to cause such tremendous change? Something very big happened. No question.'

'Too many bloody corpses to go digging great holes in the earth any longer, I'd say.' Dufferdill crushed his glass to his chest as somebody pressed by. 'Dirty great population explosion.'

'Same thing happened in all the churchyards,' agreed Father Starkey. 'No room. When I was at Denton Abbas – in sixty-eight – we kept digging up parishioners we'd only put down a few months before. Most embarrassing. Just had to close the churchyard down. Oh, the arguments it caused! People like to know where they're going to be buried, and it's no earthly – oh, ha-ha! – no earthly good telling them the soul doesn't remain in the plot, you know. The prospect of death intensifies a sense of property like nothing else does, and really, you'd think it would be a man's last worry. *Last* worry! Oh dear, do forgive me!'

Dufferdill, unrepenting, raced on: 'Population build-up, overcrowding, undertakers pressed for time and labour. What do you do? Well, I tell you what you don't do. You don't detail twenty, thirty chaps to start digging a socking great trench God knows how many of your megalithic yards round. No, you burn our late Celt. Chuck your deceased pre-historic person in the sea, in the river. All of a sudden, you're not in the commemorative trade any longer. It's the disposal business. No choice. What's the alternative?' He peered about him with lugubrious expression. 'Barrows on top of barrows, back-to-back barrows, multi-storey barrows. No, no, not on. They just chucked 'em away, that's what they did. Take it from me.' He flourished an empty glass triumphantly, the mystery solved.

It was Reggie's turn to storm the bar. As he was shorter, less bizarre-looking and, more to the point, less well known to the proprietor of the Gallows Tree than Dufferdill, the task took him some time, and when he returned to the staff corner, his colleagues were discussing the ineptitude of the Archbishop of Canterbury. 'Going back a minute,' he tried. 'Just to take you up a second . . .' He made several attempts, and failed, to re-engage Dufferdill's rambling attention. Eventually it was the jolly, silver-headed priest who turned his sentence (the first half of which was devoted to the complete mishandling of ecumenical developments) to Reggie's account.

45

'Speaking of which,' said the good Father Starkey, checking the proper cloudiness of his beer, 'I'm interested in your feeling that it was some *cultural* change affecting, you know . . .'

Reggie was slowly grasping the irregular course of school-masters' conversation – only a day before and this change of current would have left him blank-faced and empty-mouthed. Only a day earlier and the gap left by this hesitancy would have been flooded by another participant astride his topic.

'Yes, yes!' he cried, to claim the space. He assembled his thoughts as rapidly as he could. 'Duffer's explanation doesn't quite do. Population explosions – unlike nuclear explosions – don't just happen overnight. There's no sudden end to things. And *that's* the oddity.' He jabbed a bold finger. 'No, if it were simply a matter of population explosion, the cultural changes would be more gradual; you'd get a greater transitional over-lap. All right, very occasionally – *very* rarely in this country – you find an Iron Age cemetery – ashes, urns, no barrows. More rarely still in this country – in the north – you have a chariot burial. Indisputably Iron Age. What you *don't* get' – his fingers essayed a snap which was feebly muted – 'is any continuation or use of the rounded barrow form. Death seems less importantly observed, and that posits fundamental changes in thought. As though the use of iron itself in some way altered the thinking and the whole structure of living. Established forms of be-haviour cease.'

'Fiddlesticks!' claimed Dufferdill airily. 'They just went about it in a different, labour-saving way. I mean, *look* at the Battersea shield.'

This time he was ignored. Reggie made no attempt to accommodate Duffer's tangential flourishes into his own reflections. Encouraged by Father Starkey's amiable murmurs of agreement, he went on. 'As if iron was the agent that trans-ferred power – political and economic power. There's a fasci-nating parallel with our own time, if you ponder it a moment. A new technology, a new material easily mined, easily fashioned. Iron, the pre-historic plastic, the first form of mass production, first consumer boom. The aristocracy, who'd been buried in the grand style, were no longer honoured. Right? Why should they be, when weapons and domestic terms were commonly available? It must have made for a real political re-emphasis. Iron and the birth pangs of social democracy?'

'Or,' reflected Father Starkey, calling on his own expertise, 'spiritual change.'

'What about the Battersea shield?' repeated Dufferdill aggressively.

'Well, all right,' conceded Reggie. 'It was found in a river. Grander chieftains were certainly buried in rivers. It still doesn't explain why the old burial forms were suddenly inappropriate.'

'*Spiritual* change,' insisted Father Starkey. Reggie paused to consider this widening of his own political viewpoint as Father Starkey kindled to his own theme. 'The parallel is really very exact,' he said. 'Materialism eroding spirituality.'

'Magic, you mean,' queried Reggie, 'resides in the iron rather than the natural elements?'

'Mumph, if you like, *magic* . . .' The priest inferred that this was not his choice of word, then explained himself by adding that, whatever view modern man took of pagan belief, to the pagan it was still religion. 'However, it's certainly probable that the increased effectiveness of the ordinary man, greater material prosperity . . . all those things that flowed from the use of iron, both lessened the esoteric power of the priesthood and helped to consolidate the notion of man as controller of his own destiny. My guess would be that their gods ceased to be less cloudy, elemental forces and corresponded more closely to themselves. Would I be right?'

'Well,' ventured Reggie cautiously, 'I'm a bit weak on the Celtic pantheon, though it's certainly true they developed a warrior aristocracy; and Teutates, the one god I know of – I think their principal one – *is* a warrior god.' He began to feel excited by the light being thrown on the little mystery he nursed. 'I'll find out as much as I can. You're right; you can't separate the spiritual aspect. They re-assembled the deities to suit their militaristic nature, and made their own decisions by the sword. Whatever the spiritual significance of the barrow, it clearly no longer applied.'

'O-oh-oh,' yawned Dufferdill and began packing his pipe with loving care.

Reggie's head started to thud horribly. A small hammer descended metronomically on an anvil between his eyes. Idiotic, drinking at lunchtime. 'They certainly didn't *abandon* belief,' he murmured.

'Oh, crumbs, no,' the priest agreed. 'Abandoned belief is an entirely modern luxury. Atheism and the electric toothbrush.'

'Simply *adapted* . . .' Reggie pressed two fingers to his forehead. No bowel movement this morning either. Fatal. 'Yes, I must look into it further.'

Dufferdill now had his bonfire going. He began to fade behind the smoke.

'Yes, man gained power over his surroundings. To a degree, anyway,' mused Father Starkey. 'The elements still presented a knotty one. Agriculture guarantees faith . . . Farming and poverty – the two great supports of spiritual observance.' He gave a jovial cough and ran a finger inside his dog collar. 'When are we going to wean you off that shredded compost, Duffer? It'll lose you friends.'

Dufferdill, delighted to have brought attention back to himself by however foul a means, grinned. He was not a man who cared to stay silent for long. 'Anyway,' he sucked, then puffed, 'whatever it was they thought up, it didn't do them much bloody good. Along came the Romans and trounced the lot of them. "One must remember we are dealing with barbarians",' he repeated with the radiance of a man who has definitely ended the argument. 'What can you make of a shower who spend generations digging a fortification like Maiden Castle – all done with antler teaspoons, I dare say – and then let the Romans storm in by the back door? You can put your clever megalithic yard in this pipe of mine and I'll smoke the jammy thing for you. But speaking of maidens, I'm going to have a word with Garsington about this little co-educational venture of his. Immediately prior to that however, Ned, it's your turn to fill the empties. Bless you, Father!'

*   *   *

As the bell for afternoon school rang, Reggie abandoned any attempt to relieve his lower intestine and, groaning faintly, retrieved his trousers. At some point in his life he had been infused with the notion – from Nana, perhaps – that retained stools led to an accumulation of poisonous vapour in the body, and he was as incapable of ridding himself of the idea as he was of the offending stools. As a small boy he had sent away for free samples of laxatives whenever he saw them advertised, and then passed whole moments in contemplation of the faecal variety he was able – with difficulty – to produce. Black, ochre, olive and rust-coloured turds all received his wondering attention as samples of expelled evil. Evacuated, one was a good boy.

His headache undiminished, Reggie began – at Amis's behest – to read *The Tempest* with his senior class. Warily, he had queried this choice of play.

'I want to do it as my summer production,' Amis had answered. 'Anyway, you've got to start them somewhere with Shakespeare and this is perfect; it's pure pantomime. They miss all the jokes in the comedies and the tragedies make them giggle. Besides,' he'd added, 'Grenville would make a gorgeous Ariel. Sings like a crow, of course, but we'll get round that. You'll see what I mean.'

So Grenville stumbled through his 'I-thank-thee-master's, his 'no-Sir's, his 'Ay-sir's, while Reggie wondered what peril surrounded this child with navy-blue eyes and petalled hair. As Prospero, he declared

> *If thou more murmur'st, I will rend an oak*
> *And peg thee in his knotty entrails till*
> *Thou hast howl'd away twelve winters.*

To Grenville the threat was as routine as that of a schoolmaster's detention. With dull, uncomprehending monotony the boy read on, his lashes dark crescents on his cheeks. Caliban, played by Astin Major, squinting through his elastoplasted spectacles and sticking inky fingers in his sandy hair, stumbled like a lame horse over the pronunciation of 'Sycorax', and shouted 'Oh no! Oh no!' with the beauty of a pair of bellows.

49

But even Astin Major's unrhythmic delivery did not prevent Reggie's carrying

> *You taught me language: and my profit on't*
> *Is, I know how to curse . . .*

all the way, alongside his headache, the mile and a half walk back to Sunnybank.

*   *   *

Mrs Pike was all concern.

'No really, I should never have mentioned it,' protested Reggie feebly as she set Codeine and a weak, sweet cup of tea before him.

'Are you sleeping properly?' Her eyes anxiously fished for the truth.

'Beautifully,' he lied.

'You shouldn't have walked all the way home – couldn't *somebody* have offered you a lift?' Her tone condemned all those who'd failed Reggie. In fact he'd turned down three offers, but he couldn't be bothered to explain. 'I thought the walk would do me good,' he said.

Mrs Pike made disapproving noises and removed her cheery apron. 'You could always use my little Austin,' she said. 'It's just sitting there.' And she explained that she left it there as a challenge to encourage her to pass her test more quickly.

'I see,' said Reggie warily. He'd noticed the old A30 with L-plates hanging drunkenly from it.

'The problem,' Mrs Pike mused, 'is practice.'

'Ah,' murmured Reggie, scenting a stratagem.

'Frank, that's my son-in-law, he's very good, of course, and Daphne too. They both give me a little practice when they can.'

An ungentle dread pulled at Reggie but to his astonishment he heard himself say, 'Well, perhaps we could help one another then. Mind you,' sense returned, 'I shall have to get myself a little car.'

This fired a fresh enthusiasm in Mrs Pike. 'Oh, Frank could help you there! He's in the business, Frank, well . . . a little bit of everything he does.'

Frank, it appeared, scrapped metal, fattened pigs, hauled hay and straw, and owned a twentieth part of a racehorse. It was, as Reggie observed, a remarkable clutch of interests.

'It's all for Phoebe, of course. They live for that child.' Again, the gravity of her tone, her slowly shaking head, all indicated that something ailed Phoebe. But Phoebe's health and intelligence were so obvious, it seemed impertinent to ask what was wrong with her. He might have misunderstood the implication completely.

Her sighing over, Mrs Pike again outlined her gratitude to Reggie. It was of great proportion.

'Oh, I shan't *teach* you to drive,' he protested, 'but I'll happily sit beside you.'

'That's why Edmund never taught me,' she smiled. 'Could end a marriage, he said.'

'Indeed.' Reggie made to move, and was struck by a new explosion of blood in the head. For a second, his vision darkened and was scattered with odd shapes, crotchets, quavers, other abstract scratchings.

' . . . supper upstairs,' he heard Mrs Pike promise.

'It's only a headache,' he insisted, weaving backwards, 'but thank you, yes, most kind.'

As he picked up *Pre-historic Wessex: Monument and Legend* to read over his supper tray, the fiery glow was receding from Reggie's room. The burning of the light had made his eyeballs feel like pickled onions, but now, fortified by Mrs Pike's care and a supper of creamed sweetbreads followed by caramel custard, he was able to read fairly comfortably. He noted the abundance of mounds and earthworks in the area and spent a long time studying a stone head said to be housed in Tidworth's museum, evidence of the cult of the severed head. Its features were crude, with gashed eyes and a roughly shaped nose and mouth. But his attention wasn't firmly on E. F. Whittaker's mammoth work. Drowsiness made his eyes slip from a paragraph here and there. Twice he slipped into a half-dreaming state and saw again the vanishing loops and runes of his earlier headache.

Eventually he gave up the battle and went to bed early. His

sleep was not undisturbed. First, he discovered a pebble which must have dislodged itself from his pocket somehow and was pressing upward from beneath his pillow with all the force of that dried pea under the princess's twelve mattresses. Then he was alerted by a curious, regular thumping coming downstairs – finally, after an hour or so's slumber, he was awakened by a noise overhead, not the hairdryer this time but faint song – unaccompanied and wistful, in a minor key. It broke his sleep and then so permeated it that the singer glided into view. A pale, indistinctly featured maiden in a simple grey worsted shift, she hung above the foot of his bed, hands clasped, feet pointed downward. She was like a painted angel faded by time.

4

Morning school on Saturdays wasn't without its disadvantages, thought Reggie as, much refreshed, he slunk from Sunnybank at eight-fifteen on the following day. Bright, cloud-scudded skies and roads that were shedding their holiday queues might seem all too ideal for driving practice and he had plans of his own to implement. The Turtledown Army ranges that ran up behind the school and curved away to embrace six miles of coastline would be closed to the public this week-end. If he didn't seize his opportunity immediately, he would be robbed of the glorious walk until next June.

Weighed down by books, he took a short cut across the parkland surrounding the school, and regretted it. An odd collection of pale-coloured horned cows observed his progress with watchful interest, one of them advancing uncomfortably close. It lowered its great head, splayed its legs as though about to charge, then swerved after the other beasts.

Nervousness possibly eased the bolts on Reggie's system. As he headed for the cattle grid and the rugger pitches beyond, a sweet turning in the gut presaged the kindest relief imaginable. The pleasure of anticipated release was so acute, it was almost tempting to prolong it.

At the side of the pink stuccoed, Georgian building, around the bike-sheds, small boys struggled together, cast marbles and swung on a tyre suspended from an evergreen oak. Its leaves were wearied and dusty by the dry summer.

'Morning, sir!'

'*Morning*, boys!' Oh, the joy of it.

'Morning, sir!'

The northerly entrance to Reggie's anal passage bulged luxuriantly.

'Morning, Montis!'

Oh God, was Garsington going to stop him? There came a

point when protraction swallowed itself and became retraction. 'Morning!' cried Reggie, trying to look urgent.

'Must chat sometime.' Garsington passed on, his gown billowing about his athletic figure. Garsington was a Cambridge Blue.

Thankfully, Reggie stumbled on, briefly impeded by a day boy's mother, who reversed rakishly and disgorged five ebullient creatures from her car.

'Morning! Morning! Morning!' hallooed Reggie, and swept towards the staff cloakroom in a state of near ecstasy.

Blissful post-faecal stupor gave a buoyancy to everything. Reggie faced 3B with a benevolent air.

'Well,' he said, 'we all start together. ' His heart went out to the evident new boys, drowned in their clothes and pinched about the mouths with misery. 'And we all start at the beginning. Let's see what you know.'

They knew little and what they did know seemed to have come from Goscinny's *Asterix* rather than Reggie's predecessor. He crouched and drew a line marked BC at the bottom of the board. 'OK,' he said. 'Let's fill in the space.' And then, catching the subdued expressions, 'It's all right. I used to think this was the most boring bit, too. But it's not. Just wait!' Eschewing all its subdivisions, he drew another line two-thirds of the way down the board, and chalked STONE AGE right across it. 'That takes us a good way back,' he exclaimed, but found 3B's sense of time unable to leap 500,000 years. He coaxed them closer towards the Neolithic, which they plainly thought of as time when ape men dragged women around by their hair. He showed them a photograph of the Laussel Venus, to try to explain how, on the contrary, the female form was venerated. He was himself moved by the angle of the neck as it leaned towards the cornucopia, by the five scratched fingers resting on a swollen belly. Giggling interrupted his perusal and Reggie realized that he'd stimulated the wrong sort of interest. Nevertheless, it *was* interest. He seized it and diverted it to his own purpose. Matravers, who had been to Stonehenge, helped him by describing the guide, an ex-pilot who had seen so many strange formations from the air during his flying years that, when he left the service, he could think of nothing else. 'He said

54

his wife thought he was barmy,' said Matravers confidentially. Still, the fact that a fighter pilot could now spend his life within a stone circle was enough to make 3B look on Reggie's chart with a gleam of curiosity.

'Let's say . . . what? 1500 BC for the start of the Bronze Age. All dates are approximate. There was no public announcement, you understand. No bloke to say "All right, chaps, down stone axes; pick up your bronze ones." '

The class warmed. Even one tear-stained child at the back began to blink away his grief.

Reggie drew a long barrow beside NEOLITHIC STONE AGE and a round barrow beside BRONZE AGE. He drew a short-bladed knife beside the round barrow and a long-bladed one beside IRON AGE. It was all looking rather professional. He stood back and admired it. 'About here,' he pointed to IRON AGE, 'the Celts arrive. What do you know of them?'

They knew they had a football team.

And Reggie said no (through the laughter), not to shriek – the Celts really did still dwell in Scotland and Ireland, living descendants of a people who fought and feasted, boasted of heroes and satisfied their restless energies with cattle raids if a battle was not easily to hand. A people who severed the heads of their enemies and kept them at the door to ward off the evil spirits, a people who sacrificed their fellow humans and, less reliably, ate them on occasions. Oh, yes, they lived still.

The boys looked in awe at O'Rourke who suddenly acquired a new playground reputation and was later to be propitiated with crisps and caps and conkers.

The general excitement was interrupted by a tidy-minded child who wanted to know when the Iron Age ended so that he would know how far down his page he could go.

'We're still in it,' said Reggie.

'Sir?' The child looked at him with disbelief.

'Oh, yes,' nodded Reggie.

'But, sir,' interrupted Tidy's neighbour, a boy with badly cut hair and a glass eye, 'aren't we in the space age?'

'Nuclear age, you twit,' hissed Blackstock from behind Tidy and Eyeball.

* * *

55

Reggie smiles at them. He is ridiculously happy. As happy as once he was at his own prep. school. It is a recollection that has faded, but now comes back: an interval of jokes and gangs and games, of linked arms, whispers, stolen fruit, and dens. Why did he ever leave the classroom? He is native there.

He banged the blackboard with his knuckles. 'No,' he said. 'We still principally use the same metal for our tools today. The Iron Age, we're still in it.'

And thus he closed for 3B – in the space of forty minutes – an alien half million years. Time contracted and held them.

*　　　*　　　*

The staffroom lament continued.

Ogilvy, rubbing the remarkable promontory of his nose, was getting up a petition to head off Garsington's plans for the future of the school, and so anxious was Ogilvy to sign it, that his yellowed features were tinged a living pink.

Reggie, approached for his support, still felt too light-bodied, too light-spirited to take it as seriously as he was intended to do.

'Newcomer's restraint?' Amis drew his close-cropped and curly head confidingly near. His breath was not good. He had one of those unfortunately jutting jaws that impose an unintended leer on their owners' faces. He came closer. 'The chief objectors,' he whispered, 'are those who feel Garsington was promoted over their heads.'

'Oh?'

'It's all right. Tomorrow the topic will have changed. I'm taking odds on nationalization and the price of beef. We keep in touch with the outside world – in our way.'

*　　　*　　　*

Walking away from school through the copse whose outer perimeter formed a boundary with Army territory, Reggie was still amused by the English master's detachment. He admired it. Thought he might model his own manner upon it. At this distance, Dorothy seemed like a raging goddess lost in her own sacred maze. He tried out the feeling of being without any convictions whatever, and found it suited him. It was a form of freedom.

Ironically, the notice at the barrier, stating that the ranges were Army property, listed a long collection of prohibitions and cautions. Keep to the paths, beware unexploded shells, avoid fire hazards, and venture near the cliff edge at one's own risk. These prospective perils fitted ill with the tranquil, gorse-burnt heathland which interleaved and reached away to a shining sky. Beyond, invisible, lay the sea. The air was filled with the restless tick of grasshoppers and small cream, brown, blue and orange butterflies.

Reggie stood at the lowest point of the rising land and examined the map of Turtledown ranges. From here he could take a path which joined up with the main walk reaching from Swale Harbour in the east to the back of Tidmouth, six miles away in the west. It was the shortest route, but some quarter of a mile back from the headland. If, instead, he were to go on beyond the crossed, sandy routes, he could fork down to Wimble Cove, pick up the cliff path there, and walk back over Turtle Hill itself to Tidmouth. It would still amount to six miles if the curves of the coastline were taken into account, and was probably much harder going. He wriggled his toes inside his new walking-boots to test their comfort, and set off.

The landscape, riven by tank tracks and scattered with square, yellow targets, was empty of all human life. The only movement was the slow, cropping advance of distant sheep apparently exempt from the dangers of unexploded shells, since they grazed on the forbidden side of the wire. Indeed, the very frequency of the warning notices about shells, adorned with cautionary skulls, was self-defeating. In no time at all, Reggie was oblivious to them. He drew at the air and caught the scent of wild rosemary. Head high, he strode towards the crossroads marked as Shepherd Hill, and from its rounded height saw the wild, outrageous upflown frill of cliff racing out of the down and ahead of him. Below it lay the stunning glitter of the English Channel.

As he forked left for the descent to Wimble Cove, his eye was fixed on a collection of stone buildings, largely obscured by trees, about a mile away in the valley. They nestled around a dried river bed. The only clearly visible feature was the small towers of what seemed, at this distance, to be a Norman church. This must be the deserted village of Maidenwell. There was still, so Ned Starkey had told him, a depth of bitterness felt by the older villagers who had been turned out of their homes by the Army some fifteen years before. The younger ones, now married and conveniently rehoused on the East Tidmouth estate which Reggie passed on his way to school each morning, were happy to be nearer the shops, happy to have the Army provide work and trade. They rolled their eyes with tolerant exasperation when their elders sang of their grievances.

As he drew downhill, flints scattering beneath his stout shoes, Reggie became aware of hammering sounds. There was life of some description in Maidenwell. The church was now clearly visible, a small sturdy building in surprisingly good condition. On yet closer inspection, Reggie noted that many of the gravestones were new, their bland colour unblotched by lichen. He turned the corner of the graveyard wall into the village, and realized that the hammering came from within the church itself. Ladders and buckets were stacked outside the porch and a small blue van, emblazoned with the golden words 'Orlebar and Gedge, Building Contractors', was parked at the gate. Always eager to explore churches, Reggie pushed his way in and up the path. A workman stood at the half-open door and stared at him.

'Good afternoon!' Reggie saluted the large, elderly man. He regarded Reggie with suspicion, and slipped a chisel in his dungarees. 'Afternoon,' he responded guardedly. The silence round them was immense.

'Is it possible to – er – look . . .?' Over the workman's shoulder Reggie could see the walls had been freshly plastered and a frieze picked out in red and gold.

'No visitors allowed in.' The man stared discouragingly, the lower rims of his eyes damp and sore-looking.

'Ah.' The lack of welcome made Reggie back away apologetically. 'Sorry to intrude.'

The hammering did not resume until Reggie had clicked the

churchyard gate behind him. In passing, he had noticed fresh flowers on the new graves, and a date: 1834. Odd.

He stood on the unmade road and looked about at the tiny collection of ruined buildings. No more than half a dozen roofless cottages and one larger house set back behind a disintegrating wall. The blindness of the buildings confronted him through their screen of beech and ivy, giving forth a sense of dumb hurt.

Following the sandy road towards a bridge that spanned the silent, unrunning river, Reggie saw other signs of incongruous repair: the well, a round, stone-walled circle was newly pointed. It looked like a feature in some prosperous suburban garden, an insulting, unfeeling piece of restoration. He peered into its dark centre and dropped a pebble. He heard the pebble clatter on others. He hurried on.

Directly ahead, blocking any view of the sea, rose the weird lonely shape of Wimble Toot, which he knew from the map to be a protrusion jutting into the sea from the shore, but looking, from this position, as though it was a pyramid set on the land. Reggie, becoming accustomed to the deceits of this turbulent geology, hastened his step towards it. On his right stretched the densely tangled, impenetrable woodland that clustered over the last of Maidenwell. Ahead of him, to the left of the Toot, the cliff rose as if trying to wrench itself away from the earth. The whole coastline articulated struggle and upward flight as if its relations with the sea had always been savage, a reflection made yet more apparent when he stood on the little ridge connecting the Toot to the mainland. It clung on, this large, thinly-grassed mound, it clung on by a rocky thread, refusing to be abandoned to the sea as a steep-walled island. On its easterly side the main cliff-face flared up out of deep, dark green water, fan-shaped, rucked, as generously striped as a humbug. At its base was a sizeable cave which the sea, with hungry slapping sounds, seemed to have licked out of the limestone.

Reggie stood alone on his small peninsula and exulted in his solitude. In the other direction, west towards Tidmouth, reached the graceful curve of Wimble Cove. Here was one of those astonishing variations in geology. Here, where the dried river bed opened out into the sea, the cliff rose low and slowly, a red sandstone which lent itself to a fine, pebble-free beach. Then the cliff began to rise at an ever-increasing angle until, at its most precipitous point, it again blazed white before a pale-green sea. Unprepared for the immense height of it, Reggie realized that this would amount to a stiff test of under-exercised legs and, putting his head down, he began a steady haul up to the dizziest point of Turtledown.

Half-way up he was forced to rest. He sat, perched danger-ously on the slope, and gloried in the cove below. Although there were no large waves, the movement of the water sounded busy. A lobster boat rode the sea at a bluer distance. To the west a thicker sky began to gather and momentarily turned to the colour of putty the white face of the eagle cliff.

He resumed his climb, negotiating the last twenty yards or so on hands and knees, flints slithering away beneath him with sickening speed. Even here, as he neared the crown, there were notices about shells on the barbed-wire fence, though Reggie found it hard to imagine that much firing was attempted here. The greater hazard was the bitten cliff-edge. He no longer wanted to look down. No birds called.

Scrabbling his way to the stile that separated the top of the slope from an interesting banked earthwork, he leant over it a while, panting, and looking curiously at the formation. He hadn't discerned it from below at all and, as he'd climbed, the need to keep his head down had prevented his glimpsing it until this moment of arrival. As he hung there, a wretched bag of middle-aged parts, a cheerful voice hailed him. Dufferdill's domed head with its lavish, whiskery embellishments appeared over the ridge.

'Good God, Montis!' Dufferdill sounded concerned. 'Are you all right? Nobody ever climbs Turtle from the east side. Not more than once anyway. It's a killer.'

'Just . . . getting . . . my . . . breath.'

'I bet you bloody are. All feak and weeble, I'd say. Just you rest a jiffy while I do the talking.'

He was as good as his word.

'Seen the Toot down there? It's a corruption of "tit", well,

60

"teat"; well "tits" a corruption of it, if you see what I mean. Can you imagine anybody these days – imagine the monarch – having the nerve to say, "I name this place Tit Hill"? Actually, it would be Tit Avenue, wouldn't it? Tit Crescent? Like all the estates round Maiden Castle. Seen 'em? Caesar Close, Caractacus Crescent ... bloody hell! OK? I usually have a stroll Saturday when I'm not supervising games or orchestra practice. The wife goes shopping in Swale; got a discount card for the Rush and Hurry. Picks me up t'other end. Next time you come along here, Montis, you want to approach it from the ridge path – there – do you see? Come straight up from the East Tidmouth Gate. I suppose you've come through Maidenwell?'

As Dufferdill sprang up and pointed, Reggie realized that a straight walk ran all along the spine of the downland and, had he not forked left at Shepherd Hill, attracted by the deserted village, he would have been here exploring, some half an hour earlier.

'I expect you've come to see the fort. Not a lot to look at, since half of it's fallen into the sea. Still, I suppose you know all that. The wife's always telling me not to teach grandmothers about the sucking of eggs, but there we are; it's a vice of the teaching profession.'

'A fort?' Reggie stood up, genuinely surprised. The single raised bank suggested nothing so grand. Nothing was marked on the map.

'Good heavens, yes! Come and take a gander.' Gamely, Dufferdill was struggling back the way he'd come. Reggie took in the full oddity of his appearance: knapsack, bottle-green corduroy plus-fours, and thick, green, hand-knitted socks.

'Tour first, then aperitif? Or perhaps you need a drink straight away? Of course you do; how thoughtless of me.' Dufferdill slid down on his bottom, unfastening his knapsack. Reggie's fretting curiosity was made to wait.

'Whisky? Beer? Lager?'

'Lager would be just the thing, thanks.' It was hard not to smile. Reggie took the can handed to him and ripped off the tab. 'I can see why I was deceived,' he said. 'There's no need to build defensive ramparts at all on this site. Nature has done the job very effectively.'

'And on the sea, the south-facing side too,' agreed Dufferdill, opening his own can messily. 'Absolutely unassailable.'

'Strange position, though,' mused Reggie. 'I mean, it doesn't command any vital trackway or crossing of valleys.'

'Unless,' considered Dufferdill, 'you want to repel an invading fleet of coracles.' Reggie laughed. He was beginning to think that his colleague's confusion of periods was deliberate. An obscure kind of joke.

'On the other hand,' continued Dufferdill, 'they'd've had a devil of a job keeping out any callers from the north, and that, as I've recommended to you, is the natural approach point. In fact, considering all the trouble they've gone to, digging ramparts on the western side, you might well conclude the whole thing was the work of Irish jobbing builders.'

Mildly light-headed from exertion and drink, Reggie staggered after Dufferdill, who pointed out the relevant contours with the brisk enthusiasm of an estate agent selling a property. 'Useful double ditch; embankment; quite a decent mound here ... considerable damage on seaward side ... now for the impressive bit!'

He strode so fast over the worn path that wound its way over grass-covered dips and bumps that Reggie, after pausing to glance hurriedly at this feature or that, had to run to keep up with him.

'How about that!' Dufferdill stood, legs apart, knuckles resting on his hips, looking down the western descent of the hill.

'That's more like it,' breathed Reggie. A substantial series of ditches and ramparts descended below them, uniformly cropped by rabbits and sheep: three ramparts in all.

'Looks as though they meant business on this side, eh? Warding off rates demands from the Tidmouth urban district councillors maybe.' Dufferdill approved its shape. 'Still, small beer for this part of the country. Better stuff round Casterwich, especially Roman – much more interesting. I don't, as I said, go for the non-literate periods. Lends itself to wild guesswork.' Reggie felt this was intended for him. 'Where sources are limited to unwritten evidence, the amateurs have a heyday. All sorts of romantic nonsense.'

'Or the strictly scientific.'

'As you say, the strictly dull, scientific. Lists, classifications. Monumentally tedious, if you'll forgive the pun. Still, it improves the view, this kind of thing!' He waved a hand expansively.

The view was superb. Far to the west, the pale, humped shadow of Portland Bill was visible. Rambling towards it, the yellow headlands rose and fell convulsively. To the north, before the plain stretched away in a geometric pattern of fields, a purple belt of heather engirdled the pale, alien stacks and buildings of Winburgh's atomic research station. Tiny, sharp movements of light showed where cars passed along the narrow roads. Far away, a small red combine cut shadows in the wheat. Toy cows speckled the yellow fields. But everything was powerfully removed. Around them, the space and the silence were vast.

'It's a pity,' sighed Reggie, looking regretfully at the barbed-wire fence, 'that we can't poke about a bit more. There can't seriously be unexploded shells up here.'

'Oh no?' Dufferdill pointed solemnly to a shallow ditch twelve feet to their right.

'Good God!' Reggie caught sight of a rusted metal canister up-ended against a stone.

'It's mostly quite safe, but the Army's not going to risk its reputation on the odd exploding rambler. That's why they're doing up the church.'

'At Maidenwell?' Reggie was learning to tag on to Dufferdill's erratic conversational course.

'Bit of a stink about the church being shelled.' Dufferdill wiped his nose noisily with the back of his hand and, in so doing, caught sight of his watch. 'Holy eels! Half-past three! The wife'll play havoc if I'm not in Swale by five. Yes, the villagers still regard the place as sacrosanct, as indeed it is. Consecrated ground and all that. There's a woman I know believes that a piece of consecrated ground, applied to bruises, grazes or sprains, heals them instantly. I don't know about instantly; I dare say it works after a week or two. Anyway, all the fault of some johnnies with less than twenty-twenty vision. Should never have happened.'

'Ironic, isn't it?' Reggie nodded towards the blunted, visible end of the shell. 'Just as well there are no residents of this fort left to complain and demand a special pass for grave-tending. How we do insult the sensibilities, generation after generation! Still, sacred places have a way of remaining sacred places – in the countryside, anyway. I don't suppose the removal of a Methodist church hall in Bromsgrove would have much impact.'

Dufferdill laughed ruefully. 'Each new civilization makes it its business to try and smash the religion of the last, but they always end up adapting, incorporating, somehow. Makes you wonder what we have left for the invader to adapt, doesn't it? The corporal who took a pot shot at the tower probably thought all religion had come to an end, and he has certain grounds . . . Still, the Army's not all bad. It leaves the plant and wild life to flourish. I'll show you some of our rarer species another time but must get on now, I fear. The wife! It takes me well over the hour to reach Swale. See you, Montis! Enjoy your walk!'

He swung his arm dangerously in a form of salute. Reggie accompanied him to the stile and watched a little of his friend's cautious, slithering, arm-wheeling descent of the precipitous slope before turning back to survey the fort at leisure. Half a mile away sheep, bleating at some imagined terror, ran bobbing through the gorse.

Returning to the north entrance on the ridge, Reggie was struck by the lack of any serious fortification, remarked upon by Dufferdill. Even allowing for the erosion of three, maybe four thousand years, it was quite evident that the ramparts of the western side had not been continued as an effective encirclement of the site. Although there was an outerwork, normally a sign of a defensive entrance, it was so modest that it barely mattered. Any marauding tribe advancing from the hinterland could enter virtually unimpeded. It made no kind of sense.

As far as he could judge, the site, looked at from above,

would have a slight figure-of-eight formation, the larger bulb lying to the west, most rigorously fortified end. It was hard, of course, to know how much of the area – roughly an acre and a half on the top – had crumbled away into the sea. Tempted, Reggie glanced about him and, seeing no walkers in any direction (Dufferdill must still be shuffling down the lower slopes of Turtle Hill), he squeezed under the barbed wire that flimsily barricaded the seamost part of the site. He climbed down the bank formed by the slip. Ten feet in front of him, the violently bitten-off edge of the cliff brought the dangers of trespass home, but between himself and the edge lay the modest remaining contour of a barrow. At least, the disturbance of the ground suggested that. It was only a small, shallow depression and mound of the disc-barrow type associated with female burials and appropriately shaped more like a nipple than a bowl. A far less common type, but it did look a little like it ... Reggie hovered, and wondered if he were guilty of the wishful thinking which Dufferdill so abhorred. He looked out to sea. A pale star seemed to float below the surface of the now grey water, reflecting its radiance upwards. Screwing his eyes up, he saw that this strange image was a reversal, a form of mirror image – that the submerged star sapphire was a reflection of the sun leaking through a layer of cloud. A drowned sun.

How easy it would be to fall into a trance, induced by the quiet hypnotic rush of the sea and the glowing, sunken star! Reggie shook himself. The place was not safe.

And yet, for a second, victim of the spell he has recognized is possible, Reggie walks nearer the edge and lies down. He is not, he is not an imaginative man.

The plunge was dreadful. The sea moved stickily some five hundred feet below, the unsteadiness of its surface transmitting nausea. His sense of gravity seemed pulled over the cliff. He gripped the hard, chalky edge and steadied himself. As he did so, the sun broke through its prison of cloud, expelling the star and once again releasing the clear, green radiance of the water. Now Reggie could see more clearly the rocky ridges that ran out from the base of the cliff, out under the water – part, perhaps, of the fallen cliff-top where he lay. They had the appearance of two giant legs, the shins and thighs of a vast drowned figure whose body was submerged beneath a net of weed. The water shifted caressingly over the limbs. Reggie could not get up.

Turning his head to one side to avoid staring any longer at the watery tomb below, he glimpsed the reassuring, bottle-green figure of Dufferdill toiling up the eagle-wings of the neighbouring cliff. Dufferdill could not have guessed what comfort he offered at that moment. Cautiously retreating on his stomach, his eyes fixed on Dufferdill's knapsack, Reggie re-gained a safe position and scrambled on hands and knees below the wire. So hard was his heart beating that he had to rest a few moments before he had the strength to continue down the official pathway and on to the much gentler rise of downland.

As he walked, moving shadows encircled his progress. Look-ing up, he saw gulls which seemed silently and suddenly to have appeared from nowhere. They flew above his head in a snowy garland, though every now and then a pair would peel away from the circle and alight a few feet ahead, gazing out to sea, then take off again as Reggie approached. The underside of their wings – thin, pure shapes of flight – was gleaming white. They made little sound, just an intermittent, gentle chatting. As they escorted Reggie westward, their shadows, spinning round and round on the turf, became more numerous. They were joined by two birds with black plumage that Reggie couldn't readily identify. He spun on his heels, watching them, and assumed – rightly – they must be jackdaws.

The closer he drew towards Tidmouth, the greater the company of gulls became. Their attendant presence might have seemed sinister but, as it was, Reggie welcomed the company of these sighing tribunes.

5

On Sunday morning he lay in bed longer than he had intended.

The Misses Cox were away for the week-end and he had begged Mrs Pike not to make breakfast for him. When, with a touching ignorance of the world's common hunger, she had insisted that no human being could possibly survive a day without breakfast, he had sheepishly admitted he had cereals of his own. 'Well,' she'd conceded eventually, her face relaxing very slowly on this point, 'you must let me give you Sunday dinner then.'

So, aching in every limb, he lay in bed at half-past ten, looking out on the cheerful clutter of houses that gripped the hillside beyond, glad of something to look forward to. The darkness of his room chilled him briefly. (Sunnybank really was a most unsuitable name.) The dimness of the room, the silence of the house now Mrs Pike had left for Mass, or perhaps the fact that it was Sunday – a closed day with no family excursion or argument to fill it – prompted an unexpected bout of homesickness.

The smeared, lachrymose faces of one or two new boys flashed across his mind.

Chiding himself, he swung his legs out of bed, felt fruitlessly for his slippers and forbade all recollection of crumpled Sunday paper, pop records, roasting lamb and Dorothy's gin on the kitchen window sill. This was not a memory of the recent past, but a general recollection of a life four, five, six years old, when the children could still be seen at home.

It was their departure, he thinks, polishing his glasses on his pyjama jacket, it was their going that left us staring at one another like strangers.

He padded to the door and, opening it, found his feet smothered in a warm, wet, ticklish embrace. Enraptured to find her own loneliness ended, Bundle thrust her tongue between

Reggie's toes and made him squeal. He bent to pick the puppy up and, laughing, pulled her close to his body. Her furious licking was redirected to his stubble, his ears, his open, half-protesting mouth. 'Hey! Hey! *Silly!*' Her wiry body wriggled in every part of itself as he strove to hold her still. 'Steady on!' he cried and held her away from himself a little. 'Good morning, Bundle. Good to see you.' And with an affectionate shake he put her down. She jumped round his ankles, gripping a pyjama leg for reassurance every now and then as he struggled to the kitchenette alcove down the passage.

It was not a space intended for much cooking. Little more than a larder, contrived by partitioning one end of the bathroom wall with tongue and groove, it had no window and allowed for nothing that could not be achieved on two rings. The ventilator above the original washbasin let in a few threads of light, but not enough. He wondered whether it was possible to peep into the bathroom through the tongue and groove, and quickly pulled the light switch to prevent himself finding out.

As he emptied his All-Bran into a plastic bowl, whisking the dried milk powder to a watery, lumpy substitution with a fork, a fragment of melancholy returned. A feeling that blew straight in from his student days. A chill and anxious combination of new-found independence and a fear that one could not handle worthily the freedom it offered. A fear that one's own inadequacy, second-rateness, would be cruelly exposed by the space now opened wide for their display.

Bundle stood against him on wobbly hind legs and begged his affection. He picked her up and, holding her under his left arm, carried both her and his cereal back to bed.

*　　　*　　　*

He bought a *Sunday Times* from the newsagent's down by the harbour. A smell of bacon drifted from the back of the shop. The proprietor, almost obscured by postcards and sticks of rock, remarked on the continuing fineness of the weather, showing that he thought Reggie was a tripper. To a resident he would have remarked on the drought.

Although warm, it was such a pale, hazy day that the far

headland was invisible, the seam of sea and sky unmarked. A veil of azure, suspended from space, hung over the shore, diffusing the light in a way that made it difficult to focus on anything for long. It was the sort of weather that attracted visitors anxious to seize the last of the summer. Soon, the tired dry leaves would fall. Many of the trippers were already unpacking picnics and setting up striped canvas screens on the beach.

Thinking the museum might be open, Reggie walked along the promenade towards the small turreted building, enjoying the light September warmth, but wishing he had a pair of sunglasses. He screwed his eyes up, feeling the needle points of brightness that flew inland off the water prick behind the retina. Trying not to look towards the sea, he kept his gaze on the gabled and balconied houses to his left, but even their soft, pastel colours flared in the refulgent morning, and he blinked away, catching, between slats of darkness, the splendid movement of a horse being ridden through diamond sprays at the water's edge. He was compelled to look again at the silhouette. More striking even than the proud and beautiful curves of the animal's architecture was the smallness of the mounted figure. A child. A girl whose hair flew out in starry, gold-tipped trails.

As horse and rider cantered away towards the harbour, no longer in a direct line with the sun, Reggie could see the animal was purest white. With its plumy tail and rounded quarters springing rhythmically through the water, it resembled some newly emerged sea creature. Reggie blinked. And blinked again. For he was sure the tiny figure astride the animal was Phoebe. But no, it could not be – a child of five or six? No, she could not possibly control so large a beast. His eyes hurt. He looked away. Every head on the beach was turned as if by an incredulity that matched his own. The conjunction of white and gold and glittering spray marked the passing of a princess.

The museum was closed until two.

Reggie cursed and, finding a bench in the shade, tried to absorb reports of a world that seemed absurdly distant. But the apprehension that had stood angel to his waking was not so easily dismissed. He found he was skimming the news pages uncomprehendingly, and turned with relief to reviews of films, plays and exhibitions that would never be seen by the residents of Tidmouth, least of all by the newly self-exiled, who had to justify their arrival here by clinging to its amenities as if they could nowhere be bettered.

* * *

Mrs Pike was standing on a chair, hanging a new flypaper from the lamp flex when Reggie entered the hall, smelling out his lunch.

'Ridiculous!' cried Mrs Pike, who was looking very trim in a navy suit with a navy and white shirt tied cravat fashion at the throat. She lowered her arms. 'The number of bluebottles!'

'Is it?' said Reggie.

'For the time of year. Disgusting!' She stepped down off the chair. Reggie rushed forward, too late, to offer his hand. 'It's the drought,' she said. 'Never known anything like it.'

'It can't go on,' said Reggie comfortingly.

'We can only pray,' sighed Mrs Pike, then, altering her attitude, she clasped her hands briskly before her and inquired whether he would like a sherry before his dinner.

'So good of you!' gulped Reggie, thinking he must resist. He mustn't succumb to the continual offer of comfort she embodied. 'But, sorry, I've got . . .'

' . . . one or two things to do,' she supplied.

'One or two. *Exactly*.' He was released.

'One-thirty sharp!' she called up as he reached the first landing.

He wondered what form the lunch arrangements would take. Would he eat at his own table, with his mirror image for company? Would they eat together? In the dining-room? In the kitchen? He became agitated by the possibilities of the ritual, and was still wiping his palms on his handkerchief (having done nothing but start and abandon a letter to Dorothy in the meanwhile), when he entered the dining-room and found the problem solved.

'Hello there!' Father Starkey, sitting at Reggie's table, rose to his feet.

'Good heavens above!' They shook hands. 'What an agreeable surprise,' added Reggie, wondering if his first exclamation amounted to blasphemy.

'I help out at St Teresa's occasionally,' explained the priest, 'and dear Bella insisted I eat here. It takes very little pressure . . .' He turned as Mrs Pike reappeared with an apron over her good suit. 'Very little pressure required to accept an invitation. I suffer from bachelor greed. Allow me, Bella dear.' He took the plates, already filled, and gazed on them devotionally. 'Sunday lunchtime marks starvation peak.'

'Just give me a coo-ee when you're finished.' Mrs Pike slipped away, her fingers making twinkling movements.

'Ah!' Reggie understood. 'Mass, you mean?'

'Precisely. Whatever can be said for the food of the spirit, I haven't in all truth found it much fills the belly.' Father Starkey flicked out his napkin and tucked it in at the neck. 'Forgive the nursery trait, but grease on the cassock . . .'

'Of course.' Reggie pushed the apple sauce towards his friend and examined the contents of his own plate with interest. The helpings of roast potatoes, pork, stuffing, peas and carrots were generous, and unspoilt by glutinous dollops of packet-mix gravy.

'We've been praying for rain today,' remarked the priest. 'Delightfully pagan. I enjoyed that.'

'I hope it works, if that's what's needed.' Reggie began eating. He had the dimmest notion of the exigencies caused by drought. In Hounslow there had been no obvious problem at all.

'Oh, the farmers are getting very desperate – you've probably noticed how poor the crops have been.'

'To be frank, no. It's rather shocking, but I doubt if I'd know a good crop when I saw one. I did, mind, think the downland looked burnt out yesterday.' And he gave an account of his walk.

'You visited Maidenwell?'

'I passed through. Bit spooky.'

'It's a sad business. I say, I wonder if I could trouble you for a little more apple sauce?'

A silence fell between them briefly, and Reggie was moved

71

to ask how it was that Father Starkey ('Ned, my dear fellow; Ned, *please.*') how Ned had arrived at . . . Lost for the proper phrase, Reggie waved his fork.

'The celibate state?' offered Father Starkey.

'That wasn't exactly what I meant, no.'

'It's what people generally mean when they ask about one's faith or vocation. There's always that unspoken query lying at the back of their curiosity.'

Reggie began to demur. 'I meant nothing so personal, I promise you, Ned.'

'Faith *is* personal, my dear chap. Heavens above, *I* don't mind. It is very curious, after all, and if I were a younger man I should be actively with those who are campaigning for a married priesthood. I'm with them in spirit. With them in prayer. Now that I'm not much troubled' – he ducked to catch a falling scrap of crackling – 'not much troubled by carnal desires, I can see how ridiculous it is to ask chastity of a young man. When one is troubled by them it seems, on the contrary, to be perfectly sensible to keep them at bay. Or it did.' He chewed thoughtfully for a while.

Reggie tried to frame a less blunt inquiry. 'But when did you realize your vocation?' he ventured. 'To be honest, I've always wondered what people meant by a "calling" in the religious sense. It seems to mean so much more than strong personal inclination. Are you called in the exact sense?'

'Voices, do you mean?'

'Well, yes, I suppose I do.' Reggie coughed faintly. 'If that doesn't sound naïve.'

The priest swallowed and digested. 'Looking back,' he began, 'I'm inclined to think I was carved out for the Church by three factors – a country upbringing, a remarkable mother, and a pronouncedly sensual temperament – but at the *time* – when I was in my early twenties, that is – yes, I could say I felt called in the literal sense. However,' and the priest cleaned the corners of his mouth the better to lean forward and converse, 'I can't pretend I heard a cultivated English voice urging me to enter the priesthood. Had I done so, I think I would have concluded, even in those unpsychoanalytic days, that my own voice was masquerading as the Almighty's.'

'*Not* a voice, then?' Reggie put down his knife and fork, curious in spite of himself.

'*No* . . . A *sense*! I imagine that sounds frightfully vague to a non-believer. I can see from your face it does. You *are* a non-believer, aren't you?'

'Oh, absolutely.' Reggie was firm. He was nursing a new-found existentialism.

'You think man limits himself by harbouring notions of God?'

'At its briefest, yes.'

'Mmm,' said Father Starkey. 'The standard opposition. I, you see, think man can achieve his highest potential through God. There's little meeting-point. I respect your position.' He was perfectly amiable about it. Relieved that he was not about to be converted, Reggie turned, alerted by Phoebe's arrival in the doorway.

'Granny says do you want any more?'

'It's hard to say no,' admitted Reggie.

'Indeed it is,' agreed Father Starkey, surrendering his plate. 'Tell Granny the crackling was de-licious. She might have a fragment more to spare.'

But the little girl was scowling as she concentrated on scraping the plates.

'Didn't I catch sight of you astride a white horse this morning?' Reggie asked, his voice ingratiating.

'There's no such thing as white horses,' said Phoebe, and retired with her burden of crockery.

Reggie was taken aback. He had a dim recollection of Antonia in her jodhpur era saying much the same thing with much the same scorn. All white horses were called grey, she'd groaned disparagingly. Perhaps that was Phoebe's drift. Or perhaps he'd been seeing things.

The priest was talking, continuing his earlier theme. 'I woke in the middle of the night,' he was saying, 'intensely aware of a presence within my room. I wasn't *afraid*; there was nothing malevolent about it, but a very real sense of something there.

So vast that it pressed against the walls and ceiling. As real as the nose on my face. No, I wasn't dreaming,' he averred, anticipating Reggie's question. 'Literally, I pinched myself. *I* wanted to be quite certain I wasn't dreaming, naturally, before acknowledging a quite overwhelming sense of this presence. And I . . .'

' 'Scuse me.' Phoebe placed their replenished plates before them, and stood back to recite 'Plums and custard or steamed chocolate sponge and custard. Granny is sorry the cream's gone off.'

'Sponge for me, dear, thank you,' replied Reggie. 'Ned?'

'Plums and custard, Phoebe, please. Thank you dear. And as I lay there pinching myself, something I can only describe as a message appeared on the air. Now . . .' He paused to make the experience solemnly clear. His broad and humorous countenance was narrowed by gravity. 'This was not a bit of sky-writing, you understand. No letters of smoke. No visible words at all. The only way I can conceivably describe it is by saying I heard with my eyes.' He laughed. 'Well, there we are! It just shows one shouldn't attempt to articulate the mystical experience, *but* . . . the interesting thing was the message. Now if it had come in answer to anything I'd been thinking or praying about, my suspicions would have been alerted. But it was something totally unconsidered.'

'Yes?' said Reggie eagerly.

' "Go and preach".'

'That was the message?'

'Yes. "Go and preach".'

'That was all?' It was a bit disappointing really.

'The implications were quite far-reaching.'

'I imagine, yes. But *preach*. The message didn't suggest which faith, which branch of the company you might favour?'

'What a mischief-maker you are, Montis! I never supposed it was Mahomet in my bedroom.'

Pudding was discreetly produced by Mrs Pike who whispered another apology about the cream and the heat, then slipped away, delighted by the evident pleasure the two men were taking in one another's company. There was a loneliness in Mr Montis.

'So why Catholicism?' Reggie pressed.

The priest nodded over Reggie's shoulder. 'It had a good deal to do with her.'

'What!' gasped Reggie. Some long-forgotten, unconsummated love affair between Mrs Pike and the priest! The astonishment that flooded his face communicated itself.

'No. *Her!*' Father Starkey pointed above and to the left of the hatch. Reggie followed the finger's direction. 'Ah!' He understood. The Bellini virgin. 'I see.'

'There I was, degree in Greats, half a desire to go into the theatre in some capacity, repelled at the same time by the frivolity of the Twenties. I was a depressingly serious young man.'

'You surprise me.'

'I surprise myself when I think about it.'

'With an instruction to preach?'

'Yes. I thought for a long time that maybe I'd got the message wrong. Maybe He or It had said "teach". Imagine the horrors of receiving a message from God and mis-hearing it. You can hardly say "Pardon?" Hardly ask Him to speak up a bit. That wouldn't do at all . . . Anyway, after a little resistance, it made perfect sense. My mother was a saint. A widowed saint – my father was killed in Flanders – and she brought me up single-handed. A very beautiful woman, with a quite extraordinary, radiant gift of peace. Not especially religious in any conventional sense, but probably the most truly *good* person I have ever known. And of course, because I loved and valued her so much, it created problems.'

Reggie pulled his pudding plate towards him nervously. Confessions of a homosexual nature were not in his line. Not over Sunday lunch. But he was saved by Ned Starkey's unabashed description of himself as disgustingly goaty. It sounded like a normal, heterosexual condition.

'And you couldn't, you mean, reconcile your desire for women with the perfect model of womankind you had before you?'

'In a nutshell. Your problem too?'

'Oh, every man's problem to one degree or another. Marry the nice girls, lust after the others. Or we did.' Reggie sounded wistful. He supposed it was all changed now. 'But your problem,' he said, applying himself to the priest, 'was obviously more acute. Not a nice enough girl about.'

'Oh, I don't think I could have brought myself to approach the nice ones. I thought I was contaminated, contaminating. The degree of self-loathing! Once – I've never told anyone this before – once I even tried a bit of the old self-mortification. But I suspect you have to rather like self-mortification to keep it up, and I didn't; so I abandoned it without feeling a scrap better.' Father Starkey slithered a plum stone from his mouth to his spoon and laughed. 'What a prig, eh? But anyway, this is all told with hindsight – the important thing is that I found then – and for different reasons still do – *great* comfort in Our Lady.'

The priest himself had been so frank that Reggie felt not the least hesitant in asking whether this wasn't a flimsy sublimation.

'Self-deceiving? Oh yes, and of a kind that permitted me to go on thinking of women in a quite false light for years later. The Hail Marys I handed out! The absolutions, if I thought them wronged! Shocking really. By equating purity with non-sexuality I was fraudulently resolving my own problems and clinging to a view of women that made me unjust as often as blind. So . . . why didn't I leave the Church?'

Reggie smiled. 'You might say.'

'Tell me if I'm boring you. We could continue this after lunch with a walk. Look, since there are two of us and you plainly enjoy walking, let's try Granny's Sleeve. It's not a place one should venture to on one's own.'

'Granny's Sleeve?'

The priest explained that this was the true cliff above Granny's Gate, the black face there being undercliff which had been pushed forward by successive landslips. The terrain, he said, was now a nature reserve and deliciously dangerous. 'You'd like it. Anyway, you wanted to know why I didn't leave the Church.'

This time Reggie grinned from ear to ear at the priest's

attractive presumption. He obviously adored to talk. They declined coffee to save on water, collected Bundle, congratulated the cook, and struck off through the ornamental gardens that rose on a slope above the promenade.

'By the time I realized my errors, you see,' Father Starkey said, pursuing his narrative beside the clock-golf course, where they sat awhile on a bench in the sun, 'my temperament had quietened. The fires *had* to die down before I could realize the truth, and by then it was all too late to matter. The Church had given me so much and I was – still am – in love with Our Lady for reasons that would undoubtedly be thought heretical in a younger priest. Me? I'm not a danger in the Church, not like Lefèvre, though even that danger I think overrated. No, as I grew older, I became infinitely more tolerant – of myself especially, you must be thinking, and you could be right. No, I'm more and more of the view that God, having given us minds and imagination, would rather we used them than submitted them with dull servitude to inflexible doctrine and liturgy. How *boring* it must be for Him to hear the same chant rising from a million throats! To have created man in such variety and to see him made quite uniform by faith! I don't believe that could have been His intention, do you?'

'You're right, Ned.' Reggie rose and stretched. 'You're a heretic priest. How exciting. I thought you'd all been burnt at the stake three hundred years ago. It's a novelty meeting you. Now take me off to Granny's Sleeve and show me another.'

'Oh, look!' cried Father Starkey as they reached the exit of the gardens. 'There's Bella!'

An A30 hiccoughed slowly down Harbour Street with Mrs Pike clutching its wheel, nose close to the windscreen. Beside her sat her plump and henna-ed daughter Daphne, who waved darkly painted nails at them and pulled a face.

'My turn later,' said Reggie.

'Oh, good! Are you on the rota too? I do Saturdays. We'll have her through her test in no time. I say, what did we do with the dog?'

Guiltily they retraced their path through the gardens where

Bundle, fastened to the leg of the bench was about to be claimed by a small boy whose face she was busily licking.

'Not a word to mother!' The priest warned Bundle, after thanking the boy profusely. 'By the way,' he cautioned Reggie. 'Driving practice. I do urge you to go out of Tidmouth. The hills here are very taxing for the passenger.'

'They're very taxing for walkers!' laughed Reggie, whose legs were still aching abominably after his hike from Turtle-down.

'Nothing like a good pair of stout, country-bred legs!' Father Starkey patted his left thigh approvingly as they headed back towards Harbour Street. 'Last you a lifetime. Now then, you asked me earlier, why Catholicism. And I, I think, mentioned something about a country upbringing. Well, that was it. I absorbed my religion from the hedgerow long before I knew it was religion at all. I just thought it was the miracle of ants and beetles and birds' eggs and new blossom in May. Oh, yes.' They crossed the road and made towards a gate at the far end of the car park, Father Starkey waving up at the windows of a somewhat follied Georgian house. A stern row of urns crowned its front façade and at the side its mathematical lines were abutted by an improbable tower. It was to the upper window of this nice excrescence that Father Starkey waved. 'Mrs Cheeseman,' he explained to Reggie. 'Reclusive old bird, but we need to borrow her house for a charity do near Christmas. Oh yes, creation had impressed me long before I met its architect and, being a young amateur naturalist, I never cared for Protestantism, which has always seemed a very male, urban, cold, northern kind of Christianity to me. It lacks mystery and a proper sense of ritual.'

'Are you sure it isn't superstition you enjoy?' teased Reggie, pulled along by the excitable little dog.

'What do people mean by superstition? Of course, judged by your criteria, I'm superstitious, since superstition is misdirected belief and you don't believe in belief.' Father Starkey thumped his own chest with pleasure and led the way across a fissured field. 'See how broken the ground is? Wait till we get into the wood and see how dramatically the cliff has shifted.

Belief offends because it stems from a simple readiness to believe.'

'Out of ignorance.'

They passed through a gate leading into a lane, and the priest observed that it was possible *not* to believe out of ignorance; but Reggie, momentarily tangled up with the dog, didn't hear him. Father Starkey greeted a cottage owner and sympathized over his garden, which led to a discussion of the pests which flourished in drought conditions, and lasted until they reached the silent woods. In spite of the dry weather, a green dampness prevailed under the trees. The place was full of unseen, calling birds and a rich smell of decay. In single file, they followed the statutory path marked by yellow arrows, Bundle bounding ahead of them to investigate rattling movements in the undergrowth.

At times the path was so narrow, no more than a ridge between thickly overgrown chasms, that Reggie was content to watch his footing and let the priest chatter on. The profusion of growth impeded any view he might have hoped to have of the sea. They were closed in on one another's company.

'The way I look at it is,' called Father Starkey, ahead of him, 'that the readiness to believe is a very marked impulse in all human beings. You can't wholly dismiss it as the longing of the unknowing to know. Equating it with ignorance is misleading. Good gracious, even today it manifests itself – the need – in political and all manner of odd convictions. Rational commitment, it's jokingly called.' He paused to slither down a short, steep decline in the path and rode it on his bottom. 'Take care!' As he took Reggie's arm, he observed that the only truly irreligious people in the world were those incapable of forming any kind of commitment. The two men resumed their course.

'Even if you were right,' argued Reggie, 'and the need to believe was as fundamental to human nature – which I *don't* believe – as the need to eat, it's surely wiser to believe in provable facts than – a contradiction in terms – to believe in mysteries.'

'To be in a state of mystery is very largely, even today, the human condition,' the priest began.

'That's not the same as *believing* in mysteries.'

Father Starkey seemed to ignore the distinction. 'The human capacity for *faith* has certainly been weakened by being forced to coexist in a world of documented fact. A place where fact is pre-eminently respectable. But facts can't demolish faith. They can only achieve a superior reputation until they're discovered to be wrong.'

'Whereas mystery can never be faulted because it's not susceptible to proofs. Oh, come on, Ned!'

They passed a still, small pool sunk in a dark bowl of earth. Above them, an impenetrable mass of leaves stopped all brightness. Reggie wasn't sure he cared for this place. Even though the full extent of the slips and subsidence – which seemed to occur in lines roughly parallel with the sea edge – was concealed by the wild growth of ivy and elder, hazel and beech, it was evident that a simple fall could end in one tumbling a considerable and hidden distance. It certainly wasn't a good place to bring Bundle, who kept darting off the prescribed path after rabbits. But Father Starkey, oblivious to his friend's wary pursuit of him, was cheerfully acknowledging that many so-called religious facts have also been found wrong, but it didn't matter, because religions were merely various metaphors created by the religious sense as it grasped to express the essential mystery of existence.

Reggie stopped and laughed aloud. Birds flew up in alarm at the sound. 'Then how on earth,' he cried, 'are you able to settle for one metaphor in particular?'

The priest stopped, turned and looked at him with some surprise, waiting for Reggie to catch up. 'No difficulty at all,' he exclaimed. 'Christianity *is* the one revealed religion, but it corresponds very closely to earlier apprehensions – particularly in the crucial tenet of the Resurrection. Look at the vegetation mysteries. That's why I'm so very partial to Catholicism, my dear fellow; it's allowed Our Lady increasingly to fulfil the perceived function of the goddesses responsible for the rebirth of the young god. She is our principal intercessor, and the Catholic Church in its wisdom has gone on, over the centuries, augmenting her position and importance. I can feel part of a much greater religious comprehension within Catholicism than would ever be possible in the Anglican church.'

It was pointless, if pleasant, challenging him directly. 'I suspect you,' said Reggie severely, 'of devising a church all of your own. On the one hand you've incorporated into your faith a goodly pinch of paganism, and on the other hand, your mamma.'

'Yes, well,' the priest sighed, 'put like that it does all sound a bit wonky. But then atheists *are* awfully easily shocked. Well now, I've jabbered quite long enough on my own account. Tell me everything about yourself.'

'Do you think,' pleaded Reggie weakly, 'we might turn back?' He looked at the implacable, shadowy woodland all round them, at the wicked thread of the path. 'I'm worried about the dog.' Then, more ingenuously. 'And I'd awfully like to visit the museum before it closes.'

They escaped from the dark tent of leaves and broke out into the light, Father Starkey making exclamations of concern as Reggie told his own tale.

'But this is dreadful, dreadful!'

They walked along the promenade beside a coruscant sea, the early haze having now lifted, while the priest uttered mortified cries. 'There was I, prattling on to no good purpose. And you in need of cheer. It's too bad of me! Oh dear, oh dear, oh dear! Let me buy you a choc ice. Would you care for a choc ice?' They were nearing the kiosk.

'Gladly, I'll have a choc ice, but I shall buy them. No, I insist. Can you hold Bundle? Ned, listen. I don't need cheering. And if I did, I think I would choose to listen to you prattling on, as you put it. Give me heresy, Ned; I like it.'

'Oh, well,' responded Father Starkey doubtfully. 'Ah, do you think I could have one of those lemony things? They're awfully good.'

He made Reggie have a bite of it to see how good the lemony thing was.

'Delicious!' mumbled Reggie, his mouth expanding gingerly around the icy lump.

Poor Bundle had to be tied again outside the museum but swiftly managed to attract sympathizers with peppermints and bacon-flavoured crisps, while the two men wandered round the fossil cases, remarking upon the ichthyosaurus remains, the coprolites and the beautiful inner structure of the ammonities. The head that Reggie wanted to see was in the British Museum for a special exhibition, but the keeper said a replica had been made; so they climbed the spiral staircase to a small, circular room upstairs and gazed at the crudely engraved ball on its plinth.

'So this is the severed head,' said Father Starkey dubiously. 'And I never even knew it was here before. He looks a bit down in the mouth, poor chap, and no wonder.'

The features were rudimentary gashes.

'I don't know.' Reggie stepped back. 'All things considered, I think he has a rather placid air.'

The priest shuddered. 'Bounty hunters.'

'Oh come now, Ned! No worse than and very little different from the gargoyles you're so proud of. It has the same apotropaic function, exactly!'

Reggie circled the rough and touching stone: the spirit's lodging place, the fount of wisdom and magic.

'I wonder what he would find to say if he could?' Father Starkey patted the stone head, and ran a finger over the coarsely indented nose and mouth.

'Sh, sh.' Reggie pressed two fingers to his own lips.

'Yes?' The priest looked startled. 'What?'

Outside, distantly, a band played 'Rock of Ages'.

'Don't you hear him?'

'Him? Who?'

Reggie nodded knowingly at the head.

'Good heavens, no. Did you?'

Reggie smiled. 'No,' he said, 'but then I'm not an imaginative man. He speaks for those who *can* hear .. Tells tales at the feasts of the Other world.' And he gave the other an affectionately mocking smile.

'Ah, well, well! Who am I, with my experience of disembodied voices, to question that old boy?' Father Starkey addressed the head and gave it a fond and final pat. 'Perhaps you're right, Montis. He's not so very gruesome after all.'

*   *   *

And the two men, for all their differences, stroll back along the promenade in a blithe appreciation of friendship.

6

'Indicator!' screamed Reggie. Then, one hand over his lowered face, 'I'm sorry. I shouldn't do that. I didn't mean to scream.'

'Please don't worry, Mr Montis.' Mrs Pike kept her own gaze on the road. 'I'm quite used to it.' She drove on, jaw set, fists clenched round the wheel, elbows protruding.

'Perhaps, you could . . .' Reggie struggled for expression.

'Relax more,' Mrs Pike concluded for him. 'They all say that. I expect I will in time, dear.' She spoke soothingly.

Now that they had made the right turn he'd suggested in order to shed the angry tail of day trippers who had thought they knew a quiet, country road home, Reggie attempted to look about him.

'Lovely part of the world,' he remarked in a strangled voice. Discreetly, he wiped his upper lip with the back of his hand, while stealing a look at the high, deserted headland road they now travelled. This was Isle of Purbeck country. Stubble-yellow fields flowed into one another. The two furthermost, meeting in a gully which revealed a triangle of sea, were steeply ridged in a series of descending lynchets. It was a fine, pearly blue evening. It could all have been most enjoyable.

'Change down,' he ordered, and they roared and moaned and lurched for a while until Mrs Pike engaged the gear successfully. 'Down is so much harder than up,' she said.

'I wonder,' ventured Reggie kindly, 'whether you haven't had enough for one day?'

Mrs Pike laughed gaily. 'I give in, then,' she said. 'I won't have you worried out of your mind. I tell you what. Why don't we call in on Frank and Daphne on our way back and get those things sorted out?'

She was referring to a car for Reggie and the chance she thought might exist for him to visit the ranges during the winter months if he had a word with Frank. Frank, it appeared, was an

Orlebar, one of the Orlebars of Maidenwell. He seemed capable of anything, to judge from Mrs Pike's admiring accounts of him.

* * *

There appeared to be no problem. Any Sunday between October and June, when the ranges opened again, Reggie could visit Maidenwell. 'Don't go meself,' said Frank, 'but you could go along of my mum and dad. No trouble.'

Suddenly Reggie remembered where he'd seen the name before. '*Orlebar!*' he exclaimed. 'Of course! Is your father a builder?'

'Does a bit of that, yes. Been restoring the church down there after they'd made a pig's breakfast of 'un.' Frank was a big man with a rosy, open-featured face, who conveyed, despite a handsome beer belly, the impression of immense physical strength. 'All best forgotten, strikes me,' he said. (Could he really be the son of that surly old man?) ' 'Course, he can't take you beyond the village itself.'

'Oh.' Reggie's hopes were dashed. That's that, he thought. And the idea of being kept from the hill for a further eight months was peculiarly saddening: more than that, frustrating. Its contours swam in his mind intriguingly.

'I'll show you what I've got,' Frank was saying, motioning him to follow. 'Shan't be long,' he called to his wife and his mother-in-law as the men passed through the kitchen, though whether they heard him above their own chatter and the bawls of a toddler smashing his high chair with a spoon, was doubtful. They smiled warmly, however.

In the concrete yard behind the bungalow, Indian game cockerels, guinea fowl and a few bantams with feathered legs hopped about among the heaps of scrap. The yard was bordered with ramshackle huts and pens.

'That bloody fox has been about again,' said Frank as they negotiated the various obstacles.

'How do you know?' questioned Reggie, looking vaguely about for depredations of a foxy nature.

Frank sniffed lavishly. 'Can't you smell he?'

'At this time of day? At this time of year?' Reggie assumed that foxes were nocturnal, but he sniffed. The rich amalgam of odours told him nothing specific.

'He'll come when he pleases if he's hungry enough.' Frank was wandering about, eyes to the ground. 'Thought so!' He kicked two droppings with the toe of his heavy boot. To Reggie they looked like the droppings of any smallish dog.

'See that twist at the end? That tapered thread?' The two men crouched over the ordure. 'That's Charley all right.'

Reggie expressed a reserved interest, then leapt backwards in fright as a guinea fowl flopped off the roof of a nearby shed with a whooping screech. Another followed it, thin neck and balding head outstretched.

'Trouble is,' Frank was scratching an armpit gloomily, 'this weather. It's reduced his prey, see. And look what it's done to my vegetables.'

This was plainly to be an extensive tour. Reggie followed as Frank led the way out of the yard through a home-made, uncertainly hanging gate and cast an arm despairingly in the direction of his vegetable patch. It looked dry and weedy. 'I'll wager you've never seen potato plants so small!'

Reggie made incoherent sounds of agreement, and hovered as Frank then lamented the condition of every cabbage, parsnip, carrot and curly kale plant on the dusty patch.

Next, Frank invited inspection of his hay stacked in one half of a large Dutch barn. It looked all right to Reggie.

'That barn should be full!' laughed Frank as if he couldn't sustain his own indignation for long. 'Shocking! Still, it'll give you some good beef prices this winter. The farmers won't keep their stock on.'

Uncertain whether this, on balance, was good or bad, Reggie gratefully espied the object of their search. 'The cars, eh!' he cried, his gaze lighting on three exhausted and incomplete vehicles parked beside the barn. Black-headed doves were using the roofs as a flight base.

'Nun doves,' said Frank lovingly, in answer to Reggie's inquiry about them, and he started making warbling sounds to attract one on to his shoulder.

'So. This is what you have in stock?' Reggie studied the selection.

There was a grey Morris Minor with no front wheels and a smashed offside wing; a red Anglia which appeared to have had its jaws prised open, so far had the bonnet been forced by impact; and an elderly Hillman Minx without either windscreen or headlamps.

'I use the parts, see.' Frank looked admiringly at his museum. 'I can patch anything up good as new if there's something there you fancy.' A flight of doves took off from the roof of the Hillman as the client drew nearer to inspect its virtues. A tabby cat lay asleep in the back seat with one eye open. Or perhaps, Reggie concluded after a more searching look, it had but one eye. Its tattered ears clung to its head like a pair of fritillaries.

'I tell you what I'd recommend.'

'Please. Do.'

'You'll not be doing a *lot* of driving about? Just the school and thereabouts? Well, I'd take the Morris. Most reliable car ever made.'

Looking guardedly at the derelict vehicle, Reggie mumbled something about its chances of passing the MOT.

'No problem!' Frank pressed a large, work-chipped finger to his nose. 'I can fix that easy. Go to a garage and they'll charge you two-fifty straight just for the MOT certificate, and that's before you've started on the car. With a bit of work I can get the whole thing done up and passed for £200. Cash. How about that? I can't do fairer.'

'What year is it?' inquired Reggie faintly.

'Sixty-one,' said Frank. 'A nice vintage.'

'That seems,' said Reggie, 'very reasonable.'

*　　　*　　　*

They wandered back past a redolent collection of squealing pigs, who all scrambled on one another's backs to catch a glimpse of Frank. He scratched the topmost one, a huge pink beast with sticking-up ears, a mean expression, and tiny, white-fringed eyes. 'Nice creatures, pigs,' said Frank. He seemed to entertain a warm view of creation generally. 'No money in them, but I like them.'

They re-entered the yard. The top of a small head appeared above the lower door of the smartest shed, a cedar-wood building. A hand fumbled for the bolt.

'Just coming, my love!' With surprising agility in so large a man, Frank sprinted across the yard and unbolted the door. Following at a slower pace, Reggie saw Tenniel's Alice looking cross. 'I can do it myself,' said Phoebe.

Behind her, a white horse reached for hay in the corner of a darkened stable.

Phoebe herself closed the door and the bolts while her father hung back. Then she turned and said, 'It's *cream*,' to Reggie before walking off to the house.

'Albino,' elaborated Frank.

At closer quarters the genetic oddity was not terribly attractive. Cream, yes, with very pink parts and a pink-rimmed lilac eye which it rolled threateningly as it ate. 'Wonderful little horsewoman,' murmured Frank of his peremptory daughter.

'Come on, you two!' Mrs Pike was standing at the back door. 'My supper'll be late if we don't rush!'

'That means me,' smiled Reggie, with an almost pleasant sense of domestic captivity.

Hurrying towards them, Mrs Pike made popping gestures of self-reproval. 'Oh, I've let time fly! Fortunately, it's all cold tonight.'

'I wanted to show Mr Montis here the fireplace I've made.'

'Another time, Frank love,' she cried, climbing into the passenger seat. 'Mr Montis, would you be so good?' He took the wheel. 'Let's hope the girls are a bit late back themselves, eh?'

'The Morris suit you, then?' Frank hung over the driver's side.

'Perfect,' agreed Reggie thinking no word – unless it be 'Sunnybank' – was ever more misused.

'I *have* heard,' mused Mrs Pike, smoothing her skirt as they drove back home, 'they'll be taking girls at Turtledown.'

'It's been proposed. And opposed. Not a popular move, apparently.'

'I've heard that, too,' said Mrs Pike, adding confidently, 'but I daresay it will all go through in the end.'

'I daresay you're right.' Reggie changed down for the descent into Tidmouth.

'I wondered,' Mrs Pike began again after a slight pause, 'whether you might put in a word.'

'A word? I'm sorry?'

'For Phoebe.'

Phoebe! Before Reggie could voice any surprise or objection, Mrs Pike had moved in very swiftly with, 'She's extremely bright, you know. Very, very bright.'

For some reason he did not immediately understand, Reggie was filled with resistance. All he could think of to say, however, was, 'The expense!'

'Oh, that's nothing,' countered Mrs Pike quickly. 'I don't like involving you like this, but what are friends for?'

Since, Reggie reflected, it would be some four or five years before Phoebe was old enough to enter Turtledown, his sense of being imposed upon lessened slightly. By that time – who knows – the private system might be abolished altogether. 'It needs some thinking over,' was the most encouraging sentence he could frame before they reached Sunnybank, and Mrs Pike bounded out to arrange her cold collation.

'Well, I know you *will* give it some thought!' She paused at the kitchen door and smiled over her shoulder, presuming a generosity of spirit Reggie wasn't at all sure he possessed.

* * *

It bothered him.

After supper, for which the two girls did not even appear, Reggie retired upstairs and tried to compose a letter to his wife, suppressing the agitation brought on by Mrs Pike's soliciting his help over Phoebe. He filled his old-fashioned pen and leaned over the pad, wondering what form of address or endearment was acceptable.

How much pleasure it had given him to despatch her weekly cheque for £25 from different postal addresses! There was a triumph in travelling by Tube to Cockfosters, the Angel,

Vauxhall, Parson's Green, Chalk Farm, and on one occasion, Ongar, to post her envelope, while all the time living round the corner in Hounslow. Now the ruse would have to end. He would have to disclose his whereabouts.

Reggie rose and switched the lamp on. It was very nearly dark outside.

*   *   *

Summer is drawing to an end.

*   *   *

He is saddened that the slopes of Turtle Hill are forbidden him for another eight months. It is as though a woman has said they must not see one another until summer comes. After the wintry separation they will know how steadfast their love truly is.

*   *   *

Impatiently, Reggie returned to his notepaper and tried to draw the fort's contours on his letter to Dorothy. 'My dear Dorothy,' it said. His mind held the details imperfectly. More walks were needed. He crumpled up the sheet of paper and began afresh. 'Dear Dorothy,' he wrote.

*   *   *

Now his mind slides back in contemplation of the unease he felt at 'being used'. Next he rebukes himself for being so unlike the members of Mrs Pike's family, with their close and total readiness both to give and ask favours, as if that were the point of being human.

The only truly irreligious people in the world are those incapable of forming any kind of commitment.

Phooey! Reggie cannot agree with Father Starkey's view because he doesn't accept the idea that everybody is possessed of a religious sense. *Ethical* sense, now that's a different matter. Confusing ethics with religion is slipshod.

A blob of ink drops from his pen.

He thinks of his wife, and concludes that one has to be committed to a point of fanatical irrationality to be effective. Dorothy is certainly effective.

He sighs. What is bothering him is a sense that his fine new freedom is being invaded in tiny ways. He soaks up the blot with an old paper hanky and writes: 'You must be wondering what has become of me.'

Then he crosses out the 'must' and substitutes 'might'.

Bundle's yapping could be heard downstairs; then a confusion at the front door; voices and sounds of the girls' return. Swiftly, Reggie got to his feet, pulled out the old gramophone and put *The Magic Flute* on at full volume as a hint to his upstairs neighbours that sound travelled.

Biting the nutty top off a coffee-flavoured walnut whip, he began wielding his pen vigorously.

'I have now settled at the above address and would be pleased to have any outstanding bills or other correspondence forwarded . . .'

The letter remains unfinished.

To his utter astonishment, the music seizes him. He sits, pen poised throughout the growingly familiar overture. And then the next side, rapt, although he can't understand a word of German. Again, the sense of acute happiness fills him, scattering earlier discontents. He, who has never in his life listened to a piece of music without feeling the need to do something else at the same time, drips ink over his Basildon Bond for two-and-a-half hours.

He sits through the entire performance, enchanted.

*   *   *

Crawling, dazed and sweetly sated, into bed, Reggie was especially enraged by the bloody hairdryer buzzing overhead again. He knew, from experience of living under the same roof as his daughter, that girls were always washing their hair or waxing their legs or tearing their eyebrows out – all manner of disgusting self-improvements – at any unacceptable hour of day or night, but this was too much.

He pulled on his dressing-gown, stepped into his slippers,

and marched upstairs like a parent about to reprimand its children.

He tapped at the door. Plainly, the noise of the hairdryer drowned his first tap; so he knocked more firmly and pushed the door open. Angrily, Reggie strode into the room.

He halted. He stared.

Anna, the Athenian games mistress with her level gaze and curling helmet of hair, was crouching on one of the twin beds, facing him. She was stark naked. Raising her head, she used her free hand to place one finger to her lips and indicated by a glancing nod that he should come in and sit quietly on a chair until she had finished what she was about.

If Reggie hesitated it was because Anna's other hand, with a steadily increasing rhythm, was pumping a vibrator up and down between her sister's thighs.

Stephanie, who lay on her back, the top of her glistening head towards him, seemed unaware of his presence as, softly and deeply, she continued to moan.

Reggie found himself sitting obediently on the hard-backed chair by the door, watching this spectacle with a mixture of horror and intense excitement.

Stephanie's writhings became more desperate. Anna, hovering above her, small breasts quivering, lowered her head. Passionately she sucked and bit her sister's left nipple.

Reggie was agonizingly erect.

As Stephanie's cries deepened to a more frenzied growl, Anna's head and tongue moved swiftly down the recumbent body. Her own spine athletically hooped, she brought her tongue into fierce labour between her sister's legs. When the cries of the spread-eagled girl spilled over in a shuddering succession of gasps, Reggie felt his own juices explode from his skin like the pulp of an over-ripe fruit.

Shamed, shocked by himself, by what he had witnessed, he leapt to his feet and fled.

*   *   *

Later, as he lay in bed shaking, he tried to assemble his untame thoughts. What in God's name were they doing? – doing *that*?

92

What would they think of him? How was he ever going to be able to eat breakfast or supper in the same room as them again? How was he to contain this re-awakened, long quiescent sexuality? Could he venture upstairs a second time?

They were disgusting. They were unnatural. They . . . his disapproval transformed itself into involuntary, pumping fantasy.

He dreamt luridly

He breakfasted early, suffering the sight of two transparently underboiled eggs in consequence. He ate rapidly and endured indigestion. As he flew past the bathroom to collect his briefcase, Anna emerged in a towel.

She caught hold of his arm. Flushing, mumbling, he tried to pull himself away. Anna was smiling.

'She was *pleased* you were there.' She spoke quietly and calmly. 'She would like you to come again.'

The ambiguity of this last remark reduced Reggie to struggling discomfiture. 'Sorry! Sorry!' he barked, wriggling free. 'None of my business, so sorry. Excuse me!'

And he crouched in his room until certain the coast was clear before flying from the house.

Part Two

SAMHAIN

7

'Oh, he's settled into the routine wonderfully! Happy as a king at the school, aren't you, Reggie?' Bella Pike turned to Reggie for confirmation. 'Except for those headaches, of course,' she added with a sympathetic tilt of the head.

And my hill, and those girls, and my bowels. *And those girls.*

They were sitting in the Orlebars' lounge on the last evening of October. Originally the day had been fixed simply as a collection day for Reggie's car, although 'originally' is a loose word to use since it was the most recent of a series of dates first proposed and then postponed by Frank over the five preceding weeks, and would very probably have suffered the same fate as all the other days had Daphne and Bella not decided (it being November's eve and half-term to boot) that a little party would be in order. The date had thus acquired a ceremonial finality which Frank was obliged to meet.

So here they were on Samhain, the night when the Other-world becomes visible to men, and all manner of strange visitations occur, drinking cups of tea seated before the great fireplace which Frank himself had made, and enjoying the munificent warmth of burning apple logs before trooping outside to a far less cosy fire.

Oh well, thinks Reggie, I need taking out of myself.

He's been making some pretty strange visitations of his own recently.

The sound of Bella's voice, describing his own general contentment with Turtledown, brought Reggie back with a jolt. He felt that the conversation was developing a current that would once more turn to his 'putting a word in'. As unconcernedly as he was able, he asked Frank how the car was coming along.

'Running like a dream!' Frank patted his belly with appreciation. 'You could have had it sooner, but I knew I could lay my hands on a better engine if I waited a bit.'

First it had been a battery, then a fault in transmission, then a worn clutch pedal, a different gear box and, finally, the engine which Frank was sure had been damaged by the previous lady owner driving with the choke out all the time. Reggie wondered silently whether the range of improvements would be covered by the forty five-pound notes he had in his pocket. 'And if you take delivery tonight, see,' said Frank enthusiastically, 'I can keep the mother-in-law's A30 for a bit of a service.'

He'd feared as much.

'Do mum good to get a bit of practice in a different car,' observed Daphne, 'now she's got the hang of the other one. Only three weeks to go, mum!' To the test, she meant.

'Don't remind me!' protested Bella vivaciously. She had been to His 'n' Hers Fashions that afternoon for her regular Wednesday appointment, and emerged with a pinkish rinse that rather became her. Or perhaps it was the soft, dark cherry angora sweater, or maybe the warmth of the fire, or the lacing in her tea. Anyway, thought Reggie, she looked very rosy and bright.

'Reggie's given up so much of his precious time,' she was saying fondly. 'I can't let him down by failing!' She gave him a grateful smile.

Gary, in his playpen behind the sofa, began to cry.

'Give him a biscuit, Phoebe,' urged his mother, spreading herself more comfortably in front of the fire, but Phoebe continued her training of Bundle, which had taken up an hour already, and nobody seemed inclined to light the bonfire until she'd tired of the pursuit. Gary cried some more, and then comforted himself by trying to wedge his head between the struts of the playpen.

'Sit!' ordered Phoebe, and nervously Bundle lowered her backside to the ground, watching Phoebe carefully. Although she was maturing fast, Bundle remained a very pretty little dog, with a brown patch round each dark, bright eye and a tremulous black nose.

'Stay!' said Phoebe and, walking across to the playpen, waited. 'Here!' She clapped her hands. Bundle ran to her, squirming with pride at her own performance.

'Good girl!' Phoebe at last fetched the biscuits – one for Bundle, one for Gary.

'Thank you, darling,' said her mother.

'She's really got a way with that dog,' Bella remarked, 'don't you think, Reggie?'

'Bundle certainly behaves rather better for you than she does for me,' he complimented Phoebe. He found he took Bundle for a lot of walks.

During these walks he had twice spotted Phoebe involved in activities that, although quite innocent in themselves, were not (he'd thought) suitable for a child of her age. In Swale he'd observed her entering the cinema alone to see *Snow White and the Seven Dwarves*. In Tidmouth, when he'd been staring in the music-shop window wondering whether he might branch out and buy himself a second record, he had seen her inside a listening booth, earphones on her head, foot tapping and (he was almost certain) wearing lipstick. He'd wondered whether to mention these matters to Bella, but thought better of it. Her indulgence towards Phoebe was limitless.

'All right,' said Phoebe. 'Let's get on with it. Bundle's had enough. I'm going to enter her for the pet show next year.'

'I'll have to see about getting it all organized,' sighed Mrs Pike as the adults clambered to their feet. 'It's one of the things we do,' she explained to Reggie. 'It raises quite a nice amount, the pet show.'

'Not a patch on the skittle championship,' boasted Frank.

'And what about the dance in February?' chimed in Daphne, defending her own effort.

'There's the Christmas entertainment to be seen to first!' Mrs Pike shook her head over the labour involved, but implied somehow that it was all worth while.

Frank fetched some matches off the mantelshelf. 'Made a good job of it, didn't I?' he said to no one in particular, approving his own handiwork. It was ten feet long, made of Doulting stone, and had taken ten months to complete. Reggie was now well acquainted with these statistics.

'Had to go all the way up to Mendip to fetch the stone.' Frank lingered over it. 'Still he's a good 'un.'

'Come on, my love,' pleaded Daphne, interrupting the charitable competition she was having with her own mother. 'Let's put our things on.'

The women put witches' hats on, snapping the elastic under their chins. Bella was careful with her hair.

'Got the tatties?' Frank pulled a rubber Frankenstein mask over his face. 'Go and fetch they, Phoebe, there's a lass.'

Coats were slipped on. Daphne wrapped Gary, who was screaming at his father's altered appearance. Phoebe came back with a bowl of potatoes. 'You do look silly,' she said.

' 'Tis only a bit of fun! What about you, Reggie?' Frank insisted that Reggie wear a mask, and put it on for him. Glancing through his slits into the hall mirror, Reggie saw that his tweed cap surmounted a toothless brigand with warts and an eye-patch. Phoebe sniggered and told her baby brother to stop screaming. 'They're only playing,' she said scornfully.

'Be careful with this fire,' warned Daphne as they stepped into the chill evening. 'If we catch ablaze there's not the water to put it out.'

'That's why I've put he in the yard, woman,' said Frank. 'I don't want my hay going up, do I?'

The yard was hung about with little lanterns and pumpkins which Daphne now lit with a taper. Their glowing grins sprang to life and cast a short radiance. 'Oooh!' sighed Phoebe at last and everybody's spirits – even Reggie's – rose.

Encouraged by a douche of paraffin, the fire sprang high. Gary gazed in silent marvel, letting his thumb lie idle in his mouth.

'We ought to dance round,' suggested Daphne, who held her son to her shoulder. He had knocked her hat a little askew.

'With no clothes on!' shrieked Phoebe.

'Hark at her,' laughed Frank and watched his fire with the mad, blank satisfaction of Frankenstein.

They drank a good deal of rum punch, Reggie and Frank peeling their masks back from the chin to get at it. Mellowed by its spicy warmth, Reggie fell more freely into the spirit of the evening.

Candlelit games followed, indoors. Biting an apple on a string; sitting in a circle, hands clasped, while Frank went out of the room and they all chose an object, then called him back and concentrated powerfully until he guessed, with the help of his assistant, the Princess Phoebe Orlebar; then more psychic guessing games, some of which Reggie had once played with his own children; and another game, new to him, in which he had to lie on the floor, legs upright, feet bent at a flat right angle while Daphne placed a glass of water on his soles. 'Now don't you spill that, mind,' she giggled. 'That's precious.'

Everybody, to Reggie's puzzlement, was weak with laughter, then they all went out into the kitchen to prepare more food and left him lying helpless in the middle of the room.

It was Phoebe who took pity on him and removed the glass, because Bundle was jumping up at his ankles.

'Oh, that's a cruel one!' laughed Bella Pike, doubled up. 'They shouldn't have done that to you, Reggie!'

'I don't mind,' he said, and he didn't. He had another glass of punch and a piece of parkin, and felt thoroughly happy.

Frank was spreading Gary's plastic mat on the floor. 'No spilling allowed!' he warned, placing a large shallow bowl of water on the mat. 'This is for washing up in, after.' And he scattered half a dozen small English apples in the bowl.

Reggie, taking off his mask, had to go first. He was so incompetent that he put his glasses on to see better; then dropped them in the water. The laughter spiralled ever more wildly.

'I'm not messing my face up,' said Daphne. 'You have a go, Frank.' And he did. So did Phoebe. So, to her credit, bearing her pink rinse in mind, did Bella. What's more, she retrieved an apple.

'Just look at the mess!' wheezed Daphne, laughing with her knees pinned together.

Frank had an idea.

'Hey!' he said. 'See if you can do this!' And going out to the yard he came back with some pieces of metal in his hand. 'Here!' he urged Reggie. 'I can't grasp it no way.'

'What trick's this?' Reggie took the objects, amused and slightly suspicious.

'It's two short lengths of copper piping, see, and two bent bits of Daphne's wire clothes-hanger, see . . . and you slip the one inside t'other, see.' He did so, holding the four-inch sections of copper pipe upright in his hands, like handles. The lengths of coat-hanger wire, bent to slip inside the copper grips, protruded at right angles and swivelled loosely.

'You've got to get they straight and steady.' Frank brought his great, meaty hands close to his chest so that the thick wires poked out like aerials.

Giggling slightly, Reggie took the home-made instruments and copied Frank.

'Got 'em steady? Right! Now keep they steady and walk over to that bowl of water!'

'What *is* this trick?' persisted Reggie, his attempts at straight-faced concentration relapsing into involuntary giggles. He had to walk with very small steps.

'It's not a trick,' promised Frank.

Everybody was watching with interest now.

As he drew near the blue plastic bowl, Reggie felt a decided pull in his arms. It was just like the feeling he'd experienced on the edge of Turtle Hill, as though the essential stream of self was being drained out of him. He paused to steady the rods, which were beginning to sway from their alignment. Another step and the pull became more pronounced. The rods agitated, swinging towards one another.

'I'm obviously no good at this,' said Reggie watching the rods cross in front of his body and trying to straighten them out again.

'You're *very* good,' said Phoebe out of the silence which had fallen.

The rods locked across his chest. He could feel a current pouring from them into his arms, down his body, where it became a great, dragging weight, and out into the ground. Perhaps, he thinks, this is how trees and plants feel. Rooted things. 'What is it?' he asks, bewildered.

'You're a dowser!' shouted Frank, jubilant. 'Come on, let's get looking!'

And he led a dance out into the yard round the buildings, round the paddock, into dark corners, scattering rubble and straw wherever he went. Reggie followed, the coat-hangers projecting from his chest. In excited procession, behind, came everyone else.

'There's a well somewhere here, I'd swear to it!' And Frank vanished among the dimming lanterns again.

Between the pigs and the compost heap the rods swung and crossed.

'It's a strong one!' gasped Reggie.

'I'll dig he tomorrow!' yelled Frank. 'Another drink! A prize for the dowser!'

*   *   *

Before they left, everybody had to stand in a circle, hold hands and make a wish.

'What did you wish for?' asked Bella, as they drove home in the flawless Morris.

'You shouldn't ask,' said Reggie. 'It's secret.'

Bella stroked Bundle. 'Oh, go on,' she said.

But he shook his head

Reggie has wished for Stephanie.

*   *   *

Bundle barked, and Bella stifled a scream.

A shadowy figure rose from the top of Sunnybank's un-illumined steps, and stood above them like a vampire.

'A-h-h!' It was Reggie who actually uttered a cry.

'I knew you'd turn up if I waited. What sort of guesthouse is this, with nobody here to welcome guests?' demanded the Otherworld manifestation. 'I've been waiting here since the pub closed.'

'Dorothy!'

'Do I smell *rum*?' Dorothy wrinkled her nose with astonishment and displeasure. Rum was not Reggie's drink.

'Dorothy, this is Mrs Pike, proprietor of Sunnybank.'

'Proprietr*ess*,' corrected Dorothy. 'I say, I'm sorry to hang about on your doorstep like a vagrant.' She took careful note of Reggie's hand at Mrs Pike's elbow.

'Excuse me.' Mrs Pike exhibited an uncharacteristic coolness. She climbed the remaining steps and tried to unlock the door. 'You must be Mrs Montis.'

'Dorothy Montis, yes.'

Dorothy resembled a vampire because she wore a voluminous grey cloak and a sort of skull cap pulled down over her forehead. An extremely long scarf, wound round and round her neck, trailed almost to the ground. She towered over Bella as the two women walked into the hall in front of Reggie. He hated the way her gaze made a racetrack circuit of the décor and fittings: she would have some sardonic remark to make later.

Later!

'My other tenants have gone away for half-term, otherwise there would have been somebody to let you in and make you feel welcome.' Mrs Pike spoke stiffly. She turned to Reggie and with the same withdrawn politeness, asked him whether he would care to sit down in the hotel lounge while she prepared a pot of tea.

'That would be nice,' responded Dorothy.

The original hotel lounge, now the best room, was never used. Bella Pike stood with her hand depressing the handle.

'No, no. Please don't bother.' Reggie tried to gather himself. 'I'll take er – Mrs Montis – upstairs and give her a cup of tea myself. It's late.'

'Very good. Will you be *staying*, Mrs Montis?'

'I don't know where else I could go at this time of night. Would that be OK?' Dorothy began the long unwinding of her scarf. Reggie felt appalled.

'I'll make a bed up in the girls' room. At least it's all aired.' And before anybody could either prevent her or add anything further, Bella Pike had stooped to pick up the dog, and disappeared into the kitchen at the end of the hall.

'Lovely evening,' Reggie called after her. 'Thank you so much!'

*　　*　　*

Bella, closing the door behind her, gives a little sob. She finds it hard to think of Mr Montis as 'Reggie' any longer.

*　　*　　*

Dorothy pulled a face. 'So!' she exclaimed meaningfully.

'So nothing,' answered Reggie, guiding his wife upstairs and trying to still his anger. 'What in heaven's name are you doing here?' Instinctively he relieved her of her small piece of hand luggage.

'I've been worried about you.'

'Rubbish!'

'I *have*!' She glanced back at him over her shoulder, her eyes an unusually enlarged and candid blue. 'I wanted to make sure you were all right. There are things to discuss. Anyway,' as they reached the landing, 'I rather fancied a few days by the sea.'

Reggie gritted his teeth.

They reached his sitting-room in silence.

'My God!' exclaimed Dorothy, as he switched the light on. 'How can you!'

'I've always thought – for a socialist – your views on interior design betrayed you.' Reggie shut the door sharply.

'Taste is acquired. It's a matter of time and education.' Dorothy was pulling off her gloves and annotating with her eyes.

'Meaning: one day everyone will have your taste?'

'Don't be so catty, Reggie. It's not like you.'

The grey woollen cap was torn off and her short, tawny hair sprang forth like a live beast. The lioness-headed Dorothy. Sekhmet. The man-devourer. The goddess with a weakness for blood.

'I also,' she continued, shaking her head as if releasing it of electricity, 'wished to return a cheque.'

'Don't tell me you've arrived here at' – he consulted his watch – 'a quarter past midnight to return a cheque. Anyway, what's wrong with the cheque?'

'I *arrived* six hours ago,' she reminded him as if she would later be needing a decent explanation for his absence. For now: 'A cheque for £500,' she said.

He looked up, confused.

'That,' she rummaged in her handbag, 'is what you've paid me over the last few months – for no reason whatever. I'm not a dependant. You've had neither bed nor board from me.' She flung down the cheque she'd written and raised a cynical eyebrow. '*Rather* looks as though you owe somebody else for board and bed.'

'Don't be ridiculous, Dorothy.'

'If, however,' and she picked the cheque up again, 'it was simply conscience money, I'll take it back and donate it to charity. That's the best place for conscience money.'

'Do whatever you like with it. But don't, please, Dorothy, stay here.'

(He is anguished at the idea of her sleeping in the attic overhead.)

'Why? Am I compromising you somehow?'

'I've chosen to be free.'

'Pooh!' She flung off her cloak, revealing a T-shirt with the CND sign on it, a pair of well-cut grey culottes and expensive black boots. She looked rather good, if somehow disingenuous. 'Don't kid yourself, Reggie! You ran away.'

'I'm building a fresh life for myself.'

'Private-school-teacher! History! You, Reggie, are not building anything. You're retreating into the archetypal womb of your past.'

'Thank you,' he said sarcastically, 'for your concern. You did say you were worried about me?'

'Yes, yes!' She sank into a corner of the sofa and thrust her head low over the arm to try to net his gaze. 'That's the whole point! It's not good for you. It's negative, regressive. Think positive!'

She straightened her own back in a positive, queenly way, thrusting her chest forward. The CND symbol, Reggie reflected with interest, was the ancient female symbol: the crutch, no less. 'That's a bit dated, isn't it?' he murmured, nodding at her bosom.

She glanced down briefly. 'We're resuscitating it for the anti-nuclear society. Now listen, Reggie. I know you think me bossy, but this really isn't the life for you. It's without purpose.'

'Oh, do shut up, Dorothy. I'm rather tired. Apart from that I'm very happy.'

There was a short silence.

'This really *is* a ghastly room, Reggie.' Restlessly she began prowling it. 'Ha!' She pounced. 'Ha! So you took it!'

She stood before him, accusing. 'Why did you pinch my *Magic Flute*?'

Reggie felt dreadfully weary. 'I hadn't heard it.'

'You don't even *like* music! You don't like anything cultural.'

An old wound re-opened bloodily. Dorothy's derisive view of his own appreciation, his view that she was all piss-and-wind pretension . . . these raw oppositions steamed so freshly still, he found himself automatically on the attack. 'Well, I must say,' he sneered, 'it's a very silly story.'

'All operas have silly stories; well, most, anyway.'

'As silly as that?' Sarcastically he began detailing its incongruities. 'The Queen of the Night sends a nice young chap Tamino to rescue her abducted daughter Pamina – the girl's been snatched by Sarastro – plainly a blackguard. But what do we find? Nothing of the sort . . . all of a sudden the Queen it is who's the bitch, and Sarastro a dear old sage. He whips black servants, mind, but that's neither here nor there—' Dorothy butted in.

'OK, OK. It's anti-feminist and racist. But I like it.'

'My wife likes racist, anti-feminist opera!'

'Don't be silly! It's eighteenth-century prejudice. Anyway, it's the music that counts.' Dorothy fished her cigarettes out of her handbag and lit one, while Reggie continued to grumble over the plot.

'I say,' laughed Dorothy, 'you *have* been paying attention, Reggie. Or have you just read the libretto?'

'Don't be absurd.'

The truth was that he'd been dismayed by the libretto when finally he'd read it in English. The bliss the music produced in him was illegitimized. There was more darkness in the opera than the score suggested. 'Anyway,' he snapped crossly, 'you haven't come here to discuss *The Magic Flute*.'

'No. But I have come to discuss – amongst other things – our daughter . . . You know,' Dorothy's tone relaxed, 'I really think you might have changed. Come alive to music.' She gave a short, wondering laugh. 'Don't worry about the plot; that's all tied up with freemasonry. But oh, Reggie, honey, this could be the beginning of something really big . . .'

'Our daughter, you said.' Reggie's interruption bordered on the rude, but it failed to extinguish the dangerously soft light that bloomed in his wife's features.

'Come on,' he said. 'It's half past midnight.'

'And right now your daughter is probably preparing for nones or vespers or whatever it is they do in convents at this hour.'

'What!' Reggie's attention was seized.

'She's gone into retreat.'

'Oh.' He subsided. 'That's different.' He wondered how many more trivial reasons Dorothy was going to advance for coming here.

'I'm not so sure,' answered Dorothy darkly, 'one thing can lead to another.'

'Well, it makes a change. I seemed to spend most of her adolescence separating her from unsuitable men.'

'Isn't this much the same thing?' Dorothy blew smoke dramatically. 'Bride of Christ, and all that?'

'No, it is not. She's in retreat, Dorothy. Some of the very best people do it.'

There was a brief pause while Dorothy, failing on this tack, searched around for another pretext. 'How are your bowels?' she asked at length.

'Dorothy, I cannot believe that you have spent endless hours fretting about my bowels.'

'I mentioned it to Gilbert, and he says nobody comes to any harm if they only shit once a week but, as I pointed out to him, *you* don't believe that, and that's what matters.'

'I should be very grateful if you didn't discuss my physical peculiarities with my son, even if he is a doctor – or very nearly.'

'It's his birthday next week. Don't forget it.'

'No, I won't.'

There was another silence. Reggie waited for a while, then stood up to make tea.

'Or does *she* supervise your roughage now?'

He stared down at his wife and gently relieved her of *The Magic Flute*. Had he heard aright? Had he perceived the toothy snap of jealousy in her last remark? The real and most astonishing reason for Dorothy's presence here dawned on him. 'I'm going to make you a cup of tea,' he said quietly, 'and then I suggest it would be better if we talked in the morning. We ought to go to bed and get some sleep now.'

'Separately or together?' queried Dorothy, confirming his dumbfounded suspicion. In the last five years of their marriage Reggie had been made to feel incompetent by his wife's sighs and clicks of exasperation as he'd fumbled his way round her large body. He couldn't absorb the idea that she might now desire him.

'Separately,' he said.

'You rotten sport. It could be interesting.' She blew her smoke sideways and gazed at him flirtatiously. 'You must be quite randy by now. Doesn't the idea appeal?' She rose, simultaneously dwarfing him and any embryonic interest he might have had by leaning over him and placing an investigatory hand over his flies. 'Oh God, Reggie! What's the matter with you?' She flounced back on the sofa crossly. 'Could you do me a sandwich, at least?' she demanded.

*   *   *

Somewhere inside, Dorothy hurts. There are qualities in Reggie that she misses more than she would ever say: the steadiness that tempers her own rushing temperament, the sheer constancy of his presence. Oh, true, he has bored her by his routine movements and unimaginative attentions to her body, his failure to see how her skin screams for sly, preliminary arousals before being fully, ardently open. But that, she has now persuaded herself, is mere technique. She has read a considerable number of books on the subject. Reading has inflamed her feelings. Here she is. In Tidmouth at a quarter to one in the morning. Jealous.

As Reggie returned with a piece of processed cheese only just glanced upon at its centre by two curling slices of bread,

Dorothy's hopes underwent an angry diminution. How could she have imagined this greying, unremarkable man – and God, what a lot of weight he'd put on round the middle – how could she have thought he would be revivified by the games and subtle lickings she'd envisaged? 'Thanks,' she said ungraciously. Reggie waited in silence while she ate. She chewed dully, swallowed, and announced she'd like a bath.

'Sorry,' said Reggie. 'Only allowed if absolutely necessary. I'll show you upstairs.'

'Jeez .. !' breathed Dorothy.

*   *   *

He hates the way she flings herself on Stephanie's bed. Resents her in this room.

This room ... twin divans either side of the fireplace, covered in woven African rugs, pillows the wrong end because to lie that end means you have a clear view of the sky – instead of the chimney – through the eight inky-blue squares of skylight set into the sloping ceiling. Anna's guitar in the corner; posters of pre-Raphaelite figures; the bursting wardrobe; the scatter of running-shoes; the mirror which now reflects Dorothy's form.

Dorothy kicked her own shoes off. They fell among the others. 'Nice, looking up at the sky,' she said.

He told her where to find the bathroom, and left.

*   *   *

As Dorothy lies on Stephanie's bed, the painful convulsions of Reggie's heart require some explanation. Did he not, then, after his first appalled intrusion of that room, devise elaborate means of avoiding the two young women? Did he not duck, gulp, gobble, sweat and mumble? Yes. But certain other symptoms affected him also.

In daylight hours he was repelled by their perversity. At night his feelings changed. Not since his teens had he suffered such ungentle lechery. Unsparing masturbation was accompanied by images of his entering first one and then the other. Sometimes all three were intertwined, Anna over her sister's body as he had first seen her, he behind, parting the fig-fruit and ramming to its core while all three cried and clasped one another in a confusion of breasts and mouths.

*   *   *

At school he was too new to go into automatic gear. The routine helped him. On free days he walked. He walked beyond the Army ranges at St Aldhelm's Head where a tiny chapel sat on new-ploughed headland; to Winspit, where the sea rolled into rock pools, where an abandoned quarry, arched and pillared like a Greek temple, stood in a gouged-out cleft of the cliff. He walked across the purple heath of Studland, its hummocked and boggy reaches encircling the great, miraculously balanced rock of Agglestone.

Then he succumbed.

Towards the middle of October he had crept upstairs, entered and sat meekly on the hard-backed chair. Anna had bestowed her grave and welcoming smile. Stephanie did not even look in his direction.

On the next occasion, Anna had beckoned him, indicating that he should stand beside her.

It was only then, not until then, as he had gazed openly at the fair, reclining girl that he had seen – the sheet tumbling back – that her right leg was a reddened stump. His gaze had travelled back, aghast, to her face. She lay with her lids tightly, hurtingly closed.

'Show her,' Anna had whispered urgently, not looking at him. But he had nothing to show.

Uttering an engulfed cry, he had left them. In bed, alone, he had wept without understanding.

The room became a sacrarium in his mind. A place where mystery, guilt, lubricity and tenderness mingled inexplicably.

He is uncertain whether inhibition or an incomplete perception holds him back from entering upon the adoration.

*   *   *

Reggie heard Dorothy come downstairs. Heard the vigorous brushing of her strong white teeth, heard her reckless flushing of the chain in spite of his warnings.

He thought of her long, shapely body on that bed. Beneath that temple roof.

When he entered her, Dorothy was astonished and gratified by the passion of his mouth in the crevices of her skin, by the ferocity of his movements.

She was encouraged, obscurely, by the tears that later streamed from him. She comforted him, though she failed to persuade him to stay beside her.

Alone, Dorothy slept deeply.

8

Reggie was already tackling his porridge – something Mrs Pike knew how to prepare properly – when Dorothy came down the following morning. The porridge had been cooked all night until the oats dissolved into their own thick, rich cream. Reggie ate it with guilt as well as enjoyment, since he always fortified himself first with his own special cereal upstairs.

Dorothy paused in the doorway.

'Darling!' she cried with marked warmth.

'Good morning, Dorothy!'

'Oh, *darling*!' She descended on his table and lowered her long form to kiss his bulging cheek. Her eyes feasted on her husband's while she strove to see whether he noted the particular care she had taken with her appearance.

Although a small stone she'd discovered beneath her pillow had left her with a mild headache, a few moments spent standing on her head, two ginseng capsules, a discreet application of the mascara she normally declined to use, and a little dusting of the *Bois de Santal* talcum powder she found in the bathroom had all helped restore her radiance.

Reggie sniffed.

'What's that?' he asked.

'There, I knew it You *are* becoming more aware! More sensitive to things around you! Once, you wouldn't have noticed if I were awash in diesel oil. Look at me, Reggie!'

He looked.

'Can't you see?'

He sees his wife. She wears the same clothes. Her short, lively hair is cut on the same flying lines as it always is.

'I'm *glowing*!, Reggie!'

'You do wear extraordinarily well, I must admit,' he acknowledged generously. 'Nobody would take you for forty-eight. You've been using Stephanie's stuff, haven't you?'

'I now think' – Dorothy was unfurling her napkin – 'that the break was a good thing. We appreciate one another better.'

Bella arrived with porridge for Dorothy. A woman who could not for long think anything but the best of everyone, Bella had recovered herself, and now said she would happily provide some dinner if Mrs Montis was staying. Actually, it wasn't entirely absent from her consciousness that Mrs Montis was no cook. Mrs Montis barely noticed the offer. Her gaze was avidly fixed upon her husband, who said that it would be most kind of Mrs Pike to go to so much trouble.

'We must walk and talk, Reggie!' Dorothy caught his finger tips. His successful arousal of her, his awareness of her new scent all betokened a sharpening of his senses. He was capable of a fervent response.

'Where would you like to take a stroll?' he was asking. 'There are some charming places round about.'

'Oh, anywhere! Everywhere! I'm too excited to eat. Can't we go now?'

'Can't I just finish my toast?'

'Oh, if you must.'

The mild dampening effect of his stolid eating was quite overcome when Mrs Pike (who had noticed she was no longer 'Bella' any more than Mr Montis was now 'Reggie') released the information that Mr Montis had proved himself, last night, capable of dowsing.

All in all, thought Reggie, quite a night.

'No!' Dorothy was awed.

'Oh, yes. And if Phoebe brings the rods with her when she comes, we might persuade Mr Montis to do a little dowsing in my back garden!'

Looking up, glancing between the two attentive faces fixed on his, Reggie understands that he is – in a modest way – being fought over.

'Probably a fluke,' said Reggie.

But the two women disagreed with him violently. It was a very special gift. When Mrs Pike left to shush Bundle out of the dining-room, Dorothy seized Reggie's arm as it travelled towards the marmalade. 'I knew it!' she breathed, 'Something wonderful has happened!'

'I once read,' he said, 'that one in three people can do it.'

'Oh, nonsense!' Dorothy dismissed the statistic. 'You've obviously got a sixth sense.'

'I've always wondered what the sixth sense was,' ruminated Reggie. 'Sight, touch, smell, taste, hearing – and what?'

'A power beyond,' cried Dorothy.

'Ned Starkey – a colleague of mine – claims it's a religious sense.'

'Oh, how foolish!' Dorothy laughed breathlessly; then not wishing to sound contemptuous of Reggie's friends, 'and how sweet.'

Reggie wishes he had not made love to his wife last night.

'I suppose,' he said, rising, 'there are many family matters to discuss. Let me show you Tidmouth and you can tell me all about Antonia.'

* * *

Dorothy enthused over Tidmouth which was pleasantly poised between the holiday season and winter dereliction. The interwoven clusters of narrow streets could be seen in all their charm, the way the buildings tried to accommodate themselves to the unwilling lie of the land be noted.

To Reggie's chagrin, his wife observed many details he had missed. The way eighteenth-century cannon were used as bollards on the harbour; the fact that plague victims were buried beneath an unmarked mound in the graveyard. She found her way to a disused fulling mill. She saw a blackboard in the sub-post office saying 'Percy Allen is much better thank you' and another notice in the closed window of the fish shop saying 'This store will re-open on November 10th as a delicatessen. Good luck to all.'

As they walked over the boulders of Granny's Gate, she stopped to watch two birds settling on the stones. 'Pied wagtails,' she concluded aloud, observing the characteristic quiver of their tail feathers.

None of this deterred her from her main theme. Tidmouth was a most unsuitable place for Reggie to live.

'You're cut off here ... You'll moulder ... There's no intellectual stimulus.'

In vain Reggie told her that he had very lively discussions with his colleagues, that the staffroom was a permanent commentary on the way of the world. (He neglected to tell her the conservative colour of the commentary. He'd come rather to enjoy the elegiac quality of discussions on the loss of law and order, the demise of the mile, the surrender of the individual to the State, falling rates of literacy and numeracy, the decline of customer service and all the other things that had made this country great.) Instead, he referred to the archaeological riches of the area, the incomparable geology.

'But that's *hobby*,' she declared. 'It will bore you eventually. You ought to be thinking of the *real* world.'

'It all seems very real to me,' he argued.

'I'm thinking of joining a commune,' she said. 'You should come with me.'

Reggie cannot imagine anything more dreadful.

But Dorothy stood on the shore, her hair leaping in the wind, her cloak flapping, and lengthily enumerated the virtues of such a plan. Not a *rural* commune – her scorn for back-to-the-landers was stinging – but an urban co-operative, a commune in London's dockland. A warehouse. Twenty-two people of all ages and backgrounds. Sexual freedom. 'The ambience might really help us.' There was to be a free school, a drugs rehabilitation service, a cheap food scheme for old age pensioners, and job opportunities for the young unemployed. 'It's the way to the future!' she insisted, her cloak cracking in the wind like a primitive sail.

'Aren't you a bit old for that sort of thing?'

'My mind is young. *My* mind is younger than Antonia's.'

Reggie was quite adamant about not sharing the only way to the future.

'It's this place,' Dorothy complained. 'It's drained your resolve. Here, you can only see the past around you. You've stepped into premature retirement.'

Although she had earlier seemed to be of the opinion that something wonderful had happened to him, on the way home she pursued her new notion so exhaustively Reggie felt that, even if he were missing the thrilling issues of the day, he didn't much care. Indeed, he felt less at one with Dorothy than ever he had.

'OK.' Dorothy stopped. She'd promised herself not to raise this topic but, faced with Reggie's obduracy, had no choice. 'It's that woman, isn't it?'

Reggie slipped on a frill of rust-coloured seaweed. 'Which woman?'

'*Which* woman?' Dorothy very nearly screamed. 'How many are there?'

'I can't think what you mean,' said Reggie, guarding his obsession for Stephanie and her sternly beautiful sister.

'You're having it off with the landlady, aren't you?'

At this he laughed outright. It was an absurd idea, he protested. But he didn't entirely convince Dorothy.

*   *   *

Bella Pike had toiled over this meal. She had poured wine and cream into the sauce for the chicken. The bird itself was garnished with button mushrooms, anchovies, bacon rolls and chopped parsley.

Phoebe served the meal. Mrs Montis's plate came back with the chicken untouched.

'Was anything wrong?'

Distraught, Mrs Pike rushed into the dining-room.

'My wife has become a vegetarian,' apologized Reggie. 'I'm awfully sorry, I didn't know. It's a new thing.'

'I'm against using Third World cereals to sustain our meat-eating diet,' Dorothy explained patiently. 'If we all become vegetarian there'll be enough protein for everybody.'

Mrs Pike stood thunderstruck. Her noble resolve to think better of Mrs Montis evaporated. She couldn't for the life of her think what a grown woman was doing in that silly T-shirt anyway. *And* she hadn't made her own bed. 'I'll see what else I can find,' she said tightly.

'Oh, please don't bother,' Dorothy waved her hand placatingly. 'I ate all Reggie's veg.'

Apparently impervious to the icy wrath that stalked in the

wake of Mrs Pike's retreating form, Dorothy hissed across the table. 'What, by the way, is wrong with that child?'

'Phoebe? Nothing, as far as I know. Why do you ask?'

'There's something wrong.' Dorothy pondered it. When Phoebe returned with the hazelnut gâteau Reggie adored, his wife's eyes were obliquely trained on the child. 'I'm going to ask her grandmother,' she declared.

'Please don't stir up more trouble,' groaned Reggie, sybaritic enjoyment of his pudding under threat. 'You've already wounded Mrs Pike's pride.'

'I can't help that,' said Dorothy. 'People have to be re-educated about food.'

'Haven't you taken a rather ecological turn?' questioned Reggie.

'One hundred per cent, I have. That's why I'm fighting a nuclear future.' She attacked her pudding greedily.

'But, my dear Dorothy, your socialist aims of more for all can only be achieved by a nuclear future.'

'I know,' she said. 'It took a lot of thinking about, but I've decided that equality of poverty is better than equality of wealth. Actually,' she concluded, 'I've decided there *can* only be equality through poverty. Wealth, by definition, undermines it.'

'I see,' said Reggie more patiently than he felt. There was absolutely no question of returning to Dorothy. He'd forgotten how upsetting her changes of policy could be.

'It's cost me a lot of friends.'

'I can imagine.'

'I belong to the Socialist Resources Group; they're the ones with the commune. They're going to generate methane from the Thames.'

'Very enterprising,' commented Reggie, wondering what the chances of a second helping were.

'We've got to use the *sun*!' Fiercely Dorothy plied her spoon.

'It's a waste of time,' sighed Reggie. 'Japan *has* to go nuclear with no resources of her own, and that fact alone determines everybody else's policy.'

'We've got contacts in Kyoto,' whispered Dorothy piercingly.

Reggie decided he wished to hear no more of this.

Perceiving the line of his jaw, Dorothy suggested they spend the afternoon in bed.

'Good Lord, no!' He had no intention of wasting the afternoon in Dorothy's snares. Besides, as he explained, he had to do some divining for Mrs Pike. 'And then . . .'

'And then?' Dorothy thrust her face as close to his as she could, over the table.

'And then . . . I thought I might get my eyes tested.'

She caressed his left ear. 'Am I being too fast for you?' she murmured. 'Truly, Reggie, I've researched some wonderful new ideas to try out.' She also had in her small piece of hand luggage a special selection of underwear bought in a shop off Windmill Street. For the moment, though, the blunter approach . . .

'Reggie . . .'

'Yes?' He sounded wary.

'Reggie . . . I haven't any knickers on.'

'I've got the rods,' said Mrs Pike, entering with her aerials projecting. A look of acute relief passed over Reggie's face.

Her other project promptly forgotten, Dorothy leapt to her feet. 'I must see this!'

They trooped out through the large kitchen, past the prefabricated extension which Mrs Pike used as her private bed-sitting-room, and into a small garden of dead bushes and bare, brown lawn. Phoebe was training Bundle to fetch a rubber bone.

The women stood back to watch the display.

Without rum punch inside him, Reggie felt decidedly foolish. Venturing cautiously down the lower end of the garden, he heard Dorothy begin chattering to Mrs Pike: making amends no doubt. He concentrated.

Gradually he worked closer to them and they fell silent.

A gasp went up.

'Look at that!' exclaimed Dorothy.

The rods were forcing themselves across one another.

'Water!' shouted Dorothy.

'That's where the drain runs through,' said Mrs Pike disappointed.

'Never mind! It really works.' Dorothy had to have a go of her own. She was useless.

Abandoning the attempt, she said she was going to borrow Reggie's car to take Mrs Pike for driving practice. Perhaps Reggie would like to ring Father Starkey and put him off his Saturday turn.

Failing to get through to Ned, Reggie trailed down to the optician's on his own.

*   *   *

'She's a dwarf!'

Dorothy burst in on Ned Starkey and her husband as they sat in Reggie's room, playing poker with a pack of cards confiscated from one of the Lower CE boys.

'I beg your pardon?' Reggie laid down his hand, revealing a royal flush. Father Starkey quietly abandoned his two pairs.

'She's a *dwarf*!' repeated Dorothy, her scarf swinging. '*Phoebe!*'

'She's . . . *what?*' Reggie needed a further repetition if he were ever to get this fact knocked securely into his skull. But the others remained silent, staring at him with their own form of disbelief.

As Dorothy's expression of incredulity deepened to condemnation of her husband's blindness, Ned Starkey removed himself with a small cough and interested himself in the view beyond the window. 'Heigh-ho, so Bella's returned your car with no parts missing,' he sang out, unnaturally cheerful.

'A dwarf!' repeated Reggie. He was stunned. He turned to his friend. 'Is that right, Ned?'

'Rather presumed you knew, old chap . . . look, why don't I go down and get Bella interested in a pot of tea?' His exit was hurried.

'How *could* you not have realized! After two months here!'

Dorothy was beginning to sound her old self again. It was peculiarly comforting.

'She doesn't look like a dwarf.' Reggie thought all dwarves had flattish faces and a rolling gait.

Enraged, Dorothy hurled herself on the sofa and cried out bitterly that he hadn't changed at all. *Not at all!* She lit a cigarette and began smoking feverishly. 'For two months she's been right under your nose and you've failed to see anything amiss! What did you suppose all those collecting boxes were for, in heaven's name?'

'What collecting boxes?'

'Oh God, you drive me insane! There isn't a flat surface in this house without a collecting box on it.'

Reggie sneaked a look around the flat surfaces of his own room and saw nothing. In a foggy fashion he had been conscious of the odd collecting box downstairs, but since he had never visited a boarding house or a hotel that did not have collecting boxes prominently placed, he regarded them as furniture and fittings of the drearier kind. In other words, he ignored them.

(Reggie is not a mean man exactly, but he does need to have his better impulses activated.)

'PRG in large letters everywhere!' ranted Dorothy.

'I suppose I imagined they were something to do with regional government,' tried Reggie lamely.

'You didn't imagine anything. That's your trouble – you don't. *Imagine.*' All Dorothy's raised expectations of a transformation in Reggie were dashed. 'Persons of Restricted Growth,' she spelt out acrimoniously.

'Oh, well,' remarked Reggie, 'if it had said *dwarves . . .*'

'Don't be such a fool – you can't call dwarves, dwarves.'

'You just did.'

'You're avoiding the point. That poor child!' Dorothy drummed her fingers thoughtfully on the arm of the sofa. She had the dangerous air of one hatching a plot.

'She *is* a child, then? She's not one hundred and forty-three?'

'My God, you're disgusting!'

'I'm sorry. It's the way she behaves.'

'Have you *no* feelings?'

Acerbically Dorothy addressed her husband with the facts.

Phoebe was twelve years old. She suffered from a form of dwarfism – there were, it transpired, many forms – in which the victim simply failed to grow. There was no obvious malformation, but she would probably be incarcerated in a child's body for the rest of her life.

'Surely they can do something?' With an effort Reggie recalled that the collecting boxes were black with large orange letters. He should have seen them. The design was fairly striking.

'That's just it,' said Dorothy purposefully. 'More money for research. That's our task. I've given that cheque for five hundred to Mrs Pike. I explained it was your money.'

'You did what!'

'You're not going to complain about that, are you?'

On due reflection, Reggie supposed he was not.

'Mrs Pike, by the way, assumes you know. I let her think that.'

'That was good of you,' he muttered humbly. 'It really was time I had my eyes seen to.' The optician had chided him thoroughly for letting ten years elapse between testings, and prescribed two pairs of glasses, one for reading, one for general wear.

Dorothy stubbed out her cigarette vivaciously. 'It's not your bloody eyes that need seeing to.'

'I've been getting dreadful headaches . . .'

'A blind man with a stick could see certain things better than you.'

'At last,' sighed Reggie contentedly. 'You're talking like a woman who's got her knickers on.'

Dorothy ignored this. Something else had been tossed up in her turbulent mind.

'Do you have your binoculars here?' she asked.

'If it's a failure of imagination I suffer from, binoculars are not going to help me see the calamities of others.'

'For *me*, you idiot. I need some binoculars.'

'What on earth for?'

'I've developed an interest in birds.'

'Oh no, you haven't.'

'Oh yes, I have. Who identified those birds on the beach?'

Reggie shrugged. Perhaps she *had* taken up ornithology. Perhaps it was part of the ecological framework. 'If I let you have my binoculars,' he said cunningly, 'can I keep *The Magic Flute*?'

'You bastard! Oh ... OK.' She submitted with extra-ordinarily bad grace.

Stiffly, Reggie said, 'I take it, you won't then be popping me into *your* birdcage and taking me back to Hounslow now?'

'There are vital things to occupy you here,' she said briskly. 'Your job is to get Phoebe into that school. It will give her just the start, just the confidence she needs.'

And thus, with another flexible alteration of principle, she strode from the room.

Ten minutes later – during which time Reggie had reflected on his gross stupidity – there was a soft knock at the door.

'Oh, Mr Montis ...' Bella Pike's eyes were a little damp behind her gaily rimmed glasses. 'It's a very wonderful thing you – and your wife – have done. How can I possibly thank you!'

And lunging forward swiftly, she delivered an impulsive kiss to the side of Reggie's nose.

*   *   *

During the month that elapsed after Dorothy's departure, an uneasy torpor set in. It was partly the weather, of course. Had Reggie still been living in that gingery, narcoleptic outer sprawl of London, he might not have noticed much change beyond the very obvious – leafless parks, boiled office temperatures – but here, in Tidmouth, the alteration was more profound. Behind the outward screen of briefer days and barer woodland a new, submerged routine came into sleepy action. Animals made ready to retreat into the deepest recesses of their warrens. Others, after the autumn rut, separated themselves, male from female, until the slow period of gestation was over. Further inland, where mist drifted over the dry, ploughed pasture, there were still people who kept within their dreaming consciousness a faint memory of the young god's ritual dismemberment. This was the season of his interment and, in the sly way of these things, it affected Reggie.

A stranger to the slumbrous season, he mistook the languor, the sense of coming epiphanies.

Perhaps it was not headaches he suffered from at all, but a mysterious virus. Dr Cassidy was grumblingly prepared to treat it as such, though without any noticeable effect. Next, Reggie wondered if Dorothy's warning that Tidmouth would bore him eventually might have some basis. A certain deadness reigned in the streets. Shutters were closed, beach huts padlocked, boats rested hull upwards on the beach, deck chairs were piled beneath tarpaulins. The odour of doughnuts around the harbour disappeared, replaced by more robust scents: tar and seaweed. Postcard stands were withdrawn. Most of the hotel owners locked up and left for the Mediterranean, spending their hard-earned profits on somebody else's seafront. The retired remained on benches, mummified in their wrappings.

There were even days when he felt he was being kept in reserve for some manoeuvre of Dorothy's. Days when he felt she studied him through his own binoculars.

Looked at from certain points of view, this sense of stasis was unjustified, incomprehensible even. After all, there was much to do, much going on.

Mrs Pike had promised to pick Reggie's brains when it came to drawing up the programme for the Christmas entertainments she planned next month. The school routines were enlivening, in both mental and physical ways. Two afternoons a week Reggie ran up and down the touchline with one of Popplewell's whistles round his neck. He derived a certain beaten pleasure from the exercise.

But most of all, in the greying light of the cramped classrooms, he enjoyed his role as teller of tales. His collection was growing most satisfyingly. And the response was better than he could have predicted. When he described Vercingetorix's stand against the Romans, the warrior's lonely submission at Caesar's feet, his manacled removal to Rome where, after six years, despite all vows made to him, he was dragged through the Forum and strangled, Blackstock in 3B burst into tears.

So overjoyed was Reggie by the sight of this cheeky little beast's weeping that he was encouraged to launch into the stranger mythologies of Ireland. Legends like that of *Táin Bó Cuálnge* or *The Cattle Raid of Cooley*.

*   *   *

It gives him the oddest feeling to stand as bard amid the hungry countenances of children. His voice rises to a higher, singing pitch . . .

Cú Chulainn lies wounded surrounded by his northern enemies. Across the battlefield, through the slaughter, there comes towards him a wondrous warrior. He is yellow headed. A great silver brooch pins his green mantle. In his hand a five-barbed spear. Who is this man who strides among the enemy unseen? 'I am Lugh, the sun god, father of the Other-world!' cries the fair warrior. 'Sleep Cú Chulainn and I will fight the hosts on your behalf!' And so saying, he bends to each wound and heals it. For three days and three nights Cú Chulainn sleeps, embodied in the radiance of the warrior god. When he awakes, the battle is won!

A thin beam of sunlight pierces the dusty schoolroom air. There is a slaked silence.

*   *   *

Reggie is himself told tales.

By Dufferdill.

As the two men walked, toiling up ridges that broke upon vistas of a jagged coastline and a grey sea curiously sliced by silver blades, Dufferdill talked ceaselessly. Past and present carelessly occupied the same sentence. 'Three of Monmouth's supporters,' he said, as they descended Barrow Down and approached Harman's Cross, 'were hanged from here. Ghastly business. Should never have happened. Poor fellows, they are not forgotten. This is now an accident black spot. We hang rebels at your peril, eh? Damn this traffic.' Cars whizzed past on their way to Swale.

Over one of several Sunday lunches served by Mrs

Dufferdill – a calm woman, a bishop's daughter – he threw historical light on a musical mystery. Reggie was again complaining about the inconsistencies of *The Magic Flute,* when Dufferdill interrupted him with a gleeful shout, declaring that all the women in the opera were bitchy because Schikaneder – Mozart's librettist – had just had his wife walk out on him.

'Pamina's a sweet girl,' murmured Mrs Dufferdill, scooping things quietly out of silver bowls. She spoke as if the girl lived down the road.

But her husband wasn't deterred by one exception. The whole piece was a warning against female wiles, he insisted, and explained how all the characters of the original story – on which Schikaneder had based his libretto – had been transposed, so that the wicked magician and the good fairy exchanged personalities. 'In *Lulu* the good fairy brings the lovers home by playing her Magic Flute; in the opera she becomes that hysterical old cow, the Queen of The Night.' Dufferdill fondled the ears of his highly-prized labrador dog who was casting a hopeful eye on his master's plate. 'Who seems,' he added, 'to be summarily eliminated by a thunderclap. Would it were Mrs Thatcher could be so easily dealt with.'

'*Darling!*' sighed his gentle wife, reprovingly.

'As it is,' grumbled Dufferdill cheerily, 'one must maintain a stiff lower lip.'

*   *   *

So life was not without its incidents. But for all the school's exigencies – and these included negotiating a future place for Phoebe at Turtledown (an exchange not helped by Frank's fulsome interventions about Reggie's great virtues and a lengthy account of certain vital interruptions suffered by his own well-digging programme) . . . for all these little twists of daily event, Reggie still experienced the sense of floating in a tideless pool of time.

Apart from his heads, the rainless suspension of season, and a suspicion that Dorothy was not yet done with him, he himself could only clearly separate two factors that he knew for sure contributed to the fretful mood: a longing, more and more pronounced, to revisit the windy heights of Turtle Hill whose incomplete and puzzling ridges imprinted a maze upon his mind, and the desire to understand, but not (oh God, no!) not explore the yet more baffling territory inhabited by the two sisters.

They preyed upon his thoughts.

In the dining-room, upon the stairs, he escaped with averted civilities. He knew they awaited him. Once, in the dim light of the stair-well, Anna had stepped out of the shadow and bodily prevented his passing. 'Don't be afraid of us,' she had urged quietly. The half-light had emphasized the straightness of her nose and brow. A rare honesty dwelt in her face.

It frightened him.

It was no part of the reasoning he had invented for them . . He was intended to be a component of their corruption. An erotic device. Or worse, the object of their desire to humiliate the male.

But when occasionally he dared to raise his eyes, he saw the painful gait of Stephanie, the frank dignity of her sister, and knew that they wanted something more difficult than he could name. He was not an adept.

It was easier to dodge them and charge them with depravity.

*　　　*　　　*

None of these surface movements stirred the sleeping god who lay in fourteen severed fragments. The hills were stripped to their monumental winter outlines, the branches blackened in the cold; gulls sat on the slow grey shift of the sea. Sometimes, out of sheer impatience, a wind sprang up, angrily striking the water, rattling windows.

Reggie, standing behind the glass, waits.

*　　　*　　　*

Dorothy arrived with a late November gale.

Or perhaps she just gave the impression of a gale. Whichever it was, she turned up one Saturday morning before Reggie arrived home from school, and made use of his absence to befriend the Cox sisters and to discuss with Bella plans for a major PRG gathering in the Bloomsbury Hall next February. The afternoon she planned to spend – so she alleged when

Reggie trudged in, wearied by a Parent-Teacher Association meeting – doing a bit of bird-spotting. He cross-questioned her quite closely about it and she rattled off some packaged facts about this being a well-known migratory point for certain species, referring briefly to redwings and fieldfares. He was confirmed in his suspicions that she was actually keeping an eye on him, and ill-humouredly announced that he would be going for a walk in the opposite direction.

*   *   *

Mrs Pike and Father Starkey, driving cautiously up Harbour Street in Reggie's car that afternoon, saw the vehicle's owner striding, head down, towards Granny's Sleeve. Bundle trotted at his heels.

'It's his wife,' confided Mrs Pike with a less than careful change-down on the hill. 'She upsets him dreadfully. But she's really very well intentioned. Just a bit ... *forceful*.' Mrs Pike had come to the conclusion that if anybody could advertise the needs of the PRGs nationally, then it was Mrs Montis, whose talk of contacts in high places had impressed Mrs Pike slightly more than it should have done.

Father Starkey was preoccupied by the sensation of Reggie's Minor sliding downhill towards an oncoming Vauxhall Viva. He yanked on the handbrake. He and Mrs Pike jolted in unison.

'Whoopsy ...! Thank you, Ned dear. I'd never have thought of that ... When we get home, remind me to give you one of my ashtrays as a little thank-you gift for all the trouble you've taken.'

A non-smoker, Father Starkey smiled. Sunnybank was now aflood with lop-sided, lumpish bowls and ashtrays which Mrs Pike had contrived during her Thursday evening classes. Soon she would progress to the wheel.

The wheel she at this moment clutched between two strangling hands was pushed leftwards in order to enter the gateway of Mrs Cheeseman's Georgian house on the corner of Shilling Street. There were one or two other permissions to be sought before the Christmas entertainment could be happily staged there, and for this Mrs Pike needed the priest's support, as Mrs Cheeseman frightened her out of her wits. Could the geyser be used? Would paper chains be acceptable? (They would certainly help to conceal the tarnished décor.)

Grimly, Mrs Cheeseman believed that she was obliged to do something of a charitable nature in order to achieve grace. At her age — she'd convinced herself — one act a year was quite sufficient. The gross unpleasantness of the act more than compensated for its being the solitary giving gesture on her calendar. The vulgarity of the visitors and their entertainments, the fears she suffered for the safety of her ornaments, left her feeling indescribably seedy for weeks afterwards.

It was not surprising that Mrs Pike made a hash of negotiating the gateway.

The old lady heard the rumpus, but did not stir from the drawing-room in the tower, where she sat not only for the duration of the party but throughout all the preceding and succeeding days in which Mrs Pike and her helpers cleaned the woefully neglected rooms, the splendour of whose adornments and proportions were heavily obscured by dust.

Hearing all the throttling and grating below, Mrs Cheeseman thought pleasurably of the objections she would raise. She might, quite reasonably, refuse the drawing of any water.

*   *   *

Father Starkey, being blessed with a far more generous nature, had proportionately more demands made of it.

The combination, in a single afternoon, of Mrs Cheeseman and (at the wheel) Mrs Pike might, for many a churchman, have represented a greater strain on reserves of goodness and kindness than would be thought tolerable. Father Starkey, a singular man, not only contended cheerfully with these two ladies: by the time Reggie regained Sunnybank, he found his friend sitting on the stairs, clutching a brown glazed pottery object while Dorothy, in marmalade fun furs, binoculars swinging from her neck, brown leather boots firmly braced, stood over him in haranguing attack of his faith. Father Starkey listened placidly. He knew her sort.

'Anti-sex and anti-women!' Dorothy declared, giving only a casual glance in her husband's direction. And she reeled off a fluent string of standard criticisms. The attribution of original sin to Eve, rather than Adam; the absurdity of the virgin birth and its cruel implications for women's view of their own sexuality; the malign influence of Paul; the brutal refusal of the Pope to allow either birth control or abortion; the bigotry behind the doctrine of apostolic succession, which prevented women administering the sacraments of the very religion she was hotly asserting no sensible women could subscribe to ...

Reggie attempted to sidle round her so that he might return Bundle to the kitchen, where Mrs Pike, one ear pressed to the door, was listening with enthralled horror to Dorothy's diatribe.

'I sympathize with much of what you say,' Father Starkey conceded, while Dorothy struck the stair rail for emphasis and refused to allow Reggie past. 'But now people realize it's the old Judaic element responsible for so much of the continuing prejudice, it's bound to subside.' And he returned to his favourite theme of Our Lady's promotion in Catholic theogony, so disarming Dorothy that Reggie was at last able to squeeze between her and the grandfather clock.

'He's already had Mrs Cheeseman this afternoon,' whispered Mrs Pike with a worried air.

'You needn't fear for Ned,' Reggie reassured her. 'By the end of the afternoon he will probably have Dorothy converted.'

'Do you really think so?' Mrs Pike took the possibility seriously, and indeed, as Reggie again attempted to clamber round the animal form of his wife, he noted that Ned Starkey had seized the initiative and was describing with some enthusiasm to Dorothy the existence of a fourth-century, Middle Eastern sect called the Kollyridians, women who worshipped Mary in a way offensive to the early Church. 'Epiphanius, who wrote a book reviling eighty distinct heresies ... so heresy was already tremendously popular in 375,' he said tangentially to Reggie as his friend's right leg straddled his head. 'He, Epiphanius, was tremendously heated about these ladies because they placed Mary on an equal footing with Christ and, although there's no mention of the cult anywhere else I know, it's interesting that Mahomet condemned the idea of a Trinity composed of God, Christ and Mary, so clearly, somewhere in those lands, it's probable that such an idea *had* evolved. Odder still . . .'

'Do forgive me.' Reggie lifted his left leg over Father Starkey's head. 'Perhaps Dorothy ought . . .'

'Don't interrupt!' snapped Dorothy. 'This is jolly interesting. Go on, do. Odder still?'

Reggie hovered on the stair above.

'Odder still,' continued Father Starkey with unequivocal willingness, 'is the suspicion that this form of devotion was so widespread, so popular, the Church eventually had no option but to incorporate it into orthodox belief. Mind you, the great council at Ephesus – 431, as you'll recall – was the most awful charade. Frightful piece of one-upmanship between Cyril of Alexandria and Nestorius of Antioch. Still, that's beside the point. The *important* point . . .'

'Yes, yes!' Dorothy hooped her arms between stair rail and wall, looking more than ever like a lioness in her orange furs.

'. . . was that Mary, with Cyril's connivance, you appreciate, was declared *Theotokos*!'

Dorothy stared blankly at the priest's beaming countenance.

'*Theotokos* . . . Mother of God,' he explained.

She still didn't grasp the full import of this promotion properly.

'If she was mother of Christ and Christ was God, she was mother of God,' clarified Reggie from his perch.

'She was divine?' queried Dorothy.

'Precisely,' exclaimed the priest and, seeing that he had momentarily defused Dorothy's attack by this fifth-century piece of feminism, added, 'Something else that will amuse you . . . I don't need to explain the significance of Ephesus to you.'

'Temple of Artemis, Seventh Wonder of the World?'

'Exactly, but did you also know that Mary, who was committed to the care of John after the crucifixion, very likely went with him to Ephesus and it was the goddess-worshippers there who gave Paul such a headache?'

131

'You mean . . .?' murmured Dorothy, trying to think what he did mean.

'That the Marian cult absorbed all the old pagan forms, and it's my belief that had that *not* been the case, Christianity might have collapsed with the end of the Roman Empire. She – Mary – provided the thread needed to keep the whole thing going, and by golly!' he declared warmly, 'she still does. More revised – or as we have it, revealed – thinking attaches to her than any other figure . . . the Assumption in 1950; and only a couple of years back the late Pope – bearing vigorous, questioning women of your type in mind – said it was a mistake just to think of her as a *mother* figure.'

'Oh, I know.' Dorothy's cynicism revived. 'She was suddenly a women's libber.'

'An important, active agent in the apostolic community's faith.'

'A canny piece of sophistry,' contended Dorothy. 'He still left women double-locked between the legs.'

'Excuse me.' Reggie, pained, climbed away from the debate. He heard Father Starkey remark that Mrs Montis had a pungent turn of phrase and that, much as he'd enjoyed their conversation, he had a boy to cram.

The last sound that reached Reggie as he turned the handle of his sitting-room was his wife's roar of lubricious laughter. Then suddenly, she was gone.

He thought he saw her several times. On the cliffs, her huge grey cloak enwrapping other figures. Disappearing round the corner of Fossil Street, furred and prowling. He put these glimpses down to paranoia, his failure to wear the right pair of glasses for the right purpose, and the deceiving folds of this plunging landscape. Of these various explanations, paranoia surged uppermost when, on the Friday before the Christmas entertainment, Antonia rang from Casterwich station asking to be picked up. Without a doubt, he was being watched.

Mrs Pike, who was in receipt of various secret messages from Dorothy about national expansion of the PRG movement, who had in fact invited Dorothy to the fund-raising evening and been informed that Dorothy had a nasty cold, seemed unsurprised by this latest development. Antonia, she presumed, was deputizing.

Reggie, ignorant of this, has darker impressions.

'Perhaps,' suggested Mrs Pike brightly, 'your daughter could do a turn. Is she any good at anything?'

Reggie racked his brains. 'I don't think so,' he said. 'She used to do a daisy dance when she was small, but I don't suppose she'd feel . . .'

'It was quite the thing?'

'. . . at her age,' Reggie concluded, and he sailed off through the pitch-black lanes to meet his daughter off the 18.30.

'You might have warned me,' he said, suddenly affectionate as the homely, dimpled girl with Dorothy's colouring but half her height, hove towards him, scattering carrier bags. They kissed.

'You'd have made excuses or worked up a lecture if I had,' she grinned and started bundling herself into the Morris. She wore a long, rabbity coat with square unbecoming shoulders that took a lot of piling into the car.

'You could be right,' he sighed, nursing the splitting bags and arranging them one by one on the back seat. 'Your mother says I've got to talk you out of becoming a nun.'

Antonia screamed with laughter. 'Me a nun!' she whooped.

Could she be sent to spy?

*　　　*　　　*

Reggie eyes his daughter cautiously as he switches on the ignition. Her curling, uncombed hair, her plump disarray suggests a certain ineffectiveness as a spy. He has always thought of Antonia as a fat and sullen girl. Something is changed. She has an irenic air.

*　　　*　　　*

A fox stared into the headlamps and slithered through the brambles at the side of the road. Antonia shrieked again. With excitement this time. He was wondering how to broach the nunnery business when she broke into a bubbling explanation of everything.

133

Antonia's ineligibility as a novitiate was beyond question. Antonia was pregnant. 'The convent was just a cheap place to stay on Social Security. And the best sort of hidey-hole.'

'Who were you hiding from?'

'Who do you think?'

'Your mother?'

'In one!'

'But why?' Dorothy, whatever else might be said of her, was not one to be shocked. He enjoyed taking a corner dangerously as his daughter's condition sunk in.

'You won't be doing the daisy dance then.' He laughed to himself.

'I won't whatter?'

'Never mind.' He was pleased to discover he wasn't shocked himself. Just aged slightly by the announcement of his forth-coming grandfatherhood.

'I want you to tell mummy.'

'She doesn't know?'

'I want you to tell her to leave me alone.'

'She'd enjoy helping.'

'That's precisely it.' Antonia wound down the window to see if the air smelt different here. '*You* know,' she grinned; 'she'd either insist on delivering it herself, or make sure I aborted by the self-suction method, or feed me on wheat-germ patties and molasses, or . . .'

'Yes, I know, I know.' This was better. He, not Dorothy, was in conspiracy with Antonia. He quite liked the feeling. He was less sure about Antonia's somewhat careless attitude towards her own condition. She didn't know – or wasn't saying – who the father was; had the sketchiest idea of how far gone she was and seemed, initially, to have the vaguest appreciation of the economic difficulties that faced her.

'That's rather what I came about,' she said eventually, after he'd pressed her on the practicalities.

Reggie took the hill into Tidmouth at such speed that he flew the crest with all four wheels off the ground.

'You don't mean, *live* here?' For an awful moment he saw her sharing the top floor with Anna and Stephanie.

She toyed with the idea and dismissed it. 'No, I meant bread, basically.'

*　　*　　*

For a moment, Reggie wonders whether he can be sure this isn't an elaborate ploy of Dorothy's to keep him peripherally involved in family affairs. His suspicions then shame him so deeply that he says, 'Of course, darling. An allowance. Of course I'll help out.'

*　　*　　*

A light blazed from the attic as they drew up outside Sunnybank. A dimmer glow from the hall crinkled in the frosted glass.

'But as for telling your mother . . . We're not really in contact, you know.'

'That's not,' announced Antonia, peering out of the window to see if he'd parked straight, 'what she thinks. She says you need an eye kept on you.'

Reggie's heart went into a spasm.

'So you *have* talked to her?'

Antonia began hauling out her carrier bags. 'Only over the phone.'

Walking up the path behind his daughter, Reggie tried to divine Dorothy's Byzantine mind.

He can't be blamed. The sleeping season lends itself to fancies. In the darkness, the entombed and dreaming god gently stirs his mutilated body.

9

Sitting rigidly before her single-bar radiator on the upper floor of the tower, Mrs Cheeseman ran a bony hand so fiercely down the spine of her aged tortoiseshell cat that it leapt from her lap with a squawl.

The invasion of Steeps House was under way.

It had begun with a lengthy demonstration of handbell ringing by a young Salvation Army group, whose repertoire had so far ranged from 'Crimond' to 'Drink To Me Only With Thine Eyes'. They were now winding up their performance by inviting the audience to join them in 'There was a Farmer had a Cow' with all its jolly multiplicity of verses and animal grunts The audience, of near enough sixty people, took up the invitation with gusto. Mrs Cheeseman's Edwardian pendant earrings (her one concession to the evening) trembled with revulsion.

And there would be crumbs all over the floor! (That she, whose house had long been favoured by Tidmouth's mice, should be exercised by crumbs, was unreasonable except that there existed in her mind a major difference in kind, quality and quantity between her detritus and that of others.)

'Ee-i-ee-i-yo!'

Her ancestors glowered in their frames.

'With a quack-quack here and a quack-quack there,

Here a quack, there a quack, everywhere a quack-quack!'

Mrs Cheeseman allotted herself a modest throne to the far right hand of God.

*   *   *

Bella was delighted with the way things were going.

The audience was enjoying itself thoroughly.

At a pound a ticket, she'd been quite surprised to attract such a number, but then people were always anxious to see the interior of this grand, melancholy house at the corner of Shilling Lane. She looked around, smiling at her friends and neighbours, re-knotting her rope of artificial pearls, and calculating the returns. With luck she could raise another forty pounds on the raffle – first prize a toy panda large enough to terrify a small child; second prize a bottle of Cyprus sherry, and third a box of chocolates Mr Partridge had reluctantly offered from his top shelf, persuaded only by the almost certain knowledge that half of them would have gone powdery white with age.

She popped out to see how the sausage rolls and vol-au-vents were going in the vast, black, unruly kitchen range. She had to keep taking them out and putting them back again. Antonia had pre-empted her and was blowing on burnt fingers. Such a sweet girl, thought Bella and thanked her profusely, asking if she would mind stirring the cider cup which – in view of Mrs Cheeseman's unimpeachable water restrictions – they'd substitute for the usual orangeade. 'It'll cut back on the profit a bit,' Mrs Pike lamented, 'but the bulk of it is Frank's homemade.'

Antonia sipped some and suggested the addition of a little sugar.

In the other room the applause was still wild. The Salvation Army was bound to do an encore, which would allow time for the cider cup to be poured into individual paper beakers. More helpers crept into the kitchen and scurried round. Everybody had brought her own tea towel.

The handbell ringers changed mood as the applause died away, and embarked on a skilful rendering of 'In The Deep Mid-winter'.

Reggie did not join in the general humming. When it came to the last verse the simple words were softly voiced by the audience. Reggie's neighbours on either side were weeping.

The applause was tremendous.

Food and drinks were passed along the rows during the interval, while Bella raised Phoebe like a ventriloquist's dummy and spoke of the tragedy of restricted growth. Phoebe who, according to Frank, always ailed at this time of year, looked dreadful. Although she wore her usual stony expression

137

throughout her grandmother's description of the limited opportunities facing such kiddies as herself, her transparent pallor, the flying halo of hair, specially ringleted for the occasion, made her face look shrunkenly small. The two large, glazed blue eyes protruded like gems in a burial mask.

After the peroration, during which there was a further clinking of small change in handbags and pockets, Phoebe remained standing on the chair where she'd been placed and, with a watchful chord from Dufferdill on the piano, she sang in a thin, clear voice 'My Love is like a Red, Red Rose'. Clearly it was a great favourite. Gravely oblivious to the applause, she gathered the skirts of her long white dress and climbed off the chair. The audience cheered the chair for ages but Phoebe, resisting the nudges of her parents, remained impassively on her seat in the front row.

When the woman next to Reggie whispered what a shame it all was, he found himself agreeing with genuine compassion, though it was not Phoebe's frailty so much as the public exhibition of it that primarily moved him.

The turns followed thick, if not fast.

There was a tendency for everyone – in Reggie's judgement – to go on too long, but then he failed to understand the provident need to have one's poundsworth.

Dressed in a smock and tattered hat, Frank told stories in a Dorset accent so thick that Reggie couldn't understand a word, but everybody around him was screeching with laughter.

Upstairs, Mrs Cheeseman drew nearer her one bar of warmth and screwed cotton-wool pellets into her ears.

Some of Anna's pupils did a gymnastic display, which had the chandelier swaying.

Father Starkey's recitation of 'The Jabberwocky' was well liked, though it had quite plainly been heard many times before. Still, Ned Starkey had been responsible for rounding up much of the evening's talent and had left himself little time to learn a new trick. The gloomy Ogilvy, his small, fringed wife, Mr Kean, the French master and his girlfriend, a rather sexy creature with hair so fashionably frizzed by Swale's leading stylist that more than one woman in the room thought something must have gone wrong with the perm, all solemnly arranged their chairs and instruments, and after many furtive looks at one another to check that each was tuned and ready, set off on one of the most unco-ordinated string quartets Reggie – whose lack of musicality must be remembered – had ever heard. But the supporters of the evening were quite untroubled by the quartet's inability to end together, and were so intrigued by Mrs Ogilvy's frequent scowls at her husband's fingering of the cello, that they felt they'd had a really good time and showed their appreciation frenziedly.

The response encouraged Reggie who, lacking any performing talent and thinking quite wrongly that brevity was the thing required, read Yeats's poem, 'The Cloths of Heaven'.

'Tread softly,' he ended, daring a brief and imperceptible look at his audience, 'for you tread on my dreams.'

If they were disappointed that the recitation was over so soon and was read rather than uttered from memory (as was the convention) nobody was going to show it. They accorded Reggie the same heartfelt thanks as all the others.

'Beautiful!' breathed Mrs Pike as he passed her. 'Absolutely lovely, dear.'

He blushed and settled sheepishly back in his chair as she rose to announce the last turn of the evening. 'A very pretty duet ... Anna, Stephanie?'

The two girls came forward. Anna, her lean and graceful body clad in dark, close-fitting brown velvet, leaned forward to help her sister on to the dais, taking both hands in her own and smiling at the silvery girl. Everything about her – her skin, her long, fine hair, her simple dress – all had this silvered quality, as if a pale radiance from within her body illumined her.

Reggie rarely had either the temerity or the opportunity to look as openly at Stephanie as he did now. He drank her up. She had the poignant, oval-faced serenity of a painted angel. Was this slender, ethereal creature the same girl whose wounded body could arch in such frank sensuality? His blood raced.

A subdued silence fell.

Placing her recorder to her lips, Anna played an E-flat.

Looking directly into her sister's eyes, Stephanie, unaccompanied, began to sing.

As the pure sound issued forth, Reggie's heart missed a beat.

> *Bei Männern, welche Liebe fühlen,*
> *Fehlt auch ein gutes Herze nicht*

And then the slow, sweet echo of Anna's warm contralto expressed Papageno's view of love:

> *Die süssen Triebe mitzfühlen,*
> *Ist dann der Weiber erste Pflicht.*

Together, their voices rose like doves, each face reflecting the rhapsodic joy of the other in this, the loveliest of Mozart's duets.

Again, Stephanie's unfalteringly liquid voice took up Pamina's vow of love:

> *Die Lieb' versüsset jede Plage,*
> *Ihr opfert jede Kreatur.*
> (Oh love doth sweeten every sorrow
> Each living creature pays its due.)

The two girls, the light and the dark, two tongues of autumnal flame, quivered before Reggie. His vision was disturbed by tears.

When once again the voices met in final unison, declaring that nothing in all creation is more noble than love, he saw Anna's gaze rest unmistakably on him. As Stephanie took Pamina's line more ornately and ecstatically above that of Papageno, a faint smile touched Anna's lips and lingered on him before she turned more radiantly to her sister. Together they sang the triumphant final phrase:

> Man and woman, woman . . . man,
> Their love the gulf with the gods can span!

It mattered not a jot that the residents of Tidmouth gathered in the draughty salon of Steeps House knew barely a word of German between them. It was of supreme unimportance whether or not they recognized the music as that of *Die Zauberflöte*; whether or not they knew Papageno was a man,

Pamina a woman. The silence that elapsed before their wildly tumultuous applause rang out showed how deeply aware they were that an unusual beauty had been unfolded in their presence. The peeling room itself recovered something of its former simple grandeur. So long did the cheering and stamping go on that the two girls, gravely smiling, performed the final verse again. As the unaccompanied song carved the air afresh, Reggie looked about him at the stilled faces and thought he saw in these good, plain, open countenances an understanding that he himself lacked. His sense of loss was almost beyond bearing.

Above them, Mrs Cheeseman stroked her cat and wept.

There was much kissing beneath the mistletoe that night.

* * *

Shortly after that evening, the drawing of lots began.

Mrs Pike pressed Reggie to join her family at Christmas. A telegram arrived from Dorothy urging him to join her and the children for a week's trial in the commune. A trial indeed he thought it might be. On the other hand, three days in the Orlebars' bungalow before the great stone fireplace seemed little less of an ordeal.

Alternately they pressed their suits.

In the meantime there were celebrations in the staffroom where Dufferdill and Sopworth, who were supervising the bar, became horribly drunk and devised a limerick competition between themselves which rose to such heights of rhymed obscenity, that Matron left the room in tears for the second time that day. The earlier outpouring had been provoked by 4A's presentation to her of a razor, a gift she took as personally as had been intended. She was an unhappily hirsute woman.

Eleanor Straker danced with Reggie on the square foot of parquet she fought clear for them, appropriating him until her husband unprised her and took her home, whereupon Mrs Popplewell drove him into *her* corner and, as the bun on top of her head slowly fell to pieces, spoke without apparent drawing of breath about a wide variety of barbarous things she would do to football hooligans if somebody gave her half a chance.

* * *

Almost permanently drunk in the last few days before the holy festival, Reggie was incapable of clear decision. He compromised. He said he would attend the carol service in the tiny church of Maidenwell and immediately afterwards, catch the afternoon train to London.

* * *

His palms on the wheel sticky with Frank's Drambuie, he drove down the valley towards Maidenwell, peering desperately for a vista of the great hilltop that occupied his aching thoughts, but neither the curve of the road, nor the low-lying cloud allowed for it. As he climbed out of the car, he cursed.

* * *

' 'Twas a curse done it,' announced Frank's father, speaking of the drying of the well. 'They drove us out from here when the maid was in the womb,' muttered the old man, removing his cap. A cold wind blew off the land down the valley.

'You don't want to take no heed of Dad!' Jovially, Frank clapped Reggie on the back. 'You're a gloomy old bugger, Dad!'

'What's that?'

'You're a gloomy old bugger!'

'Art without feeling.' Old man Orlebar looked about at the ruined buildings of the village, almost lost behind the rapid growth of silent woodland. The few remaining walls were still greenly swagged about with ivy and bramble. Some of his facts, it was true, had acquired the distortion of legend, but they hung together well enough in his mind.

' 'Twas there I were born.' Red-eyed, blue-jowled and grim, he pointed towards a tumbled line of cottages, lost amid bracken.

'Get a move on,' urged Daphne, pulling Gary's balaclava round to the front of his face. 'He'll catch his death.'

Reggie stood aside to let the family crowd past him into the tiny church. When he looked back he caught sight of a figure among the trees, wild-haired – man or woman he couldn't tell – somebody muffled in a cape.

'Are you coming, dear?' Mrs Pike, who took an ecumenical view of carol services, was calling.

Reggie looked again.

Fallen stones, sentinel trees. Nothing more.

*   *   *

The clangour of London!

Buses, taxis, lorries drive at people, one another, like vehicles in the front line of a desperate war.

For an hour he stands, staring into one shop window like a moth at the light, thankful for the stillness of the fashion dummies with their fringed eyes and rouged cheeks. Then, buffeted, taken into the insensate babble of the human stream, he is borne down the tidal passageways of the underground and finds he has caught a train that takes him back to Paddington instead of going the other way, east, towards Dorothy's warehouse. There is a connection to Casterwich in five minutes.

He stands all the way, the narrow band tightening round his skull, his eyes open moulds for the pouring in of hot liquid metal.

By nine o'clock on Christmas Eve he is back inside the chill emptiness of Sunnybank. He climbs upstairs, past his own room, on, up to the narrower landing, and there he sleeps on Stephanie's bed until woken by the pale, hard, blue glare of the skylight and the sound of Christmas bells.

*   *   *

Reggie ignored the phone, preyed on Bella's larder, and listened to a special service on the radio. Never, in all his life had he spent this day of all days on his own, and the experience – in spite of the nauseous headache which still troubled him – had a distinct novelty until about lunchtime. At that moment, the sense of retrieved freedom began to wilt and was replaced by wistful thoughts of turkey, three kinds of stuffing, little sprouts, glazed carrots, roast potatoes, rich, dark pudding with old sixpences inside, mince pies, brandy butter, Stilton, crackers, bad jokes, marrons glacés, a glass of fine old port . . . freedom seemed to have a lot in common with loneliness.

For half an hour he picked at his fragments of incised Samian ware, separating them from other, less easily distinguished shards; then he took P. J. Fowler's *Recent Work in Rural Archaeology* into the bathroom, spending a long and ultimately profitable time on the seat there. As he presided over the sluggish quartan stirring of his bowel, it struck him that the more demands and invasions were made on his freedom, the less efficiently his lower intestine worked. Doing his duty. There was some connection.

'Have you done your duty?' Nana would ask when he descended into her dark basement kitchen where, because her eyesight was failing and nobody dared tell her the truth, a film of grease clung to the stove, the sink and all the eating utensils. And then, one day, when he was about twelve, he had realized that if nobody told kindly Nana the truth about her filthy kitchen, there was no need to tell her the truth about anything. Nana, not expecting fibs, never perceived them.

'Have you done your duty?' she would say.

And he learnt to answer 'yes', without so much as a shifted eyelid. The only penalty had been a sense of containing a lie within his bowel, a terrible withholding of truth and obligation and all that was decent.

Nana's ashes had been scattered off Brighton pier thirty-five years ago.

Duty still hung on by its little loveless claws. Duty made him feed the black collecting boxes that gaped on every windowsill. Duty made him agree to a monthly allowance for Antonia although she was already receiving a moderate subsidy from other British taxpayers. Duty had made him go as far as Oxford Circus to spend Christmas with his family, but somewhere between Oxford Circus and Wapping his sense of duty had rebelled. Or rather, he supposed with some pleasure, he had rebelled against it. Reggie sighed and tore off a sheet of pink tissue.

The pleasure was short-lived.

He watched a two-hour comedy spectacular on Bella's colour television and wondered what damage duty had done him. And pondering the complexities of a giving that was done without any desire to please those to whom the giving was directed – a giving that was executed according to some behavioural rule book (Oh Nana! Nana!) – an insight of the utmost simplicity came to him.

With a dully-felt clarity he knew why the rituals of the attic room so frightened and affronted him. Oh, the objections he had presented to himself: the perversion, the corruption, the degradation of the two girls – his own timidity, his sense of outrage, his puritanism, his offendingly brutal burst of lechery ... all these disqualifying attitudes that turned with bewildering difference through his brain concealed from him the simple, fundamental reason for his self-exclusion.

*   *   *

Gazing unseeingly at Danny la Rue, he knows that the act he has witnessed under the attic roof is one of supreme tenderness. Of purest love.

And he cannot enter upon it.

Part Three

IMBOLC

10

In mid-January, it rained.

The nation raced to its various windows and looked out at the foreign moisture. Some ran into the streets, faces upturned.

It was a very short wet spell.

Trying to avert blame from his own government, the Prime Minister declared that the weather was an international problem to do with a change in prevailing wind patterns. Things were far worse in America. Productivity under the present three-day week arrangement was remarkably high, though there would have to be further cutbacks in the steel programme. Desalination plants were now currently – he said – under construction on the coast, although until now, given our average rainfall and temperate climate, such schemes had been considered uneconomic.

The Church announced a week of prayer.

* * *

Arriving at the Orlebars' bungalow one grey Saturday afternoon with his belated Christmas present for Phoebe, Reggie was unable to elicit any answer at the front door. He wandered round to the unsightly yard at the back. Between the pig pen and the compost heap he saw Frank's head on a platter of mud.

'Can't be much further down!' A spadeful of clay flew about Frank's ears.

Reggie gazed down the hole. 'I wish you wouldn't take my powers so seriously,' he said, thinking at the same time that anyone who had allowed two and a half months to elapse since the original divination could hardly be described as *seriously* determined to strike water. A wind blew through the yard, making the loosely patched corrugated iron rattle.

'But I *do*,' insisted Frank, digging furiously.

Reggie gently kicked a hen off his shoe. 'By the way,' he said, 'your father . . .'

'What's the old fellow been saying now?'

'Oh, I haven't set eyes on him since the carol service. But the curse . . . what did he mean by it?'

'Oh, that's just his way of looking at things. He's a great one for putting two and two together, and making five.' Another slab of mud flew through the air and the hens ran to explore it for worms.

'Did the village well dry up then, when he said?'

'I don't know when he said.'

'When Phoebe . . .'

'Oh, 'twas dry afore she were born. The water table on the downs, he's been dropping for years.'

'I see.'

'They found all sorts at the bottom, mind. Old stuff, what did'un call they?' Frank paused, sweat running down the reddened folds of his neck.

'Not votive offerings?'

'That's right, votives . . . that's it. Superstitions. If you've got summat there for Phoebe, you let yourself in. The back door's open. Last room on the left.'

'Oh, I'll just pop it in the kitchen.' Phoebe had been unwell since Christmas and unable for that reason to take up the precious place Reggie had helped secure for her at Turtledown. He wasn't keen on a bedside visit.

'She'll be pleased for a bit of company.' Frank seemed to be disappearing further down the hole. 'I'll not be long meself,' he added, 'but I like to see a job done.'

Reggie knocked gently at the last door on the left. 'What is it then?' a voice yelled, and he let himself in.

A gasp escaped him.

He understood why Frank's approach to all his other jobs appeared so dilatory. This, obviously, was his craft-shop.

'Well,' breathed Reggie, 'what a magnificent bedroom you have.'

'Is that for me?'

Supported by a pile of gold, satiny cushions, Phoebe sat on a bed that was a miniature replica of an oriental queen's canopied litter. A large white cat was draped across her legs. Slippery, haunting music came from somewhere. He handed over the gift which, remembering how appetizing it was to unwrap and unwrap, he had secreted under many layers of paper. 'What is it?' he murmured, wondering.

'You should know,' she said. 'You bought it. Didn't you?'

'The music, I mean?' he stuttered, thrown by her rudeness.

'*Gymnopédies*. Satie.'

'Ah.' He nodded and continued, dumbly, to stare about him.

Satin folds of the same glowing golden colour fell from a tented peak above the bed head and were tied back to admit the light. Raised embroideries in gilded thread whirled in curvilinear shapes behind Phoebe's own flying hair. The foot of the bed was scrolled on the Egyptan pattern and carved with imaginary beasts picked out in green and gold. It was the handiwork of a craftsman with no sense of period, somebody who had just pursued his own littered taste, a taste accumulated from film sets and, possibly, Victorian drawings of romanticized earlier eras.

Phoebe was still unwrapping.

'Is it something very small?' she demanded to know, crossly.

'Quite,' said Reggie marvelling over the thick, soft white carpet which billowed and lapped like spume round the miniature and bulging *boule* chest of drawers, a small red lacquer cabinet hand-painted with dragons, a curved rosewood desk with a red leather top and little inlaid drawers, a circular green and gilt table with two matching chairs, a genuine Victorian birdcage with – yes, a stuffed canary inside it, and another chair with a shell back, again ornately gilded. On a low table by the wall, a Bonsai garden was placed, alongside an exquisite dolls' house, its Georgian, porticoed front half open to reveal a perfectly architectured interior, furnishings for every room, and a family of dolls no more than two inches high – father in his book-lined library, mother pouring tea from a silver service in the dining-room, a mob-capped maid at a kitchen range with copper pans above, and two children in a nursery where another tiny dolls' house stood. The girl child had a numinous head of hair just like Phoebe's own, and was dressed in pink with white, frilled knickerbockers.

'Thank you very much,' said the real Phoebe doll, and Reggie jumped up from his crouched examination of the dolls' house to see her studying the gift he had chosen: a small geode lined with glittering iron pyrites.

'Is it real gold?' she asked.

'Fool's gold, it's called,' he muttered, embarrassed by the fabulous wealth of her possessions.

'Could you put it with the others?' Small, pale, imperious, she held out the geode and indicated the windowsill which, he only now observed, was lined with fragments of haematite, quartz, sulphur, calcite and a number of fossils – ammonites of smaller sizes, gastropods and, very special, a trilobite specimen which he picked up and admired.

'This didn't come from round here, did it?'

'I don't know,' she said. 'It was given me.'

The rest of the large sill was filled by five neatly ranged rows of pebbles. There must have been nearly a hundred in all. Apart from a few smooth black pennies of Kimmeridge shale at one end, they were entirely unremarkable beach pebbles. Only the uniformity of their oval shape and size was of any note. He picked one up.

'Why these?'

'I like them.' She sat up against her pillows, the bones of her face unnaturally prominent, her eyes blue headlamps. 'I like the feel of them. Sometimes I paint them.'

He gazed again around the heuristic room. So. The little princess.

'You're fond of painting, generally?' He nodded towards the pinned pictures. 'You did them?'

'Mm.'

They were crammed with tiny stick figures, rather like Lowry drawings, except that in each one there featured a single, large, halo-ed figure, as if, in her imagination, she had reversed the proportions of her own world. The image was profoundly moving.

The music ceased, leaving a hollowed-out silence. Reggie made some confused, limited movements.

'Would you like to hear something else?'

He looked at her, surprised. It was the first gracious thing he had ever heard her say. 'Thank you,' he replied faintly.

She leaned to one side and pressed one in a range of buttons set in a white quilted plastic panel on the wall. From all around the room came the lament of an unaccompanied counter-tenor: *King Henry lay weeping*.

The child sat upright and stared at him. He stared back.

'Your tastes,' he attempted, trying to fight back the weirdness of the situation, 'are very . . .' He was going to say 'strange', but faltered, and came out with 'grown-up'.

'Don't you like it?' She pressed another button and this time Brahms flowed out into the white room. *Variations on St Antoni Chorale*, not a piece of music Reggie knew, but he heard, beneath its bright, sweet bravery, a sadness.

He stood awhile, listening.

'Will you be teaching me?'

'I beg your pardon? Er, I don't know, I don't know for sure which form you'll be in.'

'You could have found out.'

'I will . . . I *will*.'

'Tell me,' she said, switching off the music and activating a television screen on the far white wall, 'if it's not time for *Dr Who* yet . . .' (it plainly was not, and she switched off the image of the sequined conjuror who had appeared) 'all about the school.'

Reggie looked about in panic. There was no chair large enough to sit in. He would get stuck in the Shaker-style rocking chair beside her bed. Where did Frank sit, for goodness' sake? He remained standing at the foot of her Cleopatra couch and told her who taught what, which rules mattered, how many hours a week were taken up with games, who were the most despised masters, who the most feared. She listened patiently while he gabbled.

'I think it's time for *Dr Who* now,' she said eventually.

He felt dismissed.

Reggie mumbled something about speaking to her father, then something about how nice it was her granny had passed her test at last. He was on the point of adding how much he hoped she would be up soon when she said, quite sharply, 'I hope you were right about that water.'

'Pardon?'

'The well. I do hope you were right.'

'Ah! Oh! Yes. I hope so too.' And stepping carefully backwards through the grotto, he let himself out. As he closed the door he heard, above the electronic theme tune of *Dr Who*, Phoebe's small, stern voice. 'Thank you very much indeed for my present,' she said.

*   *   *

There seemed no end to the abnormal season.

Up on the downs the clouds first gathered around him, then raced past as a wind howled off the sea with a note so near to pain that he abandoned any idea of walking the long way home. In the screaming, milky mass, he could barely see where he was going. He stumbled along narrow, ridged pathways, floundered through dead vegetation. A figure loomed, then vanished ahead of him as the cloud streamed by. Dorothy, watching through her (rather, his) binoculars. Not Antonia. He had sent her money on the first of the month.

It was a signpost on which an old fertilizer sack had blown and now flapped. He darted on through prickling gorse and blackthorn beaten flat by the wind.

A pale host of silent gulls allowed themselves to be blown sideways, inland, over the fields.

*   *   *

Bella Pike was also a little disconcerted.

Although Mrs Montis made a scrupulous point of leaving before Mr Montis came home at six, and thus gave no impression of trying to lure her husband (or was it ex-husband? Bella wished she was a little clearer on the legal situation) back home to Hounslow or Wapping or wherever it was, Bella found being sworn to secrecy very disturbing. She was happy to discuss forthcoming plans for the PRG conference, happy to see how warm a friendship was developing between the two Cox girls and Mrs Montis, but Bella liked things to be orderly. She liked advance warning, and Dorothy's wild entrances were never announced. She wouldn't take her coat off or settle down to a proper tea, either. Worst of all, Bella suspected that Mr Montis suspected something. He was very distracted these days. Always going out to supper at his colleagues' homes. She wondered if her coooking was failing to satisfy and promised to do him a special menu – with wine – if he wished to invite any of his friends back in return for their hospitality. But he said he preferred to take them to Lower Moigne Manor or Seabrook House (where the prices, she knew, were terribly expensive). And then, to her intense disappointment, he declined to come to the dance arranged for the first day of February, the St Brigid's Day dance – which marked, in the Irish calendar if not in the British climate, the first day of spring.

It was a very popular affair with a running buffet and the Black Spot band.

First, he'd said he had no dinner jacket and when she'd said that didn't matter, lots of people didn't bother with such things, he'd said he couldn't dance and when she'd said that didn't matter either, he'd said the noise and heat would give him a headache. She then refrained from further blandishment. But a faint unhappiness still persisted, even though he'd given her the price of a ticket to put towards the funds.

On the eve of the dance Bella Pike popped into St Teresa's for a quick prayer that all would come right.

It didn't feel quite right. Partly because the nice religious smell of the church was swamped beneath the closer scents of shampoo and lacquer freshly applied by Piero at His 'n' Hers Hair Fashions, partly because she was troubled by the morality of keeping Mrs Montis's visits secret from her (please God) ex-husband. A good confession would clear the air.

Father Starkey, who was helping out with confessions that afternoon, heard of Dorothy's visitations with some astonishment, but regarded the swearing to secrecy as no more than acceptable discretion on the part of the wife aforementioned. Mrs Pike's mind was put completely at rest.

* * *

Reggie was upstairs compiling his notes on Celtic religious festivals in one book, and any good stories that came to light in his researches into another book reserved for classroom telling, when Frank, in a badly strained dinner jacket, bounded into his room and said he'd struck water that day. He was thrilled. His face shone, and he insisted Reggie come downstairs for a quick one to celebrate, before they pushed off to the dance.

So he downed a cherry brandy while the women fussed over one another and gave off hothouse gusts. Mrs Pike, in a pretty, long-sleeved navy chiffon with a single spray of cherry blossom printed across the skirt, couldn't decide whether to take her glasses off or leave them on. Frank said she looked better with them on, which he meant as a compliment, but Daphne said that was cheeky of him and told her mother to pop them in her evening bag. Daphne, in gold lamé, looked like a foil-wrapped French praline. Phoebe, outside in the car, preparing to be hoisted for the Lucky Programme Number, refused to come in; so the women were quite anxious to be on their way, but Frank was just as determined that another cherry brandy per man would do no harm at all. 'Anyway,' he said, 'we've struck water haven't we?' It was vital to drink to it.

At length, in a swirl of stoles, sparkling bags and freesia scents, they left, Frank boisterously patting his departing mother-in-law on the bottom. She squeaked.

'Have a good time!' waved Reggie and returned thankfully to his list of festivals and their patron deities.

Only two – Beltaine (May 1st) and Lughnasa (August 1st) – appeared to have any connection with specific gods. Lugh, the sun god, was associated in Roman times with Apollo and Belenos or Belinus, which meant Shining One. There was a connection here with Bran of the *Mabinogion*. The story of Bran's insisting on his own head being severed and thereafter borne by his fellow warriors so that he might entertain them at their feasting went into Reggie's book of classroom tales.

Imbolc (which, ironically) fell on February 1st, seemed without a deity. It marked the hour when the sun emerged from its winter sleep (Reggie made a note that the climate was warmer and dryer during the period in question), the time when the sacred flame was lit and trial marriages made in celebration.

He heard movements overhead which surprised him, since he'd thought the girls would be in some way involved with the dance. (Mrs Pike, however, had felt it would be tactless to involve Stephanie on such an occasion.) They seemed to be dragging heavy objects across the floor.

A puff of the smoked haddock he'd hurriedly gobbled down at supper escaped his throat. The girls, who had tackled their meal in a more leisurely way, had been laughing over a member of staff who'd taken a party of children orienteering and then got lost himself on a boggy part of the heath. He couldn't help hearing. He'd taken his jam roly-poly upstairs with him on the pretext of getting on with urgent work. Anything to avoid the oppression of contact.

The noises went on pretty regularly for an hour or so. His urgent work went untended while he listened.

Then he went upstairs.

*   *   *

'Come in.' Anna, dressed in jeans and a navy, roll-neck sweater, opened the door, unsurprised. Stephanie lay on the bed, reading by lamplight. He was vaguely aware of muddle, as though they were having a spring clean. Clumsily, he hesitated. 'Would you have such a thing as a bottle of ink?' he inquired, 'I seem to have . . .'

'It's kind of you to come.' Anna smiled her grave, clear smile. 'He's come,' she called softly over her shoulder and, going over to Stephanie's bed, she knelt and kissed her sister. 'There, I said he would,' she murmured.

They seemed to enter a private world. But he watched.

Anna removed her sister's book and drew back the sheets a little. With her lips she slowly pressed her sister's neck and shoulder. Then she stood and removed her sweater. The arms of the fair, recumbent girl rose and drew Anna down. They just lay very still, cheek to cheek, Anna whispering something – of comfort, it seemed – until she glanced up at Reggie, standing petrified by the door. 'You're both nervous,' she smiled. 'You must help one another. It's all right.'

And she rose, her small breasts quivering, curiously innocent, as she unzipped her trousers and kicked off her track shoes. Unselfconscious, utterly naked, she walked towards Reggie, took his head gently between her hands, crushed his mouth to hers and forced it open with her tongue.

Instinctively, Reggie stepped backwards, devising some reference to ink. But as his resolve drained, his desire, treacherously, was kindled. Anna was removing his tie, unbuttoning his shirt, her nipples brushing his chest. Although he stood rigid and unhelpful, the slyness of her touch was irresistible. Her fingers slipped round his body, down his spine, over his buttocks. Now to the front they moved and dismay brought him almost to impotence, but she slid to the floor in front of him and with her juicy mouth, restored him.

Somehow, his eyes still fixed on Stephanie's inert form (she had placed one hand over her face, hiding her eyes) he allowed himself to be extricated from his clothing. With a brusque, embarrassed gesture he flung away his glasses. Anna, on her knees before him, laughed softly, her hand never leaving its maddening craft. He could not look down at the wickedness she performed upon him. And then, his whole body surging with desire, he was suddenly activated.

He was ready to be led to his altar.

*　　*　　*

As if she found her own nakedness – or the witnessing of it – intolerable, Stephanie's hand was still gripped over her eyes.

Anna gave Reggie a little push and he gathered from her what he should do. He placed his own hand over Stephanie's rigid knuckles, stroking gently, kissing between the gaps of his own fingers until her hand had eased enough for him to lift it and hold it, palm against his mouth.

His eyes searched the clouded blue of hers.

This was a different kind of entry. A subtler knowing.

There is a blue whose invitation lies in its very hardness: a challenging blue that dares. And a blue so soft a man can be foolishly melted in its false tint.

Stephanie's eyes were of a wounded blue.

She offered no lures, no sensual cunning, no expectation at all. Her eyes held only the several fears that are the residue of pain.

It is open to him to withdraw from this strange new duty that is being asked of him. Some men, perceiving such authentic vulnerability, would be excited by it. Would feast their carrion appetite. Reggie sees, almost academically, the possibility of mere self-satisfaction and knows, as if the hand that Anna cradles at the nape of his neck transmits the message, that such an approach will only compound and magnify all existing injuries.

The fear lay like a deeper nakedness in Stephanie's eyes.

It is *this* nakedness he is being asked to confront, console, conjure. It is a wooing that requires a lover of infinite experience or – as he begins better and better to understand – love of an order that has no source in care for self at all.

A small pulse throbbed at her throat. Nervously, he kissed it. He touched her face. Kissed her closed lids, her brow. His kisses stole across her body as light and warm as spring rain and, all the time, the other sister's touch spoke to him, making him delicate in his proficiencies. She did not guide him. Did not insert a gesture of her own. But he felt her eloquent approvals through the cells and nerves of his whole being.

Even as his lips met Stephanie's directly for the first time, he felt a current channelled through him. Just as he had once felt the gentle pull of the water's flow. Between the sisters he became an instrument of divination.

Her tongue, her skin, nipples, hair and thighs, all these human geographies were explored with her pleasure as his only motive. And the blessing of this hieratic journey was that as he travelled, licking her skin alive, his own achieved a degree of responsiveness beyond anything he had ever known before. He was able to look straight into that released blue gaze, knowing that it beheld a tenderness in which sexuality was servant.

For hours, it seemed, they underwent this sweetly painstaking investigation. Time ceased to be a factor. But there came a moment when it was apparent to him that she would entrust herself to his deeper, fleshly penetration. She had arrived at the knowledge that she was neither pitied nor carnally desired, but truly adored, and the change in her understanding was betokened by her profile, for although her head was turned aside and her gaze was not on him, the spacing of her lips, the rapt and lovely strain of her throat made sufficient signal of her readiness.

*   *   *

He finds he is able without any slackening of love to part the imperfect V of her legs and enter her. He is able to gaze at his own entrance of her body. He is able to smile at her as he senses a renewing fear in her that will fail the test that is being made of him.

Not until he was moving in a deep, prolongedly sensual rhythm did she completely relax again. Her whole body opened up to him like soil parting itself for planting. And then, when the honourable manner of his lovemaking was assured – not until then – did Anna join herself to their embrace, enlarging every pleasure with her own erotic ornament.

The disembodied sense of slowed movement in space which has dogged him all the long dark months of winter now occupies its proper form and place. As he flows into her, he flows into himself. The alternately furtive and thuggish prodding which he has hitherto understood as textbook intercourse is unrelated to this space-surrounded union.

*   *   *

When she cried out aloud and cried again, aloud, he thought he had heard no moaning like it since his wife gave birth to their first-born: their son ... the sounds now meet and echo in his memory and it seems to him that he is the new issue.

'You make me feel beautiful,' was all she said in the silence later.

And that was all that mattered.

160

II

She used the same words in the note he found pushed under his door the following day. Just those words with the initial S below.

He had come from Saturday morning school, arms filled with a tissue-wrapped green sheaf of unopened daffodils, heart filled with such sparkling elation that he kept smiling foolishly to himself. Indeed, he was just thinking how fortunate it was that he had not been witness to a bank robbery or kidnapping or car crash that morning, since he would have been too euphorically distracted by his own happy fantasies to make accurate report to any long-suffering police officer, when he opened his door and trod on the note.

His spirits took another sweet leap.

Reggie has no idea how close he is to confronting a police officer.

*   *   *

He heard Mrs Pike calling his name frantically and, slipping the note in his pocket, smiled down over the banisters. The expression on her face instantly cleaned the smile from his own.

'They've gone!' she screamed, clutching her throat and tumbling upstairs.

'The pearls!' he thought she said.

Mrs Pike gained the landing, and repeated herself breathlessly.

'The girls!' she cried. 'They've gone!'

'The *girls*?' Reggie stood stock-still. 'The *girls*!' he repeated stupidly.

She came at him incoherently. She held in her hand a sheet of azure blue writing paper identical to the one folded in his own pocket. 'I don't understand it . . . I don't . . . what can have made them . . . so suddenly? Without warning?'

He took the paper from her agitated hand and scanned it. His perplexity was greater than hers. He felt quite weak.

'Do you believe it?' she demanded, a touch indignantly.

'What?'

'Do you believe' – she pointed at the letter – 'what they say?'

The note, written in Anna's hand, expressed the very deepest apologies, begged forgiveness for this sudden departure, gave profound thanks for the care and excellent attention they'd received (as well as a further month's rent, enclosed) but explained that an important, long-sought job had come Stephanie's way. Since the opportunity had to be seized immediately, they had no choice but to leave forthwith.

No, he did not believe it.

'The school wouldn't let them go like that!' Mrs Pike now sounded angry as well as hurt. 'There's something very odd about it, wouldn't you say, Mr Montis? A matter for the police?'

'Police!' He was absolutely stunned. What could he have done to provoke this?

Mrs Pike was talking rapidly. It had been quite carefully calculated, she claimed. *They'd* been the ones who insisted that she stay with her daughter after the dance last night. They'd been the ones . . .

'When? When did they say that?'

'Yesterday afternoon. In fact, I have to admit it, Mr Montis, but the way it was done, you know . . . the *manner* in which . . . well, I'll be quite frank with you, I've had *a good look round*.'

He slumped against the wall, open-mouthed. Mrs Pike had the grace to blush. 'I'm sorry,' she muttered, tight-lipped, 'but I find it all so very peculiar. So . . . *upsetting*.' She began to cry and hurriedly held her apron to her nose. 'I still don't know whether to call the police,' she sobbed.

'There's . . . nothing missing, then?' he forced himself to say slowly. He, whose heart had been robbed from its body. *He* felt vandalized.

'Not that I can see. Please don't mind me asking,' she sniffed, dabbing against her eyes, 'but could you just . . . well, look over your belongings?'

Dazed, he did as she asked though in so blind and forlorn a way that he saw nothing missing. How do you tell the police your heart has been thieved?

As he moved about in a dilatory fashion Mrs Pike trailed behind, making small, choking sounds. He wanted desperately to be left alone to think.

'What do *you* feel . . .?' she repeated beseechingly.

'Feel?'

Emptied! Broken! Utterly confused!

'About the police?' she persisted.

'I can't think why the police should be informed,' he said rather more sharply than he intended. Mrs Pike fell silent, suppressing her anxieties behind a clenched fist.

'You can't imagine they've been kidnapped or . . . or . . . in some way taken against their will? Abducted?' It was a relief to voice his own absurder fears as if they might be hers.

'Good heavens, no. People who are being kidnapped don't pay a month's rent in advance,' said Mrs Pike.

'Of course not. Exactly. Well,' he concluded and swallowed hard, 'we must simply accept their word – there may be some other, more personal reason which they didn't feel at liberty . . . which they didn't wish to burden you with . . . *with which* they didn't wish to burden you,' he corrected himself, distraught. 'Otherwise – though I confess it's strange the school should have agreed to their leaving only three weeks after the start of term – still, they're acting within their rights and perhaps the matter should be left there.' His voice tailed away.

There was an awkward pause between them.

Mrs Pike felt she wasn't getting the support she needed. 'I'll have your dinner ready in ten minutes,' she said, subdued, seeing this migration as a criticism of herself, and sure that Mr Montis was trying to avoid saying as much. Numbly, she turned to go downstairs.

'Here!' said Reggie abruptly, thrusting the flowers at her, 'these are for you.'

Mrs Pike descended to her kitchen in floods of tears.

*   *   *

When she saw his barely touched plate, she thought perhaps that was it. Perhaps he and the girls liked their food a bit more spicy. Perhaps she ought to add a few more herbs and garlic and such. She'd try hotting things up a little. The idea of losing Mr Montis was so frightful that the girls' departure seemed less distressing by comparison. To cheer herself up, Mrs Pike spent the afternoon reading books on oriental cookery.

She had to turn the light on to read. The room turned quite dark when it began to rain.

*   *   *

It began to rain. Ye gods (ye gods indeed) it began to rain!

Reggie strode out along the headland, bent against the downpour. The seaward end of the hills was enveloped in driving cloud and his waterproof anorak was soon giving the lie to its guarantee. Drenched, cold, bitter, he walked into the painful angle of the weather, his boots gaining little purchase on the slimy clay footpaths.

A horribly cruel hoax!

He had woken to the feeling that his life was changed in a profoundly important way and now ...! How he wished he hadn't made use of Mrs Pike's absence the night before.

Had they scuttled for fear he would be constantly knocking at the door?

He saw himself as they must see him. Leering, ridiculous, comic, boring, middle-aged: a stock figure of theatrical farce. The ageing, unbecoming lecher. All that he had thought so wondrously changed in him, so tender, was a joke, a folly that even now they must be laughing over.

Injured rage carried him through the storm, steered him dangerously near the cliff top. A change in the wind's direction could easily have bowled him like a scrap of litter into the boiling sea.

My God, he thinks, looking down on the wickedly heaving race of water ... how cruel, how angry it is! And something of his own bewildered fury is carried on the back of the waves that fling themselves at the unfeeling cliff face.

Slipping and slithering through the vengeful weather, he was able to isolate three factors that curbed his grosser mortifications. One: the fact they had urged Mrs Pike to stay away on the afternoon *before* his visit. Two: the fact that the noises and muddle he had dimly detected might well have indicated preparations for departure *before* he arrived in their attic. Three: the note bearing its single sentence which lay in his dampening pocket.

Again and again he went over all that had passed between them. Surely he had – please God he had – communicated his tenderness? And then afterwards, they had talked so late into the night, so closely and companionably. He had heard the whole tragic story . . . the ghastly train accident. The train had overturned in a tunnel south of Toulouse as Stephanie and her fiancé were returning from holiday fifteen months ago. Returning to Cambridge where she was working for a doctorate in biology. The darkness, the subsiding screams in the tunnel which Anna had described as if on Stephanie's behalf. Her eyes had never left her sister's face, her words progressing only as far and as fast as Stephanie's grief could bear. And then, more briskly, her own part. How she had managed, with her fortunate blend of qualifications, to get herself a job at Stoke Mandeville and help her sister's physical recovery. How she had decided they had best work together, and looked for a school where their separate trainings could be accommodated.

There was so much more. All about their home in Hampshire. The large family they came from. But always it was Anna insisting on her sister's greater brilliance, greater beauty, and slowly Reggie had understood the selfless extent of Anna's care. Understood why she had needed his help. Why it was to an older man she had turned, someone who would neither take shallow advantage nor be gauchely, evidently pitying, if the purpose of her endeavour – to show Stephanie that she was in every important way a complete and desirable woman – was not to fail. The inevitable struggles with guilt and revulsion were likely to be far less marked in someone old enough to feel that his self-esteem was of little consequence in such a relationship . . . That, surely, had been her thinking?

Had it not?

Tormented now by all the states of mind he had supposed would be more quickly and unkindly kindled in a younger man, Reggie paused, curving his back against the hurtling rain, and pulled the letter from his pocket. It was blurred by damp. As he tried to straighten it, the wind plucked it from him. A gorse bush blocked its flight. Frantic, he scurried after it and reached out, tearing his wrists on the thorns. The rain had liquefied the ink, the words had become pale, wriggling, incomprehensible distortions of themselves.

The paper fluttering in his hand, Reggie looked sadly out across the lashing Channel, and the rain, as if compounding the delusion, so flew against his glasses that even the massive, toreutic surface of the sea was melted and disfigured.

He saw nothing clearly. Nothing, nothing at all.

*   *   *

Late on Saturday afternoon there was no reply from St Nathan's when he rang. He found out the name of the headmaster – Sidney Smythe – and rang him at home. The phone trilled and trilled without response. Since Ned Starkey was acquainted with everybody and their business, Reggie tried him. It was an oblique exchange since, quite apart from anything else, the phone was in the hall, inadequately protected by a small arch which simply gave the caller an illusion of privacy. So he whispered something about Mrs Pike's *amour-propre* being a trifle dented. 'You can't throw any light, can you, Ned?'

'I know the one with a gammy leg was really looking out for a research job in industry, not a university lab, so I expect that's it. These things *can* come up pretty suddenly, of course.'

'I suppose, yes.' Reggie didn't sound any more convinced than his friend.

'The older girl is a saint, you know.'

'Yes.' Distressed as he was, Reggie couldn't help smiling at certain antinomian aspects of Anna's saintliness. He wondered how Ned would judge them if he knew, and then he realized he was ablaze with sexual longing and desperate to get off the phone. Ned, however, was seizing the opportunity to discuss a number of school matters. Reggie heard nothing of his conversation and suddenly blurted out that he must catch the six o'clock post, which was shameful of him, since the last post on Saturday went at twelve noon. There was a slightly stupefied pause at the other end of the line, then Ned's voice saying, with all its customary benevolence, 'Of course you must; off you go, then.'

*   *   *

Reggie picked at his mushrooms *à la Grecque* and was knocked back by the garlic. Fortunately Phoebe was waiting on table so he didn't have to endure a reproachful study of his plate. The dance, she said in answer to his diffident questioning, had been OK.

Later he wrote a letter addressed to St Nathan's, with *Please Forward* in the top left-hand corner. It might reach them. Then he put on *The Magic Flute*.

Although the duet between Pamina and Papageno was indestructibly lovely, the ambiguities of the opera seemed to obtrude more than usual. The references to female duplicity abounded.

Bewahret euch vor Weibertücken!

sang the priests jauntily in the second Act, warning Tamino against the wiles of women, having made clear to him that all his false assumptions about Sarastro's character were the direct result of swallowing female deceit. Their choral singing assumed a deeper and more minatory tone at the end of this passage, and Reggie found himself moved to find fault with the Queen of the Night. All that melodramatic and disingenuous grief over the loss of Pamina! Her monstrous command that Pamina should murder Sarastro! And wasn't that celebrated top F rather nervously striven for? For a while he was mildly comforted by all this evidence of female unreliability and perfidy, but as the opera came to its end and he was left in the extra silence of the house, the music that remained in his head was that of the three boy trebles bringing poor, bewildered Tamino to the grove wherein stood the Temple of Wisdom.

Their solemn exhortation, so strange, so light but incisive, eventually brought sleep. Their commands tapped thrice within his mind like the incantatory strokes of a magician's wand . . .

Sei standhaft, duldsam, und verschweigen!
Be steadfast, patient and be silent!

Patient . . . silent . . .
Silent.

Outside, the rain beat so hard upon the stone that late home-comers had to pause and peer through their windscreens as a dense white growth of water sprang like ghostly liquid wheat from the road.

Soon the streets were transformed into rivers, water coursing down the steep heights of Tidmouth to the sea.

*   *   *

Dufferdill rescued him from the prospect of chicken *vindaloo* the following day by inviting him to Sunday lunch, with a good walk later if the weather cleared.

Quite hungry by now, Reggie devoured Mrs Dufferdill's wholesome roast beef and Yorkshire pudding thankfully. The one rim of fat he had left on his plate was taken by Dufferdill to feel Honeymill Golden Bowl, or Bucket as he was called. 'Don't approve of feeding scraps to dogs at table,' said Dufferdill doing just that. And then continued his attack on Sore Knee oil, as he called his nation's chief resource. 'Just enough to rub on the ache,' he grumbled. 'Eh, mother?'

'If you say so, dear,' beamed Mrs Dufferdill who had once confided in Reggie that whatever else, 'life with Duffer is never dull'.

The leaded window-panes streamed less lavishly during the raspberry crumble. The shrubs in the garden glistened. The earth began to steam.

'Good-oh!' cried Dufferdill. 'Reggie, Bucket and myself will go to Studland Point.'

'What about the washing up, dear?' asked his wife mildly.

'Oh,' Dufferdill gestured carelessly, 'leave it till I get back.'

Both he and his wife laughed at his dishonesty. Reggie endured a small pang of domestic loss to add to his other sorrows. He was grateful for Duffer's company this afternoon.

Both stoutly clad, they climbed the gorse heights of the cliff near Studland, and tramped the margin, enjoying the view of the bay below. The sea was green again, but opaque and sulky, swinging large chunks of wood and weed in its waves as evidence of its deadly temper the day before.

'Two inches!' commented Dufferdill referring to the rainfall. 'A mere piss in a pot. Still, I daresay they all offered up thanks this morning.'

Cormorants flew alongside them, lean black arrows assuming homelier shapes as they settled on the tall, sharp pinnacles of limestone rock that stood in circlets of foam, separate from the cliff face.

Reggie allowed everything to be pointed out to him without feeling any pressure to respond much. Dufferdill's own enthusiasm served for two, as he thrust a finger at the curious cavities in the cliff face that formed an elaborate pie crust round the headland, the rock pipits that flew from under them in startled bursts, the dun shape of the Isle of Wight, the black-backed gulls whose elongated wings made such distinctive bows upon the air.

Chuntering cheerfully about the way those fools in government would regard the crisis as now over and blithely ignore the fact that thousands would starve to death next summer in consequence, Dufferdill led their descent towards the village.

'Thousands?' queried Reggie, amused in spite of himself.

'Well, millions then,' barked Dufferdill, his head and shoulders silhouetted against the curve of Studland Bay and the lagoons of Poole Harbour beyond. 'I wanted to bring you down this way,' he said. 'Something that'll interest your antique turn of mind.'

And they walked down through the graveyard of the charming little rosestone Norman church, built on the earlier Anglo-Saxon site of a church founded by the remarkably busy St Aldhelm. 'The first of the property magnates,' murmured

Dufferdill as he marched on. It was not the church he wanted to show Reggie.

'What do you make of that, then?'

Pointing ahead, he spoke as proudly as if he had put it up himself. On a mound at a narrow bend of the road stood a glaringly new Celtic cross.

'Must be fake.' Reggie peered as they drew closer.

'Depends what you call fake.'

Reggie prowled carefully round the cross.

'Carved from Purbeck stone by a mason, name of Trevor Haysom,' announced Dufferdill. 'Old, old name in these parts. Old, old craft for that matter.'

The cross displayed the Celtic loops and knots, the unfathomable knots that signified life's mystery, but the mason had entwined them round contemporary contradictions.

'First Archbishop of Canterbury was enthroned on a seat of Purbeck marble in the seventh century,' said Dufferdill proprietorially, following Reggie's crouched examination of the motifs. 'I think he still is. That,' he said pointing to different looping on the eastern face, 'is meant to be the double helix.'

The chain contained – at its base – a tip of the globe with 'Spaceship Earth' inscribed upon it, and above it, in a narrowing, ascending column, the overlapping shapes of a butterfly, a plane with the stylized outline of Concorde, a plunging bomb, a violin, and ears of wheat. Above them, amid winding vines, stood Christ, a scroll in His hand. Dufferdill saw Reggie's eyes screwed up behind his glasses. 'It's meant to say,' he translated, but had to think a moment, 'Into – no, out of mystery we come, into mystery we go.'

Reggie continued his tour. The next panel had some fierce mythical beast on it, and the western face a far more elaborate pictograph – a flowingly carved vine burdened with fruit and alert birds whose feathers merged with the foliage. At the top, growing as it were from the vine itself, was an archer, his bow drawn, his arrow ready to pierce the bird above.

The final, southern side, was less complex, and simply bore on its downward, interleaving strands, some runic lettering.

'No,' sighed Dufferdill. 'No good. Can't remember what that

is. What do you make of our Mr Haysom then? Pretty misanthropic chap, but then all the best people are.'

Reggie smiled, his eyes still travelling over the remarkably crafted composite of ancient and modern. 'I'd say,' he pronounced reflectively, 'he's a man who grieves, loves and believes.'

'Oh, very cryptic! I like that. That's good. Grieves, loves and believes, what!' Dufferdill swung a green-stockinged leg to indicate the soppiness of his friend's response.

* * *

But Reggie is intrigued by the vision of unity – of a life that embraces feeding and killing; creation, destruction; scientific clarity and eternally presiding mystery. He is not so easily mocked.

* * *

'The thing cheers me vastly,' he said. And it did. He tried to follow the lines of the insoluble knot to see how it had been fashioned, but he could not. His eye kept being diverted by an independent springing of the tie that could not be traced to a single source. He turned to Dufferdill, who was curling his moustaches with one hand and holding out the palm of the other to feel for rain. 'Thank you, Duffer! Thank you for bringing me,' he said, 'I'm pleased to have seen this thing.'

It filled him, quite inexplicably, with hope.

* * *

But for the next few days he swung between opposing states of hope and despair. The plans he made to hunt the sisters down he then abandoned as again he suffered all the horrors of rejection. Hardest to bear, and the most persistent of the horrors, was that image of himself as fool, dolt, the object of snigger and whisper. He, who had always striven (more than he would readily admit) to keep the right side of convention, had committed the most laughable of all improprieties.

There were rare moments when he wondered if anything good was to be salvaged from this humiliation, and he supposed that simply to have swallowed the bitter bread of the outcast was salutary. He now knew better how it felt to be an object of social avoidance. Ironically, though, by appreciating more keenly how Stephanie had suffered, his tenderness towards her increased.

It was at first an unending, cyclical progression of feeling.

With the passage of days, however, the tirelessly overturned thoughts resolved themselves more clearly into this good comprehension. His imagination had been bloodily extended by the experience. He knew better how it was to be deformed, deprived, one of a minority: other than.

For the first time he began, properly, to consider Phoebe's plight, which had not, to be frank, seemed so very serious to him. How, he was closer to grasping the maleficent trap posed by her own body. The perpetual imprisonment she faced. And pity took feeble root in him.

The days were beginning to lengthen. The portion of light increased. The pain of unrequited sexual longing began to ease. But oh, how he longed to tell the girls of the gift they had made him!

12

A trio of boys from 3B caught his arm as he passed in the corridor.

'Sir! Sir!'

'Matravers?'

Matravers was supported by the irredeemably scruffy Simpson and his plump friend Biddle.

'We've had an idea!' They hopped around him, exchanging glances.

'Yes?'

'Couldn't we start digging up the school grounds?'

He peered at them, bemused. 'I fear Mr Popplewell might object to that.' Poor Popplewell had been talked by his wife into sending their daughter to Turtledown, and was having quite enough trouble living this submission down. 'Do you have a special reason for wishing to dig up the rugger pitches?'

'To *dig*!' Simpson flapped his elbows in frustration. 'For treasure, sir.'

'Biddle's got a metal detector, sir.'

'I got it for Christmas, sir.'

'I see. Dig?' Reggie did not approve of metal detectors, but an idea was forming in his mind.

'It'd be terrific fun.' Matravers was being flirtatious, as small boys of that age can so unnervingly be.

'You want to do some proper archaeology?'

'Couldn't we? We might strike gold, sir.'

Reggie laughed. 'I don't know about gold. Bones, maybe. Let me think about it.'

They ran off excitedly. Reggie, hardly less excited, sped off to the staffroom and, above the babble of teachers arguing over the best way to handle hijackers, rang the Royal Armoured Corps HQ.

The Army were only too pleased to agree to anything that

might foster local goodwill. The officer who dealt with public relations sounded positively eager over the phone. He asked Reggie to call round to the mess for a drink and a chat. Certain safeguards would have to be observed, of course, but he thought the scheme had real possibilities.

*   *   *

The chance that his longing to re-explore the arcane whorls and ridges of the hill above Wimble Cove might be realized sooner and more thoroughly than he could have dreamt made Reggie act more decisively to resolve his other longing.

Pleading one of his 'heads', he took Friday afternoon off. It wasn't totally dishonest. Agitation was likely to bring one on. Even as he thought about it, he could feel it take an incipient hold.

His unconvincingly casual stroll along the wired-off playing fields of St Nathan's Comprehensive did not go unnoticed. A woman in the council house opposite, whose arthritic condition disposed her to weave interesting elements into her imposed watch at the window, spotted him immediately.

Just the type. Middle-aged, inconspicuous, generally grey-toned. The authentic paedophile. She observed his slow saunter with starved glee.

Reggie wasn't quite sure what he expected to see. But he had some dim notion that if he could recognize one of the games staff, he might stop him on his way out of school and explain himself as a cousin – more probably an uncle – of the Cox sisters. A man who had dropped by on his journey westward ... it was a trifle covert, but the idea of addressing Sidney Smythe direct appealed less and less. Smythe was a man he might conceivably encounter at an education meeting.

He was just beginning to wish he'd thought up a more salubrious approach when a new class of girls, in boots and pad-thickened socks, dawdled towards the pitch, hockey sticks over their shoulders. Behind them, at an energetic trot, whistle to her lips, came Anna.

He lowered his cap and walked quickly away to his car.

So they hadn't gone at all!

The woman across the road noted the disconcerted speed with which the suspect – the dirty-minded old fool – leapt into his car. But he didn't move. He sat at the wheel staring into space. He was letting her down. He was not gazing at the ill-shapen girls reluctantly joggling about on the brown turf. She invented a fresh plot. It had to do with Missing Persons.

* * *

Reggie positioned himself beside the school gate the moment the first children bounded out. He merged with the handful of parents who had children to equip with new shoes or a brace at the dentist's.

The woman opposite wasn't fooled. She bit her lip in delight when he stepped out in front of a young woman on a bicycle, and made a clumsy grab for the handlebars. If he'd been a bit better looking, or a bit younger, she might have enjoyed making up a love story.

* * *

'I must talk to you!'

'My God, Reggie! I nearly fell off!'

'I've been going out of my mind worrying about you; both of you. What's going on? I want to know the truth!' He gripped her handlebars so purposefully that a number of Miss Cox's pupils tittered as they drifted by. One or two remarks were made.

'Come and sit in my car.'

'No.'

'*Please!*'

Her customary calmness of manner was gone. She was looking awkwardly around, nodding briefly to those who passed.

'I can't,' she repeated. 'I can't explain here.' And she put her foot to the pedal.

'Look!' He darted round to the side of her, trying to keep up. 'I promise I won't ... *bother* you ... I won't ... *pursue* you.' He stopped running as she pulled up, and continued breathlessly, 'I won't make a spectacle of myself again, but I just want to know ...'

'Meet me at the Lower Knoll crossroads,' she said and, springing into her saddle, pedalled off at a tremendous rate.

* * *

It was, the old woman at the curtains decided, a love affair after all. She had seen the rueful affection in the young woman's face. And she had the charity to hope it might have a very happy outcome for all concerned.

* * *

Reggie parked at Lower Knoll and waited.

He waited a considerable time.

Cars passed along the lane. A woman briskly trotting out a large hunter, and leading another, passed him with a vigorous 'Good afternoon'. Dusk fell.

He became aware that the phone in the Lower Knoll box was ringing. Had several of its glass panes not been kicked out, he would never have heard. Looking around to see if the call could possibly be for anyone else, he assumed an unnecessarily surreptitious air and struggled inside the call box. He lifted the receiver.

'Oh, good. Hello!' he heard.

'This,' he replied stiffly, 'is getting ridiculous. I'm beginning to feel like Bulldog Drummond.' More to the point, he was beginning to feel idiotic all over again. The prank was being continued.

'Forgive me, Reggie. Both of us – forgive both of us, will you?'

'Where are you?'

'I'd rather you didn't know.'

He burst out then. 'I promise not to pester you. I know you must think me an awful old clown, but it won't happen again. I just want you to . . .'

'Reggie!' Her voice broke in, quietly incredulous. 'You mustn't think, mustn't talk like that. You did something very precious. Another day and we should have gone. It would all have been too late.'

'You mean . . .' He was close to weeping with relief. 'It wasn't me. I didn't . . . *disgust* you?'

'You can't have been thinking that!'

He couldn't reply. She was speaking. 'I should have written, but . . . well, it would be better if you weren't involved with us for the moment. Try to accept that. It would be wiser.'

'Stephanie?'

'She's fine. She's very happy.'

'*Why* have you gone?' He wanted to keep her talking, so desperate was he to maintain this frail contact.

'Stephy's got another job. It came up very suddenly. The school were extremely understanding about it. It's rather special.'

'I don't understand the secrecy.' He sounded almost petulant with frustration.

A man with a Border Collie had appeared in the gloom and stood glancing impatiently at his watch. It was beginning to drizzle.

'Look, you'll have to trust me, but I can't go into it.'

'You're still living nearby?'

'You mustn't try and follow me or find out. Swear.'

'You got my letter?'

'Yes. It was sweet of you to worry. You mustn't worry. It will be OK.'

'But . . . I simply don't understand.' His mind was in a turmoil. The man outside tapped on the glass.

'Don't press me, Reggie, please. We're deeply grateful to you for what you've done, for what you did. But Stephy must be left alone now. She has important work to do. Be patient. We love you. Be patient!' And she put the phone down.

The man outside was mouthing angrily.

Reggie stumbled out of the box.

'The villagers always have to wait, don't they?' said the man bitterly. Rain was dripping from his trilby. Reggie patted the dog absent-mindedly and climbed back into his car.

Be patient!

*   *   *

His anxieties were only mildly allayed.

He went back to Sunnybank and pursued home-made ravioli

round his plate with distaste. All this talk of secrecy was eye-wash, he decided. A pretext for keeping him at bay.

Very well. Anna's thinking had become clearer.

'Reggie!'

His role had been that of the releaser. He had been appointed to free her from her fears. To free her for the enjoyment of other, younger men.

'Reggie?' Bella Pike stood in front of him, nervously trying out his Christian name again.

'I'm sorry?'

'You're not happy, are you?'

'Happy?' He smiled hugely. 'Yes, I'm tremendously happy. Fine, fine. You?'

'Something's troubling you.'

He wavered a little under the force of her conviction. 'Not really . . . Only . . .'

'Your head?' she inquired tenderly. 'You've been off your food all week. Why don't you tell me all about it?'

'Nothing to tell,' he said, vaguely alarmed. He pushed his chair from the table.

'Don't go, dear. You haven't had your sweet.'

He looked at Mrs Pike. She was a very presentable woman.

'I'll get it for you. Leave your ravioli if you don't fancy it this evening.'

She returned with a sherry trifle. He had a dreadful presentiment that she was going to spoon it into his mouth.

Instead, she sat down to talk over the applicants she'd had.

'Applicants?'

'For the "Accommodation Vacant".'

'Ah.'

'Are you *sure* you're all right?' She put a hand to his forehead. The combination of trifle in his mouth and a lightly concerned palm on his brow was wonderfully comforting. He felt about nine years old.

The applicants were described and dismissed in an animated manner as 'too stuffy', 'too blowsy', 'too dreary', or 'too . . . you know, dear'.

'Too . . .?'

178

'Oh, you know.' She wrinkled her nose and raised her shoulders to her ears. 'Not our sort,' she summed up at length.

'You shouldn't trouble yourself about my opinions.'

'Well, I do,' she announced as if there were no point in arguing this. 'You're chief resident now. You've got to live with them, same as me.'

Oh, not quite the same, Mrs Pike!

Reggie ate some more trifle which was dripping with alcohol.

'It can create a ... feeling ... if everything's not quite – *compatible*,' she explained aloud and asked what colours he would like in his room when it was redecorated.

This was news to Reggie.

'Oh yes, dear, it's due for a change. And Ezra's coming to fit those shelves he said he would do. You can't manage with all those books on the floor.'

He was made forcibly aware of how alone he and Mrs Pike now were in this large house. The changed situation, now he thought about it, was a little on the cosy side, and he wasn't completely certain how he felt about that. Meanwhile the trifle slipped down, damp spoonful after rich, damp spoonful.

The sense of loss he'd endured since the girls' departure would doubtless diminish. It was almost sad to be made to admit it, but at fifty-five one knew perfectly well that time did heal.

'Finished, dear?'

'I do believe I have,' said Reggie.

'And how do you feel now?' Bella Pike rose and smiled at him fondly. She wore a new sort of shirt affair with an Indian pattern on it. Quite fetching.

'*Better!*' they said in unison and laughed a little.

Outside, the rain beat down and isolated the house.

Like Nana's house, it had a nesty warmth: a place of feathered comfort and steady provision.

*   *   *

The nest also leaked.

First it required buckets and bowls to be strategically positioned, then emptied. Next it called for a daring manoeuvre on the roof, which had Mrs Pike on tiptoe and gasping for Reggie to come down off those dangerous tiles.

'I can't let those rooms with the damp coming in,' she said with a hint of satisfaction in her voice.

Ezra arrived with emulsion paint and saws. While he stripped the variegated wallpapers, Reggie was transferred to the lounge downstairs and spent too much time watching colour television. He let the serials get a grip on him.

At the same time, he found he was returning to Sunnybank progressively later each evening.

'No family – no excuses!' Amis had equated firmly when asking his help backstage with *The Tempest*, and Reggie gave in without a flutter of protest. He was secretly relieved to stay on for the abominably dreary school supper, since it played less havoc with his digestion than the garlic, chili and ground ginger enlivening Mrs Pike's cuisine. The quartan spasm of his bowel was now accompanied by a fierce burning sensation which left him uncomfortably itchy.

And there was another thing.

'I had such a funny dream about you last night!' Mrs Pike proclaimed at least twice over breakfast, and Reggie was mildly put out that he should have wandered – in God knows what guise – within the privacy of Mrs Pike's bedroom. 'Too silly!' she smiled, not disclosing the details.

He himself a rare dreamer – or a poor recaller of his own dreams – began to dream of the hill. The sisters dwelt within its unresolved rings. He scaled its grassy heights, expecting to find either Stephanie or Anna in this or that hollow, but the pattern of the fort presented undiscovered gullies that misled him. Anna rode the ridge above him on her bicycle, back hooped, head down. He saw Stephanie struggle up the sharp incline, dragging her leg beneath a long, ensnaring skirt. He could never get near enough to help her.

*   *   *

During daylight hours his command of the hillfort was strengthened considerably. Major Bittern of the RAC was a most accommodating man, perfectly frank about the ill-feeling he knew was still current among the 'natives', and keen to extend the various conciliatory projects which the Army had undertaken during the past fifteen years. He regarded it as an 'ongoing operation'. All outside suggestions most welcome.

There *were* problems (his manner intimated they were minimal). A heavy gunnery exercise which would make the place simply too hazardous until the beginning of April; a complete prohibition on the use of bulldozers (the terrain was far too dodgy for that), and a need to prevent small boys from falling into the sea. Apart from that, he was only too happy to re-route the public path in order to keep onlookers at a manageable distance, to clear the area of shells and to supply any tents, posts, wire, workshed or whatever that could conceivably be of use.

It was all so astonishingly easy that Reggie couldn't think why he had waited so long. The Major didn't even question Reggie's own competence. 'Only too pleased to oblige!' he assured him with a vigorous assault on Reggie's shoulder, and they shared an excellent malt whisky until quite late in the evening.

The rearing white face and ringed crown of the cliff moved inexorably into the forefront of daydream. He saw it as he tramped across the sodden playing-fields, as he popped his umbrella in the puddle that constantly occupied one corner of the staff cloakroom. He saw it on the windscreen of his car as more clouds rolled in from the sea and discharged their burden of weather. He thought of it, talked of it even, when fulfilling his new commitment of picking up Phoebe from Lower Knoll crossroads each morning and running her into school with him. So obsessive did the image become that when Dufferdill growled 'Unbalanced!' over his skin-flecked coffee one dark and louring break, Reggie jumped guiltily. But Dufferdill was grumbling about the weather.

'You're the hardest man to please . . .' Reggie tried to apply himself to weather conversation. 'It was you said we needed it.' And he looked at the long, fog-wadded windows of the staff-room.

'Out of kilter,' said Dufferdill ominously. 'All wrong.'

If Nature had failed to conjoin her elements happily and presided over conflict rather than marriage, Reggie, staring at those opaque oblongs of glass, did not notice. He saw, imprinted on the bulging, sullen grey, a sparkling cliff crowned with ancient coils of turf.

13

On every side, Reggie was surrounded by tiny people.

They buzzed, scurried and squeaked like the more vivacious insects – like grasshoppers, cockchafers, ants and fleas. He did not know where to look next.

A steward's badge swung from his lapel, an unnecessary, additional identification, since his height was quite conspicuous enough. He flexed his knees to lower himself a little, but was still obliged to lean down when one of them asked what time the major speech began. Flustered, Reggie dropped all his papers. The little person – the person of restricted growth – crawled nimbly beneath the line of plush seats and retrieved them.

'Two-thirty, it seems!' choked Reggie, and looked wildly about him for someone of his own size, as the small, indeterminately-sexed person thanked him profusely.

Dorothy's mighty, mane-headed figure appeared on the platform above him and the buzz acquired a different key. She wore flowing black, and seemed luminously pale skinned. Bella, coming out of the wings behind her and wearing a sporty yellow suit, spotted Reggie, noted his aghast expression and waved consolingly before settling herself at the table beside Dorothy's standing form. Gradually, the platform filled.

Down in the body of the hall the chaos was beginning to assume direction as the little people bobbed towards their seats and put their sandwiches away in bags and boxes. Reggie was caught in the tide that swayed around him. Men and women no higher than his chest climbed over his feet. Some had additional handicaps: a humped back; a foot contained in a huge, dragging boot; crushed-up features. Their happiness shocked, mystified and disorientated him.

All through the hour's lunch break the hall had been filled with vibrant chatter and peals of laughter. Even now, they jabbered away at one another, pointed to coats, offered sweets, read through their agendas, plunged hands into muddled handbags just like any other delegates at any other conference – except for the uniquely joyful pitch of their congress. If he closed his eyes and merely listened, Reggie was reminded of children at a circus, an incongruous image, for these, surely, *were* the clowns!

He remembers the greasepaint tear on the clown's cheek.

He sat down and felt better. Felt more like one of them, although his feet rested firmly on the floor while those of his neighbour swung some six inches above it. His neighbour, a diminutive man in a navy, double-breasted suit, had already told Reggie that he and his wife possessed three full-sized children. Reggie had not known whether he should congratulate the proud father. It seemed only to advertise the man's own handicap to remark on his good fortune in producing normal offspring; so he'd mumbled feebly while the man had said what a joy his children were and how his children's friends quickly got used to 'having us around'.

Like pets, thought Reggie with dismay, as he had attempted, and dismally failed, to imagine the homestead scenes.

The little man was speaking now.

'I'm as strong as an ox,' he said, as if in contravention of the thoughts he imagined Reggie must be entertaining. He bent his arm. 'Feel my muscles.'

And Reggie assessed the rounded biceps beneath the navy suiting. 'Wouldn't like to tangle with you!' he joked infelicitously.

'Used to do a spot of wrestling,' his neighbour whispered as the general hubbub began to subside. 'Floored a bloke sixteen stone. No rigging. No messing. Straight.'

'*Very* good.' Reggie's whisper was articulated in a way that implied the conversation must now end.

His neighbour hissed louder. 'Painting, nowadays.'

Reggie flicked him a little dart of reproof. 'And decorating?'

'Pictures. I paint pictures.'

Before further predicaments could develop, Dorothy struck the table with her gavel and drew the packed hall to order.

There was a delayed twittering like that of small exotic birds in high-grown jungle.

And then she began.

At this distance Reggie could admire his wife. He could admire her on more than one ground. He could admire her appearance – it was a kind of kimono she wore, of fine black wool; an orange begonia at her breast. He was also unwillingly obliged to admire her energy and organizing genius. Good God, she'd roped *him* in, for a start. That was no small feat. Hardly less of a feat than pulling together this first national meeting of the PRGs whose plight, Dorothy now explained, was so woefully ignored.

Distantly, Reggie tried to apply 'plight' and 'woe' to this ebullient gathering. But no matter! Dorothy's rhetoric worked in mysterious ways.

She introduced a speaker on the medical aspects of dwarfism, and sat down. The young doctor was a friend of Gilbert, who had said he also would try to be here this afternoon. Reggie would have liked to see his son, and during the talk periscoped the hall for him.

The woman, two down, began quietly to knit. In fact most of the PRGs who had found the morning session so rewarding – stating their togetherness, bearing witness and proposing practical measures of help like lower bus seats, higher clutch pedals and a clothing exchange centre – seemed to find the medical lecture far less engrossing. But then most of them, as Dorothy pointed out, when she rose again for her major address, were beyond medical help. It was the remaining children they had to strive for.

'And not just those children whose problem is dwarfism,' she cried. '*All* those children who face a future in which their healthy growth and development is imperilled ... The children of the nuclear future!'

A charge went through the hall. This seemed not strictly to be their field. 'Is it widely understood,' she demanded, ringingly, 'that at present we are accepting as safe a level of radioactivity some experts feel is three times too high? That we have based our estimates of safety on survivors from Hiroshima and

Nagasaki, who are now known to be unusually resistant to radiation?'

There was a great deal of shifting and stirring going on. Reggie was part of it. Dorothy was unperturbed. 'Isn't it right that we, who know and understand the problems of malformed growth, should take it upon ourselves to fight this fearful threat to coming generations? Yes, we understand the problems – we have a vigour that *must* be used!'

Her oratory was impressive even though her subject-matter seemed mistaken on this occasion. Reggie wondered whether his wife had come out with the wrong set of notes, or whether she would soon start applying the PRG situation to that of blacks or threatened species. Bella Pike was looking very bewildered indeed. But no, Dorothy was repeating her point that the people gathered in the hall had a special understanding and thus a special responsibility.

'Is it generally known by the people of this country that the Atomic Energy Authority has a private armed constabulary with unlimited powers of search and arrest? Is it fully understood that a nuclear society must, by its very nature, by its very, mutually agreed, need for stringent security, be an undemocratic society? Democracy! The right to meet and speak out publicly as we do today is not compatible with the nuclear age! And we – you – who, in your thousands, physically, powerfully represent the underprivileged, underdeveloped, unheard, unseen, *you* are the natural messengers of this warning! *You* can have what you now lack – the full focus of public attention!'

It went on.

It went on a good long time.

Reggie, who had tried to withdraw into a tiny inner particle of himself, became slowly aware through the layers of his disquietude that the mood of the conference was swinging exuberantly towards support for his wife and her startling call for commitment to something (literally) far greater than themselves. As he gazed upon the shiningly attentive faces, he came to the conclusion that Dorothy was an unprincipled, incorrigible genius. Her sense of the theatrical, the political and the compassionate had been brilliantly met together. He gained a small glimpse of her larger vision ... the spectacle that could not be ignored ... the march of the dwarves, all the little people in the world made tall by their total commitment to the human race.

She ended strongly with the words he recognized, Miranda's words:

> *Oh brave new world,*
> *That has such people in it!*

Incredulously, he stared at row upon row of intent, perfervid faces. His eyes then swung to their single, focal point. The white-faced, black-robed figure of his wife – a woman whose humourless fanaticism might be quite impossible to live with, but who was, in public, breathtakingly persuasive.

He recalled the words of *The Tempest* that preceded those Dorothy had quoted:

> *How many goodly creatures are there here!*
> *How beauteous mankind is!*

In a hall holding maybe three thousand dwarves, Reggie feels very, very small.

* * *

Neglecting his steward's duties, he fled. He had an excuse – an arrangement to meet Norman Herrington at the British Museum, but he knew his hurry was pure evasion.

Would Mrs Pike be able to join in the general admiration he had seen race and bubble through the hall, or would she think she had been tricked by Dorothy? He couldn't face her for the moment.

* * *

The tranquillity of the Museum was marvellously restorative. He entered from the north door and, instead of going upstairs to reach the pre-Roman British room at the far end of the building, where he and Norman had agreed to meet, he approached it by walking through the Egyptian gallery of large sculptures on the ground floor. He particularly liked the massiveness and the space of this long hall. The rapidity of his step decreased in the calm, wide corridor.

He came to a halt between two still, black figures. Almost, but not quite identical, they faced one another across the intervening space of some twenty feet. Sekhmet, the lion-headed goddess, her leonine face, surmounted by a large disc, the crown of Hathor, perhaps an emblem of the sun, was not in the least fearful. He drew slowly towards the one on his right.

She sat straight, slender waisted, nubile breasted, her hands laid quietly in her lap. From the Temple of Bubastis, said the inscription. She was about twelve feet high and had rather touchingly long toes. In her left hand she held the ankh, the hieroglyph meaning 'life'. She held it pointing downwards along her thigh, her fingers firmly folded through the bulk-like loop, to Reggie's mind, upside down. He stared up at the contemplative, faintly sad face. The unpupilled eyes stared back – into him, as though trying to behold a braver Reggie.

He must have stood there a long time, because he obviously attracted the attention of a young boy, who now tapped his arm.

Reggie swung round.

'Are you particularly interested in Egyptian religions?' The boy was thin, fairish haired, with dark, almond-shaped eyes and a very sharp nose. His expression was intense.

'Er, not particularly, not especially.' Reggie felt he had to account for the time he had spent in front of the black granite goddess. 'No, I just think she's rather nice.' There was a pause. Then he said with feigned politeness, 'Are you interested, yourself?'

'Yes,' replied the boy, his sharp profile towards the seated figure.

'Student, are you? Research?' Reggie put his hands in his trouser pockets and flapped them up and down a bit.

'I have esoteric reasons of my own,' said the boy solemnly.

'Good. Yes.' He *would* have to attract a nutter, wouldn't he? Reggie took a step backwards, but the boy seemed eager to continue their stilted conversation.

'People don't yet realize how very complex the Egyptian

religions were,' he said gravely. 'Every single mark, every single placing means something. Nothing is random.'

'No,' said Reggie. Then, trying to be friendly, 'Tell me about the ankh there. Isn't she holding it upside down?'

The boy stepped into the middle of the hall, directly between the two almost identical figures of Sekhmet. Tourists walked slowly by, unheeding.

'They hold the ankh in their left hand, do you see?'

'Yes.'

'They would have stood either side of a portal.'

'Yes?' Perhaps he wasn't a loon after all.

'Well, the left-hand side in the woman is the most developed side of the brain – the side where the greatest psychic energy is stored.'

Oh, crikey! He was a loon.

'And so their power would have flowed down their arms, through the ankh towards one another, forming a powerful barrier against evil spirits.'

'I see,' said Reggie slowly, as though he really did, though he longed to point out that a good few evil spirits must have passed down the Egyptian gallery unimpeded. Then he realized that he himself had been halted. So, however, had the boy with the young Pharaoh's profile.

'Must rush,' he exclaimed, moving purposefully backwards. 'Nice to have met you.'

Reggie practically ran up the wide, shallow staircase with the colossal Pharoic head commanding a view of all comers at the top of it. He was still thinking of Sekhmet's hand through the vulvine loop of the ankh, male end pointed firmly down – a jolly good talisman for Dorothy – when Norman Herrington bumped into him on his way down.

'Hallo there! Just coming to see if you were waiting downstairs!'

Norman was a big, ruddy man, his face empurpled with broken veins, his fingers calloused, split and blackened. He looked more like a farmer than an academic in his rumpled corduroys and a tweed jacket with leather-rimmed cuffs and elbow patches.

'Just got a bit delayed by Sekhmet,' grinned Reggie. 'Sorry.'

'I know the one. She's a hypnotic piece. Well, good to see you! Shall we go to the coffee shop?'

They eventually sat down in the cafeteria, having sorted out a Japanese visitor's confusion over Cornish pasties and steak and kidney pies in the warming-up machine – much to the indignation of the girl behind the counter, who said if you'd fingered something you couldn't put it back. If that principle were taken too far, responded Norman giving her a very meaningful scrutiny, some people would be in dead trouble.

'Well, now!' Norman squeezed himself into the narrow space provided behind the formica table. 'I've looked it up and can find no record of any dig there at all. Old Pitt-Rivers did some barrows very close by in the twenties, but the fort itself . . . it's not, to be frank, even marked on the map I have of the area. Is it really as big as you say?'

Reggie tried to do one of his inadequate diagrams on the back of his PRG agenda. His memory had now faded by five months. Three large ramparts on the western side, petering out at the northern entrance. A single bank and inner ditch on the precipitous, easterly side. His sketch of the entrance and its outerwork was particularly unhelpful.

Norman pondered the drawing while Reggie pointed with his pencil to indicate the supposed disc barrow near the cliff edge. 'All this has subsided, so Lord knows what's been lost.'

Norman scraped thoughtfully at an incisor with a dirty fingernail.

'What puzzles me,' prompted Reggie, 'is its purpose.'

'A beach-head?'

'Maybe. There's a good landing-cove below. A long haul for anyone needing fresh water, though; so I doubt if it was ever settled.'

'You don't think it's just an animal corral or some such?'

'The ditches at their deepest are up to forty feet.'

'Mm. Bit excessive.'

'I wondered if it could be purely ceremonial,' ventured Reggie nervously.

'Can you strip it?'

Reggie explained the prohibitions on a bulldozer.

'The whole thing looks bloody dangerous. You'll have to keep the kids on tethers.'

'Yes, the children worry me a bit, frankly.' Reggie bit into his tasteless éclair. 'Otherwise I'd be tempted to tackle the barrow at the edge. If it is a barrow.'

'Is there a sweetshop, ice-cream stall within walking distance?'

Reggie looked puzzled at the question. Norman laughed. 'If not,' he said, 'the kids'll soon tire of it. Have it all to yourself, lucky man.' And he suggested excavating the entrance and cutting a random section through a ditch and bank. 'Perhaps I could come down, myself, some time,' he offered.

'I hoped you might say that,' laughed Reggie, relieved. He didn't want to make a mess of his dream.

When Reggie left to go back to the Russell Square entrance where he'd deposited his coat, Norman, companionably, came along with him.

In the Egyptian gallery they paused, involuntarily, between the two Sekhmets. Reggie gave a sudden shout of laughter. 'Inimical spirits!' he yelped. 'Both of us. The boy's theory works!' And he described his earlier encounter to Norman.

'He could even be right,' conceded the bluff archaeologist. 'One man's guess is often as good as another's in this businesss.' Then, with the same louche kind of music-hall wink he had bestowed on the girl behind the tea counter when discussing well-fingered objects, he announced, none too discreetly, that he'd always understood that the ankh symbolized the genitals of Isis.

'Well, whadderyerknow!' exclaimed Reggie in very poor imitation of casual American. Some of Norman Herrington's remarks and gestures drew such attention to themselves that they became needlessly embarrassing.

* * *

Perhaps it was this parting shot – or maybe it was simply a question of leaving the calm and scholarly halls behind him – alternatively it might have been the frenzied clangour of the station – or even the fact that, having paid the price of a ticket, Reggie found himself standing crammed in a corridor of the train, just down from the buffet where all the potential drunks and rowdies were collecting. Whatever it was, and the options were manifold, his earlier state of perturbation returned, and like many another human being whose apprehensions are aroused, his emotion became displaced and reproduced itself as irritability. Certainly, it can't only have been Norman's leering reference that fanned his rancour into fresh exasperations over *The Magic Flute*.

> *Dank sei dir Isis, Dank du Osiris, gebracht!*
> Thanks be to Isis and Osiris!

What in heaven's name were they going on about? What, he had always wondered bemusedly, was the entire cast doing in Egypt, anyway?

And what, you might equally wonder, what is the quite specific apprehension, underlying all the other aggravants, that drives Reggie to vexation over Mozart's opera while squashed between homegoing shoppers and their sticky, whining children?

Well, rather than confront his extreme discomfiture over his wife's radical redirection of the PRG movement, rather than anticipate the mood of his landlady when he returns to Sunnybank – will she be cool, tearful, enraged, bitter, savage, icy, hysterical, hurt, acerbic, wounded, wrathful or any one of a thousand other possibilities he is trying hard not to imagine – he might just as well become exercised over something as harmless as the silliness of an eighteenth-century plot.

Good God, he thinks . . . if the entire thing is bound up with freemasonry as Dor – no, Dufferdill it must have been who mentioned it first – if *that* is its concealed burden, is one to suppose that otherwise perfectly sober, down-to-earth fellows like councillors, policemen, drapers, hosiers, bakers and publicans not only roll up one trouser leg and bare one hairy tit to the knife, but also fling themselves about in worship of Isis and Osiris!

Reggie loosed so loud a deprecatory snort that he attracted

the wonder of a small boy blowing a prize-sized bubble of gum. A small shred of the exploded bag hung from Reggie's elbow and was doubtfully eyed by its owner. But the middle-aged man who'd appropriated his, the boy's, bubble gum, was too preoccupied by the follies of other middle-aged men to notice.

Two great mountains. One throwing water, the other spouting fire.

Enter Tamino between two soldiers, ready to undergo the trials of fire and water that will, if successfully essayed, conquer all fear of death and make him participant in the mysteries of Isis. Two very short-lived trials, thinks Reggie disparagingly. Dramatically and musically, the least significant part of the whole opera. As if the freemasons themselves were just a trifle embarrassed about the dottiness of the whole thing.

As well they might be!

Reggie sighed again over the gormlessness of all men masquerading as honest burghers and civil-tongued small shopkeepers who, on certain appointed nights of the year, left their comfy wives at home watching 'Celebrity Squares', rolled up their trouser legs, donned embroidered aprons and participated in the mysteries of Isis!

O brave new world (he reflected ironically)
That has such people in it!

The reflection was a mistake. He was compelled very quickly to shut his mind down on a promptly released image of his wife, an orange begonia at her breast, in declamatory stance.

A little further down the train a gang of teenagers turned their transistor up louder, terrorizing the other passengers with Rock.

Dufferdill, Reggie remembered, had also said, over a Sunday lunch, that Mozart once planned to make a musical out of *The Tempest*. 'Now that would have been a bit of a hit!' he'd wagered.

The punk group on the radio were singing *Shitty City* but nobody, fortunately, could hear the words, as they were all thrown forward when the train lurched and slowed to let another one by. The rush of the passing train drowned all sound. Reggie saw a string of colour frames, each containing perfectly posed bodies, like film being pulled horizontally through a viewer.

How curious a coincidence it was, he ruminated, as the guard uncertainly announced they were nearing Reading, that the last works of the two greatest creative minds in all European history should have been both their most fanciful and their most unfathomable. They resembled one another in many ways. The ordeals for instance; surely poor Ferdinand's allotted labour of piling up logs (*logs*, Reggie reminds himself, being in charge of props for the school play), surely the log-pile couldn't be another bit of freemasons' ritual? Did freemasons exist in Shakespeare's time? If they derived from the old medieval craftsmen's lodges, he supposed they must have.

Shakespeare a freemason?

Reggie dismissed the idea as he was squeezed breathless by Reading folk fighting to be first off the train.

The similarities between the two works were not negligible, though. He amused himself by compiling a list, as somebody slowly ran a large case against the shins of all those standing in the buffet corridor . . . Sarastro and Prospero, two elderly men preparing with some unwillingness to hand over their powers, subjecting rival incumbents to tests. Both men inconsistent; from all accounts sagacious, but quite plainly testy and capricious on occasion. Both pieces darkened by the idea of wrongful usurpation or abduction; both coloured by the rival ambiguities of liberation and captivity; both according more power than the merely playful to magical transformation.

What had these two shining imaginations, so close to expiry, really intended?

Reading!

Reggie's own imagination (which shows perceptible signs of stretching) was put out of action by having his feet trampled on for two solid minutes.

Sinking at length into a vacated seat, he tucked his tenderized toes under him and weakly reached for somebody's abandoned *Evening Standard*.

The great reredos he has been inwardly erecting for the past half hour is rudely pulled away to reveal the truly ineluctable matter of his mind. All incorporeal fancies flee in the (photographed) face of Dorothy. There is a picture on the back page of his wife springing waist-high from a mêlée of dwarves. 'PRGs pledge Anti-Nuclear Move' read the headline, but in fact the copy beneath was mostly devoted to the morning's resolutions. Well, that was a minor relief, at least, but Reggie's worries about Mrs Pike and his resentments over his wife, are none the less re-activated.

Why is it that the moment he so much as thinks of Dorothy, he has the impression that she has walked through an open door into his mind and sits there conducting careful observation of him? His whole sense of freedom is invaded and taken from him as she sits on a woolsack in his head. *Damn her!*

Rain silvered the black glass of the train window and Reggie resolved to cease all contact forthwith. No letters, no phone calls, no pretexts, no helping out with the PRG movement which – he now half suspects – is a quixotic cover for her pursuit of him.

The little sapling pity, so shallowly rooted in the cold season, looks dangerously like dying.

No more Dorothy!

He then remembers that he has still not plucked up the courage to fulfil Antonia's commission, now two months old, to inform Dorothy of her daughter's *enceinture*. Blow it and blast it! Antonia could tell her own mother. He would simply sign the cheques.

The familiar, nauseous sensation that preceded a pain in the head – stiff neck and swollen glands – was upon him as he walked up the path to Sunnybank. He needn't have worried. Not even the dog barked. Mrs Pike had gone to the Orlebars for the evening and left him a cold supper.

He took his strongly dressed salad up into his newly white-painted room. ('White! All white?' Mrs Pike had queried, distressed. 'So bleak! So monastic, dear!') Well, he wanted the monastic existence. It suited his purpose, suited the exclusions he'd been forced to make.

If ever a picture of the sisters drifted unprompted towards him, he changed it to an image of the hill. He made that the heart of his yearnings and, thinking about it, fell asleep.

14

Sunday.

Easy enough to avoid Bella on Sundays.

Reggie always undertook to do his own breakfast on Sundays. And once Bella had left for Mass, he would slip off for lunch at the Dufferdills.

He spilled his All-Bran over the edge of the bowl. God, he felt ill! As carefully as he could, with a shaking hand and swimming head, he scooped up the surplus cereal and shovelled it back in the packet. (He'd encountered enormous difficulty purchasing this packet, trying at least five groceries before he'd found one that stocked his special cereal. 'Don't tell me there's a world shortage of All-Bran!' he'd quipped, and the man behind the counter, lugubriously earnest, had said he thought there must be: the suppliers kept making excuses. His gloom was contagious. Reggie had bought all there was in the shop and now restricted his daily intake with the watchful foreboding of a junkie.)

His eyeballs seemed to be fixed too high in their sockets. Soon the band would tighten round his skull and the distortions of vision would follow.

The moment he heard Mrs Pike depart for Mass he rang the Dufferdills to say he really wasn't up to lunch.

'You should get this thing seen to, Reggie,' sympathized the kindly Mrs D. 'You shouldn't let it go on like this.'

He promised to do something about it and retreated to bed where he planned, after completing his Sunday session on the bog, to hide for the rest of the day. He was now fully convinced that constipation brought these attacks on. It was a build-up of the frightful vapour.

Downstairs the dog whined for a little, then fell quiet.

There was no good, roasting smell; so Mrs Pike was probably eating at her daughter's.

Inside the house the silence spread like fog. Outside, the percussive rain intensified. Beyond the dulled window the houses clung to the hillside, resisting the downpour dumbly, like stoic animals left out in error.

Reggie groaned in the silence and pulled the bedclothes over his head.

He was sharply surprised by a prompting which reached him through the tumescent pain. It was this: that of all the things his mind rushed instinctively to exclude, he must fight to keep remembrance of his own exclusion in the days that had followed the girls' departure. The days when he had for once been too wounded to crawl back inside the safe, bare cell of his own mind. When he'd been as exposed as those beaten dwellings on the hillside.

Reggie rubbed his nose in a self-rebuking way. Why was he rambling in this peculiar fashion? Because, responded the voice located in some unknown void inside himself (startling him dreadfully), it is important to feel as others feel. That is the springing of the imagination.

Reggie pulled the sheets further over his head and lay in a state of mild fright. 'Springing' was not a word he ever used – not in the sense of springing from a trap, which seemed to be the implied use ... Perhaps this illness was making him hallucinate. He remembered Ned Starkey's account of the voice of God, and pulled himself together.

Oh no! Not me!

'Voices don't come chatting to me,' he claimed out loud – muffled, that is, by blankets. And the sound of his own voice was even more crazed than any corybantic inner conversations he might have thought he'd heard. He stuffed the sheets in his mouth and, thus protected, slept.

*   *   *

He was awakened by a soft knocking, and the sight of three heads poking round the door.

They all belonged to Bella Pike.

'You haven't left yet then?' she whispered. 'All right if I come in a tick? I've been meaning to pick your brains.'

In his condition, this last remark amounted to an imprecation. His brain whimpered.

'Just having . . .' he moaned.

'A lie-in?' she concluded. 'And why not?' All three overlapping Bellas wore orange belted raincoats of so violent a hue that he was obliged to close his eyes to avoid retina damage.

'Don't mind me,' she was (they were) saying. 'I wanted to catch you before you go. It's,' she paused, obviously to check her watch, 'after eleven o'clock, by the way.'

'I'm sorry. I . . .'

'Oh, I'm not criticizing!' She was anxious he shouldn't think that. 'Two things,' she said more cautiously. 'First, has Gilbert rung?'

'Gilbert? *Gilbert?*' he repeated, astonished, allowing his eyes to open a chink.

'Oh, what a delightful boy! I so enjoyed meeting him and *he* was so hoping to see you.'

'I know. I had . . .' The matter of the conference was undoubtedly coming up.

'To go to the British Museum. I told him that. I said how sorry you'd be to miss him. I said he ought to come down and stay a few days. We could put him up easily enough.'

'He's very . . .'

'Oh, awfully busy, I know. These young hospital doctors. Still, he said he'd give you a ring.'

There was a pause.

'No, no,' said Reggie vaguely. 'No, he hasn't rung.'

'You're not well again, are you?'

'I'm all right.'

'That's not what *I* would say.'

'I'm fine, truly.' The orange was advancing in a phalanx. Reggie closed his eyes once more. A hand searched out his forehead.

'No temperature,' he gasped. 'I never do have a temperature.'

'Don't be silly,' said Mrs Pike. 'Everybody has a temperature. What's 98.4 when it's at home?'

'It's nothing, nothing.'

'If you didn't have a temperature' (her hand was smoothing his hair gently) 'you'd be dead.' He heard a little laugh. He tried to respond with one of his own.

'That's better,' she said, glad to have made him smile a bit. 'Well, I'll let you rest. I won't bother you with the other thing.'

He knew what the other thing was going to be. He couldn't lie here for ever, too ill to take the worst. 'Of course you must,' he murmured valiantly.

But she went for Codeine and a wet flannel to press blissfully to his tender head before she could be persuaded to divulge the other thing.

It was not, as he'd dreaded, a complaint about Dorothy's manipulations. It was a simple question (by comparison, simple) of her tax forms which would soon have to be filled in. 'I can't manage this VAT,' she said in a worried voice, 'but this is no time to bother you with VAT. I'm going to poach you an egg before I go out.'

'No, please, nothing,' he protested and said how very happy he would be to help sort out her tax problems.

'Shush now,' she soothed. 'You get your rest. But, just one little thing!' The three Bellas spun on their trajectory with the impeccable timing of Busby Berkeley girls. 'Wasn't she wonderful? Your wife? Dorothy, I mean. Wasn't she an inspiration to us all?'

'An *inspiration*?'

'I can't put it higher than that!' She seemed to feel, from his tone, that he would have preferred a more elevated term. 'An *inspiration*! It should raise us a lot of money.'

'Money!' he found himself repeating dumbly beneath the wet flannel. It was a perfectly adequate substitute for conversation as far as Mrs Pike was concerned.

'For the PRGs,' she said. 'There's no such thing as bad publicity, you know. Daphne's got all the papers this morning. She's going to show me when I get there.'

Either Bella Pike did not fully understand what Dorothy was up to or she was so involved in her own cause that she saw Dorothy's as innocently supplementary to it. 'It will highlight all our efforts,' she was saying; 'catch the public eye. PRGs get overlooked, you know.'

'Indeed.' Reggie pursed his lips at the solecism.

'I'd *like* to talk about it.' The Bellas lingered wistfully. Reggie gave the faintest moan. 'But now's not the time. Still . . .' In triplicate she screwed herself up to this announcement. 'I can't thank you enough!'

'*Me!*' Now he was truly amazed.

'The way I look at it, if you'd never come here, none of this would ever have happened.' There, she seemed to indicate, I've said it. A fibrillating, orangey gratitude flowed from her persons.

Reggie sank back in his pillows. By what awful route could the recriminations, that should have been hurtling towards Dorothy, be diverted his way in this unrecognizable form, as gratitude.

After a lot more gentle quibbling over his need for a poached egg, the three Bellas slipped away, each overprinted on the other. 'Miserable weather!' they called out cheerfully and sang in trio down the stairs.

Hang on! That feeling, hang on! Therein lies the path.

Reggie beat off the bodiless voice.

*   *   *

Ding-dong!

Reggie surfaced.

Ding-dong!

The bell. The dog was barking. He couldn't fathom what time of day or even which day it was. He tried to assemble these puzzles slowly.

Ding-dong! Ding-dong!

Sunday! He looked at his bedside clock. Three? In the afternoon? He digested this information and realized that Bella was not going to answer the door. Neither was he.

But Reggie's is not a fundamentally rebellious nature. His refusals, when they occur, generally arise from timidity, not hostility. If a bell rings, he's inclined to answer it.

*   *   *

'Are you unwell?'

'Good lord! Good heavens above! Come in!' Reggie ushered his sons inside. There were, he was glad to note, only two of them.

'You look terrible,' said Gilbert, whose own attractive appearance was a little spoilt by the growth of scanty moustache much paler than his dark hair – hair which, his father noted, was considerably shorter than when he'd last set eyes on his son. 'I've obviously,' said Gilbert, 'come at a bad time.'

'If you're a doctor, there's a case for saying you've come at a good time. Since you're my son, a case for saying the time couldn't be better.' Reggie grinned weakly and staggered towards the stairs. 'Come on up.'

'I tried to ring earlier but the line was engaged, so I just risked it and took off!'

'Ahah!' Reggie caught sight of the receiver slightly apart from its cradle. He must have done that while ringing the Dufferdills. Thickly, he attempted to explain, but it all became too much for him. He gave up and tipped the phone back into position.

'Good to see you!' he attempted genially, and led the way upstairs.

'What's the matter with you?'

'Mystery virus,' supplied Reggie.

'If I'd known . . . still, this is my one day off and I'm lucky to get that.'

' 'Svery good of you. I know they don't give you youngsters much of a break. Kind of you to come and see your old runaway, reprobate dad.'

Gilbert, who has decided to let his girlfriend cool off for a day since they're just not making it one hundred per cent, trod carefully upstairs behind his father and wondered if he was drunk. It wouldn't be surprising if he'd turned to alcohol. Mother could be right – withdrawal brought these problems of loneliness. 'Mystery virus?' he echoed doubtfully.

'Hasn't got a name. Hasn't got a cause. Doesn't appear to have any cure either. Still, you didn't get away from the hospital to talk about that. How's the weather now?'

'It's drying up. Improving.' Gilbert's suspicions were deepening. He threw a quick, practised look round his father's sitting-room. It was rather bare and very cold.

'Well, what do you think? Has my wife, your mother, gone off her rocker at last?'

Gilbert hated seeing his father bend to light the mean gas fire.

'This is pretty bloody, dad.'

Reggie, who was trying with genuine effort to rise out of his painful stupor, blinked owlishly, and fumbled for whichever pair of glasses the situation required. 'So she has. It's serious, then,' he said.

Curse it, the last thing he wishes to discuss is his wife.

'She has what?'

'Lost her screws.'

'I don't know what you mean.' Gilbert deposited his youthful, skinny form on the sofa and felt its prickles through his jeans.

'Your mother.'

'Oh. *She's* all right. It's you I was worrying about.'

'No need to worry about me, old son.' Reggie drooped over the fire and wondered who'd sent Gilbert. 'It'll pass. Bad weather seems to bring it on. Thundery weather especially. I thought you must have come about your mother.'

'Let me make us some tea,' suggested Gilbert. He wanted to examine the larder.

'No, no. Let me!' Reggie insisted and rose unsteadily. A wave of nausea hit him . . . This was too awful, with Gilbert here. He made an effort to hold himself upright. 'Really very nice to see you,' he mumbled again.

Reaching the little kitchen, he pulled the light cord and jumped to find his son right behind him.

'You go and sit down,' pressed Gilbert, anxiety too old for his face somehow.

His father, pyjama collar sticking above his old dressing-gown, hair on end, looked shocking.

Reggie gave in.

Gilbert, conducting a quick survey of the shelves, found an unopened bottle of dry sherry, three packets of All-Bran, several varieties of proprietary pain-killers (suicidal, too?), a bottle of herbal aid to constipation which Gilbert sniffed before being satisfied that the label was a true indication of the contents, and some antibiotic pills. No incriminating empties anywhere.

'Perhaps,' said Gilbert brightly, returning with two mugs in which tea bags palely floated, 'perhaps you could do with a stiff *brandy*?'

'No, thank you,' his father responded emphatically. 'Drink is the very devil. Drink brings it on. Now,' he settled himself, made himself decent, 'I want your assessment of yesterday's débâcle.'

He looked with pleasant disbelief at his two sons. Amazing to think people so newly out of short pants could be licensed to slice open members of the public, rearrange their organs, re-determine their lives.

Gilbert lowered his dark head to his mug and grinned over the edge of it. Had it not been for the scrappy, blond-ish moustache and his more unguarded expression, the likeness between father and son might have been more discernible. Gilbert had Reggie's well-shaped, regular features all right: they just seemed more alerted to the funny side of life.

Gilbert shrugged. His mother was much as she'd always been. The nuclear twist to yesterday's conference was only her astride an old, old hobby horse – and, well, if some of the PRGs were taken by the idea, so what? Why shouldn't they campaign as she suggested? No harm could come of it.

'No good, either,' declared Reggie.

'What do you mean? Where's the harm?'

'I mean the issue's decided.'

'Oh, sure, yes.'

Father and son stared into their mugs. The natural ambivalence of men in these matters meant that they could not take altogether seriously the mind of a woman whose body they had both, in their different ways, occupied. It wasn't Dorothy's nuclear cause that raised passion in Reggie. It was her unscrupulous – as he saw it – use of Mrs Pike's cause. Gilbert's apparent unconcern, coupled with Mrs Pike's somewhat ingenuous response, didn't appease him much.

In the silence a smile flooded Gilbert's face that made him

look about fourteen. 'She wants me to deliver the Ant's baby.'

'You mean she knows?' Reggie was enormously relieved to be released from facing Dorothy with announcement of this imminent birth.

'Oh sure, she sussed it out. The Ant says she'll call the police if I lay a finger on her. Says we're too old now to play doctors and nurses.' He gurgled with laughter and squeezed his tea-bag.

Reggie managed a painful smile himself. 'It wouldn't be quite proper.'

'She's wangled herself a bed in my hospital, though, so I may frighten her yet.'

'Antonia?'

'Yep. By the way, she says to remind you about the money.'

'I'm only a day overdue.'

'Oh, she's quite a fixer, the little Ant. That's the great thing about a sociology degree. It really equips you to play the system. There isn't a grant or a subsidy going she hasn't got tapped!' Gilbert seemed to think this admirable. Reggie was less sure. His daughter evidently had more of her mother's grip on the bureaucratic udder than he'd supposed. 'Ah!' he exclaimed suddenly. 'Good! There's only one of you at last. I told you the weather had something to do with it!' He swallowed his tea noisily and urged that they take the dog out for a walk.

The pain had ebbed a little, leaving him only mildly vertiginous. Quite well enough to walk without staggering, as long as they observed an unambitious pace. As Reggie went to change he remembered that Gilbert had been quite a runner at school.

His son was reading 'Peanuts' in the *Observer* when Reggie, in tweed cap and anorak, returned to the sitting room. (Mrs Pike was right. The room was very bleak. He wished it could have been more welcoming, and felt abruptly grateful for his landlady's well-meant though biliously glazed vase and the few terminal anemones it contained.)

'Remember telling me about that boy at your school . . .?' mused Reggie.

'Which boy?' Gilbert barely looked up.

'The boy who always wanted to be in the athletics team and never was? Was only ever reserve?'

'No.'

'Oh, *you* know,' Reggie insisted. 'The one who was always dying to have glucose tablets like the rest of the team and then in the flu epidemic or the measles or whatever it was, had his hour of glory at last?'

Gilbert gave a shout of mirth. 'Oh, Peebles! Poor Peebles, who was found solemnly rubbing the glucose tablets into his legs!'

'That's the one!' his father cried with amusement.

'What on earth made you think of him?'

'I don't know,' said Reggie. 'Come on!'

*　　*　　*

They strolled towards Granny's Gate, with Bundle forcing welcome halts on them every three yards or so. When they reached the shore itself and Reggie let her off the lead, she promptly scampered up the low initial incline of the grey cliff and darted along the top. The scrub-grown chasms of Granny's Sleeve were sufficiently far back for her to be safe where she was.

A strong wind was blowing off the sea. It slowed their progress as they leaned into it, and mischievously removed their words if they fell more than a foot apart.

Gilbert was fascinated by the brooding cliff-face. On a day like this, his father said, he wasn't seeing things at their best. Everything was made grey – cliff, stones, sea, sky. Only the rebellious breakers beating against the harbour wall lightened the monochrome. But Gilbert didn't mind. He drew a deep breath and felt the rough salt cleanse his lungs. 'Great!' he pronounced. After the centrally-heated stew of the hospital it felt pure and astringent.

For all the private vows he had made the day before, Reggie was moved to pursue the matter of his wife and her motives.

'Oh, you know *her*!' exclaimed Gilbert. He was old enough now to regard his mother's vagaries with affectionate amusement. 'From time to time she even does a bit of good.'

Reggie pondered a while and pulled his cap further down

over his eyes to secure it against the tearing wind. 'Has she mentioned bird-watching?' he inquired.

'Has she *what*?'

Reggie repeated the question. No, Dorothy had not mentioned bird-watching at all.

'I thought so,' declared Reggie grimly. 'Would it surprise you if I said I thought she was spying on me?'

Gilbert was very surprised, but concealed his astonishment with some professionalism. Paranoiac symptoms, he noted, and turned up the collar of his inadequate denim jacket. He'd forgotten how bracing weather could be. 'She hasn't any reason for watching you,' he replied reassuringly. 'Nobody can sue for adultery or desertion these days. Anyway, that's not her speed.' He sprang from one large boulder to another. 'Is that dog all right up there, by the way?'

Bundle was scampering along at a height of fifty feet now, too small to be troubled by the blast.

'She doesn't like the stones on the beach,' said Reggie absently. 'She's fine. So, she doesn't mention birds at all?'

'Flying birds, do you mean?' Gilbert shouted, having lost a bit of distance, and he thought briefly of the new girl he felt might supersede the old in his affections.

'Of course I mean *flying* birds. Feathered birds. The kind that flap their wings and sing.' Reggie did an irritable imitation.

'Well, no.' (His father, thought Gilbert, *needed* watching.)

'Hmm.' Reggie paused to gaze at a distant frigate making slow work of the sea. Apart from a bearable thudding at the base of his skull, he didn't feel too bad. 'I'll be frank with you,' he said, raising his voice. 'I can't help wondering whether this entanglement – this means she's developed for keeping in close touch with Mrs Pike – whether it hasn't got something to do with keeping tabs on me.' He had the grace to look slightly ashamed of this reasoning.

'I think it has to do with persons of more restricted growth!' chided Gilbert, his smile belying his concern.

'In *her* eyes,' countered Reggie acrimoniously. 'I *am* a person of restricted growth. I have no imagination, you know.'

Gilbert made a vain attempt to brush his vision free of flapping hair. 'You really shouldn't let yourself feel so persecuted, Dad! She's genuinely interested in the problems of dwarfism. Dwarfism *is* very interesting. That child – what's her name?'

'Phoebe.'

'Phoebe, that's right. It's an intriguing case. I shall be fascinated to see whether she ever achieves maturity.'

'You mean she might *die*?' Reggie was surprised by his own degree of shock.

'Oh no, no,' Gilbert clarified. 'No, she may never ovulate properly. Never experience the usual puberty, you know. Remain a child, but an increasingly elderly child.'

Assured that Phoebe's life-span at least might be normal, Reggie returned to the more persistently mystifying matter of his wife. 'But why, why, is she using them in this way for her anti-nuclear nonsense?'

Fretfully, he resumed his irregular journey over the boulders of Amun, and Gilbert leapt after him. 'Looked at from her point of view,' he called in his father's wake, 'the end of civilization is everybody's business. Destruction doesn't discriminate.'

His anorak filling with wind, Reggie poised for a moment like a stout bird on its rock. 'Ironic really,' he mused.

'You what?'

'Ironic. That she and I should really be thinking along the same lines and yet be so far apart.'

'I don't quite follow.' Gilbert had discovered the eternal pleasure of popping seaweed underfoot, and gave only half his windblown attention to his father.

'Here am I, investigating – in my small way – the patterns of events that contribute to decline in civilizations . . . to be even more honest, *brought* here by despair at the various ravages I see. And there she is!' He cast an arm at the sullen horizon, 'trying – in *her* small way – to forestall destruction.' He made a rueful grimace.

'Well . . . that should help you understand her better.'

'Such an impossible task . . .'

'What, understanding mother?'

'No. Though God knows, that's not easy. No, trying to forestall it.'

'It's a rather marvellous lunacy in its way.' Gilbert came and stood shoulder to shoulder with his father, staring out to sea. 'You and I are just going to let it happen.'

'There's no alternative.'

'Oh!' laughed Gilbert. 'Mother can weigh you down with alternatives.' He nodded at the expanse of water before them. 'Tides, for a start.' He gestured again at the elements. 'Wind. Sun.'

Reggie heaved a quiet sigh at the pathetic alternatives his wife championed. Queen Canute. 'Sad, really,' he said, and even as he said it he thought he really didn't know which was the sadder – the fact that the world had brought itself to the brink of such a grave decision or that he and his wife, with their common anxiety about it, would never agree on a common solution. But then he didn't have Dorothy's manic belief that she could, single-handed, save the twentieth century. Or, perhaps, he didn't find the twentieth century *worth* saving? He expelled this disreputable thought.

'Personally,' Gilbert was saying, 'I think the risks of going ahead outweigh the risks of going without it. Nuclear power,' he clarified, noticing his father's distracted air. 'But I respect her position. She'd rather fight for something she thinks better, knowing her chances are poor, than simply settle quietly for the inevitable.'

'Fight by whatever means,' Reggie pointed out dryly, adding that Gilbert's mother had never settled quietly for anything.

'The risk she's prepared to face,' reflected Gilbert, 'is failure. Most of us aren't. It takes nerve to gamble on the long odds she gives herself. I think so, anyway.'

Or a spectacularly flamboyant form of blindness, Reggie was about to propose. He checked himself. He listened for a moment to the irascible rush of wind and water, then briefly clasped his son's shoulder. 'You understand her better than I,' he acknowledged softly.

The bank of cloud, which had gathered over them with

increasing weight and darkness, lifted a little from the horizon, exposing a thin, brilliant line of light. The surly grey of the sea was suddenly silvered as if a million small waste stars had been tipped into it.

A pleasant, unexpected stirring turned in Reggie's gut. Instinctively, he turned towards the town.

'Are we going?' asked Gilbert, disappointed, though his skin was stuck to his bones with cold.

'I need to get back.'

The light, cutting into the lower strata of the blue lias, made its weeping surface glitter. Reggie looked up for the dog. She was running ahead of them, occasionally stopping to turn and check on their progress.

Consumed by the need to assess his father's symptoms better, Gilbert questioned him closely on the school, his work, his leisure activities. With the wind now behind them, talking was easier.

His father proved amusing on the shambles of the school play. Amis, who desired mists, storms and a chariot to lower Juno on stage, had put Reggie in charge of all such special effects. 'He's creating the largest possible margin for disaster,' laughed Reggie, cheered by the promising tremors in his bowel as much as anything else. 'You'll have to come and see it. Shakespeare on roller skates.'

As they passed the harbour, Gilbert looked longingly at the few boats still moored there. The masts rose black against the band of bright and greenish light.

'Perhaps we could go fishing some time,' he ventured.

'Perhaps we could!' Reggie looked with anticipatory delight at his son. 'My God, I feel better! What a good thing you came!' He whistled Bundle inexpertly and clipped on her lead. 'Easter maybe? If they let you off the removal of ladies parts then.' (Gilbert was specializing in obstetrics.) 'Only three weeks to go.'

'That'd be great.'

'*And* I could show you my hill.'

'*Your* hill?'

Excitedly, Reggie explained. They walked the length of the

promenade and up Chandler Street, deep in conversation about one another's lives. It was the beginning of a new companionship.

Unshackled from the statutory resentments of adolescence, Gilbert found his concern for his father was genuinely fond, while for his part Reggie felt a deepening pride in his son. The boy had developed a most mature and sympathetic manner. He would make a splendid doctor.

That evening was pure happiness for him. An evacuated bowel; the clamp around his head loosed; beside him, his son in a relaxation of gossip. They sat in the Ship Inn, whose ales Gilbert said must be tested. Reggie's only previous visit there had been with Mrs Pike – a treat after passing her driving test. She had become very animated and found occasion to touch his arm many times. Now he sat before the blazing log fire nursing a tonic water – a choice Gilbert noted and thought augured badly – absorbing the amiable melodies of human friendship which flowed around them. Cheers greeted darts that found their target, jeers the darts that didn't. Jokes were funnier than usual. The copper pans gleamed.

'We've enjoyed ourselves, haven't we?' Reggie smiled into the warmth of the fire.

'We have. And next time we'll go fishing.'

'Fishing it is!' declared Reggie and allowed himself, after reservations, to be talked into adding a gin to his tonic.

Gilbert found this protest indicative of the secret drinker.

For a while Reggie quite forgot to worry what despatches his son might carry back to Dorothy.

*   *   *

As he sat awkwardly the far side of the GP's vast desk, Reggie thought Dr Cassidy's manner compared very poorly with Gilbert's.

The man's brusqueness was famous in Tidmouth for discouraging all those whose symptoms did not yet border on the severely acute. He listened with evident impatience to Reggie's apologies for calling yet again with his mystery virus.

'The antibiotics seem not to have worked,' said Reggie

tentatively, feeling that the failure must lie in his bodily re-sponse rather than in the chemical composition of the drugs. That much, at least, was communicated by the tiniest upward flicker of Dr Cassidy's eyebrow. Briskly, the doctor rehearsed the symptoms again. 'Sounds like migraine,' he concluded.

'*Migraine?*' echoed Reggie with bold scepticism, thinking that migraine was a complaint suffered by women who did not want to be troubled by their husband's attentions. 'But that — that's just a headache. I promise you, I feel rather ill.'

'You *do* feel ill with migraine,' responded Dr Cassidy tersely. 'Some people feel very ill indeed.' Iller than you, he implied.

'Can it be prevented?'

'It's a bit of a mystery, frankly,' said Dr Cassidy, consulting his drugs catalogue for the latest thing.

'Not another one,' sighed Reggie. 'Couldn't you diagnose a totally unmysterious complaint? Something easily remedied?'

Reggie was rewarded with the rare spectacle of Dr Cassidy's none too friendly smile. 'It's mystique that keeps me in business,' he grinned, the wrinkles of his scowl smoothing out. The skin on top of his bald head looked terribly tight. 'No,' he said, apparently more ready to talk, 'there are masses of theories. The most popular current idea is food allergies. Look, here's a list of things to avoid.' He pulled three stapled, mim-eographed sheets from his desk drawer.

'My God, I'll starve to death.'

'Well, that's one solution.' Cassidy scribbled a prescription. 'Here,' he said, 'if you don't have the patience for all that, take these as well. They're also liable to make you feel rather ill so it's a matter of deciding which unpleasant sensation you like least. Follow the directions. Too many and you can contract gangrene. Let me know how you fare.'

By the time Reggie arrived back at Sunnybank with his lethal pills certain crucial intelligences had travelled. Certain key figures been posted.

'I've often thought,' said Bella, 'you might care for a sherry before supper.'

Out of courtesy he shared a glass with her. Unless he was

very much mistaken she seemed to be inviting confidences. Her endeavours were cut short when Ned Starkey rang to ask Reggie down to the Ship Inn 'to talk things over'.

* * *

Over the following three days, Reggie drank more industriously than he had since Christmas. His friends seemed quite preternaturally anxious to unburden themselves of their most intimate worries. They discussed tensions and loneliness and 'that certain age' when disillusion and a sense of personal failure became alarmingly pronounced. They asked him whether he too ever felt like this, and Reggie said he didn't, but if they did, then they must let him buy them another drink. In this wise he spent a good deal on Frank and Ned and Daphne and Duffer and Bella. About each he learned much that he had never suspected before: some of what he learned he would have far preferred not to have known . . . such as the discovery that Daphne possessed a third, vestigial breast for example.

On the third day, Gilbert rang.

'You must think me very stupid,' he said, 'I've just realized the problem. It's migraine.'

'I know,' said Reggie.

'Nausea, head pain, distorted vision, vertigo. Yes, migraine.'

'I know,' said Reggie. 'I've been told not to eat anything in case I'm allergic to it.'

'Oh, crap,' answered Gilbert. 'It's excessive releases of blood to the brain. At least, that's one theory.'

'Any others?' asked Reggie.

'Well, tension.'

'I'll let you know which one I decide to choose,' said Reggie.

* * *

His original diagnosis having been proved faulty, certain counter-directives were issued.

The rush of confidences suddenly ceased, as did the patronage of the pub. Only Father Starkey, the last to be informed, kept up the welfare work, confessing, one lunchtime in the Gallows Tree, to bygone onanisms.

If Reggie was at all baffled by this peculiar onset of alcoholic outpourings and its equally inexplicable cessation, none of it – except possibly Daphne's small surplus – troubled him long, because something of real value was achieved by his call on Dr Cassidy.

Having given lengthy study of his list of forbidden foods, he told Mrs Pike that he'd been advised to avoid spicy items. She looked at him for a moment as if he'd said something risqué, then, grasping his proper inference, set about the organization of his new diet with enthusiasm.

For, he profoundly hoped, the last time, Reggie scratched his bottom.

15

Be patient!

The trees refused to leaf. The land was too engorged with water to be sown. Stealthily, the school holidays passed, without any hope of excavating in this weather.

*   *   *

Dear God! thinks Reggie, made tense by the terrible prolongation of this waiting, watching season. In a dilatory fashion he expands his notes, studies maps of Hampshire and plans unreal tours of the county in which he chances upon the sisters who wait beside a cottage gate, their arms heavy with sheaves of bluebells.

Surely something should by now produce a bud?

Reggie finds himself looking at the bare, sealed branches in people's gardens with impatient fury. They have a Lenten restraint, an almost pious refusal to indulge their boughs with modest green ornament.

*   *   *

On April Fool's Day he rang Major Bittern, and said he would like to make a few preliminary reconnaissances on Turtledown. Within the hour a pass had been prepared for him.

It was a wild and tearing day. Even Bundle kept her small white body sideways to the blast as Reggie climbed higher along the ridge. Through the racing trails of mist below him he could see the tiny church of Maidenwell. Behind it the ruined buildings remained invisible beneath their brown and leafless tangle of woodland. A thin column of smoke, bluer than the dun trails of fog, was carried, vanishing, inland.

A faint bleating of lambs reached him, the sound weirdly detached from the yellow blobs huddled round whatever poor gorse cover was available. He turned and headed into the weather, making slow, angled progress towards the coast. Sparse, sharp needles of rain hurt his face and made his ears ache. His glasses were peppered with silver shot.

* * *

And yet the sheer difficulty of gaining the fort is peculiarly elating. Reggie sees himself as the lone invader despatched to breach the walls. He imagines a shield at his chest, a sword in his hand. He imagines the ferment in the camp.

The closer he draws, the slower his progress. His role changes. He is a lover of the chivalric age come to pay court to his lady. It is in a state of adoration that he finally enters the ruptured walls and stands on the great, encircled height, staring at a sea that howls and boils in warning.

* * *

Too high to be touched by the rising spray, he listened to the murderous clash of the water beneath him. He could see the curdling withdrawal of its soured but tireless onslaught.

Face down, Reggie lay full-length on the turf, running his fingers through the rough, salt-bitten grasses. Then he turned and let the sky roll over him until the earth itself felt wonderfully unsteady. Bundle came and licked his face, between futile pursuits of baby rabbits.

Cold, wet, excited, Reggie jumped to his feet. He measured. He paced. He decided on which methods he would use. The dubious disc barrow called for a quadrant excavation, carefully sliced into quarters like a grapefruit. The principal area would best be tackled on the grid system. Complete stripping was too major a task and required more meticulous recording than he could guarantee with small boys as his assistants.

He prowled against the wind, noting bumps, dips, differences in grass coloration, the odd clumps of nettles that suggested disturbed earth, and longed for the use of a proton magnetometer which would cut down on the guesswork. But having no access to such a thing, he furtively withdrew from his pockets the copper piping and bent bits of Daphne's coathanger. Trying to hold the wires steadily in front of him, he traversed the ground. Either the place was a mine of treasures or the wind was playing havoc with his instruments.

*   *   *

As he quarters the area slowly, approaching nearer and nearer the perilous edge, does he feel a definite charge in his arms, a dragging of his essence into the ancient soil? Or is it just a japing of the gale that makes his wires cross?

*   *   *

Oh, this unyielding season!

At least, now that he was dieted as an invalid on steamed fish, milk puddings, soft roes, sweetbreads and all the other bland white nourishments that indicate a tenderness of care, he was excused Bella's frugal Lenten table. She ate like an anchorite, forswearing flesh of any sort. Ned Starkey's observances were far less slimming.

As Mrs Pike's intake fell, her output of good works increased in due proportion, and Reggie found himself with shambling reluctance going from door to door selling raffle tickets on her behalf, sheepishly asking for awful old clothes to sell as jumble, and wondering whether certain householders would care to sponsor walkers at one p. per mile. Some were decidedly angry at being approached, and asked him if he'd never heard of inflation. Others found it quicker to get rid of the caller at their door by agreeing to anything. Several welcomed the opportunity to recall their long and eventful histories. Reggie hated all of it. It intensified that sense of being watched. Eyes at windows. Windows, eyes. Any winking light or knotted trunk or gaping letter-box acquired the special gift of sight as he stood before it. Reggie took to glancing over his shoulder. He stopped before shop windows to see if another figure stood at his back. Only the innocuous Bundle panted beside his reflection. He stepped quickly into Tidmouth's many unexpected alleyways in the hope that whatever followed him would then pass by.

He blames Anna for this. Be patient! she had said and, thus saying, created the sense of something imminent.

*   *   *

One sodden brown afternoon, seizing a dull interval in the weather, Reggie and Ned Starkey trudged over the bridle paths to Casterwich. Ned said he needed the exercise. He had to pay his library fines and pick up a briefcase being repaired at the saddler's. Reggie needed company of a reassuringly solid kind. He plodded through the mud, gazing at his friend's water-proofed back and incongruously yellow, sou'westered head with the sense of thankful salvation which a small child feels towards the form that leads him out of nightmare.

In the rain's short pause the birds had begun to sing re-lievedly.

They had been talking in the desultory fashion of the single-file walker about the mathematical impossibilities of cutting taxation and increasing public expenditure, a subject on which neither was expert nor short of opinion, when Reggie inquired of the priest ahead of him, 'Do you feel ... *watched* all the time?'

'I'm neither rich enough nor poor enough for that,' shouted Ned. 'Now the business tycoon – or the pauper – poor devils, both, they *must* feel the object of every bureaucrat's beady eye!'

They trudged a little further, pulling brambles out of their eyes.

'No,' Reggie corrected himself. 'I mean by ... *God*.' The word was unaccountably difficult to pronounce. It was like a splinter in his tongue. 'Don't you feel continually peered at by *God*?'

'Aha! I get you!' The sou'wester bobbed vigorously. Ned swung at some brambles with his stick, and dislodged a clump of tired wild clematis. 'No, I can't say I do. Not in any policing sense – which is, if I may say, the way you infer. Watched *over*, maybe.'

Sufficiently troubled by his own sense of being surveyed, assessed, as if he were not a *culprit*, but in some sense a candi-date – the most improbable of possibilities *had*, it must be confessed, at last been allowed into the high-security cell of Reggie's mind for consideration. Was he, could he conceivably be, undergoing a religious experience of the kind Ned himself had once described? Paul, when all was said and done, had not been *expecting* visions on the road to Damascus. Anything but. Maybe this was the unpredictable way of these things. His questioning proceeded with caution. 'But you're always, I imagine, conscious of it – Him?'

'Look about you!'

Father Starkey sprang on to an exposed part of the low bank bordering the lane and thrashing about him with his stick, created a vista for Reggie. 'Behold!' he cried, and again, *'Ecce!'*

In a spirit of scientific co-operation, Reggie beheld. He beheld the high, swooping line of the downland, the evenly coloured patches of tan and pale green field. He beheld water dully glinting in the flooded valley grass, clotted tangles of copse, rooks against a slate sky and, through a dip of the downs, the faded point of a pyramidal hill crowned with Scots pines. The fields were empty of beasts. He beheld land awaiting the decision that would release it from this cold, late spring.

'Everywhere!' Ned performed a gesture worthy of Riccardo Mutti.

'You *must* feel watched.' Reggie's murmur was addressed more to himself than to his friend. But was it right to equate this mild sense of persecution with God? Was that entirely fair?

'If I have a bad conscience, I suppose I feel as I think you mean,' said Ned, and jumped off the bank noisily, his wellingtons plopping deep in the mud. 'But that's as it should be. If I were breaking a safe, then undoubtedly I would be thinking: *Thou God seeth me.'*

'It would get me down awfully,' sighed Reggie, as they resumed their course, able, now the path widened, to walk alongside one another.

'Don't be silly! That's the God of guilt I'm talking about. The image of my own naughty conscience. Any sense of being watched – your sense – is generated by the one watched over, don't you see?'

Reggie wondered what he felt guilty about and couldn't immediately think of anything. In fact, he thought he'd been quite abnormally good and helpful recently, begging alms and shrunken jumpers for Mrs Pike.

Ned Starkey took his glum-faced friend by the arm. 'Does the company of friends get you down?'

The look Reggie flicked at him turned into a smile. No other response was possible in the mirror of that rubicund face, squarely framed in yellow plastic.

'Is that how it is?'

'Of course! Companionable. God be in mine eyes etcetera. It's a pity,' Ned sighed, briefly saddened, 'about the commissar God, the God-outside. But it's awfully hard to communicate God-inside to small children; it alarms them rather, so we have to settle for God the Father – a major improvement on Yaweh, to be sure – beastly old God of wrath – but still misleading. Of course,' he went on, transferring again to single file as they squelched onward, but this time falling behind Reggie, 'the idea of mother-inside would be so much simpler, so much more accessible to creatures all of whom have *been* mother-inside.'

Reggie stopped to pull his gum-boot out of the mud and, wobbling on one leg, tried to dip his toe back into the retrieved boot. He was laughing at himself and Ned. 'It's not one of our clearest recollections,' he observed, 'so I doubt whether you'd make your mysticism much easier that way.' He didn't expand on the commoner male memory of female admittance. It seemed crude, unwarranted. And yet, while they chattered on about planning timetables for the summer term, the alternative image interfered. There was a pleasant grain of blasphemy in sex, an attacking return on the womb. An 'up you'.

By the time they reached Casterwich and went their separate ways – Ned to the saddler's, Reggie first to the home-made fudge shop and then on to the museum to look into the recent acquisitions case – Reggie was feeling pretty confident that, whatever unease it was he experienced, it was neither guilty conscience nor the unbidden onset of religious fervour.

As he left the museum, collecting his coat from the desk and walking down the stone-flagged hall, his confidence on this point was unexpectedly confirmed for him. Pressed against the window which looked out on to the main street beside the entrance was Dorothy's face.

His first reaction, naturally – apart from plain shock – was that she was looking for him. But even as he stepped back into a slight recess, he realized that she was in fact studying the antefixes displayed in the window, and very likely couldn't see into the darker interior of the hall.

Briefly, he hesitated. Then, as if given special strength by the discovery that he was not paraphrenic at all, he straightened his tie, adjusted his anorak over his arm and strode forth from Casterwich Museum like an officer about to claim his prisoner.

*   *   *

'Oh *Jesus*!'

At Dorothy's cry, people skirted her quite suddenly as if the pavement space she occupied reeked of profanity. 'What,' said Dorothy, not demandingly at all, but rather bemusedly, 'what are *you* doing here?'

Suddenly Reggie found himself enjoying his wife's disconcerted expression. It was a novelty, and he wished to savour it. He tapped his wellington judicially on the evacuated pavement. 'Shouldn't I,' he pronounced at length, 'be asking *you* that question?'

Dorothy seemed to have lost her wits entirely.

'A little cold for spring migrants,' remarked Reggie with a casual look at the shivering sky.

'What?'

'Migrants, dear. You seem not to have your binoculars . . . *My* binoculars,' he corrected after a delightfully timed pause.

Busily, Dorothy began gathering the grey folds of her huge cloak around her as if it were vital she should search for something within its draperies this very second.

'I thought I ought to come and talk a few things over with Bella,' she blurted unconvincingly. 'The march.'

'I'm not certain Bella – Mrs Pike – is expecting you. In fact I'm quite certain she is not,' said Reggie smugly. 'Otherwise she would have warned me of the impending event.'

'Not necessarily.' Dorothy swung one fold of her cloak over her shoulder and looked more defiant. 'Anyway, it was a spur of the moment thing. That's why I was just stopping off to buy a cake.'

'A *cake*?' Mrs Pike was never short of home-made cakes. A very clumsy error.

'Well, a few flowers, maybe. How are you, Reggie? What a surprise, eh? Why don't we go into that nice-looking café for some tea here, instead?'

'I'm meeting a friend here shortly, thank you.'

'Oh? Who?'

Disbelieving it, he none the less hears that same scrape of jealousy he has heard before in Dorothy's voice. Reggie looks at her very hard. He has to look up, slightly. 'Ned. Father Starkey,' he says.

'Ah.' Light, dismissive relief.

Is it more than mere nosiness which drives her into corners after him, despatching agents, conducting these covert investigations? Is it fractionally more than a genuine concern for his welfare which has, in Dorothy, this unfortunate way of presenting itself as officiousness? Is it possible . . .? But he can hardly bring himself to ask the question. Instead, he thinks merely of Dorothy's occasionally brazen sexual needs, the little vermilion scraps of underwear with which she once threatened him.

'We really must,' he said, 'once and for all, talk this thing out.'

'Yes?' Her eyes darted between his.

'Why' (and he stepped back against the wall as if to brace himself, and glanced about for eavesdroppers) 'why are you pursuing me in this clandestine fashion, for example?'

'I'm not!' she retorted indignantly.

'Good God, Dorothy, I know life is reputedly full of funny little coincidences, but, tested against any system of mathematical possibility you care to name, the number of chance encounters we have is beyond the limits of pure hazard.'

'Try not to sound pompous, dear,' she said. 'You don't know anything about maths. And I haven't the faintest what you're talking about, anyway.'

'What about . . .' he began.

'Couldn't we go somewhere else to talk? This is awfully public.'

222

'I thought you enjoyed a platform.'

'Don't bitch.'

'I want to be left alone,' he said, immediately regretting it. He sounded just like Greta Garbo. The same thought had obviously occurred to Dorothy, who grinned, showing all her remarkably fine teeth.

Hastily, Reggie continued, 'It's unnerving having you pop up like this all over the place.'

'When? What place?'

'Well ...' He thought furiously and with dismay realized that his complaint was mostly about his sense of her always being there. 'Like now, for instance,' he ended lamely. Then, 'Was it you sent Gilbert?'

'Of course not,' she said quickly.

'Antonia?'

'Reggie, you're not well.'

'Don't try that one,' he snapped. 'Anyway, far more important, I don't like the way you're using Mrs Pike.' He faltered. Dorothy was waving to somebody, as friendly as you like.

'You're sly,' he said weakly, 'and unprincipled.'

She wasn't listening. Her superior height had given her first view of Father Starkey who, yellow-headed, hand outstretched, was crossing the road towards them, ignoring the traffic. 'Well, well, well!' he cried genially. '*You're* a sly one, Reggie!' he grasped Dorothy's hand. 'Didn't breathe a word to me. Oh!' He had caught sight of Reggie's tight-stretched face. He gave a small sniff as if scenting some atmosphere generated by the couple. 'Oh, goodness me and heigh-ho. I mustn't interrupt whatever business you two have to discuss together, but it's most awfully pleasant to ... Shall we be meeing at the bus-stop later, Reggie?' He made this inquiry on tiptoe, as if conscious of peeping over a private wall.

'I'll run you back.' Dorothy hoisted her bag. 'I was on my way, in any event,' she said, forestalling the incipient protests.

'Well, I must say that for two middle-aged gents we've really satisfied our exercise quota for the day,' beamed Father Starkey. 'Besides,' he looked up, 'I wouldn't vouch for the weather.'

It was true. Angry bars of cloud were piling in from the

coast. Reggie found himself trooping after the others. Something in Dorothy's demeanour had changed. She was once more assured. With a grand swirl of the cloak, she led the way to the car-park and kept up, all the way back to Sunnybank, so fluent and well-judged a barrage of chatter that Reggie found himself quite admiring her technique.

But he was going to have it out.

*   *   *

Bella Pike was not at home.

'Hell!' stamped Dorothy. 'I really need to see her.'

'Then you should have rung or written. Never mind! I need to see you. Would you step into my room, please?'

Deliberately, as much to calm himself as to ruffle her, he kept her waiting. He fiddled around in the kitchen with tea-spoons and sugar bowls that were quite unnecessary. He even found a jug for the milk which needed a good wash first. It pleased him to hear her fidgeting movements; then, to his annoyance, he heard her, very softly, start playing his record.

When he returned with the tray, she was listening with that bogus air of concentration which had always put him off cultural appreciation. And indeed, the readiness with which she turned at his appearance simply proved how very weak her own appreciation was.

'All right,' she said. 'I've been thinking.'

Reggie sat down. Dorothy rose. Two pink spots flushed on her cheeks and made her look surprisingly youthful. Even her height, for a second, seemed to make her awkward, like a schoolgirl unpoised by the lengthening of her own body. Then she gathered herself more capably and paced the room twice before resting in front of the table in the bay window, where she stood darkly silhouetted in the unlamped April evening light. Outside, a wind was gently stirring the tips of the trees. Inside, the overture drew to an end.

Enter Tamino pursued by a serpent.

'I am *not* pursuing you,' announced Dorothy, quite unconscious of her timing.

Tamino then babbled with melodious fright.

'My purposes are quite different. *Quite* different.' She paused and turned her profile against the sinking light. 'My purposes have nothing whatever to do with you. In fact, I've been at such pains to keep them from you that I may have misled you – seemed furtive. I'm sorry.' She turned towards him again, but he couldn't discern her features any longer. The shadows were too deep.

The three veiled ladies, servants to the Queen of the Night, pierced the serpent with their silver spears, sang gloriously of their triumph and the freedom they had now bestowed on Tamino, who still, the feeble chump, lay swooning on the ground.

Dorothy seemed to stand, head bowed, listening to the music. Her hands gripped the table behind her. The spread of her cloaked arms seemed unusually, angelically wide. But in fact she was thinking, weighing carefully what she had to say.

Reggie, distrusting anything stated from the declamatory position, urged his wife to sit down and drink her tea, but she shook her lowered head fiercely.

There was a pause. Then, lifting her featureless face towards him, she said undramatically, 'I haven't talked of this to you before – partly because it doesn't concern you – but chiefly because, if you knew, you might misconstrue it . . . Might think I was, well, thinking up some preposterous device to get you back. Get your attention, at least.'

'I don't understand.'

'You might, you see, feel you had to prevent my doing what I plan to do. Keep me under close surveillance.'

This was a fine reversal!

'Too cryptic for me,' said Reggie and sipped at the good normality of his tea. If Dorothy was applying the word 'preposterous' to one of her own actions, then truly it must be something very special indeed.

'*If* I'm to tell you,' she went on with the utmost gravity, 'you have to swear absolute secrecy first. You have to give me your solemn oath not to interfere or in any way prevent me from what I intend.'

'All right,' nodded Reggie willingly.

'No, *really*! Swear!'

'All *right*!' he repeated, laughing gently. 'I swear.'

The three ladies ceased their squabbling over which of them was to have Tamino for herself and the music ended. In the ensuing silence Dorothy appeared to be having difficulty in expressing herself.

Then she flung her head back, stood upright, and announced, 'I'm going to expose myself to an isotope!'

'Couldn't you expose yourself to something rather more rewarding?' inquired Reggie, and then, involuntarily, he giggled. 'You can get arrested for that sort of thing.'

'I'm well aware of all the risks.'

Reggie stared at her blackened, eagle form and, leaning to one side, pulled at the cord of the standard lamp. The light sprang on. Dorothy stood just beyond its brighter orbit.

'Are you serious?' he queried, not for one moment thinking that she was, except within the confines of her own lunatic fancy. He was perfectly sure Dorothy didn't know what an isotope was. One certainly didn't go around exposing oneself to them.

'Perfectly!'

'But . . .'

'You're not to ask any questions at all,' she intervened sharply. 'If you know anything, you become an accessory. Don't you see?'

'I think I am one now.'

'As far as I'm concerned,' declared Dorothy, 'this conversation has never taken place. All you *do* know – and this is my sole reason for raising the matter at all – is that I am not trying to interfere with whatever life you lead here. I expect you to reciprocate that fully.'

'I don't believe in this conversation,' said Reggie stubbornly. 'Look, do sit down and drink your tepid tea, there's a good girl. You really will have to tell me a bit more, you know.'

Dorothy sat down, at least. Beyond that she refused to do his bidding. Instead, she told him he really must chuck that repulsive picture of Venice out. 'It's so vulgar it's not even *kitsch*,' she said and drained her cup.

And try as he might, not another word could he coax out of her on the more serious matter she'd raised.

* * *

Later, she went downstairs to talk over the PRG march arrangements with Bella. Bundle trotted upstairs and jumped on Reggie's knee. He scratched behind the dog's ear distractedly.

Reggie didn't doubt that Dorothy could dream up such a damn-fool scheme. Nor did he doubt that it was totally impracticable. He wavered between anxiety, thinking these manic symptoms of hers were in need of professional attention, and increasingly, waves of extreme anger. Just suppose she did attempt to break in somewhere, or to board one of those trains that went into nuclear installations; just suppose she even tried it? She would be so sure to be found out that she could only bring unremitting mockery and disrepute on Mrs Pike's PRGs.

Middle age was making Dorothy more and more ridiculous. If Reggie didn't pause to feel any worry for the injuries his wife might inflict on herself, it was only because he couldn't conceive of such a remote likelihood. If he felt any pity, then it was the vaguely exasperated pity men have for the mysteries of the menopause and the eccentricities it engenders.

His more protective feelings were unequivocally reserved for Mrs Pike and her PRGs. Immediately he thought of the various warnings he could issue to prevent Dorothy's ever doing anything to damage his landlady's passionate involvement.

But!

Be silent!

And he had sworn, thinking it a trifle. (Oh Nana, Nana, what is my duty now?)

* * *

After Dorothy had completed her farewells in the hall, he seized her and pushed her outside.

Both of them shaken by his roughness, they sat side by side in her car, breathing heavily.

'You *must* not attempt this absurd thing!'

'I know what I'm doing,' she said calmly, and turned to look at him, touched by his concern. 'I'll be all right.'

'It's not you I'm worried about,' he snapped. 'It's the others you involve.'

'Oh, I see.' Dorothy, now gauging his concern more accurately, couldn't prevent herself sneering. 'Nobody's going to think *you're* involved,' she said.

'Oh, for God's sake, I don't care about myself. It's Mrs Pike I care about!'

Dorothy adjusted to this new knowledge – or this new confirmation of an old suspicion. '*Really?*' she pronounced, her lips pressed tight against some large bewildering emotion. 'I see.'

'If you still want – at forty-eight – to go around being an Angela Brazil brick, well, that's your affair, but any silly scrape you get yourself into, any scandal, any criminal act you stupidly commit . . . that's going to stick on her.'

'You have no vision whatever,' announced Dorothy loftily, gripping her steering wheel and staring straight ahead.

'Vision!' spluttered Reggie. 'This isn't vision; it's delusion!'

'If that's what you want to call it.' She shrugged.

'You're pathetic.' Reggie buried his head in his hands.

Dorothy just tapped a forefinger on the wheel.

'I shall warn them at Winburgh,' said Reggie firmly. He knew now what all the birdwatching and trespass on Bella's unquestioning good nature was truly about. Clearly, he had hit the mark.

Dorothy turned on him. She seemed to fill the small space of the car with her fury and venom. 'Don't you bloody meddle! You promised me! You *swore!*' She choked with abuse. Her great flapping arms tore round him. He was a coward, a betrayer, a bastard, a spineless, timorous, treacherous, ageing deadbeat!

He stopped her flow by gripping his hand across her mouth. She bit him. He hardly felt it. He was more keenly aware of hurting her. He knew that he hurt her and he wasn't going to let go until she stopped struggling. The sight of a young couple walking arm in arm up the dark street seemed, surprisingly, to make her slump into some sort of submission. 'I won't do her any harm,' she spat.

'Don't come back here again,' he said, low, but more fiercely than he would have believed of himself. 'Just don't come back.'

'You really are a prize turd, Reggie.' Dorothy leaned one elbow on the wheel and stared at him in the feeble glitter of lamplight. 'To think I was vain enough to imagine you might care sufficiently to try and stop me harming myself!' She came perilously close to tears. '*Jesus!*'

'If I thought there was any serious risk of your harming yourself, then I might.'

'I shall regard that as a challenge!' Dorothy smiled and turned the ignition on. 'Back to Kosy Kot you go, Reggie dear. Back to Mumsy and potties and pudding! Which of us, I wonder, has *really* failed to grow up!'

Reggie got out of the car with as much dignity as he could, while Dorothy manoeuvred her vehicle into a getaway position. 'At least,' she called out, leaning across to the open passenger window. 'At least I've given the world a try!'

She roared off.

Reggie stood in his slippers. A light drizzle speckled his glasses.

Be patient!

Be silent!

'You'll catch your death out there!' He heard Mrs Pike's voice at the door, calling. And for a moment he turned, mesmerized by the sheer comfort of its homely tone and cliché.

*   *   *

Round him, in the classroom, he can keep this wadding of happiness.

Before the kindly tightening of Nana's régime, before the humiliations of his minor public school where the senior boys carried whippy canes – in the days and years of his own prep. school, Reggie was at his happiest. *Is* at his happiest here, now, in a new term, on a wet April morning in a room where the maroon jerseys steam and smell of muddy gun-dogs. Here, telling stories, he feels safe, content, and takes his revenge.

'If you see two swans linked by gold or silver chains,' he says, 'you have seen goddesses in one of their favourite forms.' And he tells them how Cú Chulainn, wishing to harness the sun-servant swans to his chariot that it might fly higher and faster, closer and closer to the orb itself, tries to bring down the birds in flight. 'They fall, the one with the injured wing dragging the other, who is chained to her. They fall, sinking slowly beneath the waters of the lake, then re-emerge. Two beautiful women, rising together out of the lake, and what do they do? They come towards the warrior Cú Chulainn and beat him unconscious. There's women for you!'

(He thinks of Anna. Thinks of Stephanie.)

And they all laugh with him, and look sidelong at Caroline Popplewell, who takes the sniggering of the boys as proof of their irredeemable silliness. She has a severe fringe and a more endearingly gibbon-like face than her father.

But Reggie is not done.

The stories, oh so beguiling, well up, spill forth. From his much-thumbed reference book by Stokes he reads *'Dá Choca's Hostel'*. He reads:

They saw coming towards the hostel the big-mouthed black swift sooty woman, lame and squinting with her left eye. She wore a threadbare dingy cloak. Dark as the back of a stag beetle was every joint of her from the top of her head to the ground. Her filleted hair fell back over her shoulder. She leant her shoulder against the door post and began prophesying evil to the host and to utter ill words.

And in the Badb – the Badb meaning 'crow' – he sees Dorothy.

He does not tell them that, in other tales, the Badb, or the Mórrígan or the Macha, the three-in-one, the all-in-one goddesses, are accompanied by birds whose song is sweeter than any imaginable sound. He fails to tell how they can heal, make the listener fall into magical sleep; how they reign over the rivers and wells of healing.

Oh no. Instead he tells of the crow-women, the black-clad,

230

screeching figures who, brandishing burning torches, rushed out from the blood-stained sacrificial groves, hurling themselves upon Paulinus and his terrified troops as they assembled on the shores of Anglesey.

*　　*　　*

Evil birds. Harbingers of ill-tidings, of war. The carriers of the curse.

Reggie is not to be blamed. He is in a ferment of feeling and has not, as yet, discovered any good or brave or proper means of releasing and directing it.

*　　*　　*

'Woe! Woe!' Amis was moaning, fingers buried in the thick, brown fleece of his hair. He rocked to and fro on the edge of the big wooden table where much of the marking was done.

Reggie, coming a little late into the staffroom after one of his more striking renditions, was at first disturbed, then amused by Amis's tormented writhings and rockings.

'How now!' he cried merrily, putting his books down.

'Too awful!' Amis raised his face and lengthened his prognathic jaw still further at the sight of Reggie. 'Little Billy Grenville!' he groaned.

Grenville was the beautiful boy Amis had selected as his Ariel.

'What of him?' asked Reggie. 'Both legs broken?'

'Far, far worse! Not his legs ... his *voice*! Gone, completely!'

'I always thought we were going to have to mime his singing,' said Reggie, recalling the awful flat sound that wrongfully issued from that seraphic face.

'Never mind his singing! Have you heard him *speak*! He's come back this term with a voice like Satchmo.'

'Well, *hardly*.' Eleanor Straker's sympathy was thin. She'd rather feared for Grenville's safety in the dressing-rooms.

'But I've built the whole production round the horrid boy. How dare he drop two octaves at this stage!'

'I've never heard them described as octaves before,' mused

Eleanor. 'And don't be silly, Mamie; you've built the whole production round yourself.'

Amis had certainly made some judicious cuts in the text.

'Help me, Montis!' The English master's head fell back in his hands.

'Phoebe Orlebar,' said Reggie. 'She'd be perfect. And she sings very sweetly.'

He couldn't think why he'd said it. So convinced, so unhesitatingly.

'A ... *gi-ir-ir-l*!'

What Edith Evans had once done for 'handbag', Amis now did for 'girl'. Disbelief, distaste, and a profound sense of disturbance rolled through his gurgling extension of the word.

'Well,' said Reggie, cheerily, 'since you have the opportunity these days, I don't know why you haven't thought of recasting Miranda as well, frankly.'

'My dear Montis, the whole *point* of Ariel is his strangely androgynous quality. As for Miranda, that will do, thank you! Just *try* finding me something prettier than little Jason Caldecott!'

'Phoebe Orlebar,' pronounced Eleanor Straker, as emphatic in her own way as Amis in his, 'does have a strange quality.'

Reggie lent her a grateful look. With her support he felt less partisan and more to the point, less surprised by his own promptitude in suggesting Phoebe. In some obscure way he was making reparation for Dorothy's mischief.

'She would be perfect!' said Eleanor firmly. 'Now pull yourself together, Mamie. Sulking doesn't suit you.'

'You think?' Amis cleared his face and smiled with grisly charm. 'Very well. If you think she can learn the lines in time. But don't you dare try robbing me of little Caldecott. On that, I'm quite resolved. As long, at least,' he sighed, 'as the little beast doesn't grow a beard by half term.'

*   *   *

The way Reggie put it was this: 'It means, you see,' he explained to Phoebe and her mother (Daphne was already hot with pride), 'that I shall be able to run Phoebe home more regularly during the week, since both of us will have to stay on late for rehearsals.'

Daphne was blind to Reggie's dissimulation. 'Oh, you'd love to be on the stage, wouldn't you?' she urged, prodding her daughter into some acknowledgement.

'Well, I've had plenty of practice,' the diminutive girl said dryly. 'Still, I don't know about being a fairy.'

Together, Daphne and Reggie declaimed that Ariel wasn't exactly what you'd call a fairy, and that Phoebe would make an absolutely lovely fairy.

'Make up your minds,' said Phoebe.

'I can do you those wings with cellophane and silver glitter,' beseeched Daphne. '*You* know, lovey.'

'Whatever turns you on,' responded Phoebe, but not unkindly.

*   *   *

Until now the journeys from Lower Knoll to Turtledown and back had been – to be perfectly honest – something of a strain for Reggie. He simply hadn't known how to react to this ancient, dry, inscrutable child with the face and proportions of an Edwardian porcelain doll. On the very first day, when he had stupidly drawn up on the wrong side of the road and crossed over on foot to fetch her, he had taken her – quite automatically – by the hand, as one would a five-year-old. The anger with which she had snatched herself from his grasp was a rebuff from which he'd never fully recovered. Her whole manner was charged with a defiance which, dimly, he had begun to understand as something more than mere rudeness. As though, wearied by the archly modified approach and speech of adults assuming her to be other than she was, she had developed a cynical, highly perceptive intelligence which she kept in reserve until, discerning a rare moment when it could be put to devastating use, she stepped out of her silence and cast it with shocking effect over idiot heads.

It would be an exaggeration to say that all Reggie's daily encounters with Phoebe were as alarming as this. They weren't.

For the most part the pair of them got on either in small, undeveloping bursts and starts that were tolerable enough, or, considerably simpler, without speaking at all – beyond noting small changes in the hedgerow or the behaviour of birds, the arrival of certain butterflies, the alert shadow of a roe deer in the woodland beside the road. These observations were made by Phoebe and countered with a range of encouraging noises from Reggie. It could scarcely be described as conversation, but it passed well enough for it. She never spoke of her family.

'I like the sound of it,' Phoebe said grudgingly at last, listening to Reggie's diffidently expressed reasons for his suggesting her in the part. And then, with an eagerness the poignancy of which didn't strike him until later, 'I like the idea of being invisible.'

At the time, Reggie laughed and said he wasn't sure his special effects were up to that. But he was having 4A build a tree with a ladder inside it. Would that suffice?

'I'd like to fly,' she said wistfully and drew the pictograph V of a bird on his steamy car window.

'It's awfully painful, flying,' smiled Reggie. 'I did it once. In a school pantomime.'

'Oh, *well*,' she replied matter-of-factly, 'it *would* be painful for *you*.'

Before her first read-through – which he wanted, profoundly, to be good, and not solely to justify his own declared faith in her – he tried to explain the problematic play. It was an exercise which compelled him to address her as the intelligent twelve-year-old she was rather than as a precocious oddity of five or six. The insultingly patient manner, the involuntary simplification of matter was abandoned. Not because he strove consciously to shed it. Because Shakespeare just didn't allow for simple accounting.

'He's a rather private, withdrawn man, really,' Reggie said of Prospero, cornering the Morris dangerously on a wet bend, 'fond of his daughter but not terribly open in his affection. Not forthcoming with her. There's ... how can I describe it? A sense of unexpressed bitterness and resentment about him,

234

something you feel is based on older, deeper events than the usurping of his dukedom. He's very hard on Ferdinand, and he doesn't really forgive his brother even at the end when everything is, ostensibly at least, happily resolved ... And his attitude towards Ariel – *I* think – is thoroughly equivocal. Almost ...' he pondered this, aware that Phoebe listened carefully, 'almost ...' and yet again he hesitated, aware that what he *was* struggling to express did not actually manifest itself in Amis's grandiloquent performance. Nevertheless, Reggie pressed on, knowing that the androgynous quality Amis so valued in Grenville's Ariel might be given a yet more reverberant ambiguity by Phoebe, if she could somehow embody the enigmatic modes of the relationship. 'Almost as though Prospero is jealous of Ariel, as though he knows all his own powers are borrowed, mortal and diminishing, whereas those of the sprite are evergreen.'

'I thought,' said Phoebe in a sensible voice, 'that Prospero had freed Ariel in the first place; so how can he be jealous?'

'That's true.' Indeed, it was. How could he convey the peculiarity of the play? Reggie drove slowly over the cattle grid between the school gates. Before the car's advance, the pale, long-horned beasts dispersed. 'But there's still a suggestion,' he insisted, 'that Prospero's magic has definite limits – in fact the play suggests it's limited to a critical four-hour period, though we have to suppose he's done a spot of dabbling before that, since there's all the Caliban-Sycorax business to account for. Anyway,' he closed his left hand encouragingly over her frail arm, 'I hope you can play it with spirit in every sense of the word!'

*   *   *

All that Sycorax business! Reggie shrivelled inside as he sat in the school hall listening to the first read-through. The awful aptness of the lines had entirely escaped him until he heard Amis give a sneering summary of the manner in which Sycorax had 'in her most unmitigable rage' imprisoned Ariel within a cloven pine:

> *within which rift*
> *Imprisoned, thou didst painfully remain*
> *A dozen years, within which space she died,*
> *And left thee there, where thou did'st vent thy groans*
> *As fast as millwheels strike.*

Reggie stared aghast at Phoebe's small figure. How could he not have realized the impropriety! But her face retained its customary detachment, and the effect was strange. The English master's florid delivery was reduced to mere bluster by it.

Reggie relaxed a little. Yes, Phoebe promised to bring something to this play that would lift it subtly above the dull literalness of the usual school production.

Part Four

BELTAINE

16

Beltaine. The true Spring festival. The first day of May when the old fires are quenched and the new freshly kindled.

When the sun broke out of the sky, unfamiliar lamp.

*   *   *

It brought people early from their beds that morning. Bright fingers plucked at drawn fabric and tapped sleepers awake. Joy travelled through the air.

Farmers, shuffling their cattle into the milking parlour, began to whistle, knowing that they could at last herd their beasts down the sparkling lanes on to drying pasture. Grain, sown late, might with luck – given a long growing season – prosper after all.

Carrying his steaming buckets of boiled potato peel, cabbage leaves and barley mash to his pigs, Frank's dreams turned to expansion . . . he'd buy in a few steers, keep his ewe lambs on, fatten the others for meat, get his potatoes in – pink fir-apple, he fancied – raise a small stand of barley, a third of an acre, maybe.

He leant over the gate between his toppling corrugated iron sheds and enjoyed the wealth of vision the celebrant sun allowed him, before turning his daughter's pony out to snatch at grass quite suddenly green. He heard a cuckoo in the next valley. The latecomer come at last.

The sharp, tender green shed its dew and unfurled itself, a festive cloak swiftly embroidered with small gold and silver flowers. Beneath the cloth, the downland stirred like a woman's body stretching out of sleep. The glass of the sea cleared, its translucence recovered.

Bella, rising early in readiness for Mass before the journey to London, found her excitement sharpened by the alteration of light. Each heartbeat was a gorgeous hurt.

Phoebe, sliding from her scrolled couch, smiled and brushed her hair until it crackled and glittered like a satellite sun.

The birds were furious in their song. And, touched in their turn by the busy god's caduceus, the straining buds flared open.

Successful union at last seemed made between the floundering seasons, whose sulky, sterile courtship had lost so many of the new year's lambs.

Reggie woke with piping vigour. His first thought was for the hill. He rose, washed and shaved quickly, gobbled down his cereal and made to creep out.

Mrs Pike, returning from Mass, accosted him in the front hall. 'We've got a grand day for it all right!' she cried. 'Are you *sure* you'll not come with us?' This last question was put hesitantly. Aware that some more final rift had occurred between Mr and Mrs Montis, Bella was pretty certain he wouldn't join their march that day, although his interest in the whole PRG question had indefinably quickened. He'd even talked to her with great kindness about the irrational guilt she and her daughter shared over Phoebe's plight – fear that they had transmitted the stunted gene. That, he had said, was impossible. Her fear, he had said, was just an evidence of her love, proof of its intensity. And so, now, she dared to ask him again whether she might not join them.

Reggie was adamant. He had the excavation to mark out. But he wished the family well. He did not, Bella noted, ask for any message to be passed on. 'You'll very likely see the Wellspring if you stay,' she called as she went into the kitchen to pack their picnic lunch. Reggie, wondering how to wedge his grid into the boot of the Morris, having filled the back up with tools, find bags and tarpaulin, gave a vaguely benign nod. His mind had many occupants.

The sun splintered on the sea, then again on the cobbled stones of Chandler Street. Reggie's eyes filled with fragments. Oh, God, no! Not today!

Standing at the boot of his car he immediately – without water – swallowed two of the tablets Dr Cassidy had given him for migraine. As the doctor had promised, they made him feel very stupid and queasy. Still, better that than the pain. He fumbled for the dark lenses that he clipped to his glasses when the need arose.

He was too late, of course. The light had already delivered its sharper volleys. He turned his face away from the deep shimmering stripe of sea, and as he did so heard a faint medieval piping and drumming.

For a moment he supposed it was all part of the migraine syndrome; then he realized that was ridiculous and stood, head down, listening to the distant sound. The intervention of a flute drew him. Rapidly, hand to his eyes, he walked across the lie of the hillside through the narrow alleys that unwound into Harbour Street.

Bunting fluttered between the flashing upper storeys. Whole families hung from windows, watching the crowd below. Through unreliable eyes and tight-packed shoulders he saw the shifting figures of the band, hopping and spinning as they played. Sprigs of blossom were stuck in their hatbands, bobbing sprays of blackthorn and apple. They looked for all the world like a spinning mass of flowerheads.

The players were dressed in white full-sleeved shirts and breeches, with scarlet tabards worn over them, and ribbon and bells at their knees. Behind them, slowly, followed another group. Reggie, pressed against the chemist's window, stood on tiptoe. He saw a bier pass above the heads of the crowd, bearing a prostrate figure veiled from head to foot in white, the gauzy stuff strewn with petals and leafy garlands. She was carried, this dead or sleeping queen, by stooping women in black. At least, he thought they were women, but as he wriggled downhill, closer and closer to the harbour itself, the women began a wailing that made the people laugh. Not only a contradiction to the gaiety of the music, it was also a mockery of moaning itself. The black-robed women were unnaturally large, unnaturally broad-shouldered. Their bowed faces were white-painted, mouths and eyes grotesquely enlarged with black and red. Painted on each white cheek of the bearers nearest to him was a swollen droplet of artificial grief.

Unresistingly, Reggie was swept down with the crowd to the harbour, his eyes closing from time to time to prevent the

241

lasers of light from finding his brain. Already the sensation of molten jelly inside his head was being aggravated by the pulping beat of the music. Silently, he prayed that the ergotomaine would start its counter-attack very soon. Meanwhile the noise and the light punished him.

Fluttering open for a second, his eyes beheld Phoebe standing on a wall above the curving strip of harbour as the mourners passed between himself and her. With difficulty, he looked again. Thin, prismatic rays sprang from her face. He pressed both hands hard against his eyeballs this time. The source of the extraordinary light, he was sure, was a single, authentic tear stealing down the child's cheek.

There were cries ahead. Officials, trying to keep order in the crowd, were forming the spectators in a semi-circle round the mainland end of the harbour. The dancers, musicians and mourners, bearing their wind-fluttered corpse, wound on round the curving causeway of the harbour wall until, reaching the far end where the customs shed stood, they turned to face the crowd – the band halting first, piping the cortège on.

Slow and measured in their movements, the eight black figures wheeled to face the water. The music slid into a melancholy key. Breezes played with their black robes. The white faces were raised, mask-like features distinct across a hundred yards of glittering dark green water.

As the white gaze transfixed the crowd, a silence fell.

Then, slowly, those to the rear of the cortège began to raise their burden so that the white-clad, faceless figure they carried appeared to stand upright, resting a moment on their shoulders before abruptly slipping into the water.

At the splash, the cheering began. The laughter. The music renewed itself more vigorously. A further cheer greeted the re-emergence of a sleek head on the surface of the water, and the black-robed figures, hoods thrown back to reveal a white division of face against short-cropped hair, helping their sporting fellow-participant up the rungs against the wall. He stood, his white veils wretched, flimsy, ludicrous rags clinging to his strong body, and took a bow. The crowd called out its appreciation. He waved. The drums were struck. Petals floated aimlessly upon the water.

The raised section of the wall where Phoebe had stood was now occupied by a knot of wrestling adolescent boys. Reggie looked dumbly.

Phoebe, surely, was on her way to London!

The thickness of impact which this realization had, told him that the ergotomaine was at last working. The dry and turgid weight of his tongue confirmed it.

On shambling and heavy legs, Reggie wandered to the outskirts of the crowd. He needed space. He blundered over the stones of Granny's Gate, the stones on which Tolkien had played as a child, had first (perhaps) decided that England stood in need of a mythology.

Reggie gasped at the sea air, unable to explain what he had seen, unable to explain the disorder of his responses, unable least of all to explain why he now returned to Sunnybank, clambered into his Morris and drove, half sensible to London.

Having left his car in a back street in Shepherd's Bush, he surfaced from the Tube at Piccadilly Circus, a stop before he meant to. The squalor, the smell of pickled dill, garlic, cheap wine, charcoal kebab and bodies no longer Englishly odourless made him feel that London was relocated on a different landmass, or was pure masquerade. He was offended by the profusion of souvenirs; bewildered by the incongruity of Asians selling them; dismayed by the ubiquitous wall-display of breast and buttock that seemed to signify the common denominator of the new cosmopolitan mind. Dizzily, he staggered off down Coventry Street, aiming for Trafalgar Square. It was half past three. He sat on the steps of the National Gallery and waited.

At ten to four the front ranks appeared at the north-western corner of the Square, to Reggie's left. Heaving himself painfully to his feet, he leaned over the balustrade, shoulder to shoulder with others. Quite a crowd was gathering in the Square itself. As he glanced down into its well he saw, her body cut off by the angle of the parapet, Stephanie's fragile profile. She was talking to somebody hidden from view.

As Reggie stared, the beat in his heart became as heavy as the synchronous beat in his head. She turned towards the Gallery, towards him it seemed. But in the second it took his hand to flutter at his chest in greeting, her animated face had again turned in response to the unseen figure. His hand dropped and gripped the sun-warmed stone. Then, a ripple of sound, of movement, alerted her attention. She pointed and withdrew backwards, beneath the scope of his vision.

Scrambling free of the throng, Reggie ran down the steps of the Gallery, his head thundering ponderously, and attempted to cross the road. But a line of police was now holding people back until the marchers had passed.

So agitatedly did Reggie bob and weave that he was not immediately aware of the nudging and soft, rustling laughter around him. When the silky amusement reached him he stopped, thinking he must be the image of the foolishness provoking it. But nobody was looking at him. They were looking at Dorothy who, with half a dozen others, led her lengthy retinue of dwarves and midgets.

She passed him, her stately, flowing black emblazoned with an orange rosette that burned scarcely less brightly than her hair. Bella, Frank, Phoebe and Daphne, clasping Gary, were to her right. Behind her reached an endless succession of tiny people who waved their banners and raised their fists as if in good-humoured challenge to any who might find them risible. They waddled, trotted, panted and grinned in curious disarray. One man, dressed in blue satin and small, shining patent leather boots, did a cartwheel under Reggie's nose. Reggie, pressing against the formidable navy-blue line, almost wept with frustration.

He tapped a constable on the shoulder. 'Excuse me,' he said frantically, 'I'm one of them.'

The policeman gave him a long, considered look. 'One of them, eh?' He winked and let Reggie through.

He was enveloped immediately by PRGs, two of whom recognized him and seemed to skip, jump and swing their way towards him over the backs of their fellows. Their arrival set off a friendly clamour, surrounding him as securely as any lassoo. Reggie's plan, to slip crosswise through their ranks and down the steps of the Square at its eastern corner, was confounded utterly. Before he could ease himself out of the column, he had been pressed by small hands past the steps and round the corner alongside St Martin's-in-the-Fields. His gaze, dragging wistfully behind him, was rewarded by the clear, heart-shaped impression of her face printed upon a backdrop of milling figures, sunlit water, lions and irregular architectural patterns.

As he was pushed around the final corner into the Square, his spirits soared. The impulse to come here – so strong, so baffling – was providential! Destiny, the flaccid pennant of the sloppy-minded, suddenly became a sprightly flag in Reggie's own imagination – as jaunty as the one that wagged in the weightless skies of the moon.

He grasped the hands of his nearest companions and raised them cheerfully, putting to shame those who stared.

'P ... R ... G ...!' he chanted. 'PRG Power!'

*   *   *

The platform party was already assembled when Reggie was swept into the body of the Square, so elatedly escorted.

Dorothy witnessed his arrival with a mixture of astonishment and apprehension. Bella Pike followed his course with astonishment and affection.

'Well, bother me!' said Frank, nudging his wife and thus, in succession, all the women standing beside her. 'If that isn't old Reggie over there!'

Phoebe didn't even lift her head to look. Her eyes filled.

'Crafty bugger!' laughed Frank, and slapped his immense thigh.

*   *   *

Craftier than Frank guessed, Reggie directed his course against the buoyant current of the PRGs who swirled to face the platform party contained between two carved lions, and presided over by the lioness herself. Reggie took an independent line, away from his leonine wife, searching, searching out the eastern corner for a more beloved countenance.

*   *   *

In stunned, reciprocal salute, he raised his arm.

'Hi!' shouted Gilbert above the babble.

'*Gilbert!*' his father mouthed silently. Gilbert stood where he'd believed Stephanie would approximately be. There was no sign of her. Frightened by this second experience of dubious sighting in a single day, he stood still in the crowd, facing the wrong way – facing that is, his son, who struggled to reach him with the good news.

*   *   *

That glimpse of Reggie settled matters for Dorothy. She resolved to make her announcement that very afternoon. Standing flanked by Bella and Phoebe, she smiled at each in turn, then gripped their hands impulsively. 'We'll make this a day to remember!' she promised them and turned again to witness the bubbling, growing lake of faces before her, carefully seeking out her husband's taller form.

*   *   *

But Reggie was at the back among those onlookers of more average build, who were, for the most part, maintaining a distinct gap between themselves and the dwarves, as if their difference needed emphasizing.

'I thought you'd decided against,' said Gilbert, who was keeping himself in this corner for sheer convenience, as he was on duty in Casualty at five and needed a quick escape route to Gower Street. 'It's great you came, anyway. What a turn-out! Every form of dwarfism represented . . .' He stared greedily at the clinical variety, too intrigued by it momentarily to tell the good news. A film crew, all three members of it linked by wires, passed in front of them, crouching. Pigeons hopped on and off their shoes as if searching their turn-ups.

'Anyway,' grinned Gilbert, about to pronounce, but stopped by his father's worried expression.

'Gilbert?'

'Yes?'

'Did you . . .? Does the name Stephanie . . .?'

'Stephy! You know her, of course. She was here a second ago.' He looked vaguely behind him as if she might still be about. 'I sent her off to find a safer place. She oughtn't to get wedged in a place like this.'

Reggie swallowed and stared, open-mouthed, following his son's directionless searchings of the balcony above.

A preliminary whining started up on the speakers, and Gilbert promptly spun round to listen. He'd shaved off his moustache and embarked on a beard, just as wispy.

Bella Pike, announcing herself as the regional secretary for Wessex, began a short and nervous address, emphasizing the need for funds. As she struggled to master microphone and notes, some of her words were lost to the gaping air, but she drew forth·approving rumbles all the same from her well-disposed, sun-sweetened audience.

Reggie tried one or two perfunctory turns in her direction but swivelled away again to keep up his more urgent surveillance and avoid direct light in his eyes. However, his attention was instinctively twisted by Dorothy's strong, challenging voice. He turned, dazzled. Out of a large, hazily rainbow-rimmed disc, Dorothy's voice loomed. There was no escaping the sound, since it travelled at him, overlappingly from four different directions, but Reggie's listening apparatus was in abeyance as he turned again and scanned the balustrades.

'Today . . .' (eloquent pause) 'I became a grandmother!'

'Good God!' cried Reggie, spinning twice and missing his hold on Gilbert's arm first time. Dorothy had got through in one. 'Good God, me a grandfather?'

Gilbert was laughing, as his mother's voice boomed on. 'Talk about a public announcement,' he cried. 'Well, she beat me to it. I was trying to tell you. Boy. Eight pounds nine ounces. Tell you more later.' And he stretched his neck as if to hear better. Reggie remained stubbornly the wrong way round, trying to look for Stephanie and telling himself that no grandfather, however new-minted, should be seeking out girls of Stephanie's age. Then, reminding himself that there was nothing the least impure about his search, he continued it.

A single gasp was released by four thousand throats.

'What! What was all that?' Reggie spun on his heels. His son looked rigid with shock, and stared straight ahead of him, ignoring Reggie's tuggings.

'Eh?'

'Shush.' Gilbert's concentration didn't break. Reggie became aware of a terrible stillness in the crowd as his wife's disembodied and cavernous voice echoed over it.

'I have taken this step to demonstrate to the entire nation . . . from my infant grandchild, newly born this very morning to the most elderly and longest-established of our leaders . . . the appalling dangers.'

'What step? What's she talking about?' Reggie hissed vainly at Gilbert's elbow.

'Of the future that is planned for us. The non-future!'

Non-future . . . non-future . . . non-future!

The emphatic phrase swung from one angle of the Square to the next.

'Jesus Christ!' breathed Gilbert. At last his ashen face was turned on his father. 'She's inhaled plutonium oxide!'

Reggie stared back.

'She's done it . . .?' he quavered.

The two men remained enmeshed in one another's gaze for a second, transfixed like the rest of the crowd, doubly transfixed as the dim roar of the traffic and Dorothy's minatory address encircled them.

Reading his father's face, Gilbert saw that Reggie had possessed prior knowledge of the revelation, and Reggie, interpreting the unvoiced realization, watched his son's features engorge with accusation.

'I didn't believe her! I didn't believe she could!' he whispered. And ducking the punch that came towards his already tender head, he wailed, 'I don't believe her now!'

Gilbert, diverted, looked again in Dorothy's direction. A faint hissing was being generated around father and son.

'. . . pledge myself mentally and physically against this threat to the yet unborn.'

'She looks perfectly all right,' declared Reggie defensively, although he couldn't see anything clearly. But he felt quite safe, assuming that anyone suffering from plutonium exposure would not be in any state to march two miles and address a large public gathering.

Gilbert was trying to judge for himself, growingly aware that his scrutiny was being shared by several members of the police force. His mother looked pale, though no more pale and certainly far less distraught than those immediately beside her. She raised both arms in wide invitation.

'Let us *all* pledge ourselves today! Without violence we shall none the less find dramatic ways of making our voice heard! However humble our influence, however lowly our station!'

The crowd was murmuring its way towards a consenting roar.

'*We . . . shall . . . be . . . heard!*'

Each word came like a transfusion of energy which accumulated and mounted in the tight-packed corpus of the crowd. The roar swelled. Arms were raised in answer.

'Yes . . . Yes . . . Yes . . . Yes . . . Yes . . . Yes!' cried the great Square, and the police moved forward in a cautionary line.

'She's not good at lying,' said Gilbert, aside. He sounded doubtful.

But Reggie, privately, thought Dorothy had been putting quite a lot of practice into falsehood of late.

*   *   *

They couldn't get to her.

Dorothy was surrounded by newsmen. She caught sight of Reggie and blew him a kiss.

Reggie was supporting Mrs Pike, who looked faint. 'The risk she's taken,' Mrs Pike kept repeating, 'the risk she's taken . . .' And clutching Reggie's jumper she sank down on the edge of the kerb.

Phoebe knelt down to soothe her. 'It's all right, Granny,' she said. 'It won't do us any harm.'

Startled, Reggie glanced at the small, attentive form. What did she mean? That Dorothy's condition was not contagious, or that it wasn't legally embroiling? For the moment he was too preoccupied and harassed to wonder further at the odd remark. He settled Mrs Pike and went to rescue his wife. Gilbert had already reached her and with Frank's help was attempting to clear a path. All around them, uproar.

'No comment ... I have nothing to add ... Nothing whatever to say,' Dorothy was calling graciously to the corral of newsmen.

'Get a taxi!' mouthed Gilbert.

Reggie turned and seized Daphne. 'Can you look after things this end? I must get Dorothy away from here!'

For once in his life he was highly effective.

Before two minutes had elapsed he, Gilbert and Dorothy were seated in a taxi cab speeding towards University College Hospital.

'Oh, good!' smiled Dorothy, hearing Gilbert's instruction. 'Are we all going to visit Antonia?'

'I'm admitting you to Casualty,' replied Gilbert grimly.

*　　*　　*

Although Dorothy kept beaming at Reggie in a very ardent manner, she was passively resistant to Gilbert's more particular attentions. With many sighs, she limply submitted to an examination of various accessible inner membranes, allowed her chest to be bared to the stethoscope, and gave a syringe full of blood without wincing. 'Have you finished now, dear?' she inquired of her son who was dabbing antiseptic on her arm.

'I have not.'

They were inhibited from more frank discussion of her disclosures by the moaning and screaming that issued from other cubicles.

'I'm so glad you came, Reggie,' said Dorothy tenderly. 'There's no point in anything but friendship between us now, is there?'

'I didn't believe you,' repeated Reggie dumbly for the third time in succession. 'You said *isotope*.'

Dorothy rose to her feet, the long black folds of her robe falling softly about her limbs. 'I'm discharging myself now,' she informed them.

'I want to know the dosage,' said Gilbert tersely, pen poised over his notes.

'Now stop fussing. You can't do anything about it. I shall go and see Antonia in Maternity.' She held out a hand to Reggie. 'Come and see what you make of your grandson, darling.'

'Just a minute!' Gilbert raced round her and placed himself squarely between Dorothy and the exit.

'There's no antidote,' she said and tugged more firmly at Reggie's hand. 'Anyway, you can't stop me leaving.'

'Bleep me if you need me!' called Gilbert to the student nurse regarding this family scene with the imperturbable wryness of her profession. And he plunged up the dark, sloping corridor after his parents.

'You'd better come back with me tonight,' Reggie was urging his wife. 'God alone knows who's after you.' He was thinking of the law.

'You forbade me,' Dorothy reminded him teasingly, 'ever to cross the threshold of Sunnybank again. Bella, you will recall, may not like it.'

Unaccustomed to this serenely affectionate manner, Reggie wavered, still drawn along by Dorothy's hand.

'The *dosage*!' pressed Gilbert, panting up the corridor.

'I shan't be arrested,' Dorothy reassured the pair of them, speaking over her shoulder and crossing the street to the Maternity Department. 'Small amounts go missing all the time and they can't trace a specific quantity to me. They wouldn't want to. Think of the fuss.'

Gilbert sprang on the kerb ahead of her and maintained a conversation while walking backwards. 'Your chest is affected,' he said. 'Not badly, but these things don't show up dramatically at first.'

'I am expecting you to say you could find nothing amiss, and everybody will assume it was a stunt of some kind.' Dorothy began to climb the steps.

'I've already entered it,' Gilbert skipped up the steps sideways. 'Look, mother, you could become very ill.'

Dorothy's nostrils flared with exasperation. 'I know that, you silly boy! Second floor is it? You're awfully quiet, Reggie.'

'I just didn't believe you,' he said yet again, 'or . . . or I'd have stopped you.'

'That, of course,' declared Dorothy, holding her long skirts up so as not to trip on the stairs, 'is precisely what the British nation will say when the first serious nuclear accident occurs – which is why I should have been extremely cross if you'd stopped me, Reggie. You would have spoiled the exact point I am trying to make.'

'Very, *very* ill ...' repeated Gilbert, leaping like a marionette on his skinny legs.

'I fully expect,' replied his mother, pausing between flights and thrusting her purposeful jaw upwards, 'not only to become ill, not only to become very, very ill ... I expect to become dead. Well, we all have to die sometime. Better to die to some effect.'

Gilbert's left breast emitted a shrill bleep. 'Shit!' he cursed, thumping himself. 'Don't let her out of your sight, Dad!'

Reggie and Dorothy entered the ward of milky women.

'How super of you both to come!' shrieked Antonia, sitting bolt upright in bed. Her chestnut curls covered her head with an unkempt thoroughness that was rather nice, thought Reggie. '*Together*. Oh, that's really great, really beautiful!' And Antonia grew quite moist about the eyes before proudly burrowing after the infant she was determined to call Basil.

'It's a *pretty* name,' she insisted when Reggie demurred, 'if you stop and think about it. *Basil*.'

He found himself unable to think with much concentration about the naming of the object. The great extremities of human experience that had been represented in the course of a single afternoon had left Reggie weakly, broodily philosophical.

The giver and taker of life, he thought, as his wife bent over the puce and irascible baby. The goddess.

'Oochy-oochy-coochy!' burbled Dorothy, uncharacteristically. And as she leaned over the cot, a pendant swung from her neck on a long silver chain. The ankh. It swung rhythmically to and fro. And tiny Basil, new as he was to this world, appeared readily subject to its lulling glitter.

*   *   *

Dorothy was quite intractable.

She sat patiently in the canteen while Reggie and Gilbert argued in fiercely subdued tones about what they should do, now that there was no longer anything that could be done. A political dilemma.

'I wish you'd go away and leave me in peace,' said Dorothy. 'I have a lecture tour to plan.'

'You must tell us what you've done and who you've involved.'

'I don't *have* to do anything of the sort and I don't intend to. I should, however, be most grateful if one of you would call me a cab.'

There was no gainsaying her. Gilbert, the more persistent of the two men, kept being called away to Casualty, leaving Reggie, undefended, to Dorothy's protestations of what was best for everybody.

He thought her mad but magnificent and eventually, to fill a silence, told her as much. She took his hand and held it tightly. 'You do? Reggie, you're a darling! Now go back to Bella. Placate her for me. It's up to her now. I have my own plough to furrow.'

'Don't you mean furrow to plough?'

'It doesn't matter.' She looked at him dreamily.

'You're going to dump Mrs Pike with . . . *this*?'

'She doesn't need me now. She has her publicity.'

'Dorothy, she doesn't operate on quite your scale.'

'Operatically?' Dorothy smiled. She seemed strangely luminescent.

'In a word, yes.'

'Before Gilbert comes back then . . .' She began to move.

'But Dorothy!' Reggie knocked back his chair.

'If you want to involve yourself usefully,' she advised, 'apply yourself to the positive alternatives. The sea, the wind, above all, the sun. Now, if you'll excuse me. I have to go underground.'

'No, no, I'll call you a cab!' He scrambled after her.

Dorothy turned, gently deprecating. 'Oh, Reggie, you really are – well, never mind.' And she swept out.

Reggie fell back in his seat. His head still felt as though a thick, nerveless cortex surrounded it, as though the world and its exigencies were at some unruly distance from himself.

Gilbert returned, having skirmished with his mother in the corridor and lost. He sat pouring surly patterns on the table with the sugar shaker.

'I'll keep an eye on her,' he said.

'I don't know *what* to do,' moaned Reggie helplessly.

'I should go home.'

'I *would* have tried to stop her . . .'

'Oh, I know, I know.' Gilbert was resigned. 'I wouldn't have believed her either,' he conceded grudgingly. 'I should go back to Tidmouth, Dad. You'll have some cooling to do down there. Go on. It's only just after six.'

They regarded one another hopelessly. Reggie got to his feet. 'Will you see Antonia again this evening?' he asked.

'Sure, I'll look her up.'

'Give her my love.'

'Yep.'

They shook hands in a defeated way outside Casualty.

'See you.'

'Yes. Keep in touch.'

*　　*　　*

It was a most beautiful evening.

The light held until he reached the enfolding lines of Dorset. Immediately he felt more peaceful, as though entering a landscape where life's dramas were small, extinguishing flashes on a rolling plain of tonal blues; sea, hill and sky deliciously confused. Pale stars shone in the gathering dusk as he drove crosscountry towards Casterwich. At this slipping hour, in this sweet county, Dorothy's probable death seemed neither so shocking nor so reckless as it had done only a short while before. It became a shadow that would change shape with the sun.

As he turned to join the wider, south-bound coastal road, he looked, out of habit, for the huge white form of the giant cut in the chalk hillside above Cerne Abbas. In the twilight he had to strain to see it. As he peered, leaning dangerously left of his wheel, he realized that it was not the failing light which made it difficult to see the round-headed, naked figure, club upraised . . . The fault lay in the giant's own fading outline.

The luminosity of white had gone. The giant was retreating into his own slope, buried by the day's new growth of grass.

17

'Your . . . *wife* . . .'

Frank took Reggie on one side, shuffling him towards Sunny-bank's rather hot kitchen range. He coughed self-consciously before making a second attempt at broaching the matter. 'Your wife . . . is she . . .?'

Reggie studied the peculiar gestures Frank was making and interpreted as best he could. Conscious that Frank was at pains to keep his broad body between himself and the womenfolk who chattered over their supper at the kitchen table, Reggie responded in a discreetly low voice. 'Not mad, exactly; no,' he replied, hoping that he had construed Frank's forehead-tapping and eye rolling correctly. 'Not *mad* . . .' he dropped his voice further. 'A woman of passionate conviction. Wayward rather than . . . well, mad.'

Frank brought his brandy glass to his lips and leaned even closer – so close, Reggie's own mouth practically touched the other side of the glass. The stove was making him very hot indeed. 'Only I don't care for it.' Frank sipped and swilled the brandy round his mouth thoughtfully. 'I don't, if you understand me right, want my mother-in-law troubled.'

'I understand,' whispered Reggie, glancing round the solid edge of Frank at the three females tucking into potato pasties. They seemed thoroughly over any shock.

'Only it's a bit political for my taste,' Frank went on, his belly pressing Reggie closer and closer to the burning Aga.

'Oh, do stop worrying, Dad.'

Phoebe broke out of the exhilarated chatter at the table. Her father's whispered consultations stopped. Sheepishly, he and Reggie looked at the child.

Her stare was halting. Somehow the two other women assembled themselves behind her gaze and contributed to the force of it. Their eating ceased.

'You just don't understand,' said Phoebe.

'And you do, miss?' Frank challenged his daughter a trifle uneasily.

'Yes.' Phoebe maintained her unblinking stare while stroking the dog on her lap.

In the silence, Reggie wondered giddily what peculiar currents of thought had circulated inside the women's heads since that afternoon. Did they not realize how grotesquely Dorothy was committing suicide? His own calmer sense of acceptance on the drive home seemed nothing in comparison to their tranquillity.

'She's a saint,' Mrs Pike put in. 'A proper saint. Saint Dorothy.'

Reggie gulped. 'She, er . . . she, I think, would like you to take over. As national organizer.'

'Out of the question,' said Frank firmly, releasing Reggie from his torment on the Aga.

'Very flattering.' Mrs Pike hesitated proudly. 'But I've got as much as I can manage down here. There's the Pet Show to be arranged.'

She didn't understand at all, thought Reggie.

'We've agreed to split whatever money comes in,' said Phoebe.

'Split it?' echoed Reggie.

'Half for the PRGs, half for the anti-nuclear side,' explained Mrs Pike.

'Fair's fair,' added Daphne, remarking that it had been a long day and they'd best be moving.

In the gathering of belongings that ensued, Frank held one finger up to the side of his nose and winked gravely at Reggie as if confirming some private agreement of their own.

It appeared that the matter of Dorothy's activities was now closed. No further reference was to be made.

*　　*　　*

On the face of it, that might have seemed difficult, since the newspapers the following morning were full of their hunt for the radio-active suspect. *Leading Nuclear Opponent Vanishes* they said. And *How Did She Do It? ... The Question On Everybody's Lips.*

How indeed?

But the question was not on everybody's lips. Not in Tidmouth, at least. In certain areas, such as the staffroom of Turtledown School, the question was tightly encased behind the teeth. The general, though privately expressed, opinion was that Montis should not be pressed with the embarrassing exhibitionism of his ex-wife, a woman widely known as neurotic, unbalanced and meddlesome. Her involvement of the Orlebar family was, in particular, considered exceptionally tasteless, and the best thing for all concerned (this directive stemmed discreetly from Garsington's office) would be to let Montis get on undisturbed with his term's work until the matter had blown over.

Reggie found his colleagues abnormally occupied with examination-paper preparations, cricket fixtures, Speech Day arrangements and rehearsals for the forthcoming play.

Since Dorothy herself had gone successfully to ground, responding from neither her Hounslow nor her Wapping address, it was extraordinarily easy – once the incident lost currency in the newspapers and a number of editors had been urbanely persuaded that its currency was of doubtful worth – to believe that the most urgent matter of the moment was the means by which Juno was to be lowered on to the stage.

Ned Starkey, the only one of Reggie's colleagues who had actually met the Montis ex-wife and was thus well able to judge the woman's near-hysterical disposition, took it on himself to distract Reggie by pretending a tremendous enthusiasm for the dig that had to be got under way. He actually toiled up Turtle Hill physically on a couple of occasions, and would have gone a third or fourth time if he had felt it necessary. But having seen his friend at work among the boys, the priest was happily confident that the excavation absorbed Reggie's attention totally. It was the best possible therapy available, he told anyone who expressed a quiet concern. And Bella agreed that between them they should find no difficulty in discovering things that would stop Mr Montis dwelling too much.

*   *   *

In the clear light and the cooling breezes of the hilltop, Reggie's mind runs free. As he and the boys kneel, carefully removing the turf, exposing burning white squares, their backs turn brown in the sun. Their faces are paled with chalk. From time to time, they straighten their aching spines and laugh at their own bizarre appearance. Cautiously, Reggie brushes away at the surface. The sweeping sound of the sea, the gentle badinage of the boys around him make happy, careless accompaniment to these few hours he has in the sun and the wind.

With each visit the web of life's close-woven duties slackens a little more. He imagines the people who lived here once and, imperceptibly, he shifts away from his, towards their loop of time.

Descending again to lower earth, he keeps up a punctilious correspondence with those of his family willing to answer, and this is a balm to his conscience.

From Antonia he receives minutely detailed reports in large handwriting about his grandson's development. From Gilbert he receives three letters which, in themselves slowly cauterize. The first, describing the state of his mother's lungs, says they are no worse than is to be expected in a heavy smoker of her years. The second mentions that the details of her blood count have gone missing in the hospital file system. The third refers to a postcard he has received from Dorothy, postmarked Wigan, in which she says she is remarkably well. An infectious scepticism about the whole endeavour finds Reggie susceptible.

Human beings as a whole have a marked capacity for ignoring unpleasant possibilities until irrevocably confronted with them. It is a tendency especially marked among the English — in some Englishmen, most particularly. In one Englishman, extravagantly so.

*   *   *

As it happened, this shocking but steady lapse of interest and belief in her condition suited Dorothy admirably.

'You blew it,' said Anna, as the two of them walked across the rough moorland above Bradford. 'That's the trouble; the timing was wrong.'

'OK, OK. I know, but all the same *why* – *why* don't I feel iller? It's most exasperating!' Dorothy stretched her neck and strode out like a racehorse. There was no point in making lightning public appearances until she was visibly sick. She'd been obliged to lie low for three weeks. May would soon be over at this rate.

'Stephy did warn you. She *said* it would take a few months. These things aren't as instant as people imagine. You blew it.'

'To put it crudely. To put it as they say in the American primaries,' growled Dorothy, 'I came too soon.' She edged ahead, tall and thin in black trousers and turtle-neck sweater, the ankh swinging furiously from her neck. 'On the other hand, it's possible Stephy just didn't use enough stuff. Do you think?'

'No,' said Anna firmly. 'In spite of the resounding silence, you did actually cause a discreet stir in vital places. Stephy says security's been tightened up everywhere.'

'How is she?' Dorothy paused to let Anna catch up. Overhead, a curlew spilled small silver coins of song.

'In herself, fine.' Much more, Anna reflected, the old and spirited Steph she used to be. And yet, in saying aloud to Dorothy, 'She needed to feel effective, be active in a way that mattered. It's done that much for her,' she sounded only harshly grateful, as if she, personally, had deep misgivings about the nature of the rehabilitation. Thrusting her hands deep into pockets of her windcheater, Anna added with less concealed ambivalence that Stephanie hated the job itself. 'Hates testing the poor bloody dogs.'

'Yes. Well, I'm sorry about that. That's the price we pay.'

The two women walked in silence for a little, picking their way circuitously over the tussocky grass. Anna wondered. Had it honestly been worthwhile? In the heat of the moment it had seemed so. Given Dorothy's more constant pressurizing presence, it had seemed so. Now, after three weeks away from Dorothy's blow-lamping impact, she worried whether she had served her sister as she should ... endorsing Dorothy's insistence that Stephanie plead the government commitment to employing a proportion of disabled when applying for the radio biologer job in Winburgh, and carrying through her own part in the scheme. In retrospect it seemed reckless.

'Are you *sure*,' wheedled Dorothy, 'she couldn't lay her hands on a teeny bit more?'

Anna's candid, new-freckled face expressed impatience and then, despite herself, affection. '*No*,' she said. 'You're incorrigible. No, for all sorts of reasons. The risk to Stephy. And anyway, now I've left St Nathan's I couldn't pull that one again. If I applied to take another party of schoolchildren round, it would inevitably alert suspicion. Oh, and all that ghastly, furtive business of picking it up from the disposal bin in the visitors' cloakroom, praying they wouldn't run a thin-gummybob over the school charabanc – all that was horrible. And no other establishment would do. One, because we wouldn't have Stephy on the inside, and two, because Winburgh's security was relatively lax, since it wasn't handling plutonium in any major research. And because *no*! I actually hate what you're doing to yourself. I can't take it as coolly as you and Stephanie. Perhaps I don't feel as passionately as you two that it matters. As an *issue*, of course I think it matters, but I find it hard to believe that the ending of one life, the life of a person I happen to like, is going to gain that much in the end.'

'Don't say that. It's got to. Hell, though! I wish it would damn well *work*!'

'It will,' said Anna dryly. Sometimes she was at a loss to know how she could feel so much warmth for this brave and crazy creature. But she did. Linking her arm through Dorothy's, she urged her, 'Be patient.'

'Anyway,' sighed Dorothy, glad of the company and the freedom of the wild, moorland air, 'it's good to see you. And the delay's given me time to get my stuff written up. All the same,' and she heaved a yet heavier sigh, 'I do get incredibly *bored*.'

'*Why* did you blow it? Announce it when you did?'

Sidelong, Dorothy glanced at the younger girl whose arm pressed so close to hers.

'Stupid of me.' She sounded faintly ashamed: a little sad, even. Quizzically, Anna returned the look. 'If you really want to know,' confessed Dorothy, 'it was Reggie. It was seeing him

that day. We used to share such a lot, you know, once —
thoughts, beliefs. And the less interest he showed over the
years, the more outrageous I think I became. Just to *show* him
in a way.' A truly shamefaced smile made her mouth crooked.
'I suppose I thought I was going to win him back somehow.
Instead I just freaked him and that was that. Told me to clear
off.' She ran her free hand through her hair with a brusque,
almost mannish gesture of self-despair. 'And then that day,
seeing him, I thought . . . I thought perhaps . . . Well, anyway
. . .' Her grin became more openly rueful. 'It was a from-me-
to-him, a kind of "I love you" . . . All a waste.' She made a
theatrical flourish of wrist and hand as if melodrama diminished hurt. 'Oh, you couldn't possibly understand. Barmy.'

'No,' replied Anna thoughtfully. 'I can understand.'

'To tell the *absolute* truth . . .' Dorothy was unable any
longer to look the younger girl directly in the eye. 'I'm still
really rather fond of him.'

'Yes,' said Anna quietly.

The curlew ceased suddenly, as if it had run out of small,
sparkling change, and the women walked on in a windy globe of
silence.

* * *

Bella Pike blushed beneath the even, golden powder she applied during the summer months. 'Perhaps you'd better talk to
her, yourself, about it,' she said, a little tight about the mouth.

Reggie was showing a distinct unwillingness over putting
Bundle through her paces at the Pet Show on Phoebe's behalf.
Both Phoebe and her grandmother had several grounds for
thinking it a good idea. Most of all, in Mrs Pike's opinion, it
would take Mr Montis out of himself.

'I *have* talked to her about it,' said Reggie. 'She's really very
stubborn.'

In her own fashion, Mrs Pike, too, was being stubborn. But
obstinacy found less direct expression in her. Employing the
especially indulgent tone reserved for Phoebe's whims, she
murmured, 'Well, if it *pleases* her . . .'

'What of me! What if it doesn't please me!'

Reggie felt himself fall straight into the trap, with all the grace of an elephant. He was mortified by the mean sound of his own voice.

Mrs Pike tried a franker approach. 'It doesn't look good if she goes round winning *everything* herself.' Phoebe had made a number of entries.

'But why *me*?' Reggie's protest was already substantially muted. He could feel submission coming on apace.

'One of those little fancies children have . . . it's rather sweet, really.' Shifting her ground to suit the situation, Mrs Pike acted attorney for her grandchild most skilfully. 'You wouldn't like to disappoint her, would you?'

*　　　*　　　*

And so it came about that, after rehearsals were over and Amis finally satisfied that the smoke bombs heralding the appearance of Ariel would not obliterate Prospero in a choking cloud, Reggie was to be found slinking off for training sessions on the beach with Bundle.

'Heel!' he whispered feebly, unhappily conscious of oblique scrutiny being made by other more authoritative, dog owners. And on the whole, Bundle obliged.

*　　　*　　　*

In fairness to Reggie, it must be explained that his reluctance to act as Phoebe's handler was generated by a change in the child's relation to him that he found deeply unsettling. On their journeys between Lower Knoll and Turtledown he had felt a growing solicitude flow from her. He had become rather tense at the wheel.

'You are funny,' she had said fondly, once.

'Funny?' he'd barked.

'You ought to relax,' she'd murmured, and dared to place a hand on his knee. Quickly, Reggie shifted his leg away from the gear-stick, reminding himself that, behind seeming infant innocence, all manner of strange pubescent leanings might be taking root.

The return journeys presented particular horrors. A good two minutes away from Lower Knoll, his left cheek began to twitch in nervous anticipation of the little farewell kiss she'd become in the habit of planting there.

One evening, yet more disconcerting, he had parked by the cricket pitches waiting for her, and seen her swinging from the metal climbing frame, knees hooked over the bar, skirt flopped over her face. He had waited. She had hung.

'Catch me!' she had yelled at length and, terrified that she might hurl herself off, regardless, he'd rushed to the frame just in time to catch her as she performed a somersault and landed in his arms. She had been as light as air.

Bending to lower her, he'd felt her arms firmly festooned around his neck. The shiny streamers of her hair had blinded his vision. Fighting to unclasp her hands, the word 'Spoilsport' had caught in the coils of his ear. And then, as though the rippling beams of light round her head were as sharp as sunlight itself, he had felt the pain awaken behind his eyes. Fumbling with the visor in the car, he had driven away over the cattle grid as fast as he could, jolting them both like yo-yos. Tenderly, Phoebe had inquired whether one of his heads were coming on.

'Just a bit of a one,' he'd said dismissively.

'Poor Mr Montis,' she had sighed and, raising a small, cool hand to his brow, had promised a spell to make it go.

> *I will be correspondent to command* (she had said)
> *And do my spiriting gently ...*

At that moment Reggie had seen a suitable pretext for ending this dangerous contact. 'Why,' he had appealed desperately, 'don't we practise your lines? Go over them together?'

And suddenly the lovely leafy profusion of June, the delicate roses that threaded the hedges they passed, had sprung forward into sweeter prominence.

After half-term, Reggie had vowed, the only words that would pass between them would be those with the Shakespearean seal of approval.

*　　*　　*

At half-term Gilbert came down.

By tacit agreement they avoided all but cursory reference to Dorothy. Instead, they climbed Turtledown, attacking the hill from its steepest side and picking over the first few finds Reggie had made. Fragments of pottery, which appeared early in origin; rather fewer and less easily identifiable pieces of greenish metal; part of a sheep's jawbone that could be of very recent date. Reggie explained that he was going to ask Norman Herrington if he could use his facilities for dating, talking so eagerly about the difficulties of radio-carbon dating and the need for dendrochronological calibrations that Gilbert was reduced to laughter.

'I don't think I've ever seen you so keen on anything!' he mocked, and he looked over the small, dull load on the tray Reggie held. 'What does it all mean, anyway?' he asked.

'Oh, just that it was used! Not that we've found any post holes yet indicating established settlement.' Reggie was a little disappointed about that, but planned to extend the area the boys, with increasing signs of boredom, were uncovering. He looked towards the doubtful disc barrow sliding below them towards the cliff edge, and his voice thickened with anticipation. 'I'm saving that up for the summer holidays,' he said. 'Just imagine . . .'

He didn't elaborate on what might be imagined.

Nor does he mention to Gilbert the figures he had seen one gilded morning silhouetted on his hill. His eyes are so unreliable these days that it seems unimportant.

*　　*　　*

Wearing the right pair of glasses, he studied, with Gilbert, the small blurred photograph of Dorothy in the *Daily Mirror* Mrs Pile had left appropriately folded on their breakfast table.

'She *looks* normal enough,' declared Reggie, staring at the imperfect accumulation of dots.

There was another letter from Antonia describing the precise intervals at which Basil required food and a change of undergarments. Basil had plainly not inherited his grandfather's recalcitrant bowel. Basil imbibed forty fluid ounces of milk per day, uttered twenty-three distinctly meaningful sounds, and enjoyed classical music: Vivaldi most particularly.

'Is it your impression,' quizzed Reggie, putting aside Antonia's five, loopingly handwritten pages, 'that women do go *on?*'

'She even sounds normal enough.' Gilbert was remarking on his mother's briefly reported speech. Dorothy (as, if in preparation for sainthood, she seemed simply to be known) had addressed the townspeople of Mexborough on the inherently undemocratic nature of modern technical processes, declaring that 'control of the means of production is an unattainable goal when the process cannot be intellectually understood by the operator'.

Whether this had been intellectually understood by the good people of Mexborough was not mentioned. Of more interest to the reporter, Dorothy had refused to elaborate on her alleged exposure to plutonium. The closing comment remarked on her particularly vital appearance.

'Normal, eh?' repeated Reggie dryly.

'Normal enough,' murmured Gilbert, turning to the sports page.

It was nice having Gilbert around.

'Got a little outing planned?' Mrs Pike appeared to clear the plates.

Gilbert said he wanted to swim that morning, and later hoped to get his father away from the hill for a fishing expedition.

'You *make* him,' advised Bella. 'He needs a bit of variety. Gets himself wrapped up in his work.' She scraped the marmalade off the edge of the plates. 'Not,' she added, screwing herself round to see if the paper were still open where she'd left it, 'not to mention your mother.'

'Oh well, Dorothy . . .' Reggie spoke as if the law operating his wife's behaviour was so singular as to be dismissed.

'I think they might have given her a bigger picture. Don't you think she merits a bigger picture?' Mrs Pike inquired of Gilbert. 'It's not nothing she's done after all, is it? She'll very likely,' Mrs Pike concluded with the air of one discussing the effect of woolly aphid on apple trees, '*die*.'

The two men were shocked.

*   *   *

'She's a very simple, trusting woman,' confided Reggie as they went upstairs to fetch their swimming things. 'Teeny bit gullible.'

Downstairs, Bella Pike spouted Lemon Squeezy into the washing-up water and considered the implications of Reggie's forthcoming widowerhood. She didn't think she had ever met a more generous-spirited woman than Dorothy Montis.

*　　　*　　　*

'Ha!'

Dorothy snapped triumphantly at her mirror image.

She swallowed again to test the soreness of her throat and felt a deep satisfaction at the raw sensation, though anyone who had talked as much as she had over the past few days might reasonably be expected to have a sore throat.

So far, the audiences had failed to match the effort Dorothy had put into addressing them, but on that score she wasn't disappointed. She'd made some good points, she thought: technocracy as tyranny; a dispossession of the workers at every level of their existence. They were points that could be polished up and produced anew.

They had been heard thus far by half a dozen workers going off-shift in Attercliffe; up to twenty (if you counted their attendant toddlers) housewives outside Fine Fare in a shopping precinct of Sheffield; a small but definitely interested group outside the Town Hall in Leeds – before she'd been moved on – and a varying, ebbing number of schoolchildren cannoning out of Eccleshall Comprehensive.

People were used to orators with poached eyes announcing the end of the world, and if Dorothy's audiences were small it was frankly because, in presenting herself as a symbol of the coming finale of the human race, she seemed less political than religious. She emanated the eccentric stink of religion.

Dorothy's own conclusion, sensing a yawning withdrawal and seeing the pallid, spotty, grimed and sallow countenances before her, had been that, as long as their reflection was sicklier than her own, her effect was necessarily blunted.

But now!

'Ha!' she pronounced again. Things would soon be different. Would they?

The little gatherings that paused awhile to hear Dorothy declare that the price of prosperity was too great, too exacting to pay, accumulated silent, wistful thoughts of waste extractors; eye-level grills; four-door, hatchback family saloons; ten days in Corsica; blenders with separate speeds for grating, grinding, mincing, whisking and pulping; music decks with speakers complete for £200, easy down-payments; Japanese cameras with which to snap the natural elements this foamy-lipped woman spoke of. Their realities differed from hers. Her eye was fixed on a further future than the one they contemplated, and it was that which made them suppose the alien female was a religious. Modern people all, they had acquired the infant's sense of time. There is only now.

Dorothy peers into the speckled mirror and perceives her future approaching very fast. Soon it will merge with past and present. She swallows and feels a roughness. She presses a finger along the yet unsunken line of her cheek. 'Ha! Ha!'

The sacrificial beast has, by long tradition, been the plumpest of the flock.

*   *   *

By what unfathomable transference did Father Starkey speak of sacrifice, as he bobbed horribly up and down in a mackerel boat that afternoon?

Perhaps he'd been thinking in preparation for a sermon next Sunday; perhaps he'd subliminally glanced at the *Daily Mirror*, in which his lunch-time pie and chips had been wrapped; or perhaps his thoughts were prompted by Mrs Pike's asking him to give up his Saturday afternoon to supervise the collecting ring at the Pet Show.

Whatever the catalyst, he rode high at the stern of the boat, proclaiming to its indifferent owner, Mr Cocker, to Reggie and Gilbert who unwound their lines, that the ritualistic peak of most mythologies and religions was embodied in the act of sacrifice and that what distinguished Christianity was the lamb's willing proffering of itself.

He paused. The waves were uncommonly large so short a distance out of harbour.

'Hold hard!' bawled Mr Cocker at the tiller. Mr Cocker wore a very new reddish leather jacket which didn't look the least nautical. It certainly didn't go with his little denim cap.

Reggie, grabbing Bundle under one arm and the side of the boat with his other hand, wondered how long his stomach would tolerate the motion of the water. As the sea flung itself over them, he ducked. Through dripping glasses he saw Gilbert howl with delight. Ned was sitting upright on his bench, speaking soundlessly, water trickling from his chin. Mr Cocker, feet planted squarely on the deck, rode the swell like a sea-creature in spite of his unlikely garb, and made an encouraging gesture to Gilbert, who then realized that his line was being pulled to some purpose.

At the end of the long, thin, yellow cord, racing through the green-glass current, a fish twisted.

Hauling rapidly, Gilbert swung his catch in the air, a flapping, threshing, iridescent prize.

Father Starkey's exposition on the equation of giving with receiving was cut rudely short. 'Oh Lord!' he moaned. 'I loathe this bit. Wait till I've close my eyes, would you!' And he averted his head as Mr Cocker, his neat moustaches pointing both ways above a grin, smashed the head of the mackerel on the rim of a bucket and flung the shuddering fish inside.

'Terrific!' whooped Gilbert. His lean form, stripped to the waist, was already tanned. He was not unmuscular but neither, thought Reggie wistfully recalling a time thirty years before, did he carry a scrap of unnecessary flesh.

'Is it all right to look now?' Father Starkey parted his fingers and allowed one eye cautious survey through the gap.

'My turn now!' Reggie rolled his sleeves up further and looked overboard to see if his line had miraculously tangled in a mackerel's mouth.

But Gilbert caught the next and the next in quick succession.

'You want to change over sides,' advised Mr Cocker.

'Anyway,' Ned howled at the wind, 'the point I'm getting round to . . .' But he couldn't any longer recall the point he was getting round to. The sun flew off the water and he pondered dimly over his lost thread while Reggie and Gilbert, crouched and swaying, made to swap sides of the boat. 'Anyway,' Father Starkey started up again, unwilling to lose any opportunity for a chat, 'what do you young chaps at medical school *really* think about euthanasia?'

Ned Starkey never received an answer to his question. He suffered a mighty buffet from underneath the boat as they struck a large wave crosswise on. He sailed through the air, landed in the bowl of bait which then (containing the priest) skidded into the bucket of mackerel and flung a number of fish skywards before they flopped back upon him and deposited silvery scales all over his soutane. 'Oh my golly! Oh my gosh!' babbled Father Starkey, and began banging wildly at himself, before realizing that some graver situation transcended his own.

One moment he saw Reggie, Mr Cocker and Gilbert all leaning over the side of the boat, tipping it unpleasantly. Then Reggie disappeared.

'Mother of God!'

'Dad! *Dad!*'

'Man the lifebelts!' roared Mr Cocker in a passable imitation of the nautical, and then looked around for the relevant objects.

The canopied wave that had raised the boat and flung Father Starkey among the dead fish had, at the same moment, hurled Bundle overboard.

Reggie, robbed of his breath by the icy cold temperature of the water, robbed of his glasses, conscious through a fast-travelling film of water of a receding brown and white patch, suddenly felt dreadfully weighted down by his clothes. But he didn't pause. He struck out. Intermittently blinded by fresh onslaughts of salt water, he seemed to gain on the small, pleading head. He swam with slow, relentless strokes.

Mr Cocker swung the boat and sent the lifebelt skimming through the air. It fell just short of Reggie's head. The swimmer, oblivious of the efforts to help him, swam clumsily on through a cruel weight of water.

All around, other boats, sighting an incident, began pulling towards him – at some distance yet, but forming a constantly narrowing ring.

Father Starkey prayed aloud as the lifebelt flew a second time.

Reggie saw it smack the water a little to his right. To his left, the pathetic upturned triangle that marked his quarry.

Do not approach till thou dost hear me call.

He heard quite distinctly. He swam on.

'The crazy bugger!' screamed Mr Cocker, thinking of trade.

'Give it to me!' Gilbert snatched at the rope, but Mr Cocker fought him off. 'Hold on to the tiller, for Christ's sake!' he ordered.

Father Starkey silently endorsed this involuntary petition.

The throttle was fully opened. The boat gained on the two blobs that marked the water like buoys over lobster pots. 'We'll get him this time!' yelled Mr Cocker.

*   *   *

One arm round the small, but threshing form, Reggie first paddled desperately with the other to keep the pair of them afloat, then made a successful grab for the lifebelt.

. . . appear and pertly.
(he heard through the crash and race of the water)
No tongue! all eyes! be silent.

He nearly lost his grip on the dog, but then grabbing her the more fiercely to him, he hooked his right arm through the lifebelt and felt himself cleave the green glass as narrowly as the mackerel had before him.

Be silent?

*   *   *

Gilbert pumped his lungs out. A rough towel hung about his head. Weakly, he took the towel and began to rub the trembling Bundle. He looked at her giddily.

Be silent?

Reggie slumped against the comfortable arm of Father Starkey until they reached harbour. There he stumbled up the rungs on to the safe and steady stone, conscious of his photograph being taken.

'Can you hold the dog up a bit, sir?'

He held Bundle and stood a second, unable to discern anything.

Gilbert propelled his father towards the car and drove up Harbour Street, cursing the limits of the ancient engine.

Mrs Pike took in the crisis at a glance and, guiding Reggie into the kitchen, began removing his clothes.

'Hold on . . . hang on!' he demurred, still clutching Bundle to him.

Phoebe was there, resembling – if that were the right word – a sultana, her head bound in a huge towelling turban. Gravely, she stared at him.

'Oh, Mr Montis,' she said.

The facts, tersely reported by Gilbert and Father Starkey, were punctuated by gasps from Mrs Pike while she stripped Reggie of his vest. 'Go and fetch grandad's dressing-gown,' she ordered the mesmerized Phoebe. 'Quickly, Phoebe!'

The child deposited a kiss on Reggie's cheek and ran off.

*   *   *

Later, the return of warmth to his body paining him pleasantly, Reggie sipped brandy by the Aga. Phoebe's own drying hair rose like radiant gauze around her head as it was bent over Bundle's recovered form. Her grandmother remarked how very nice Reggie looked in Edmund's dressing-gown.

'I think I might lie down for a bit,' said Reggie, excusing himself at length, and he allowed Mrs Pike and Gilbert to pack him comfortably on his own sofa upstairs. After the landlady departed with promise of supper in an hour or so, Gilbert wandered about, looking for something to read. He found *The Magic Flute* and put it on. 'Jeez!' he said after a little of the overture had crackled by. 'You've played it to death.'

'Probably needs a new needle,' murmured Reggie sleepily. He was feeling lovely now.

*   *   *

The congratulation, the concern, the sweetly scratchy music all conspire to make him feel content, until the more melancholy lyricism of the famous duet begins, and first Pamina's voice, then that of Papageno, strive to make him understand the transcendent power of human love. Something of Reggie's contentment seeps away. He is, he knows, more ready to receive than give.

Not even receiving is easy.

He thinks of the two glowing girls. And what has he done with that lesson Stephanie so subtly taught him? With that identifying sense of tenderness for the damaged?

Nothing.

Resistance, that old, wilful bush, has stubbornly flourished again and put its thicket between him and the world.

Rescuing a *dog*!

* * *

The three boy trebles brought Tamino to the Temple of Wisdom.

Gilbert looked at his father. He would have liked to talk to him about Stephanie, this strange, elusive, lovely girl he'd met. But she'd so passionately insisted on his silence. He forbore.

Anyway, he glanced at his drowsing parent – mouth open, thinning hair tousled – interruption would not be welcome now.

Be silent.

As though the end of a particular action must be reached before he could speak of her. He lay on the harshly patterned carpet and thought about Stephanie.

The insight came to him like a blow on the head!

He sat up suddenly.

> *Bald prangt, den Morgen zu verkünden*
> *Die Sonn auf goldner Balmx!* sang the boys.
> (Soon the sun shall herald morning,
> In all its splendour gild the sky
> Then, clouds of superstition parted,
> Wisdom shall the victor be!)

Ah yes ... Reggie experiences a moment of purest understanding. True, maybe ... he has been used to prepare Stephanie for another. Another lover. But the corollary of that, the part which has escaped him before, and now, like a piece of music, reveals its symmetry, is the knowledge that she, in her turn, has prepared him ... For what? Another love? For something, assuredly.

He glimpses a higher, more selfless plane of loving than anything he could ever before have imagined.

*   *   *

As Tamino's swiftly executed ordeals began, Reggie slipped to a profound, exhausted and exalted sleep.

The angel, who had once hung in the air above his bed, returned. Less dusty now, her gilding palely gleaming, she resumed her guardianship of Reggie.

18

In the breeze that ruffled the cliff edge the yarrow and thrift waved sturdily without bending. Below, the sea had again become seductive, moving easily into the shapely elbow of Wimble Cove.

It was very early.

Reggie moved in a dream still, not wholly awake. Or perhaps he was still in a mild state of shock. He had wondered whether the glittering expanse of water, so deceitfully gentle, would now terrify him, whether he could approach the edge. Warily, arms outstretched, he neared the barrow. His fingers were trembling.

But it was not the weird lure of the sea that drew him. The pull came from the earth itself. He crouched, wobbling slightly.

*   *   *

As if responding independently of him, his hands fall to the grass like magnets. His nails tear at the sacred mound. He scrapes and claws till his nails bleed.

I am mad, he thinks, and is momentarily glad that Matravers, Biddle and Simpson are not there to see him.

Then he fell full-length upon the blemished mound. Mockingly, the sea sucked and discarded the shingle.

Hearing a soft laugh some distance behind him, Reggie turned his head sharply, only to drop it swiftly back upon the grass.

Upon the path, some twenty yards away had stood a naked man with sculpturally whitened hair. Small clusters of comets fried on Reggie's eyeballs as he paused, head down, before daring to steal another look. He drew breath, steadied his focus, and boldly looked again.

Nothing. Only the fecund green downland and, above it, the unfractured blue.

This was not the first time he had glimpsed things which later proved not to be there. Something odd was happening to him. Reggie lay on the breast of turf that had dragged him to it, and attempted to collect himself. Even without glasses, even with the incipient distortions of migraine, it was not easy to mistake a naked man for anything else. The startling dark triangle with its pink appendage was not to be confused with a certain brief style of swimming trunks, nor even, at the extreme of possibilities, a sporran.

Very well. If a man had stood there, he must still be about. It wasn't an easy matter to elude the eye in this exposed landscape – no, not even the throbbing eye of an unspectacled onlooker.

He rose and climbed up to the path where the figure had stood. He looked west and saw only distant sheep, though it was conceivable that something or someone could hide in the deep troughs of the ditches. First, though, he advanced eastwards.

Aha! Small figures scrambled up the beach of Wimble Cove. Whether or not they were decently clad, Reggie wasn't competent to judge, but the possibility of bathers using this early hour to enjoy their dip in the nude was not in the least unreasonable. He was quite happy with this solution, and closed his mind to the stiffened white hair and the gold torc that had lent the figure its singular aspect.

Comforted, he turned back towards the cliff edge, knocking his left foot against a small object which flew sideways, vanishing in a clump of nettles. Gingerly, Reggie picked about inside the stinging leaves and retrieved a small fish-hook made of bone. It had a delicately barbed edge.

He stared incredulously. Surely it couldn't have surfaced unnoticed from his own digging which, at its nearest, was fully ten yards away from the path? Turning it over in the palm of his hand, he saw that it was not only well made but also that it showed no sign of staining or encrustation. It conformed to the common prehistoric pattern.

Twentieth-century bathers, nude or otherwise, did not carry primitive fish-hooks, so it must, however surprisingly, have come off his site. He marvelled at its quality of preservation.

He was delighted to have it. He put it in his pocket and attempted to override any residual feelings of unease.

*   *   *

'Can one hallucinate with migraines?' Reggie carefully inquired of his son, who was busily erecting rope and stakes around the main ring.

'You can fall flat on your face, become partially paralysed, or see Frankenstein in a fur jock-strap,' snapped Gilbert. 'It depends on the patient's basic disposition in these matters.' He was irritated by the fact that his father had slouched off, leaving him to Mrs Pike's gently expressed demands. 'Here, hold this while I bash it!'

Reggie did so, dodging slightly, but relieved.

'A man on a bicycle, saying he was from the *Wessex Gazette*, called. To see you.'

'Rather fat?' inquired Reggie. 'Reddish eyes, walrus moustache, no chin?'

'Yep.'

'That'll be Flash Harrison.' Flash Harrison was the local reporter.

'I said you'd be here.' Gilbert sounded a trifle accusatory.

'He's probably looking for someone to give him the results.'

*   *   *

But Flash Harrison wanted more than that. He wanted a scoop.

'I hear . . .' he said slowly, his melancholy eyes and drooping moustache concealing any excitement he might nurse in his bosom, 'I hear – not to put too fine a point on it – that you, in a manner of speaking . . .'

'Get on with it Flash, lad!' urged Ezra, who was meant to be constructing the Gents but couldn't help overhearing. 'I hope they don't appoint you court reporter on the Day of Judgement.'

Unperturbed, Mr Harrison resumed at his own error-free pace '. . . that you went so far yesterday afternoon, that would be' – and he wrote it down – 'Friday, June the ninth.'

'Yes, yes,' muttered Reggie, swallowing two migraine tablets.

'You did?'

'I – er – mean "yes" with a question mark.'

Mr Harrison appeared to write this comment down, too. He was very thorough.

'You risked your life to save a dog.'

'You make it sound extremely dramatic,' Reggie remarked sarcastically.

'Would this be the dog?' Mr Harrison pointed his pencil at Bundle, who was sniffing the newsman's cycle clips.

'I'd like to see you interview the dog!' interrupted Ezra gleefully. 'Go on, Bundle, give him an exclusive!'

'Have I got my facts right so far?'

'Not really. I'm a competent swimmer.'

'Only I'd like to do a splash on it.' Flash Harrison surveyed Reggie gloomily.

'Oh, a splash! I like 'ee!' Ezra banged a tent peg with amusement.

'I do beg you not to.' Reggie's vision darkened slightly. Or maybe a shadow passed over the summer green of the primary school playing field.

'I've got a photo.' Flash Harrison held up a picture of somebody Reggie was obliged to believe was himself . . . a plump, wetly gleaming figure. An elderly, gasping seal with a dog lashed to its stomach.

'Please,' begged Reggie. 'I haven't the time.' And he began, without direction, to stumble away.

'I'll check my copy with you later,' promised Mr Harrison, writing laboriously.

*   *   *

Dufferdill, having enjoyed a long grumble about the 'frightful Budgie Wenn' with Frank, was now, in turn, having his ear bent on current meteorological peculiarities. 'They say it'll be drought again this year. T'ain't normal. To my mind it's all that weapon testing and such is affecting the climate.'

'Wouldn't surprise me,' agreed Dufferdill. 'Wouldn't surprise me at all. What can they expect if they fill space up with Dinky toys and nuclear junk?'

'Ah!' cried Frank. 'Here's our dowser friend. There'll be need of you, Reggie, yet.'

'Oh hello, Montis.' Dufferdill hoped his colleague had not overheard the word 'nuclear'.

'Look,' he said hurriedly, 'I want to put my dog in the Best Trained Class. Useful practice, but I will of course be *hors concours*. He's a quality dog; don't want to spoil the competition for others.'

Honeymill Golden Bowl, otherwise known as Bucket, wagged his ponderous tail.

'Trained by the Duke of Buccleuch's kennelman. I may have told you that before.'

'Yes,' said Reggie.

'Anyway, don't regard me as a rival.'

'No,' said Reggie, his voice growing fainter. A large black bird nested in his brain. 'It'll just give the other chaps an idea of what to aim for.'

'That's right,' volunteered Frank and added how much he fancied a gun dog, himself, or would, if it weren't for the fowl he kept. Reggie swayed off, trailing Bundle. The band was tuning up. He reeled away from its tooth-extracting noises.

As he turned, a white horse reared in front of him, its amethyst eye familiar. Out of a sparkling gold cloud, Phoebe's voice descended. 'I'll be willing you on,' she called. 'But I want to win Best In Show myself. If that's OK.'

'Of course,' assured Reggie, unable to look up, so tightly was his head bound.

'I say!' Father Starkey bounded anxiously into view. He was sweating slightly and clutched three clipboards. 'Are you sure you've recovered from your ordeal? You don't look too stunning.'

'Fortunately,' Reggie attempted a smile, 'it is not I who am to be judged.'

'Well, not *today* maybe.' Father Starkey ticked Reggie's name off. 'Look, I've marked you as "present in collecting ring". Please don't go away.'

'My class isn't for another hour yet!'

'No, but I feel happier with you ticked. Don't be a spoilsport, Reggie. Ah! Mrs Pike! All well, I trust?'

A number was being tied to Reggie's arm. Then he observed the gaily floral rear of Mrs Pike as she bent to the grooming of Bundle. 'It's a very unsettling twenty-four hours she's had,' her owner was saying fretfully. 'I do hope she doesn't let us down. Who's a pretty girl, then?' She straightened herself and smiled at Reggie. 'I wonder if you'd do the peas-in-a-jar for me till it's time for your class?'

'But Ned said . . .'

'There we are, dear!' She thrust a jar of dried peas into the bend of Reggie's elbow and a notebook into his pocket. 'It's 5p a go!' she told him and bustled off.

'How many peas in this jar, Ned?' bleated Reggie, wobbling after the black form of his steward. And then he treated himself to 30p.'s worth of guesses to keep the takings up.

*　　*　　*

The band was well into a painful rendering of *Moon River*. A group of PRGs invited from other districts passed by, lathering Reggie's thighs with candy floss. After several false starts, the loudspeaker announced the Best Trained Dog class, and Reggie fell into the wake of Dufferdill's relatively distinct form. 'Just do what I do!' roared Dufferdill, sweeping through the donkeys, goats, sheep and Shetlands exiting from the Pet with the Most Personality class. A small boy seemed to be caught in the stranglehold of a python, but Bucket was setting a tremendous pace and Reggie flew past the child.

*　　*　　*

His tongue had acquired the taste and texture of Bombay Duck.

Retrieving Bundle from the forceful attentions of a Dobermann Pinscher, Reggie only dimly heard the judge's instructions to the lined-up class.

'*Heel*, you stupid boot!'

That was Dufferdill bawling at the hapless Bucket, who was so excited that his pedigree line was beginning to tell against him. Through half-closed cracks, Reggie saw Dufferdill lurch across the grass at the end of a lead, trip, and, dragged on his back, disappear from focus.

'Heel! Stay! Come here, you bloody animal or I'll shoot you!' Reggie heard.

The crowd, appreciating this original interpretation of a gun dog's function, applauded Bucket loudly. Another contestant was hastily being waved into place by the judge's assistant, and seemed to execute the test at lightning speed – or was, perhaps a very small, very miniature kind of a dog, for Reggie saw nothing, and was now desperate to know what succession of commands he was meant to give. Bundle sat patiently watching a bull terrier trying to psych the mind of a fellow competitor's owner by thrusting its nose up her tweed skirts.

The woman with the Dobermann was nudging Reggie. 'It's you,' she mouthed, and he tottered off in a state of terror.

'Er-r-rgh,' he moaned at Bundle, who trotted quietly to heel. 'Er-r-rgh,' he tried again. And she sat firmly on her behind, looking up at him for further instruction.

'Er-r-rgh,' he offered, and deduced from the look in her eye that he was meant to walk backwards several paces while she remained where she was.

When she winked, he uttered his omni-purpose croak again and she ran up to him, neatly tucking herself up at his feet. It was extraordinary. Head throbbing, Reggie gurgled a further time and felt his arms spring to his pocket. From thence he withdrew a rubber ball which he threw across the ring. Impeccably, Bundle bounced after it, bounced back, and dropped the ball between his toes.

Bending to pick it up, the blood rushed into Reggie's brain. He fainted.

*　　*　　*

Flash Harrison was kneeling over him, licking the stub of his pencil.

'Oh, do go away,' moaned Reggie.

'A memorable performance,' said Flash as slowly as if he were dictating it.

'Not now!' Bella Pike hove in view, a flowered ground which

slid over Mr Harrison's chinless visage. 'You won!' she said, beaming down at Reggie. 'I've got your rosette. *Who*'s a good girl, then!'

* * *

'You need a bloody full-time nanny!' Crossly, Gilbert took his father's pulse. 'I don't think I've got sufficient qualifications to look after you properly.'

Phoebe approached. 'Here's looking at you babe!' she said, squinting down at him. Her thumb was significantly up. 'It worked,' she declared and vanished again.

Reggie closed his eyes and wondered if – in a genuine hallucination – the naked man would have been elaborately stained with blue woad.

'The heat,' said one voice.

'Delayed shock,' said another, and Reggie drowsed off while the angel spun slowly, revealing a tri-form countenance, the revolving unseamed profiles of Dorothy and Stephanie and – good gracious – Bella Pike.

* * *

'Where are you off to?' Gilbert peered thickly out from under the sheets of what had been Stephanie's bed. He'd been late getting to sleep, shifting what he'd thought was a lumpy pillow about his head, only to find, at about three in the morning, that the trouble was caused by a stray pebble.

'I've got to go to Turtledown.' His father's anorak so bulged with tools and equipment that his form filled the entire doorway. He had an air of emergency.

'Jeez! It can't be . . .' Gilbert lifted his watch to his nose, and found that it could be daylight. It was five-thirty. 'Bloody funny time to go,' he grumbled.

'Couldn't sleep.' Reggie fidgeted.

'Hurling yourself over the edge this morning?' inquired Gilbert and then, more dutifully, 'Are you sure you're all *right* to go?'

'Of course, of course.'

'Well,' said Gilbert doubtfully, pulling the sheets back up to his chin, 'take it easy'. As his father sprang round to leave, he called after him, 'Hey, look, I've got to get on my way myself this morning.'

'Oh?'

'Yes, one or two ... Thought I'd call on some friends in the area before I get back to town.' Gilbert had decided he was going to track down the sisters who were, he knew, in the vicinity somewhere. Their evasiveness about a precise address now seemed very significant to him.

'Good idea,' said Reggie vaguely. 'It's been splendid having you here.' He meant it sincerely, but the need to be on his way was very impelling.

'See you, then.' Gilbert slumped back.

'See you. Love to Antonia. And *Basil*. Oh, and your mother – if she turns up.'

*   *   *

He drove past the deserted gardens of East Tidmouth. Bright bouquets of wallflowers, peonies, poppies and roses sparkled under a crystalline dew.

The downlands, too, were thinly wired under a brilliant net of gossamer. It promised to be hot but, for now, the earth was rested and sweetly vigorous. The birds were mad with joy.

As Reggie's feet crunched along the white paths his heart kept peculiar pace, as if trying to run ahead of him.

The winter-long sense of being watched was delicately altered. No longer assessed, he was elect. But novitiate still: being prepared. If, that is, he understood Stephanie's function correctly.

On the opposing slope of the eagle cliff the single shadow of a small cloud was shiftingly pressed like a flower. Above the dense cluster of oak and beech and field maple that covered the ruins of Maidenwell below him, a spiral of smoke arose.

Reggie hummed, confident that he, an unimaginative man, could not be imagining things.

Inside his pocket nestled the bone fish-hook.

*   *   *

Having removed his anorak and sorted out the tools he needed, he stood above the mound, arms upraised, both hands clasped about a knife. Poised for a moment, like a priest before the ritual altar, he then dropped his arms, fell to his knees and pierced the earth.

The movement transmitted a sense, not of slaughter, but of liberation.

The knife flashed through the turf. The sea moaned. And Reggie began his dissection of a tomb already half-lost to the malevolent green waters waiting hundreds of feet below.

*　　　*　　　*

'Ah-h!'

Dorothy woke, her chest shafted by pain. Protectively, her hands flew to her left breast.

Then her mind cleared, translated the pain. Thank heaven, she breathed. At last.

Pain energized her movements as she dressed, preparing to ambush the earliest communicants at Coventry Cathedral.

*　　　*　　　*

The sun rose to its burning height while Reggie worked. His back ached and would, later, blister. His arms and face were white with dust. From time to time walkers passed along the path and paused, then moved quietly on, silenced by the concentration of the kneeling figure.

The nipple of turf at the centre of the barrow was uncovered, revealing a little cairn of stones. Each one was removed gently from its thin bed of soil. Scraping, brushing, bit by bit, Reggie cleared the darker area beneath. Its outline, measuring some two feet by four, was plain. Working in six-inch squares, he had, by noon, removed a depth of three inches. Still he went on, dry with thirst but too absorbed to stop and sip the water he'd brought with him.

In spite of the care he took he knew he was working too fast to be as systematic as he should, but nothing would induce him to stop now. His hands were drawn deeper and deeper into the little grave.

*　　　*　　　*

Crickets chattered. The skin on his shoulders burned luxuriantly as the observer sun began its slow and rolling descent to the west.

The grave was now cleared to a depth of two feet. Something protruded from the earth. Nervously, Reggie drew a plastic tray alongside him. The need for meticulous care was now paramount.

A sudden weakness assails him. He stretches upward for a moment, easing the compacted vertebrae, drawing air deep into his lungs. Far away, the sheep bleat.

Half fearful of disappointment, he begins the lengthy process of brushing.

*　　　*　　　*

'You must be very tired.'

John Pargiter, one of the younger curates at the Cathedral, drew Dorothy into a pew and made her sit down. Evensong was over, but the organist had stayed on to practise a Frescobaldi toccata.

It was pleasantly cool inside the building. Here and there figures flitted about, quietly removing the plate, snuffing the candles.

'You set up quite a rival camp today . . .' The woman, he thought, looked ill. Violet shadows enlarged her eyes.

'Rival?' she murmured. Sutherland's sacrificial Lamb of God gazed into the world he had tried to redeem. 'No, not rival,' she said, and smiled bleakly. 'Thank you for not moving me on.'

John Pargiter studied the hollowly beautiful face. So this was the 'Dorothy' of whom he'd heard rumour. 'Well,' he acknowledged, 'we seem to have a mutual interest in the saving of souls.'

'Souls!' cried Dorothy with a more recognizable (to us) note of angry derision. 'It's not the life hereafter so much as the life here *and* after us I'm concerned with.'

'Oh, me too! Look!' His pale, bony face alight with sympathy, the young man took her hand. 'Why don't you come home and meet my wife. Let us give you some supper. It would be a privilege for us.'

Dorothy stared at him a long time as the organ music rippled richly behind the screen. 'Yours *is* a much nicer generation than mine,' she sighed at last. 'Worth saving. OK, I'd like to come.' And she swung her bag on her shoulder with the carelessness of a schoolgirl.

*   *   *

In the dying light Reggie sat back on his heels and studied the brownish litter of bones. Once sorted out, the assemblage would probably amount to a full human skeleton, but as they lay now, packed in a formation maybe three thousand years or more old, they looked an obscure bundle of faggots. In the refulgent, coppery light, they glowed dully, promising little. And yet his excitement ran rapturously high. The bones presented a puzzle.

A disc barrow, if such it was, suggested early to middle Bronze Age, say 1400 BC. But a disc barrow would almost certainly contain an urn burial with ashes inside it, not bones like this. On the other hand, there were inhumations of a slightly earlier period – associated with the Beaker people, but they were generally buried in a foetal position, not in this sort of disarray, though it was always possible that a land shift had disturbed them. As Dufferdill had once pointed out, there were few burials of any kind in the Iron Age; bodies then were presumably exposed or thrown in rivers. The only inhumations of a later period – round the second century BC – were connected principally with the Arras culture of northern England and had no parallels in Wessex.

Reggie stared into the small pit as the light faded. He went over and over the possibilities. It might be a secondary burial, of much later date than the original barrow, but its central position under the cairn argued against that.

The sea below him was curiously pale and attentive as if awaiting the outcome of his thinking. But it was no good. He had a mystery on his hands, and the only means of solving it was to dig further and find whatever telling fragments might be concealed beside the bones.

Insanely weary as he was, he would have gone on digging, but a gibbous moon now floated on the green easterly sky. He must end. He removed a small sliver of bone that might help verify a date, and drew a tarpaulin over his gentle desecrations.

A few birds still flew about, but silently. Mere shadows.

As Reggie walked stiffly away along the darkening ridge of the hill he could faintly feel the current in his hands. In his present dazed state it resembled an entreaty not to leave.

Below, in the blue gloom of the valley, a fire glowed amid the trees of Maidenwell.

A beacon seemed to be lit.

*   *   *

'Clotted my bottybook rather!' joked Dufferdill uncomfortably as he caught up with Reggie when the latter scurried into school on Monday morning. Reggie looked at his colleague abstractedly. He was wondering whether Garsington would let him have the afternoon off and loan him a few boys to take up to Turtledown so that he could press on with a bit more digging before Norman Herrington arrived at seven o'clock. He hadn't been prepared for quite such enthusiasm on Herrington's part. It seemed crucial to make haste.

'Made a bit of an ass of myself,' Dufferdill continued, accelerating his own pace as they plunged into the sudden dark of the corridor. A few boys ran off tittering.

'Oh? That!' muttered Reggie vaguely.

Dufferdill strained to look into Reggie's face. 'Hope you're feeling better,' he said. 'Only I felt, well ... the wife said I ought ... Hey, you little toads!' And, relieved that the apology was performed, Dufferdill chased after the miscreants.

'Yes, yes, much better,' Reggie murmured to himself. Actually he was feeling most peculiar. Too much sun on the back of the head.

Herrington had promised to take the bones back to the BM for analysis. 'Don't rush at it,' he'd warned in the friendliest way.

*   *   *

But it is no good telling Reggie not to rush.

His brain crawls. His fingers itch.

*   *   *

The faithful trio – Matravers, Simpson and the rosy-mouthed Biddle – watched Reggie draw the exact position of the bones, then helped him number them and rearrange them accordingly in a cotton-wool bed.

'Good thing you didn't bring your dog up here,' observed Matravers, brushing most professionally. This made the boys giggle inexplicably. Then Simpson, tow-headed and daring, with a permissory look at his friends first, said, 'Oh go on, tell us about the bait old Daffodil got himself into.'

While he continued scraping at the vacated area of the interment, Reggie obliged and guiltily enjoyed the laughter he provoked.

'This person,' remarked Simpson, a split appearing in the seat of his trousers as he bent to his work, 'if it is a person . . . hasn't got a head.'

Reggie didn't reply. A hard, curved shape was beginning to emerge.

As he worked on it, the boys kept up a barrage of questions which he barely answered. 'Is it our size, sir?' 'How old is it, sir . . .?' 'Will it haunt us do you suppose, sir?'

'Look!' Reggie sat back on his heels and pointed at the sizeable fragment of dark, coarse pottery.

Briefly the boys gave it their attention but, finding bones more interesting, soon returned to their own job. As the sun burnt through his shirt, further inflaming his tender shoulders, Reggie turned the pottery ware over and over thoughtfully. 'This could be the significant find,' he said with some nervousness.

The boys looked at him doubtfully.

'Doesn't look very significant.' Biddle wrinkled his nose and sniffed with an ugly contortion of his face.

'It could,' said Reggie slowly, 'give us the age of the bones.'

'How?' they wanted then to know.

As he continued his digging he explained, but he lost his audience. Soon the boys were lying down. Next they were playing laser warfare behind the trenches. Then they were thirsty.

More fragments of pot were unearthed.

'Can we go for a swim, sir?' The plump Biddle looked

particularly hot after his campaign. 'I *think*,' he wheedled, 'I must be getting sunstroke.'

'Oh, very well.'

Reggie kept up his brushing, and heard them disappear with a whoop down the steep slope to Wimble Cove.

Not until twenty fruitless minutes had passed was he struck by his dereliction of duty. Dizzied by heat and continual bending, he reluctantly covered his work and made cautious pursuit of his charges. A swim might really be quite pleasant.

The sea was the colour of jade. It curved invitingly into the cove. Faint splashes reached his ears as the boys leaped froggishly in and out of its mild folds.

Reggie skidded a little, twisting his ankles dangerously. One couldn't afford to look beyond one's feet on this awful slope. So he sat a minute, resting and enjoying the now familiar view: the protuberant Toot, sporadically clad by gulls, the vanishing headlands, each more deeply blue than the one before, the white fans of limestone and then, inland ... his roving eye halted for a second.

The river bed, which ran down the valley through Maidenwell and out into the sea near the Toot end of the cove, gleamed with water.

Reggie rubbed his eyes and looked again. It could not be.

But the twisting line of the river glinted in the sunlight.

He rose and scrambled down, staring firmly at his feet on the slippery grass, then ran across the flattened stretch that reached as far as the river. When he arrived at its edge and looked down, it lay as dry and wrinkled as it had been these past ten years or more.

It must have been a mirage.

Taking advantage of the spot which was shielded from the boys' view by a shelled stone cottage, he stripped down to his underpants and picked his way over the finely pebbled sand to the water.

The boys, some hundred yards further up the beach, yelled and waved. Through water so clear he could see flashing shoals of fish part before him, he swam towards them. It was wonderfully cold, wonderfully bracing, a different element from the one that had cursed and thrashed him only three days before.

'Packed up for the day, sir?' asked Matravers hopefully, jumping boisterously up above the water and sinking. He re-emerged, slung the licks of hair out of his eyes and reflected that he didn't think he *would* be an archaeologist when he grew up. 'Although,' he added politely, dog-paddling in a circle round his friends, 'it's very interesting of course, sir.'

Reggie stood up, waist deep, and felt weed slither past his shins. 'What *are* you going to be then?'

'I'm going to be rich, sir.'

'I see,' said Reggie solemnly and dived beneath the water, opening his eyes on a flurry of bubbles. He surfaced. 'I've come to collect you,' he said. 'We're meant to be working.'

They groaned and promptly crawled in different directions.

'Come along!' he called a little impatiently. But they wouldn't go until they'd climbed the Toot.

*   *   *

Sportingly, hoping no one would catch them in their under-pants, he struggled up after them. From the top he looked back towards the river. And again it shimmered. Where his clothes had been a woman crouched, scrubbing hard at her washing.

The woman, her theatrically crimson linen, the gleaming river, all evaporated as he skipped and ran down the uneven Toot.

His eyes were playing tricks, but he clambered back into his trousers calmly enough. After all, he had read only the night before that the washerwoman toiling over bloodstained garments was the Celtic image of death.

As an unimaginative man, Reggie presumed that he had not previously been open to visual projections of this nature. Now, his brain teeming with dreams and mythologies, he thinks such perceptions must be common among the livelier-minded.

*   *   *

The refreshment afforded by the swim was completely can-celled by the uphill climb. Sweating and breathless, he regained the summit moments after the boys, who had gone up like goats.

Biddle knelt beside the grave. The other two stood over him.

'Look!' Matravers beckoned hastily. 'Quick, sir, look!'

Tufty-headed already, so swiftly did his springy hair dry, Biddle was squinting at a thin black piece of metal in his hand.

Too short of breath to shout, Reggie ran.

Biddle saw his expression and lowered his hand surreptitiously. 'It was showing and I just pulled,' he said. 'Sir! It just came away.'

Reggie seized the corroded metal from him, his breath coming in harsh gasps. 'My God!' he whispered. 'Biddle, you're . . . you're a wicked boy!' And he sat down sharply. 'I think,' he said at length after handling the black and pitted piece of iron wonderingly, 'I think this may be of great importance. *Great* importance. Now show me *exactly* where it was.'

It could be embarrassing having to explain this to Norman.

*　　　*　　　*

Norman Herrington arrived an hour after the boys had left on their walk back to school. He came striding through the banks in a shirt that clung damply to him and a pair of black and white check trousers the flies of which were undone.

'A causewayed camp!' he shouted, as if critical that Reggie's drawings and descriptions had not made this obvious fact plain. In other words, a neolithic structure probably intended for animals and, later, more vigorously fortified by other peoples . . . All this he managed to outline in a loud voice before arriving at the graveside with a heavy thump as he bunny-hopped from the shelf above. 'Phew! Didn't bank on quite such a walk.' Again criticism was implied. He wiped his forehead with a creased paisley cravat, and tried to sound more civil. 'Fine place! Fine place indeed! Now then, Montis, what have you got for me?'

No time was wasted on conversational preliminaries, Reggie noted. Norman had clearly been as intrigued as himself by what little he'd had to say over the phone. He sat back on his heels, silently awaiting Norman's reaction.

For a long time the portly archaeologist said nothing as he

bent, turning over and patiently considering the finds. Eventually he directed his perplexed countenance towards Reggie. 'And you say you found these objects together? *With* the bones?'

Reggie nodded.

'Very odd.'

There was another considered pause while the sea whispered beneath them.

'Very odd,' repeated Norman Herrington. 'What do you think?'

'I think it's very odd, too.' Reggie reserved any detailed opinion.

Picking up the largest piece of pottery, Norman classified it as part of a globular, finger-furrowed jar. 'Almost certainly late Bronze Age. What shall we say, for convenience? 1000, 900 BC?'

Again Reggie nodded, the excitement at his throat making his Adam's apple quiver.

'And this?' Norman picked up the curved-edge fragment of blackened metal. 'Looks suspiciously like part of a carp's blade sword. Made of iron.' The two men regarded one another evenly. 'In other words, you would normally expect to find a gap of say, at least a century, between the two objects.'

He sat himself more comfortably, hands resting on splayed knees, while a doubtful frown spread over his features. 'Well,' he said at last, 'I thought the bones sounded puzzling enough. I didn't expect you to have provided me with additional mysteries by the time I arrived ... You're *quite* certain they all came from the same level?'

Avoiding reference to Biddle's excavation, Reggie assured Norman that they had. The man's authority, which became formidable once he was professionally engaged, was comfortingly diminished by the small bulge of crimson Y-front peeping through his fly.

'Quite a hoard in twenty-four hours,' said Norman meaningfully.

'Beginner's luck,' Reggie apologized.

Norman shook his head. 'If we're thinking in terms of between 1000 and 800 BC, this form of burial just doesn't add up.'

He looked heavily round the grassy area of slip on which they sat. 'Not unless it's a secondary or satellite burial, and it doesn't appear to be. But no. You'd expect either an urn burial or a different sort of barrow to fit the facts better. Or no barrow,' added Norman.

'Or no barrow,' agreed Reggie, determined not to be caught out on any of the possibilities which Norman now began more expertly to expand. 'Naturally, when there's been as dramatic an earth-shift as this, one expects a confusion of levels. Equally, inhumations, however rare, *are* known in that broad period. Still,' he added, almost crossly, 'the only genuine Hallstatt inhumation documented in this country – apart from a possible at Beaulieu – is in Yorkshire and *that* one . . .' He picked up the six-inch fragment of sword again and examined it as if seeking forgery. 'I was going to say, *that* one, the Ebberston inhumation, contained two swords broken – ritually one supposes – into four pieces.' He glanced up from his careful scrutiny. 'I'm not sure, that's to say I *can't* be sure at this stage, but it's conceivable this too, was deliberately broken. It's not a clear case of corrosion. Still,' and he put it down briskly, as if putting fancies from his head as well as his hand, 'the bones. Their number and their disposition pose a number of equally fascinating questions. The thing to do', and he lumbered to his feet, brushing his trousers, adjusting his fly – 'is simply to see what more we can find. This calls for a fuller-scale excavation altogether.'

'But do you think,' begged Reggie, almost beseechingly, 'it could possibly be, well, culturally transitional? I mean, could it?'

'*Could* be.' Norman re-assumed his academic guard. 'We'll have to get these things properly looked at. The important thing,' he stressed with a warning flicker, 'is not to have a theory and then attempt to demonstrate it.'

'Of course,' said Reggie quickly, 'but you seriously think it *could* be?'

'Let's wait for a clarification of the evidence, eh?' Norman allowed himself a smile of mean encouragement, the kind he might reserve for a promising student. Reggie did not mistake the professional superiority. Not only his shoulders burned.

Turtledown was his. He rose. Softened by lengthening shadow and gentle light, he felt protective of his hill. Norman Herrington was not going to rob him of it.

*   *   *

Norman had other ideas.

Towards the end of the week he rang Reggie at school.

'All right, you lucky chap,' he conceded in a squeezed sort of voice. 'You may well have stumbled on a critical site. We could be seeing a unique example of transition – or even clash – between two cultures. But if it's as important as I think it might well be, then I'm sure you'd be the first to agree we can't leave this in the hands of schoolchildren. You need expert help. I'm quite certain I can raise a rescue grant to do the thing properly, clear the site completely, and really set about it the way you'd like best.'

He went on in a growingly confidential flood of programming, almost, but not quite, persuading Reggie that he, too, naturally wanted nothing more than a full-scale professional assault.

As he held the busily quacking telephone away from his ear, Reggie could think of no respectable argument to contradict Norman Herrington.

They were in this together, Norman was assuring him; might bring Reggie a bit of kudos in the archaeological world. They could prepare a paper jointly and publish it in the AA's journal. He, personally, was prepared to give up his summer vacation to the job.

'That's most kind,' said Reggie with difficulty. His mouth was dried out by an impotent fury, for he knew that Norman was right. If the site was as crucial as he believed, then only the best scientific minds, technique and equipment would do. But he felt the intrusion was unholy. His passion for the hill was barbarously threatened.

'What about my bones?' he intervened. 'What about my bones?'

'*Your* bones? Ha! Ha!' A hollow laugh crackled up the line.

293

'I'll have the report through soon. Let you know the moment it's on my desk.'

And with that Reggie had to be satisfied. He smouldered for the rest of that long, humid day, handing out a number of black marks that were quite undeserved.

Nor was his temper improved the following morning on receipt of a postcard from Norman Herrington – a colour reproduction of the Battersea shield – which said: 'Think it wiser to halt excavations until possibility of rescue dig confirmed or otherwise, Yours, N.H.'

Yours! crowed Reggie sardonically to himself.

Oh yes, *mine*.

19

The new season's drought gripped the country in its yellow palm.

On the news, the sheep-farming moorlands of the west were described as wastelands. Civic ponds evaporated. The emergency measures the government had failed to take the previous year – believing it was against all calculable odds that two such summers should succeed one another – were angrily demanded by an electorate at last able to understand that this freakish weather was neither a Continental bonus, nor a limiting inconvenience, but a serious peril to its food and livelihood.

Steel and other associated industries went back on a three-day week. Breweries were laying off men at a stricken rate. And all the while the bald sun beamed on the cracking earth like an escaped, demented beast.

Weird stories of the way it affected behaviour were recounted.

While dogs lay panting in the shade and farm animals stood paralysed on the huge, hedgeless acres of baked pasture, certain human animals seemed activated by the heat. Perhaps it merely shortened tempers, perhaps more alcohol was being drunk. Whatever the aggravating factors, the cities saw more unpleasant incidents that June than was deemed normal. Three black youths were killed in the fun-fair at Southend; the home of an Asian family was burned to the ground in Southall; a man flung open the door of a reception room at the Dorchester and shot eight relatives at his nephew's wedding; the testicles of a known homosexual were received in his lover's post. Less gruesome, but more widespread, was the rage of those laid off, who took their injury on to the streets, and there, on occasion, were discovered mingling oddly with the lines of little people flowing in the wake of Dorothy as she extended her tour of the industrial Midlands.

'It's gathering strength,' observed Bella Pike with satisfaction. She stood at Reggie's shoulder, reading the paper, a duster tucked into her waistband. Reggie sat at his table in the bay window, wildly scribbling notes. Whenever he could free himself from the hectic midsummer school schedule he devoted himself to pre-emptive notes on the Turtledown dig. It was the only way he could fend off Norman Herrington's assault. All the local libraries had been ransacked to help expand his testament of love. For it was no less than love he felt. An ardour spilled out of him which was occasionally capable of seizing all damaged and vulnerable creatures in its flow. It even, when thus prompted, lapped briefly around Dorothy.

He turned and peered at Mrs Pike's lowered paper. 'I do begin to worry for her,' he murmured.

'Worry by all means,' conceded Mrs Pike. 'But don't attempt to stop her. You can't. She's got to do what she's set out to do. That's what destiny's all about.'

Reggie marvelled at the resolution in his landlady's voice. He also wondered – having the parallel example of Norman Herrington so close to mind – how she could bear to see her PRG crusade wilfully usurped in this manner.

As if sensing his query, Bella Pike smiled. 'She's doing her job. I'm doing mine. Regional organizer – it's another job that's got to be done. And truth to tell, we're doing very nicely.'

Reggie took the paper from Mrs Pike and skimmed the newsprint. Dorothy (in the words of the report) was taking her struggle to the industrial heartland, however cool her initial reception. That was the true arena.

To judge from the accompanying photograph, she seemed now to have drawn strong support from a section of the Church. They, her strong core of PRGs, her growing band of ecologists, the politically disaffected from all parties, and the student lobby were made to look extremely numerous in the photograph. But perhaps they were confused with the car-component workers, and aerospace employees all hailing from the same area. There was a footnote to the story about a breakaway group of militant dwarves attempting to force an entry at Dounreay.

'I really ought to try and see her,' Reggie burst out. If only, he reflected in silent afterthought, to put an end to all this madness.

Bella Pike studied her lodger judicially for a moment, then seized his head and pressed it to her pinafored stomach. Twisting in his seat, Reggie listened to the kindly gurgles of Mrs Pike's workings and dwelt on the remarkable flatness and firmness of her body.

'There, there,' she was murmuring. 'You mustn't distress yourself. If you saw her you might feel wrong-headedly bound to try and stop her. It's all for the best, you know.' She released him a little to gaze into his eyes and he was overcome by the unwonted intensity of her expression. 'That would never do,' she said quietly. 'Anyway, you have your own work to complete.'

'*My* work . . .' he began to protest, his head now forced to her hip.

'. . . is of the utmost importance,' she averred.

'No, no, you mustn't exaggerate its importance. It's . . .'

But Mrs Pike wouldn't permit argument. She hushed him as she might a distraught child, and rocked him to her until certain he was pacified.

*   *   *

Later, he found himself marvelling at her power of intuition. Oh, he'd told her a little of Norman Herrington's intervention, but it took a remarkable woman to understand the full, sharply painful possessiveness he felt about his hill, the urgent need he felt to get his speculations down before they could be accredited to somebody else, simply because his name carried more weight.

Still, as he'd come to recognize over these last months, apart from her infuriating habit of talking all the time the television news was on, Bella Pike *was* a remarkable woman. She could detect his moods, anticipate his headaches with an animal keenness. At times she was able to utter the very words he was about to pronounce himself. And yet she achieved all this without his suffering any sense of trespass.

Reggie sighed and bit into the Chelsea bun Mrs Pike had brought with his coffee, then, encouraged by her belief in what he was doing, continued with his introductory chapter on the changes in burial form between the time of the Beaker people – the presumed builders of Stonehenge and other circular monuments – and the later Celtic or Iron Age period.

*   *   *

It was clear (he had written) that, whatever the more extravagant astronomical claims made by some writers in this field, a solar cult was definitely observed during the second and third millennia. The circular barrows of the succeeding Bronze Age (together with further building at Stonehenge circa 1500 BC) indicated a continuing form of this worship. Because of its otherwise impractical siting, its lack of settlement evidence and its absence of fresh water, he was inclined to think that Turtledown was itself a ceremonial centre. Its position certainly afforded a natural observation for the sun's passage across the skies.

The additional fortifications (and here he was bordering on recklessness, since he had done no digging to prove the point) were consonant with activities of a later date, namely the increased defensive activity common throughout southern and western Britain from 1000 BC. This was demonstrated not merely by hillforts but also by the abundance of bronze spearheads and other weapons traceable to the period. What made Turtledown of particular interest was the fortification of what could only be a ceremonial place or shrine, thus indicating that the native peoples felt their religion to be as severely threatened as their livestock and homesteads.

While acknowledging Professor Colin Burgess's point that the deterioration in climate and widespread flooding around this period probably had its effect in persuading people to turn from sky gods to water gods (and certainly there was considerable Iron Age evidence to indicate water burial), climate alone could not – he had argued – create such a substantial change in religious attitude. When cultures underwent conquest or absorption, it was normal for religions to develop syncretically. But there was reason to suspect that the change of belief between Bronze and Iron Ages was nothing like so fluid.

Reggie continued:

My case for positing this view rests on what may seem very limited evidence: a single burial. But the finds made at Turtledown in Dorset crystallize within one grave the long-held suspicion that the break between Bronze Age and Iron Age cultures was particularly abrupt and violent. That is not to say that elsewhere, in other regions or later phases, there was not a relatively smooth transition to the 'industrial communism' that grew out of the use of the new metal, but we certainly know from their artefacts that the iron-working invaders were a pronouncedly aggressive, warring people. Driven here by desperate pressures of population on land-use in Europe, heavily armed, it is reasonable to suppose their incursions were characterized by violence. The Turtledown dig gives weight to this supposition.

Judging from pelvic and femural evidence, the skeleton found in the grave was that of a woman. The use of a disc barrow, normally associated with burials that pre-date the bones by half a century or more, is also, of course, linked exclusively with female burials and is extremely hard to account for. Nevertheless it may help us to conclude that the skeleton was indeed female, although there is alas, no skull which would decide the issue far more clearly.

The bones themselves were laid out in a fashion that could be described as derisory. Not only were they jumbled casually together but also there was present a third femur, conceivably that of a male. Most tellingly, the condition of the upper vertebrae implies that the body was decapitated. Furthermore, a sword, placed in the grave, was deliberately broken. All these elements strongly indicate a ritually performed death or, one might more cautiously venture, murder.

We cannot, of course, tell whether the murdered body was buried in haste by relations (hence the confused state of the bones), or whether they were contemptuously disposed thus by the slaughterers. But bearing in mind that the site itself is most probably of ceremonial, religious significance *alone*, it is of interest to postulate precisely what religious beliefs and observances, later superseded by Celtic practices, might have been quelled in this place.

He paused. He put down his pen and drew the returned box of bones towards him. They generated a peculiar tenderness in him. They lay like invalids in their little beds of cotton wool: frail, injured fragments of life.

Hesitantly, he touched one of them, a clavicle, and experienced a curious, tingling recognition. That identifying love for the damaged . . . the finer part of the raging despair he felt for the depredations of his own time . . . the good emotion that Stephanie had bestowed upon him.

*   *   *

It attaches itself to these brown and brittle bones. He cannot understand the liaison, but he knows it to be a real and tangible thing.

He drew the precious reliquary closer.

*   *   *

'Come on then! . . . *How fares the King and's followers?*'
    'Oh, Mr Montis!'
    'No, come on, Phoebe! you're not too hot on the longer speeches, and there isn't a lot of time left to go.'

They drive towards the school through clouds of white dust which hover above the road. It is very strange how Reggie, who planned to repel this child to a neutral distance by substituting Shakespeare's conversations for their own, finds that, instead, he is helping her, liking her. Growing fond of her wit and fragility. He relishes her company.

Phoebe struggled on awhile, then ended with a prolonged 'Um-m-m-m'.
    She smiled as if she could charm Reggie into releasing her

from the task of recitation. 'Have you seen the costume Granny's making for me?' she wanted to know.

'No, I have not. And if you don't make some attempt to master Act V, somebody else will be stepping into that costume you so much admire. Come on now! . . . *They cannot budge till you release . . .*'

Removing a sucked ringlet of hair from her mouth, Phoebe laughed and looked out of the window at somebody's free-range hens standing with wings outspread to cool their armpits. 'Isn't it funny,' she said, 'the way everyone in this play's imprisoned?'

He glanced at her quickly. She was bright. 'Yes,' he said.

'But *everybody*.'

He thought. Yes, everybody. Not just Caliban, Alonso, Ferdinand – nor even 'the good old lord Gonzalo' he was guiding her towards in the text this very minute – but Prospero too.

'Monkey,' he said, 'you're trying to distract me.'

'O-oh-oh!' she yawned and ran through the next lines with the inexpressive speed of a diesel. *'Your charm so strongly works on 'em / That if you now beheld them your affections / Would become tender.'*

'Dost think so, spirit?' responded Reggie with a vigour that made Phoebe laugh again.

'I've got a silvery one and a green one, all leafy,' she said.

'I don't think Shakespeare wrote that.'

'OK, OK. *Mine would, sir, were I human.*'

'And mine shall . . .' Reggie began, then leapt to the end of the speech, *'And they shall be themselves.'*

'Hey, you've missed out masses!'

'I only know the cues.'

'I can't do it unless you say it all.'

'I don't know it all.'

'Yes, you do.'

'Honestly, I don't.'

And so they argued pleasantly until she persuaded him to tell her more of what went on behind the closed doors of the staffroom.

'They're rather like a chorus,' explained Reggie. He swerved to avoid a dust-paled baby rabbit making insane progress across the road.

'What do you mean?' asked Phoebe, puzzled. 'You mean they dance and sing?'

Now Reggie laughed. 'If only they would! No, they keep up a lament, a sad commentary on the world's decline.'

'Oh, well,' she nodded, gravely comprehending, 'there's a lot to complain about.'

*   *   *

One day she had not been at Lower Knoll.

He had waited for ages, more and more troubled by her absence. (That was the day when, peering out of the rear window for signs of her approach, he'd discovered Bundle guiltily curled on the back seat and eventually had taken her to school, where much had been made of her in the staffroom – even Dufferdill, though first announcing that Jack Russells were not a recognized breed, had lowered a rigid hand to be sniffed.) And at break, he had rung Daphne, who'd feigned exasperation with her daughter. 'Didn't she tell you we were going to the dentist's, naughty girl?'

And that was all it had been.

The dentist's! And he had allowed such forebodings to build in him. *Such* presentiments that he would not, once knowing the simple truth, have dared utter them.

*   *   *

Reggie no longer flinches when Phoebe kisses his cheek.

As he lowers his head, offers himself, a new receptiveness steals through his pores, a benign transfusion of capillaries, tissues and unclassified cells. For in what portion of the human body is that human gift of imagination to be discovered?

*   *   *

The dig was covered over, the little toolshed locked. But Reggie found reasons for visiting the cove and the revivifying heights of Turtledown at the end of his hot and weary working days. There were sea sounds to be recorded for the play; the dog to be exercised; a more reverent guard than the Army's to be mounted.

On one such lambent evening Reggie lay on his small private promontory, the dog panting quietly beside him, and, watching the sun burn low at the end of its marvellous arc, he puzzled again and again over the way its function must have been contained in lost imaginings.

Brimful of undirected speculation, he later sank back in his chair while his record crackled softly in the dusk. Then, as the chorus heralded the arrival of Sarastro at the end of the first Act, Reggie sat bolt upright.

Sarastro!

The key to the man's ambivalence came to him. Sarastro, the man who abused the Queen of the Night – not merely abused, but destroyed her as she came to retrieve her stolen daughter ... the man who equally dwelt in the Temple of Wisdom, who was honoured by priests and subjects alike ... He, Sarastro, was persistently identified with eternal brilliance. With the sun, the emblem of ineffable power.

Reggie found himself sitting as rigidly posed in his chair as if Julia Trevelyan herself were taking his photograph. He released his clasp on the bristly arms ... If Dufferdill were right and Schikaneder had reversed the characteristics of the principal figures ... As he sat, Sarastro's sonorous bass addressed Pamina. Reggie knew the libretto off by heart.

> *I will not force thy love's direction*
> *And yet I will not set thee free.*

Will not set thee free!

Sarastro had not merely robbed the Queen of her daughter; he was securing her entire kingdom for himself.

Reggie remained upright in wonderment, his mind racing as the Act ended with the glorious choral promise that, once virtue and justice were restored to earth, then men and gods would be as one.

*   *   *

In the silence, his gaze falls upon the darkened table where his reliquary lies. Slowly, he walks over to it, opens the lid. His fingertips run over the fragment of pelvic bone. The womanly width.

Woman ... Womb ... Sun ... Womb ... Life ... Womb ... Womb ...

The words tumble through his head like beads. Like beads they are connected. Or were, once.

*　　　*　　　*

How dim he had been! So slow in grasping the power of images that he had totally underestimated the profound identification between female and sun. Trembling a little, he looked down on the small remains of his slaughtered priestess. What deity had she served? What deity had been honoured in the great megalithic circles?

*　　　*　　　*

It had always been part of his purpose to examine the mythologies current in other lands during the second and third millennia, to see if their iconographies might help him hazard reasonable guesses about the beliefs in the Britain of that time. The idea of a single goddess he had dismissed as the crude and portly image of earlier, neolithic periods. Since then, the pantheons had become crammed. But now ... Mozart had provided a useful clue.

He would chart the progress of female divinities, note their relation to the sun, and see what vestiges of this relationship remained in Celtic thinking.

And since Mozart had been so fortuitously helpful in this one respect, decided Reggie, his whole body abuzz with plans, well then, he would accept his guidance in yet another. He would start with the very gods Sarastro swore by, with Isis and Osiris, the silent profiles of Ancient Egypt.

*　　　*　　　*

Leaving his recording of the sea in Wimble Cove with the more competent engineers of Lower CE, Reggie went off in search of Father Starkey.

He found him having a practice bat in the nets. 'Ned!' he shouted, 'I need your help.'

'Oh, tricky one, Withers! What, immediately?' The priest had hitched his skirts up and was sporting some fine purple garters.

'Not absolutely immediately.' Clutching the netting, Reggie ducked instinctively as a ball hurtled in his direction. 'With some research work in the evenings. I think we'd make a useful partnership.'

'It's the busy season, old chap!'

'I'm under considerable pressure.' Reggie was frantic to have something completed before Norman Herrington came down at the beginning of July to discuss the revised excavation plans with Major Bittern.

'Hold your fire, Withers, there's a good fellow!' Ned waved his bat in surrender and turned to his friend 'Of course ... If you really think I can be of service.' His broad face beamed through the mesh. His thick, boyishly cut hair seemed whiter than ever against an unclerical tan.

'You really are a sport, Ned.'

'I try,' sighed the Father. 'Now, tell me all about it.'

*   *   *

Although they were quickly expelled from the local library after unrestrained exchanges in the reference section, they did make a useful pair. They retired to Sunnybank with their notes, arranged themselves at opposite sides of the bulbous oak table, and developed their duet without disturbance. Except, that is, for the stealthily regular interventions of Mrs. Pike, who felt they needed sustenance to keep their strength up.

*   *   *

'Isis,' Reggie rehearsed aloud, getting the facts straight, 'is both mother and wife to Osiris. At least, their son Horus, who avenges his father's death, seems to take on the earthly powers or identity of Osiris. He is, I suppose, the chöic version.' Reggie looked up over his new and uncomfortable spectacles. 'All right so far? In later developments, Horus takes over the functions of Re, the sun god and, as Re-Harakhty, appears to gain control over both night *and* day.' He expelled a satisfied sound. 'There couldn't be a clearer pattern of the expansion.'

It was Father Starkey's turn. 'According to Frazer,' he offered, 'Isis was the more important of the two figures – reflecting the matrilineal descent system in Egypt. And I can tell you from my own knowledge of Diodorus Siculus' – he leaned keenly over his papers towards Reggie – 'that he, too, claimed that Egyptian law was based on the pre-eminent worship of Isis. Mind you, a word of caution: our friend Diodorus saw powerful females wherever he went; a bit of a quirk in the man. Ethiopia, even in Celtic Britain! Did you know that? No?' The priest scratched his lower ribs comfortably. 'Found Celtic women far more frightening than the men; so I think we ought to regard his view as a tinsy bit suspect. Caesar gives a far more downtrodden picture of the womenfolk. One poor creature had to serve the needs of all the males in the family. However . . .' He rustled his papers a little wistfully. 'Back to Egypt.'

'Now *here*'s an illuminating connection.' Reggie's turn to serve. 'Hathor – which translates 'House of Horus' – Hathor, who I always thought was a quite separate figure from Isis, is on the contrary closely identified with her. Look, here's Isis, wearing the crown of Hathor.' He swivelled his book towards Father Starkey to show him a photograph of the statuette in the Fitzwilliam Museum. 'Isis bearing the infant Horus and wearing – do you see?'

Father Starkey stared at the sun disc contained within cow's horns. Or he seemed to. Actually his thoughts were wandering. 'It is *remarkably* like representations of Mary and the infant Jesus,' he said.

'Don't be sidetracked, Ned.'

'No, hang on. I'm remembering something.' He thought. 'Yes, yes, Moses and the golden calf.'

'Ned!'

'Baal-worship, you must recall, even so entrenched an atheist as your good self.'

'My dear Ned, I've "done" Moses with 2B.'

'Well, exactly. Baal simply means "lord". Furthermore, it signifies lordship of a temporary nature – in other words, he's a sort of consort, rather like Osiris. And the calf is the female representation: Baalat or Ashtoreth. Now, I wonder how close a relation one can find between Ashtoreth and Hathor.'

They bent to their books again, their search now in danger of developing in two tantalizing directions – back to Babylonian, forward to Judaeo-Christian eras.

The connections between Isis, Ashtoreth, Hathor, Ishtar, Innana and Astarte multiplied miraculously. All were linked through the *hieros gamos*, or sacred marriage, to a consort who either died or was annually put to death. And in the judgement of Professor James, 'Innana/Ishtar, not Dammuzi/Tammuz, was the ultimate source of life and regeneration.'

And yet, at some point in the history of these figures, their power waned or was transferred.

The two men pored over a translation of the Babylonian 'Poem of Creation' written with the clear intention of adapting whatever was relevant in the beliefs of the defeated Sumerians. 'So,' Reggie looked up, crumbs of plum cake at the corner of his mouth, 'Tiamat is ordered by her husband to destroy the younger rowdy gods, her sons no less. But far from bumping off Marduk as instructed, she herself is killed.'

'And is represented as the monster serpent; Marduk as the renewing sun.'

Father Starkey and Reggie gazed at one another thoughtfully.

'The consort rebels,' mused Reggie. 'Like Gilgamesh.'

'Re-enter the serpent,' declared Father Starkey dramatically. 'This serpent gets about a bit, eh?' He flicked over a few pages before finding Pia Laviosi-Zambotti's article on the art of Crete. ' "The emblem of the mother-goddess," 'he read out,' "was the serpent: its coils led to the centre of the earth, from which sprang the supreme generative activity of the mother goddess and into which the Tree of Life, symbol of the maternal religion, sank its deep roots." '

As if expanding a musical theme, Reggie promptly summarized from Kathleen Kenyon's work on the widespread evidence of Astarte plaques found in the Middle East as late as 700 BC. 'She's depicted bearing a lily in one hand,' he said, 'and a serpent in the other.' He picked up another marked reference, this time from Professor Albright. 'The goddess's head is adorned with two long spiral ringlets identical with the Egyptian Hathor ringlets.'

*   *   *

Their reading takes them round and round in circles. They pass through different cultures, different points in time: a journey through a mirrored echo-chamber which mesmerizes them.

*   *   *

It took them two weeks. The approaching deadline made their exchanges more like those of a tennis match between two good, rallying players.

'Danu was ordered by Indra to destroy her son Vrta, thus freeing the waters.'

'Re daily fought the serpent of darkness, known as Zet. Isis is the Greek translation of Au-Set or Ua-Zit, the cobra.'

'The Slav countries observed a solar cult until the Middle Ages ... Jerome of Prague came upon a sect in Lithuania which believed that the smith Telavel had forged the sun.'

'The Finns believed in a smith called Kalevala – who forged the sun.'

'In 274 AD, Aurelian, believing the sun had brought him victory, set up the cult of Sol Invictus and declared that December 25th was the birthday of the sun.'

'In 300 AD, Constantine, after seeing a symbol of the Chi-Ro and the message "*In hoc signo vinces*" imprinted on the sun, declared Christianity the official religion of the Roman Empire and suppressed all worship of Ashtoreth.'

*   *   *

The gradual transfer of power from female to male divinities, the usurping or vilifying of the goddess's symbols – a process which reached its nadir, perhaps, in the adoption of that primitive sun symbol, the swastika – was pin-pointed by Ned and

Reggie (as clearly as such a thing was possible in the tangled gardens they explored) to a period in the third millennium BC, when northern invaders seeped down through Anatolia into the Semitic lands.

Professor Walter Emery, who surmised an earlier date, described a people 'known traditionally as the "Followers of Horus" apparently forming an aristocratic or master race ruling over the whole of Egypt. The theory of the existence of this master race is supported by the discovery that graves of the late pre-dynastic period in the northern part of Upper Egypt were found to contain . . . anatomical remains . . . whose skulls are of a greater size.'

'Whether or not,' observed Reggie, 'Emery has his date right, it's certainly true that the invading Hittites were brachycephalic, broader-skulled than the defeated Semitic people. We also know, Ned . . .' And he looked up at his friend, conscious that a twitch of tiredness, compounded with excitement, was at work in the corner of his right eye, 'that they were aggressive, charioteering people called by some the axe-people.' His voice became tense. 'Kelt means axe. Keltoi or Celts means axe-people. Ned, I have a feeling . . .' And Reggie swallowed, trying to prevent his voice rising a register, 'a feeling that we may have a clear line of connection between the Hittites, responsible for demoting female deities in the Near and Middle East, and the Celts who spread across Europe from the Danube basin. Somewhere, in the Anatolian area, these people, I *dare*, with confidence, to guess, have common root.'

A heavy pause fell between the two men barricaded behind their books.

'It's all speculation,' replied Father Starkey warily. 'We've done no original research.'

'*But . . .*'

'All right, all right.' The priest raised a hand as if gently warding off Reggie's enthusiasm. 'It's a very convincing premise. When is your friend Herrington coming?'

'*Friend!*' Reggie choked but restrained himself. 'Two days' time.'

'We'd better get on with the Celtic side then, hadn't we?'

'If you're willing.'

'Of course I'm willing. Why should I not be willing?'

'Well . . .' Reggie hesitated and deformed a paper clip. 'We seem to have cast some clods at Christianity in passing . . .'

'My dear Montis, my dear *Reggie*, don't you remember my telling you that all myth is an attempt to grasp the truth of the spirit! That what I loved about Christianity was its simple – no, more accurately, *revealed* – confirmation of earlier, complex, confused patterning? That what I *disliked* was its failure, as a whole, properly to incorporate the notion of a mother-goddess? That what inclined me to Catholicism was its gradual repairing of that omission? My old friend, and Father Starkey positively barked with enjoyment, 'if I were an Anglican I would be feeling extremely disturbed by all the material we've accumulated. As it is, I'm more than ever angry that we have secular legislation exempting the Church from charges of discrimination against women – reprieving them from the onus of female ordination – now *there*, if you like, is an unholy alliance of State and Church! But no, I'm not shaken in my fundamental belief in Christ, if that's what you fear – it is, isn't it? On the contrary,' and he leaned over the table to squeeze Reggie's arm fervently, 'I'm grateful to you for helping me understand much, much better why the cultural climate of the time made it so difficult for Christ to appoint women apostles and how . . . no, seriously . . .' Reggie had begun to laugh affectionately at the priest's rationalization. 'And how,' Father Starkey persisted, 'uncommonly good Christ was to the women who came to him. Must have raised an eyebrow or two in Palestine, wouldn't you think?'

*   *   *

The following evening they cleared the table to make space for a fresh collection of books.

'And so!' declared Reggie theatrically, 'we come to Tuatha dè Danaan!'

'Turtledown, yes. Yes, indeed, this will be thrilling.'

'I beg your pardon?' Reggie frowned.

'And so we come to Turtledown!' Father Starkey settled

into his copy of *Pagan Celtic Britain* by Dr Anne Ross.

The two words had a remarkably close consonance.

'You startled me for a moment.' Reggie drew up his own chair. 'I said, *actually*, Tuatha dè Danaan, the legendary children of the Celtic gods, Dagda and his lady wife, whoever she was, precisely, the ones whose treasures – sword, cauldron, lance and cup – reappear in the Grail literature. You know?'

'So we have another link?'

'With the hill? Only maybe.'

'No, I meant with the Grail.'

The two men laughed at the absurdity of this detection. They were met at every turn by patterns cohering to form linked histories. Already they had remarked on the similarity between the idea of the dying consort and the Fisher King. Now, the arrival of the Christian chalice in the form of a magic, pagan cauldron made both of them rock with delighted mirth.

'We *must* be careful of making everything conspire to fit our theory,' cautioned the priest with wagging finger.

'But it does!' cried Reggie and threw his head back elatedly. He was inebriated by the lovely, ceaseless locking together of elements.

'You've got one day left before the advent of your archaeologist chum,' Father Starkey reminded Reggie, and adjusted his skirts more comfortably. 'So it promises to be a heavy evening.'

'Oh, this bit I'm far more familiar with,' Reggie answered confidently.

But it was to be three in the morning before he ran the priest back to his lodgings.

20

Norman Herrington and his assistant Bob Crabbe, who waited while Reggie emptied a bowel that had liquefied under nervous pressure during the messroom lunch, passed covert but eloquent glances at one another. Then, together, all three set off to Turtledown.

'Nice bloke,' said Bob Crabbe of the Major who had hosted them. He rubbed his nose upwards as if it itched horribly.

'Very accommodating,' agreed Norman; 'very civil indeed.' They emerged into the heat which hit them like a sauna and all three reeled slightly under the impact, Reggie more noticeably than the others. But he led them, past the tanks positioned at the gateway, towards his Morris, with the dogged forward chin of a Victorian pioneer.

Reggie did not feel he'd really got his oar in at lunch. Allotted the role of interested listener, he had drunk glass upon glass of excellent claret; then failed to decline a Napoleon brandy. Through the resultant haze he found himself tangling with a skein of emotions he felt too clumsy to separate and work to advantage. Still . . . it had to be acknowledged that Herrington had continually and generously referred to him as the instigator of the dig, as colleague, as friend and, at one juncture, as 'thoroughly sound'. He had also – though this may have been to impress the Major with the need for his, Herrington's, intervention – made Reggie's finds so far sound uniquely important.

It was supremely confusing.

'I should move the dog blanket on to the shelf at the back,' advised Reggie as they hung reluctantly over the car, loth to enter its thick, still heat. Bob clambered in first and swatted at the airless atmosphere. 'Oh, boy!' he grumbled, 'digging's going to be just great in this.'

'Better than an office,' said Norman and then, to Reggie, 'I've put aside a Roman villa at Haselbury Bryan for this.'

'Very good of you.' Reggie grinned greasily.

'Alice and the kiddies are going to come down and stay for August – if I can find a suitable hotel. Seems sensible for all of us to get a bit of enjoyment out of the jaunt.' Norman wiped his face with what looked like a car rag. He jolted violently as Reggie thrust the Morris into first gear. 'D'you know of any suitable hotels? Nothing at all grand.'

Abominably, Reggie changed into second. 'I can certainly inquire,' he said, his lips beginning to stick to his teeth.

'Your gear box,' commented Bob Crabbe from the back, 'sounds terminal.' He began a quick succession of explosive sneezes. 'Bloody hayfever!' he choked.

'Better than psoriasis!' warbled Norman.

The man's obsessive determination to make everybody appreciate the situation in which they found themselves provoked Reggie. 'What,' he demanded, 'would you say to a man who was unhappy at the prospect of having electric shocks applied to his balls?'

'Better than a red-hot poker up the arse,' replied Norman, unabashed, and his shiny, scarlet face was creased by amusement. 'You've got a long walk ahead of you,' he yelled over his shoulder with satisfaction. Bob Crabbe grunted damply.

The downs, as they rose into them, looked like slumbrous golden shoulders humped against the sky. Then the road curved, and the fortified profile of Turtledown could be seen ahead of them, its yellow banks defined like a three-stranded necklet.

'Quite a size.' Bob peered against the gritty wind that rushed into his side of the car as Reggie rocked along at fifty.

'And do you know,' remarked Norman, 'if you approached it from the other side, you wouldn't guess there were any earthworks there at all.'

Reggie heard this observation with spleen. Norman Herrington had never approached Turtledown from the other side. He wondered when to slam Herrington with his theory.

They tramped the mile and a half along the ridge in comparative silence, pausing every now and then for Bob to recover an upright position after one of his nasal detonations. They reached the causeway.

'Now, Bob!' Norman marched through the gap in the banks first. 'You see ... Obvious early works here, fortifications later.' He waved his hand. His rolled-up sleeves revealed white but hairy arms. 'I suggest we take a huge section down right through the banks and ditches to look at all levels of development.' He paused in his onward march. 'Don't you agree, Reggie?'

'Whatever you say, Norman.'

Norman's rhinocerine hide seemed to protect him from venom.

'Then over here, in the first area – the one old Reggie's already got his spade into – complete clearance, yes? On the western side,' he strode towards the lower bulge of the figure-eight formation, where the land opened up in a large circle, 'I suggest is the likeliest site for settlement remains to be located.'

'I've been thinking a lot about the burial,' said Reggie in a falsely chatty voice. But Norman was walking back in the opposite direction, towards the tarpaulin covers.

'Christ!' squeaked Bob, peering over the shallow shelf towards the dug grave. 'It's nearly into the bloody sea.'

'That's why it was such a doddle getting the rescue grant through. I said it could go at any minute. It *could* go at any minute, eh, Reggie?' As if to emphasize the equivocal tenor of this remark, Norman threw a sweating arm round Reggie's shoulder. The great weight of the man lay there a second, as companionable as a yoke.

'I've come,' announced Reggie with great clarity, 'to one or two tentative conclusions.'

Bob walked gingerly close to the shelf edge and sneezed so violently that he tottered.

'Bloody dangerous!' he gasped.

'We'll rope you,' said Norman.

'I'll be OK when the pollen count falls,' Bob assured him, but he kept a distance of three feet between himself and the edge.

A cool gust stirred the dried grasses and made the crickets

redouble their chatter. Their babble seemed like an encouragement. Reggie launched himself into his summary of Hittite invasions of the Semitic lands, their demotion of female divinities, the acquiring of their symbols – then the Celtic connection. 'I mean, what we've found here virtually says it all,' he concluded, indicating the modest square of tarpaulin beneath them.

There was a pause.

'That's all very imaginative.' Norman stood, his oily black hair lifting with difficulty in the breeze. 'Very imaginative. Quite a work of fiction, eh, Bob?'

And the two of them laughed together in a comradely way.

A fiction!

Reggie halted like a man winded. Fictions! he thought to himself indignantly. 'Fictions don't have to be false,' he declared aloud. 'A fiction is simply a mode of reality, a way of understanding the truth better, not a means of escaping it.'

Already, Norman had lowered himself towards the grave and was beckoning Bob over to help him lift the tarpaulin.

'It all hangs together!' shouted Reggie from the ledge two feet above them. 'Try finding a single, supreme goddess figure in Celtic mythology! Just try!'

A trifle superciliously, Bob Crabbe lifted his fair, pink face and pointed out that all anybody knew of Celtic mythology was gleaned from Irish records written some eight centuries after their principal currency. 'There's no contemporary iconographic evidence to speak of,' he concluded with the lofty assurance of the very newly educated.

'Transformed to a horse!' shrieked Reggie, jumping up and down above them. 'Look at the carvings on the pillars at Entremont, the walls at La Roquepertuse ... Epona the horse goddess! The *horse* ...!' he emphasized as if they couldn't hear him, 'associated, presumably because of the chariot, with the sun.'

'If,' Norman shouted back at him with a loud sort of patience, 'if you admire the horse as much as the Celts did, that's no kind of demotion.' And he completed his folding of the tarpaulin.

315

'But ... but ... Epona!' Reggie was left gasping at their ignorance. 'Not only was she made to murder her son. She was compelled to stand ... to stand,' he repeated as the others presented their backs, 'for seven years at the mounting-block and carry on her back all strangers who came to court!'

'That's right,' nodded Norman, humouring him. 'Now your boys took out a very small area here and didn't go very deep. I think it would be worth ...'

He broke off as Reggie jumped off the ledge and landed beside them. Staring at him briefly, Norman took a tape-measure out of his pocket. Reggie was undeterred.

'And what,' he wanted to know, 'do you make of that account by Giraldus Cambrensis – an eyewitness account – of the Irish king's inaugural mating with a white mare who was then slaughtered and in whose broth he was obliged to bathe?'

This time there was a distinct weariness in the expressions of the two archaeologists.

'That,' murmured Bob Crabbe, 'is a *twelfth*-century fiction.'

'But he *saw* it!'

'There are,' observed Norman with an air of tolerance, 'certain physical features of the tale which strain credulity.'

But Reggie, who has been spinning in a timeless gyre for two weeks, who knows that recurrence of ritual marks the most persistent impulses of the human memory, who knows that ancient recall can compel a people to resurrect a burial form unused for centuries, whose perceptions are, moreover, wonderfully outrageously enlarged by alcohol, is not discouraged by one-dimensional fools. He gazes out over the pale, sucked downland, mottled by patches of gorse and scrub, and draws the necessary air into his lungs.

'All right,' he submitted, striving to adopt the sensible manner they will approve. 'All right, working from later sources, then. We know the Irish Celts observed one pre-eminent god – though even Caesar in a *contemporary* account, Mr Crabbe, *contemporary* account, says that the Gauls worship a single male god he describes as *Dis Pater* – which just goes to show how simple a matter it must have been to Christianize the Celts, but I digress! Irish theocracy!' He managed an indulgent smile at the runny-nosed assistant whose own fixed sneer wavered slightly. Behind the boy's head the sea winked and glittered wickedly as if adjudicator to the scene.

Reggie rapidly began running off the facts they could agree on. 'Dagda mates with – now here's the important thing: we just don't know who he mates with precisely. He's not so much polygamous as plain vague in this respect. Sometimes it's the Mórrígan, sometimes the Macha, sometimes Danu, some of them triad goddesses. Anyway, whoever, whatever they were, the offspring are known – right? – as the Tuatha dè Danaan.' He folded his arms, the proper pedant.

'Right so far,' said Norman lazily, more interested in the piece of dried turf he was prising up with his penknife.

'Now one of those sons,' Reggie went on, remorseless now, 'is Lugh – in the Welsh, Lleu – so radiant of face he can't be looked upon. Another is probably Mac Grèine, meaning son of sun .. ½ Right?'

'I honestly wouldn't know, old friend.' Norman's smile now had a thin glaze about it. It didn't deter Reggie. 'Direct ancestors of Arthur, the solar warrior, king of the round table.' Part of Reggie's persistence was now motivated by the faint but pleasurable intimation that his knowledge in this area exceeded Norman's. That's why the fellow was being so obnoxious.

'Whoopsy!' cried Bob, less judiciously restrained. 'Another leap in time!'

Dehydrated by sun and wine, Reggie struggled for a line sufficiently straight and confined to be followed by these scientific dullards, whose linear view of time simply couldn't accommodate humanity's random, archetypal images. No wonder they valued so highly their flint scrapers, their socketed axes, their adzes, their ogivally grooved daggers, and all the other classifiable artefacts they could weigh, measure and submit to chemical and other analyses. That way they remained in control. They feared possession of the mind. Revered possession *by* the mind. Oh cowards!

Reggie prattled on about the prolific Celtic deities, the

317

sacred *loci*, the hills, groves and streams that these figures, eternally transforming themselves from bull to bird to stag and back again, both sanctified and occupied. And how, despite the munificence of their variety and number, there was not one single, supreme mother goddess, not one goddess of love. 'And that, you must admit,' he insisted, 'is quite, quite extraordinary!'

Ignoring a furtive wink from Bob, Norman sat back on his heels. 'This may all,' he interrupted, 'be very intriguing. Indeed,' he corrected himself politely, '*is* very intriguing, but it has relatively little bearing on what is required of us here.'

A rare and isolated cloud drifted over the sun. The landscape dulled suddenly. The protective hand which Norman had raised to his eyes, was lowered. His voice became more magisterial. 'If we are to do some useful work here together, Reggie,' he said, 'I feel it's wiser to keep our speculations within the limitations of what we turn up. Of course,' he hastened to add, 'I understand your enthusiasm; it's most natural. Commendable. But – and you know how it is in academic circles – we can't afford to be seen claiming more than we can substantiate.'

'You bet!' echoed his raw-nosed assistant, who now seemed to be developing an additional rash on his forehead.

Reggie felt a crashing, tumbling sensation inside his body. Perhaps he'd gone too far. He kept his eyes fixed wildly on the jowled, perspiring folds of Norman Herrington's face.

'Are we together on this?' inquired Norman. A tiny threat was stitched into his question.

Reggie gawped, his mind bounding. Whatever else, he was not going to be robbed of Turtledown by this man, a man he'd once regarded as his ally in saving so much from the jaws of the twentieth century.

It came to him that Norman was just another vandal masquerading as protector, a man whose rivalries and jealously guarded self-esteem matched anything to be found in the political arenas he claimed to oppose: a man, thought Reggie, with short, wry satisfaction, of profoundly limited imagination.

'Eh?' pressed Norman, a little alarmed by the apparently vacant expression on his friend's face.

Below them, the uncoloured sea gave forth an angry hiss as it swept towards the shore.

'Oh yes, yes.' Reggie blinked. Slyly, he said, 'I accept your point of view, of course. But I won't abandon . . .'

'Reggie, my dear fellow!' In a slow succession of clambering limbs, Norman rose and came towards him, that treacherous arm outstretched. 'Don't misunderstand me! By all means, develop your notions. Of course. But if we're to prepare a joint paper, work together with the same aim in mind . . . You appreciate my point?'

As the sun escaped its cloud and branded Reggie's back, the crickets' parley rose. The sudden imprint of heat between his shoulder-blades was like a contractual reminder. 'I propose to see how things develop between us,' Reggie heard himself announce with stiff dignity.

'Fair enough!' There came the renewed and added pressure on his back from Norman's sweaty hand.

The two forces conjoined momentarily. Reggie maintained a rigid posture beneath their mutual attack.

*   *   *

But he burned, in every sense of the word, for the remainder of the week. The account he gave Father Starkey of the hilltop conference was especially heated. All attempts to soothe were ineffective. But then, all in all, Reggie had much to harass him.

The weather had turned sullen. He spent the nights unpeeling the sheet from his sleepless body and the days snapping irritably at his colleagues.

Preparations for the play, which was to be staged on the Friday and Saturday nights, had reached a pitch of frenzied incompletion. Amis was in a state of near hysteria and kept getting Reggie to check that all the leaves didn't fall off the tree when the wind machine was turned on. This encouraged Reggie to complain to Eleanor Straker that she'd made Caliban's mask look like King Kong and that no mask at all would be preferable in the circumstances. Astin Major was quite ugly enough as it was. He next insulted Dufferdill about the orchestra he conducted. 'What in heaven's name is magical, let alone *musical*, about the ghastly scraping?' he demanded to know, though it was none of his business, as Dufferdill made plain to him, pointing out that, unless the school orchestra was given a chance to perform, it would never improve.

So Reggie carried his complaint to Amis. 'Must this play be used as a training session for chainsaw players and drainpipe blowers?' he asked angrily. But Amis was too agitated by the problems of his own role to give fuller attention to the production.

'Oh, God,' he moaned when Reggie accosted him over the matter of the orchestra. 'Tell me truthfully, Montis, do I look like a flamingo in these tights?'

'Yes,' said Reggie. 'For heaven's sake keep your coat on and don't cross your legs when you sit down.'

'I should have settled for the black: I knew it!' And Amis wandered off to beg Matron to lend him a pair of her black woollen tights. 'I shall simply *melt* on the night,' he was last heard whimpering.

*   *   *

Phoebe was able to divert Reggie briefly.

The ten minutes they spent driving to and from the school were little lakes of calm. Warm air poured through their wound-down windows. By tacit, mutual agreement they forbore from recitation of the play. Instead, Phoebe made him talk of forgotten and invented things.

That he had once been a small boy was a marvel. She made him talk of suburban dens, of games, of the things he had dreamed of being. Dredging his mind to meet her promptings, he was astonished how much of his infant world was unreal. The giant, hairy toad in the coalshed; the elvish shadows in the night-time laburnums. The grocer in the corner shop, a man with a totally bald head and no eyebrows, had stored children in the cellar next to the sacks of pearl barley and sago. The woman three doors down had transmitted her cats through the identical frosted-glass front doors of Driffield Avenue to bring back information about the other occupants. He told Phoebe of the disused quarry a mile away where he'd played, and the stones with his initials scratched on them that he'd stored in secret crevices of the quarry face.

'You collect pebbles, too, don't you?' he mused, smiling at the common occupations of children. 'Why is that? Are they magic, d'you suppose?'

'Oh yes,' she answered solemnly. 'They speak.'

*   *   *

And so there was a little respite in his day. But not enough to prevent Mrs Pike worrying over the condition of her lodger when he returned home sticky and crumpled. She noted a small quickening of a pulse above the right eye, a faint thickening of speech.

'You must relax a little,' she insisted, and made him sit with her in the front lounge while the television played and he helped her to cut out hundreds and hundreds of silvery feather shapes from an old evening dress she'd kept back from the last PRG jumble sale.

'This is Phoebe's harpy frock,' she explained. 'Could you lift Bundle off that lurex, dear?'

'She's going to look like an owl,' remarked Reggie, but Bella Pike, seeing he was on edge, smiled as though he were teasing. When she worked on another dress he demanded to know whether one outfit wouldn't have done perfectly adequately.

'She's got to have her invisible dress, dear,' said Mrs Pike unperturbed. 'Oh look, it's the gymnasts. I often wonder if that sort of thing mightn't have suited Phoebe,' she murmured, biting off her thread and looking at small lithe girls performing impossible physical feats, 'but the strain must be terrible. Do you suppose they restrict their growth deliberately?'

The gymnastic display was followed at ten by the news. Mrs Pike chattered through details about the Russian build-up of arms and troops in East Africa; the Syrian invasion of Israel; the loss of animals and crops through drought in Devon and Cornwall; the despatch by kidnappers of an Italian business-man's lower left leg to his family; and the latest Test scores from Australia. One might think she hadn't heard a word, but at the sight of Dorothy's tall figure leading a meandering stream of tinier figures across the screen like some gaunt and fluteless Pied Piper, she fell immediately silent.

They listened intently to the reporter's account of the PRGs' march towards London. There was a snatch of Dorothy's address to townsfolk of Hemel Hempstead: a hoarsely delivered exhortation to rise and determine their own future, and a comment that none of the relevant authorities seemed to think charges against her were either appropriate or necessary.

'They don't want to admit the stuff goes missing,' commented Mrs Pike, stitching away at her silver feathers. 'Dorothy's been very shrewd, if you ask me.'

The contrast on Bella Pike's television set was always poorly tuned, and the extremes of colour harshly emphasized; even so, Dorothy's face had looked a deathly white beneath a cruelly blazing crown of hair.

He stirred at last. 'I ought to go and find her,' he said, ashamed.

'She's surrounded by friends,' said Mrs Pike with some finality.

'But it's not . . .'

'Oh yes, it is,' she prevailed. And Reggie desisted from saying anything further.

Later, surreptitiously, he slipped out to the phone box at the bottom of Chandler Street to ring Gilbert. A vague-sounding fellow-student from the hostel said he thought Gilbert had gone home on compassionate leave, which prevented Reggie from leaving a message lest news that his father had rung blew Gilbert's alibi.

'Yes, yes,' he said, before the voice at the other end of the line could inquire who was calling. 'I believe his mother is unwell.'

'Something like that,' the voice yawned, 'I think.'

*   *   *

The two boys playing Iris and Sebastian were also unwell the following day, the day of their opening performance. The understudies were drilled, tension mounted, the curtain rose, and Reggie's lightning and thunder worked pretty well, though there was a terrible scraping sound as the illusory banquet table was removed behind Phoebe's outspread harpy wings in Act Three. She failed to keep an entirely straight face as the racket went on behind her.

Ferdinand dropped his logs but Miranda, scampering about the stage, helped to retrieve them, and only three people forgot their lines. Had it not been for the evil howling and whimpering from the orchestra, the whole thing could have been described as a moderate success. Amis, at least, was smiling with unaccustomed radiance.

That night Reggie lay awake under a single sheet, unable to escape the relentless hug of the heat, and made up his mind that, as soon as the play was over, he'd get off school and find Dorothy.

*   *   *

Almost hidden behind the green, gold and silver clouds of her costumes, Phoebe ran along the dusty verge and jumped into the Morris.

They drove past farm buildings whose roofs seemed to droop in the heat. The sky was grey and low with gravid cloud. Neither felt much like talking.

Then, 'Is your head hurting?' the child asked at last. And as she had done once before, she knelt on her seat to reach across and touch his brow. She whispered something.

'What's that?'

'Nothing,' she said and smiled, sinking down with her back to the windscreen.

Reggie turned his head briefly and looked instantly back to the road, horrified by the erotic subterfuge of her smile.

*   *   *

A worse sight awaited him.

Amis stood in the yard under a full-bellied sky, wearing one of Eleanor Straker's Liberty-print headscarves.

'Look! Look!' he screamed, running at Reggie as if to attack him. He whipped off the scarf.

Supporting himself on the car door, Reggie stared at the malformed apparition before him. Amis's prognathic jaw was transformed by two enormous, hamster-like pouches.

'Mumps!' screamed Amis accusingly, as though the whole thing was a plot dreamed up by Reggie. Then he groaned pitifully.

'Poor Mr Amis,' said Phoebe sympathetically. '*You'll* have to do it, Mr Montis. *You* know the lines.'

Five disfigured members of the disfiguring orchestra had also been admitted to the san.

*   *   *

Standing in the wings, his face heavy and odorous with glued beard and greasepaint, his body squeezed hotly inside Amis's much appliquéd and embroidered surcoat, his tights soaked with sweat at the crutch – Matron's tights, that is – Reggie felt gently compensated by the clear, poignant note of a single recorder playing above the turmoil of the audience. It began to create a wonderful silence around itself. The tenor of the play was more truly struck.

The music faded. The curtains parted and thunder cracked across the stage.

Exit Gonzalo
    Enter (oh, failing and ancient heart!) *Prospero and Miranda.*

This part of the play Reggie did not know at all well, but if he expressed Prospero's fatherhood in a somewhat perfunctory manner, he did little less than Shakespeare himself had done. Twice he awaited the hiss of the prompter. Several times the helpful Jason Caldecott, looking deliciously pert in a blonde wig, mouthed his lines at him, and in this manner Reggie stumbled by until thankfully able to announce that his zenith did depend upon

> *A most auspicious star, whose influence*
> *If now I court not, but omit, my fortunes*
> *Will ever after droop.*

Then, briskly putting Miranda to sleep, he welcomed his servant Ariel.

This bit should be all right, thought Reggie, and quite looked forward to it as Phoebe in her number one costume – green chiffon with gold thread – slipped out from behind the cardboard rocks. He touched his beard.

They bounded along. Reggie modelled himself rather closely on Amis's autocratic interpretation of Prospero, and sharply upbraided Ariel for demanding his or her freedom. Ariel snapped back.

> *Remember I have done thee worthy service,*
> *Told thee no lies, made thee no mistakings, served*
> *Without grudge or grumblings. Thou didst promise*
> *To bate me a full year.*

The sharpness of Ariel's response took Reggie aback. He started, flustered a little, then stuttered his lines as best he could.

He couldn't recall Phoebe's speaking so vehemently to Amis. Dimly, though despite the consternation of the moment, he recollected once telling Phoebe that Ariel was more than mere servant. The burden of his own advice was now laid before him and the scene continued sparringly, with Reggie on the defensive. He caught a petulant note in his own voice and when he arrived at the hideously embarrassing lines about Ariel's twelve-year confinement in a cloven pine, he simply couldn't meet the sprite's gaze at all, and let his gaze rove blankly into the footlights.

So taunting was the small form in the green chiffon, so blazing-eyed, so burning-haired, that when he finally cried out: *Go! Hence with diligence!* he did so with such angry fright that one or two members of the audience raised their eyebrows at each other.

In mocking obeisance Ariel withdrew, spine bending until the flying mane of hair swept the stage. She exited slowly. It was the retreat of a lazy, surfeited predator.

The crash of applause which broke out was so long sustained that Miranda, who was meant to wake (and did so) was obliged to go to sleep again until the clapping finally died away.

Reggie's sense of disorientation was furthered by the softer sounds of Wimble Cove surging about him. But his faltering lasted only a short time. The production resumed its calmly plodding pace with the advent of Astin Major. And yet, relief as it was to respond woodenly to the lumpen statements of Caliban, Reggie physically felt the interest of the audience recede from the stage. He needed Ariel's provoking power to keep the thing alive.

He exited hurriedly and was congratulated by Dufferdill, who reminded him to stand in the spotlight. Thanks to the slashing cuts made by Amis whenever his presence on stage was not required, the rest of Acts Two and Three sped by. In the little time left to him, Reggie swotted up his forthcoming lines and, during that part of the third Act when he had to be on stage but was invisible (to the players at least), he kept his back to the audience and read obsessively to the point where he knew his thunder and lightning effects signalled the re-appearance of Ariel as harpy. By so doing, he inevitably missed two brief interjections, which caused the hapless Francisco and Alonso to glare at him for a while, until forlornly they concluded that Mr Montis was taking his invisibility very seriously and they'd best plough on as if he truly wasn't there.

Crash! Bang!

The effects, Reggie had time to consider, weren't half bad. He admired them. Then he eyed the astounding harpy who sprang from behind the rocks, silver-winged, harlot-faced.

Phoebe flung her feathered arms out wide, and the banquet disappeared behind her without any awkward trundling.

In clear but belligerent tones she addressed the figures before her. They drew their swords.

'*You fools!*' hissed Phoebe, her bell-like voice suddenly dropping to a stunning whisper.

> *I and my fellows*
> *Are ministers of Fate. The elements*
> *Of whom your swords are tempered, may as well*
> *Wound the loud winds, or with be-mocked at stabs*

326

Kill the still-closing waters, as diminish
One dowle that's in my plume.

So riveted was Reggie by the electric contempt of this performance that, when his own move came and he advanced centre stage, remarking how well Ariel had performed his, Prospero's commands, he heard how foolish, how pathetically vain he sounded.

*　　　*　　　*

All the aspects of Prospero's capricious, grudging behaviour that Reggie had objectively noted before – the underlying fear of impotence; the worthlessness of his bookish knowledge without the active agency of immortal spirits to implement it; the falling away of a curiously unloving life – all these things Reggie now felt. He, who had never acted in anything but the office pantomime of 1951, was now inhabited by fears and emotions that transformed Prospero's grandeur and might have diminished it, had not some enigmatic alchemy been wrought between Ariel and himself.

Again and again he heard himself promise Ariel that longed-for freedom and then withhold the giving of it one more time, as if it were his own mortal spirit he was being asked to surrender, as if that freedom would render his own life a little thing 'rounded with a sleep'.

The hopeless strutting, the bluster, the sight of a plumpish figure in a lopsided beard and Matron's roomy tights could have been comic. But the audience of parents in their middle years saw something unexpectedly saddening. They saw the pain of a man clinging to life when all is appointed against such an outcome and the very awkwardness of the performance, the inept clasping of the impossible, made them sit uncommonly silent through Prospero's last long speech.

> *the strong-based promontory*
> *Have I made shake and by the spurs plucked up*
> *The pine and cedar: graves at my command*
> *Have waked their sleepers, oped, and let 'em forth*

> *By my so potent art. But this rough magic*
> *I here abjure.*

In the front row Bella Pike and her daughter Daphne tightly held hands.

Ariel sang of summer things.

At last the promise was undertaken. Reggie raised his head and, like a dog, howled

> *But yet thou shalt have freedom – so, so, so!*

And though the play continued to unwind its coils for fully another ten minutes, those three terrible cries hung in the dark and stifling hall until the curtain itself fell and swept them away in its dusty, everyday folds.

The applause was endless.

Together, Reggie and Phoebe stepped forward. They bowed towards the hands they could see beating like netted birds.

They bowed to one another.

'Thank you,' he whispered gratefully. 'You made me do that.'

'Me?' she mouthed silently. And numinous, ethereal, she kept her eyes on his until they were compelled once more to lower their heads in acknowledgement of their audience.

Bouquets were found.

*   *   *

'Heavens above,' demurred Reggie later, as congratulations were proffered above the party din. 'It's only a school play. Anyway, Phoebe did it all. She's extraordinary.' He searched her out and pulled her from the nearby throng. 'You could make me do anything, couldn't you?'

Without a flicker of protest she let him lift her up so that she shone above the bobbing garrulity of the school dining-room.

Outside, the sky flared pink with real sheet lightning, more stunning by far than Reggie's imitations.

A rainless storm rumbled across the hills, and at the party the players sweated beneath their greasepaint.

Phoebe alone remained cool.

21

A grave had indeed been opened and let its sleeper forth.

Reggie woke on Sunday morning, elated by the prospect of searching out his wife in the northerly environs of London. In the rich texture of his night's dreaming, the imprisonments of the play were ended by Dorothy's calling upon the people to free themselves from the enslavements of a tyrant future. She embodied that paradoxical coupling of death and freedom. In sleep, Reggie had himself been freed from awareness of Dorothy's sillier side. His eyes opened on a glory.

*   *   *

However, first things first.

He dared not let Mrs Pike know his plans. He would wait for her to go to Mass, briefly attend to his own devotions, then leave.

He excelled his own previous best by accomplishing his undisturbed meditation over the shell-pink porcelain in nineteen minutes. Then, hurriedly washing and shaving (missing, in his haste, a residue of greasepaint around his eyes and hairline), he edged away from Bundle's eager anticipation of a walk, and squeezed round the front door of Sunnybank.

The Morris squatted in the gutter like a drunk, its two front tyres flattened.

Cursing, Reggie returned to the overjoyed Bundle and tried to ring the garage. It was, of course, closed. There were no more trains on Sunday until late afternoon. There was nothing for it but to await Mrs Pike's return – hoping she would not be going straight on to lunch at her daughter's – and invent some fictitious reason for borrowing the A30.

He sat outside on the wall for a while, kicking his heels in frustration. Then he kicked the Morris to improve his temper. Then, unreasonably, he damned Frank for selling him a useless car. Then, realizing he was not making time pass any quicker by hanging about, and conscious of Bundle's bouncing, exuberant form behind the frosted glass, he thought he'd risk a quick walk down to the newsagent's near the harbour.

The weather was still heavy with unresolved storm and the inevitable migraine, which had blessedly suspended itself for the duration of the play, crept back into position like a snake coiling itself on the inside of his skull. It lay there surly but, for the moment, biddable.

Escaping the sluggish air, he wandered across the stones of Granny's Gate to the more abrasive edge of the sea, leaving Bundle to run her preferred way up the low, initial rise of the dark cliff. He stood and breathed the more invigorating atmosphere at the water's edge. He needed to clear his head thoroughly before reaching Dorothy. After all, there were things he had to say to her, things he meant. Things she must listen to. He dawdled westward, rehearsing the conversation they might have. Or rather, the statements he himself intended.

He felt a genuine concern, a need to let her know that – yes, he cared.

He cared.

In the muffled grey atmosphere, Reggie gave a half-croak, half-gasp of pleasure. So much for his own freedom! He would take Dorothy back. Bring her back here with him. The freedoms she advocated were so much grander than the little burrows he'd attempted to dig for himself.

Two gulls floating on the viscid sea seemed stuck to its surface.

How could he explain to his wife that the great irony impressed on him the previous night – the realization that there was no freedom for Ariel, not for Phoebe's Ariel, at least – had brought him closer to her side? He understood better her espousal of the dwarvish longing.

He even, and this was far more difficult to confess though inextricably linked, felt a greater political sympathy. If she had risked her life as she swore she had – and her appearance offered ineluctable testimony of it – well, she was crazy, nothing would rid him of that opinion: but she had a dignity. He longed to tell her that.

You have an undoubted dignity, Dorothy, my wife.

And (oh, if you could guess how hard it is to admit this) you are right to take on the small, self-appointed gods. They are scarcely less wanton than the cloudier kind which humanity once approved. They toy with a far more terrible dimension of death.

Dimly, the church bells of Tidmouth struck their shortened notes against a padded sky.

He thought of those who still knelt and sought guidance from a higher authority on the muddles of their age. What counsels could prevail in the minds of those who worshipped the very epitome of power which men fashioned in their own image? How much sense and solace was to be derived from that mirror activity?

Dorothy?

Dorothy, you are right to guard the one bright faith of modern, rational man: his fragile democracy.

As he walked, the boulders ahead of him grew larger and larger. Those washed over by the sea resembled gleaming seals. Beneath his feet a thousand ammonites wheeled in the stone.

Too many fancies gnawed at his mind! As he dwelt on the ways in which he might make atonement to Dorothy, the sky darkened. The unsteadiness of his vision made the sea itself appear to tremble, its slow, forward surge halted and quavered.

Reggie felt for the bottle of pills in his pocket. As he glanced down, he saw the stones beneath his feet shudder. For a second he thought the dizzy motion emanated from inside himself, inside his wretched head. But no.

The whole shore was stirring and cracking. The water was spiralling unnaturally, like whipped-cream. Out of the sea, in front of Reggie's disbelieving gaze, a black ridge began to rise. A spined sea-beast. He spun, terrified, on the shifting stones and heard, above the growing subterranean roar, a piping bark.

The dog!

As he turned towards the cliff, his feet glissading uncontrollably beneath him, a still more dreadful sight presented itself. The small white form of the dog rode a black cliff advancing towards him. A whole section of cliff face was moving across the stones towards the sea, the air around it darkening with dusk. He screamed. As the implacable black tore slowly away from its anchorage and began to travel across the fifty yards or so that separated it from the sea, he screamed again. He needed to hear the howl of his own voice and could not do so in the turmoil around him. He could run neither forward nor back. He could not maintain his footing as the boulders lurched and cracked beneath him, spilling their fossils.

Incapable of sound, incapable of motion, Reggie seemed barely to exist in his own mind. There was nothing to press against, nothing to hold. The world collapsed around him, milling him in its fall. The rising roar reached its peak and broke. There was a mighty explosion. Chunks of cliff-face flew in the air. Leaping flame crowned the section of cliff that continued, inexorably, to slide over the frenzied surface of the shore.

Although he was sure he had not run backwards, Reggie felt water swirl around his legs. Swaying knee-deep in foam, he kept his desperate gaze on the one object that told him he occupied a real landscape: the one sign of life that bore witness to his own living. Borne aloft the burning mountain, the little dog cast up her head, her white throat exposed to the swirling, sulphurous cloud.

Choking with the fumes, Reggie strained every sinew forward and began to struggle towards the oncoming wall of black lias. His feet slithered on the stones, and he fell to his knees. His wrists were braceleted in spume.

Then suddenly, giving off showers of sparks, the edifice began to break, separating into thick, burning streams, while the collapsing central core still continued on its path. The dog sank with it, clearly too petrified to run down the clay slope that was gradually extending itself in front of her. Any cries she uttered were drowned by the ubiquitous roaring and wrenching that seemed, not to accompany the movement of the flow, but to come from the centre of the earth like the separate moaning of a disturbed and captive beast.

On all fours, Reggie staggered forward till his arms were out of the epileptic water. The lengthening, lowering slope of black mud was now, at its foot, only fifteen yards away, but its angle of incline was so much reduced that he was less terrified of being engulfed. He dared go towards it.

All at once he was free of fear. It sluiced out of him.

Crawling and scrambling towards the creeping spur, he managed to haul himself upright and, putting both hands to his mouth, fruitlessly called the dog's name. Still he couldn't hear his own voice, but the utter helplessness was gone. A greater need than his own strengthened him. Bundle's body was flickeringly outlined in flame.

Again he plunged forward, yelling, beneath the tumult. Dust and fumes clogged his breathing as he drew closer and closer to the thick, black, thirsty tongue. Bundle was now above him, borne at a height of about twelve feet. Reggie entered the moving mass of shale, and felt its frightful strength drive against his legs. But the dog took courage from his boldness. Abruptly, she propelled her burning form downwards. Together she, Reggie and the subsiding spur of hot, black mud travelled towards the curdling sea.

He clasped her tightly to him, crushing the flames against his own soaked shirt, wrapping his arms around her, barely feeling the pain.

Out of a white and bubbling sea the pinnacled reef rose like a Gothic ruin. In his arms, the dog whimpered. The sounds she uttered were an odd assurance.

The quiet shore he had walked along only moments before was gone. Around him was a new tormented landscape and he was alone in it save for the whining, blackened animal he held close to his throbbing chest.

*   *   *

Flash Harrison was not to be so easily deterred on this occasion. A man who has spent thirty years of his life expanding upon 'Residents Protest over Promenade Litter' and 'Local Farmer Mourned' is not going to throw away a chance of elaborating on the human drama attached to this landslip.

Reggie was not in a state to offer much resistance.

Anyway, surrounded as he was by St John's ambulance men trying to make him lie down on their under-used stretcher; by

333

goggling holidaymakers; by two vets arguing over the correct way to dress burns, *and* a hysterical Mrs Pike, the slow deliberate tones of Tidmouth's ace reporter were almost comforting. He tried to describe what he had seen. It all seemed unreal and confused.

'Like an earthquake,' he mumbled jerkily, as the ambulance men forcefully deposited him on the stretcher and broke into a trot before their trophy could get away. Flash Harrison ran beside Reggie, his personal form of shorthand becoming more irregular than ever. 'It was,' he repeated, 'like the end of the world.'

'Like an earthquake,' Reggie corrected weakly.

'Yes, but like the end of the world?' pleaded Flash, and wrote it down, anyway.

The vets tried to prise Bundle from Reggie's grip. She squeaked pitifully and pressed herself to her rescuer's chest.

'My poor baby!' wailed Bella Pike, who had been brought from her knees by a divinely directed beam and run all the way from St Teresa's to the harbour. 'My poor, poor darling!' She cast herself across the stretcher, upsetting things a bit.

Perceiving that there was a romantic element to add to his report, Flash Harrison scribbled harder, and persuaded the St John's ambulance men to pause in their uneven course (one being much taller than the other), while he took a photograph of the moving scene. A small child in the crowd, watching all this, said in a clear voice, 'Look, Mummy, that man's wearing makeup.'

Everybody involved in the photograph bent even closer to Reggie to examine his face, while Reggie himself suffered an unexpected image of the Wellspring ceremony. That travesty of original intention was as nothing compared to the spectacle he now presented.

Slipping off the momentarily stationary stretcher, Reggie strode through the crowd, unaware of his various injuries, Bundle pressed to him like the last of his worldly goods.

He was the first of a procession that subsequently arrived in the kitchen at Sunnybank. Phoebe, on tiptoe, was stirring something pungent on the stove. She looked up.

'Hello,' she said. 'You got very dirty.'

Before Reggie could apply Germoline to Bundle's charred back, the kitchen was filled with gesturing, agitated figures. The last to arrive was Flash Harrison, who had ridden his bicycle all the way up Chandler Street and was in consequence incapable of speech. It mattered little, since he would not have been heard above the commotion.

One of the vets plunged a hypodermic into Bundle and removed her suddenly inert form to the kitchen table. A St John's ambulance man attendant on each lower limb, Reggie found his trouser legs being rolled up. The laceration and bruising made Bella Pike shriek. Until she cried out, Reggie didn't even know he hurt. Now he hurt horribly.

Father Starkey, arriving with J. G. MacQueen's recently published work on *The Hittites and Their Contemporaries in Asia Minor*, surveyed the tableau and was moved to make the sign of the cross. Daphne screamed from the doorway and Phoebe, stirring steadily away at the bubbling pan, advised everyone to keep their hair on. 'There's no harm done,' she observed calmly and, dipping a mug into the redolent broth, handed it, dripping, to Reggie.

'What is it?' he sniffed.

'A punch. A pick-you-up,' she said.

He smelt spices and wine, and looked at her, stupefied. What made him stare especially was the scorched brown tips of her tendrilled hair. They looked just as his mother's used to after a session with the curling tongs. He stared and stared.

'Drink up,' urged Phoebe. 'You've earned it.'

And obediently he did as the spirit-child bade.

On Monday he stayed in bed.

On Tuesday, ORDEAL BY FIRE AND WATER! blared the *Wessex Gazette* over a special picture-spread of the recumbent hero, with Mrs Pike and her dog prostrated on his breast. The other figures, grouped earnestly round, examining his face for traces of eye shadow and rouge, resembled mourners on a medieval sepulchre. Beneath it, smaller, was a picture of the devastated cliff and a highly coloured account of the man who had twice risked his life for his 'inseparable little friend'.

Once Reggie grasped that this extravagant prose alluded to him and, in some instances, to the words allegedly spoken by him, he refused to go to work. 'I can't! I can't!' he gasped, mortified.

'Well, you can't go anywhere else,' said Mrs Pike, as if she suspected him of harbouring plans to go elsewhere. 'You're in quarantine for mumps.'

'What? But I've had mumps. Or I think I have.'

'Well, you're in quarantine now.'

'I've got to go to London.'

'Just think how many people you'd infect in London.'

A much-recovered Bundle stood up against his legs as he sat over his breakfast.

'Get down, Bundle!' ordered Mrs Pike.

Reggie picked the dog up.

'Just look at that,' sighed Mrs Pike. 'She's really made herself yours now.'

Bundle's hairless spine was greasy with ointment. Having patted her, Reggie sought a Sunnybank Guest House serviette. He wasn't going to argue with Mrs Pike. Instead, he attended to the more factual details of Sunday's dramatic events as described by a person by-lined as Oswald E. Harrison.

The landslip had been caused by a combination of extreme weathers, heavy winter rains followed by a long dry spell. The blue lias, under pressure from the saturated greensand levels, had been forced, or actually twisted, forward, the impact being so great that the toe of the lias clay slip was forced up on the foreshore like a Turkish slipper. This explained the ectopic manifestation which had seemed to Reggie so like a drowned cathedral rising from the sea. He exclaimed on this aspect to Mrs Pike.

'It's a lovely photo,' she said lingeringly. 'Except you look dead.' Then, obviously thinking this was not a very feeling remark, added, 'I mean it's so . . .'

'Pre-Raphaelite?' asked Reggie.

'If you say so. I'd like a large, framed copy. Wouldn't you?'

'Not awfully,' said Reggie. 'I *do* look dead.' He tapped his eggs and said with an element of warning, 'I don't want you making too much of this business.'

'Oh you're too modest, you!' Mrs Pike pushed at his sore arm playfully and later ordered a large copy of the photograph for Reggie, and six others for her relations.

* * *

He went to work after all. His arms were bandaged and his clutch foot hurt dreadfully. But these were nothing compared to the agonies of staying put in Sunnybank. National newspapers kept ringing and asking if they could send their photographers down to Tidmouth to get the kind of photograph their readers loved to look at. (Flash Harrison made the odd bit of money on the side as a stringer.)

'I've got mumps,' Reggie had told them and drove off hurriedly to Lower Knoll, where Phoebe stood awaiting him.

'You're late,' she said, kissing him firmly on the ear. 'But very brave, so I forgive you.'

One television company had the nerve to ring through to the school and leave a message for Mr Montis to ring back, but since Mr Montis didn't appear in the staffroom either at break or after lunch, having locked himself in the lavatory away from the gibing of his colleagues, he didn't read it.

* * *

'The television rang!'

Bella Pike stood on the top step of her yellow guest house, dressed as though for very special guests in her best (pink slubbed linen) suit. The importance of the call had impelled her to look her smartest.

Reggie clumped up the path, his bulging briefcase banging his painful legs.

'Reggie, dear! *Television!*'

'I hope you didn't encourage them. I'm tiring of these public performances,' complained Reggie, having found this day of avoidance and scuttling very trying. He wiped the sweat from his forehead.

'*Television!*' repeated Mrs Pike as if he couldn't have grasped the wonderful implications.

As Bundle appeared, limping in greeting towards her new master, Mrs Pike added, 'You'd love to be on the telly, Bundle, wouldn't you, darling?' Bundle wagged herself gingerly at Reggie's feet.

'There you are, you see!' Triumphant, Mrs Pike folded her hands conclusively.

The phone rang.

'That'll be them. I told them when you'd be home.'

Bella Pike picked up the phone and began speaking like a receptionist. 'Hello. Sunnybank Guest House speaking. Just a moment, yes, yes. I'll see if Mr Montis is free to talk to you.' She put a hand over the mouthpiece. 'Go *on!*' she urged.

Before Reggie was able to take the phone from her, Phoebe, whom he had dropped at Lower Knoll only five or six minutes before, appeared at the door.

'Is that the television?' she asked.

'Go on, *you* tell him, Phoebe!'

'I thought,' said Reggie, his own hand now over the mouthpiece, 'that I was in quarantine for mumps.'

'Oh, but you've had it, haven't you?' Mrs Pike dismissed this pretext.

'You will go, won't you Mr Montis?' Phoebe's manner was not at all arch. Rather grave, in fact, quietly presuming.

Reggie looked at the small face under the maroon-ribboned straw boater. He thought her bewitching. The child's gaze was not corrupt exactly, but it lacked innocence.

'I should very much like Bundle to appear on television,' said Phoebe politely. How could a command be so courteously expressed?

'There!' Mrs Pike had been watching Reggie's face carefully. She hugged her granddaughter.

An interesting stratagem suddenly presented itself to Reggie. He spoke into the phone.

'Reginald Montis here. You wish to speak to me?'

338

22

So how come Reggie is sitting here on board the 17.28 hours from Casterwich to Paddington, in a first-class carriage, with the sun grinding through the glass and a dog on his lap? This isn't at all his kind of thing, as anyone witnessing his reaction to that morning's national popular press would realize at once.

DOG'S BEST FRIEND ... THROUGH FIRE AND WATER ... ONE MAN AND HIS DOG: STRANGE BOND.

This was the sort of headline brought to his attention by Mrs Pike, who had run down to the newsagent's early. Most were accompanied by the earlier snapshot (traceable to Flash Harrison, who had paid a holidaymaker £2 for it and was now clearing a 2,000 per cent profit on it) of a sodden Reggie clutching Bundle at the quayside.

The phone had again gone repeatedly. Some calls came from elderly women offering to give Reggie a good home, some from people demanding to know why he didn't devote his talents to saving Eritrean rebels instead of dumb animals, and one from a rival television company offering him twice what the BBC had offered, in return for exclusive coverage.

Having already told Mrs Pike that he would give the money to the PRGs, he felt a certain twinge in turning the offer down, but he was beginning to get the bitch smell of the media and didn't care for it at all.

Yet he sits on the train smiling with unconcealed pleasure, his injured ankle propped on the first-class seat opposite.

*   *   *

At school some of the boys had cheered, some had asked for his autograph, Matron had hugged him for longer than was strictly congratulatory, and the rest of his colleagues, though restrained, had been decent enough.

Still he smiles.

The man at the ticket desk had said Bundle could travel free
– in fact Bundle conformed to a regulation size set down by
British Rail as non-chargeable, but it had made the ticket man
feel expansive to speak as he did. He shook Reggie's hand
warmly and didn't wash his own until he had placed it on a
comfortable part of his wife's anatomy after going off duty.

No, it's not Reggie's sort of thing really, but here he sits in a
state of moderate drunkenness – and he has not yet taken the
two Oblivon tablets originally prescribed by Dr Cassidy for
Mrs Pike when taking her driving test. He has reached that
juncture when present anxieties and rigid diurnal sequences are
beginning to detach themselves from one's being, when the un-
predictability of one's responses and the sense of release from
oneself are still pleasurable: the stage that precedes the insensate.

In this mood he and Bundle glide towards London. Oh yes,
he has consented to this to please Phoebe but, more pertinently,
unable as yet to drive long distances himself, he has happily
accepted the BBC's offer of first-class rail travel and an overnight stay in the Shepherd's Bush Hilton in the expectation of
tracking his wife down the following day. Mrs Pike need never
know a thing about it.

*   *   *

'Mr Montis? Great! . . . Really great of you to come!'

The hand that shook his conveyed the sense of being put at
risk by an owner submitting it to such rough pressure. Reggie
had once experienced a similar handshake from Yehudi Men-
uhin, but then the violinist had reason to imply that his hand
should be treated gently. This hand belonged to a young man
with short-cropped fair hair, gold-rimmed spectacles, gold earrings, and a provocatively opened lilac shirt that clung to his
thin body and had – Reggie observed as the boy turned – the
words I SHIT printed in scarlet on the back.

Lucky bloke, he thought to himself. And, out loud, 'Brother
to I Ching?' – a query that went unheard or unfathomed. The
boy's small tight buttocks and highly wedged yellow shoes
twinkled along ahead of Reggie until they reached the hos-

pitality room where he paused to say how terribly sweet Bundle was. He stepped back a moment to admire the now bandaged creature (the second vet's opinion having been consulted) and said, 'We're all dying to meet her. Does she do tricks?' Then, without awaiting any reply, he pushed open the door and transferred Reggie to the care of a girl looking astonishingly like himself, to whom he grimaced, mouthing the silent message, 'Dreary side, lovette.'

The girl, named Muriel, had very low pointed breasts with which she steered Reggie into a corner. While handing him wine, she explained the sort of questions their well-known personality interviewer, Irwin Napier, would be putting to him.

She did not explain that Irwin Napier had violently objected to interviewing a man about a dog, and had only submitted finally on condition he was given the major interview of the week with the statutory star mystery guest – a regular Wednesday feature designed to keep ratings up among younger viewers – whose identity everybody else in the room was now guessing. Everybody, that is, except Reggie, Muriel and the third guest on the programme (given, though, second billing), a man Reggie recognized as the notorious Archibald Clegg, Hitler fanatic and successful publisher of obscene works. Reggie hoped they would not be introduced. Clegg was currently lobbying to reverse the legislation on the protection of children from pornographic exploitation.

Muriel was busy poking him with her pointy breasts and insisting that nobody, but nobody, loved animals as she did. 'They're only human after all, aren't they?' she inquired. It was the sort of proposition Reggie found hard to endorse with any sincerity; not that it mattered, because Muriel had passed on to re-incarnation and the conviction that she had been a reticulated python in a previous existence. 'Oh? What makes you say that?' inquired Reggie politely.

'Oh, I just got this tremendous . . . *thing* when I saw one in the Reptile House.'

'You did?'

'Ahuh,' nodded Muriel.

He was plied with more drink.

Irwin Napier made a perfunctory appearance, taking his guests' hands with distaste and telling them how privileged he felt to meet them, before hiding once more in his dressing-room to complete his maquillage and practise his questioning technique in the mirror.

More drinks.

Clegg came over and was shamelessly charming. Then Reggie was guided towards make-up, where much was made of Bundle and rather less of him. While one girl pressed a powder puff to his face, she hazarded with the other whether it was Omar Sharif or Robert Redford who was on, tonight. They then went into a debate about which of them would attend to which man. As they elaborated on the kind of attentions each would be prepared to lavish on either one, or both, of the two Reggie's girl blotted and dabbed with detachment. He felt himself disappear.

He sat clutching Bundle, waiting for a while, and gazing at the soft pink countenance, the flattened hair before him.

'You're *done*!' remarked the taller girl suddenly, and whipped off his dust sheet. Reggie, trying to regain the hospitality room on his own, stumbled down several yellow-painted corridors, holding Bundle under one arm, and occasionally supporting himself with the other against the identical décor that met him at each turn, until he was finally rescued by Muriel appearing providentially at the far end of one such long corridor. She held Reggie to her most preciously, and made panicky noises about studio rehearsal, cues and camera positions, none of which made any sense to Reggie. He grinned at her amiably and said how much he was enjoying his visit to Television Centre; how much, moreover, Bundle was enjoying *her* visit. He was very insistent about that, but he failed to make the anxiety, which underlay Muriel's unhealthy smile, disappear.

They seemed to walk a very long way, up stairs, down and round, across a covered bridge, along a wide corridor, into a lift and out in some windowless basement area.

'I'm putting you in dressing-room fifty-three,' said Muriel. 'Stay there until someone comes to take you to the studio.'

342

Since he heard her lock the door from the outside and walk away, Reggie couldn't imagine what options were open to him. But he was quite happy. He talked to Bundle a bit, put her down on the divan and explored the appurtenances of dressing-room fifty-three. It had a shower, a lavatory of which he availed himself, a dusty water jug and glass, a wardrobe and a mirror excitingly surrounded by bulbs. Over a small loud-speaker placed in a quoin of the ceiling he heard a rehearsal under way, and paused for a long time puzzling over its musical nature. Nothing to do with *Newspeople* and Irwin Napier, he concluded.

'Well, Bundle,' announced Reggie, lying full length beside the dog, 'I'm blowed if I know quite what we're doing here, but this is meant to be our great moment.'

Bundle licked him gently on the nose, a small gesture of encouragement which was later to lead to Mrs Pike's remarking that the colour on her television needed some adjustment, since Mr Montis's nose seemed quite a different colour from the rest of his face.

For the moment, though, Mr Montis, wonderfully relaxed by Mrs Pike's driving-test pills, smiled at the ceiling of dressing-room fifty-three, and waited to be taken to the studio.

*   *   *

The cameramen rode their machines around the set like front-line vehicles, oblivious to everything but the commands in their earphones.

Reggie found he was not to sit in Irwin Napier's pool of light (Napier appeared to be wearing more hair than previously), but was instead escorted to another area of the set, and placed in a swivel chair with his back to the main action. He was told he could watch it on the monitor. On the monitor, Irwin Napier was adjusting his cravat, fiddling with pearl-grey lapels and trying to shove a button in one ear.

A Semitic youth with earphones and a clipboard came and crouched in front of Reggie.

'How do you do?' said Reggie.

'What?' asked the young man angrily.

'How do you do?' Reggie ventured again, but with more caution.

'Bloody dog?' queried the young man staring at Reggie ferociously.

Momentarily lost, Reggie began to explain Bundle's quiescent presence on his knee.

'I'll ask him,' interrupted the young man speaking into his lip-mike, and, freeing one ear from his director's gabble, he delivered a charming smile. 'Excuse me,' he said courteously, 'but is the dog likely to cause trouble?'

'Trouble?' Reggie stared uncomprehendingly.

'Will he bark, jump about, run away, piss on the furniture?' The young man faithfully repeated the string of words pouring into his ear.

'*She!* Good heavens, no. Bundle never gives the slightest kind of trouble,' Reggie beamed.

'Then what,' demanded the director from his gallery above the studio floor, 'in fuck's name have we got her here for?'

The floor manager refrained from interpretation.

'Good. That's your camera,' he pointed. 'Number Four.'

'Number Four,' repeated Reggie, mildly worried about the numbers he was now having to hold in his head. Obediently he stared into Number Four's darkly shining eye. 'Number Four.'

'Can we have a bit of level?'

'I beg your pardon?' Reggie was glaring rigidly at Number Four.

'Tell us how you travelled here.'

'Oh! Certainly!' Light dawned, and Reggie launched into an account of his journey, making a special point of the ticket collector's kindness and the rare pleasure of travelling first class. 'Only once before in my life, visiting an aunt in Mablethorpe . . .'

'Thank you! Fine!' The floor manager gave a thumbs-up sign and retreated backwards.

Reggie was surprised, but not amazed. Nothing could amaze him any more: not the battery of lights and cables, not the occasion, not even the thrill of seeing Irwin Napier in the flesh. A man who has, in the words of Oswald E. Harrison, witnessed the end of the world is not easily amazed. Anyway, Napier was much shorter and coarser-complexioned than Reggie had expected. A bit of a let-down. He was also plainly nervous, fidgeting, sipping weak whisky, consulting his notes, his watch, his shoelaces, and feeling, shiftily, for his hair. All this Reggie watched with detached interest on the monitor until he again became mindful of Number Four, and fixed it with a steely eye as if submitting it to an obedience test.

Archibald Clegg popped up on the screen, looking calm and elegant. Expertly, he adjusted his own microphone and smiled at someone off-picture.

'Run through titles!' shouted the floor manager, waving his arms, and Reggie heard the theme music, saw the *Newspeople* opening titles flash by, then watched them dissolve into a toothy Napier.

'Good evening!' said, or rather mouthed, Napier, for the sound of his voice did not travel far across the studio. He was describing what he had in store for his audience that night, for Archibald Clegg came up smiling, inclining his head gently, and Reggie, peering forward at the monitor (because he had suddenly thought it more flattering to himself to remove his glasses) was dismayed by the sight of his own screwed-up face on the screen. 'Good God!' he exclaimed.

'Dear God!' murmured the director simultaneously. 'Let's use that still we've got of him instead, as a teaser. It looks more ... *heroic.*'

'Four minutes to go!' called the floor manager. 'Relax everybody!'

Muriel rushed over to him.

'What's happening?' asked Reggie.

She explained that Irwin would come to him immediately after interviewing Clegg. 'Just a perfectly natural chat,' she said with the artless air of the professional deceiver. The lights in Reggie's area went down, leaving everything but Napier's chair in shadow.

'Good luck!' hissed Muriel and, bounding away over the cable, she was lost in darkness.

Excitement at last transmitted itself. The nearness of the

moment, Napier's cruel and solitary pond of light in the cavernous studio, the ill-suppressed agitation of figures flitting to and fro in search of Omar Sharif or Robert Redford, neither of whom seemed to have turned up yet ... all this was pleasantly enthralling.

Reggie patted Bundle and stared resolutely into the unblinking eye of Number Four. Not long!

The clock, the countdown, the theme music, the titles, Napier, reliably toothy. And Dorothy.

Reggie's stern confrontation with Number Four was diverted by the monitor.

Dorothy?

He looked over his shoulder at the lit set, then turned full round.

Dorothy!

Out of the darkness, luminous, glowing, caught in a bubble of light – yes, Dorothy!

Above, in the gallery, where Dorothy's voice was coming through, proud but hoarse, the director rubbed his hands with glee. 'A scoop!' he squealed. Then, into his mike, 'If she's good, Irwin, let it run. Leave the timing to me. Bit of the old aggro, boyo!'

Reggie held Bundle to his chest and knelt back to front in his swivel chair. He strained to hear what his wife was saying.

A ghost dwelt at her throat. Ghosts silvered her skin and dragged at it. Only her hair, a more fiery gold than Reggie recalled, sprang and sparkled with wonderful, undiminished energy.

*   *   *

Dorothy, oh my Dorothy, he cries inwardly, staring at the sharp white cheekbone snapping out of the burning hair.

How thin, how stately she appears in her long black robes.

*   *   *

Reggie craned to see and hear, his black plastic chair rocking dangerously on its swivel. Napier's face was the more fully exposed. A nasty smile adorned it.

346

'Very well,' Napier was saying, 'if you won't reveal your method we'll have to accept your story on trust, won't we? We'll even go so far as to suppose you are a dying woman, though you could be dying of any one of a hundred causes. But then we are all, in a manner of speaking, dying.'

Dorothy acknowledged the statement with dignity.

'Let us then examine the cause for which you are,' Napier's voice swerved sneeringly, 'prepared to die. What on earth persuades you it merits such a gesture?'

Dorothy leaned towards Napier a little, her neck a slender white stem. 'Do you have any children of your own?' she croaked.

'I don't see . . .'

'*Do* you?'

'As it happens, no, but . . .'

'Then of course, silly boy, you don't feel much responsibility towards coming generations.' She sat upright again as if the movement involved effort.

'Beside the point. Future generations won't thank you for starving them of energy,' Napier was countering huffily as he consulted his notes. He changed tack. 'A leading industrialist, if I may quote him, says the world is beset with dangers – that radiation is no greater, no more likely a risk than being bitten by a venomous snake.'

Oh serpent! Oh uraeus of Ancient Egypt! Oh Tamino!

Reggie clutched at his chair to steady himself and strove to catch the cracking tones of his wife.

'I find that a curious analogy,' she was saying.

Indeed, indeed.

'If you can die of a venomous bite, it seems somewhat pointless – though disarming, I grant – to say that radiation represents no greater risk. All risks that have human death as their outcome seem to me equal in seriousness. Comparisons of your sort only became valid when you discuss the relative incidence of such risks. I daresay I should be extremely alarmed if the country were overrun by venomous snakes.' She coughed but composed herself, her voice emanating more strongly. 'They become valid only when you're comparing the reasons for the high incidence of these risks. If venomous snakes were suddenly to overbreed in large numbers, that would be one thing: disturbing, but a natural accident which could, I daresay, be controlled and contained. If they were to be let loose in large numbers by irresponsible human decision, that is quite another question, although I venture to think that, faced by a venomous snake ...'

'Buh!' Napier was looking out of sorts.

'My chances of defending myself against it would be somewhat greater than those of saving myself from accidental radiation. I should feel on more equal terms with my aggressor. Furthermore,' Dorothy went on, her hoarse whisper rising and demolishing Napier's restraining gesture, conducted just below camera level. 'Furthermore, a snake is perfectly visible to the naked eye. Not to mention the fact that your basic analogy is weakened by the existence of known antidotes to venom, whereas plutonium, a man-made substance, is without any such prophylactic. I would also like to make it perfectly clear that the snake ...'

'Dear lady, I doubt whether there are many herpetologists in our audience, interesting as all this is. Can we just drop snakes for a moment?' Napier was wilting.

Dorothy, reflected her husband admiringly (now that somebody else was victim of it), had lost none of her style.

'The analogy,' she was saying, 'is yours, not mine.'

'Let us turn to practicalities.'

'By all means.' Dorothy folded her hands on her lap. On the black and white monitor they lay as slackly as dead birds.

Bundle whined faintly when Reggie's weight pressed her against the chair.

'Let us bear in mind that we, in the rich world, have a special responsibility,' Napier enunciated pompously, 'towards the less well-off than ourselves. How are we ever to raise the standard of living endured by two-thirds of the world's population if we abandon the nuclear option and decline as an industrial force?'

'That was very emotively phrased,' remarked Dorothy.

'Whatever you think of my phrasing, dear lady ...'

'Oh, there's a question buried there all right,' conceded Dorothy, 'but its prose garment should alert everyone to the speciousness of it. Two things. First, you've got to believe in fairies if you're to believe that an increasingly industrial world is going to find an increasing amount of raw material for manufacture, and secondly, if you *do* believe in fairies – or if we're to accept that great new reserves *will* be found – then all you're doing is putting forward a pious case for *retaining* our position as a dominant and wealthy nation. It's the argument well-to-do socialists use, I find: they feel more comfortable with it. Poorer countries could do much better if we made do with much less; but that's politically unacceptable.'

'And naïve?' Irwin Napier gave a fanged smile.

'If naïveté is to be equated with honesty or even, as it commonly is, morality, yes, OK, it's naïve.'

Thrown by the frank brevity of her answer, Napier was forced to glance down at his questions while trying to appear not to. Dorothy seized the opportunity to reflect that it was better to fail in striving for what was right than to succeed in doing wrong. Napier indulged in an apparently thoughtful examination of his fingernails.

Reggie's heart soared blithely.

Up in the gallery, the director was hooting with pleasure at Napier's discomfiture, being, as men with his obligation to entertain often are, a creature of shifting loyalties.

'Shall we abandon pious moralities?' Napier recovered the ball and returned it. 'Let's look at the matter in the cold light of self-interest. At the turpitudinous,' Napier had long sought an opportunity of using this word, and apprehension ineptly produced it, 'matter of our weakness as a competitive nation, of our vulnerability to others if we refuse the nuclear option.'

Archibald Clegg, over the other side of the studio from Reggie, quietly blunted a sneeze against his fist. In the darkness, Reggie gave him a cheering wheel of his arm.

The goddess lives!

'Certainly there will be many sacrifices,' the divine creature was saying, her hair seeming to cast heat on Napier's flushed countenance, 'but if one of the perils you refer to is the particoloured peril – the yellow, the red, whatever shade your fancy dictates – then, my dear Mr Napier, just imagine how the communist invader would be disarmed by the true spectacle of socialism confronting him. How dismayed! How bewildered!'

'I don't think,' responded the dear Mr Napier, who didn't like his own form of diminishing address being turned on him, 'that the communist invader comes on foot.'

Dorothy's sense of humour, never marked, did not impede her now. She drove straight through the nationally renowned screen of sarcasm. Napier resorted to the number two trick of embattled interviewers by turning to his camera and raising one eyebrow at the invisible millions, thus engaging them in a conspiracy to deride. Dorothy was describing the idyllic co-operative-based socialism available to the post-industrial age. Much of it, delivered in a hoarse, fierce, but increasingly faint whisper, escaped Reggie. Spurred on by the insufferable Napier, however, he was now firmly on Dorothy's side.

What one is, what one does, that matters!

Her bones were like a truth laid bare.

Bundle barked.

'Sh-sh!' Reggie tried to trap the little dog's jaws together. She struggled at this unwonted behaviour.

'What was that?' queried the director. But the sound was too faint to dwell on.

Dorothy was putting the case for alternative, self-renewing energies.

'We're over-running wildly on this interview now,' commented the production assistant, consulting her stop watch. 'Shall I give him the wind up?'

'I'd rather drop the last item,' replied her boss.

Bundle wriggled free and barked again.

The nations saw Napier's eyes shift unhappily, but remained ignorant of the real reason. It assumed, as one person, that he was being defeated by his interviewee. The spectacle had a definite piquancy.

Dorothy, deep in solar energy, was too absorbed to notice the interruption.

Reggie was dazzled by the nimbus about her head.

ArinnaInannaAstarteIshtar!

He rolled on the floor, his arms locked around Bundle, whose bandages were unwinding.

Dorothy compared renewable energies, their small scale of distribution and administration, the simplicity of their technology, with the monolithic mysteries of the threatened alternative. Her husband bowled along the floor, then lay panting, staring upwards at the huge lamps.

*   *   *

Yes, man the forger, the maker, the smith, the smelter – the usurper of the sun – now reaches after a yet greater means of power.

The sun, abandoned, rolls, waste, about the sky: lays waste.

But now (and Reggie hugs Bundle with joy as he sees), the newly emergent goddess retrieves her orb!

Oh, source of life!

*   *   *

Bundle sprang from his arms.

'Is something the matter?' inquired Dorothy, as Irwin Napier was seen to leap on his seat, tucking his feet beneath his haunches and gibbering. At the age of five, Irwin Napier had been bitten by a sealyham and had never forgotten it.

'Good lord!' said Dorothy. 'A dog! It has been calculated that there is sufficient windpower available around the coast of the British Isles ... Good Lord!' she said again, as a figure, dragged at the end of a length of crêpe bandage, appeared at her feet. 'Reggie! What are you doing here? This,' she continued, addressing Irwin Napier, who babbled like a gibbon, 'is my husband, Reginald Montis. Oh!' She clapped her hand to her mouth as she released her surname to the Press.

'Jesus!' breathed the production assistant and covered her head with her arms.

'Keep running, Camera Two!' ordered the director tersely. Then, into Napier's earpiece, 'Get your bum back on that chair and effect the introductions, sunshine!'

Irwin Napier gulped and tenderly checked his hairpiece.

'Well, well, well,' he gurgled. 'Let me just explain this fun scene to all of you out there watching ... Would you mind picking your dog up, sir, so the viewers can see him?'

'Get hold of that dog, Reggie, and sit down here.' Dorothy patted the free seat between Napier and herself.

'This,' said Napier, his pupils like pinpricks as he subsided back into his own chair, 'is our hero of the week. *Husband* ... of our heroine.' He hoped this was right. If it was, even he could see through his perturbation that the story improved by the minute. Somewhat disjointedly, he explained the circumstances of Reggie's heroism. Camera Two showed Reggie unwinding a bandage from his neck and Dorothy kissing him. 'How wonderful of you to come,' she said warmly, paying no attention to Napier's fractured exegesis. 'I didn't realize it was a "This Is Your Life" sort of show. Isn't it cosy, Reggie?'

It was at this point that Mrs Pike was driven to comment on the discoloration of Reggie's nose. Phoebe was asked to adjust the set, but the child seemed to have left her body, and remained immobile on the pouffe.

*   *   *

'What view,' asked Napier, recovering what he could of the nightmarish situation in which he found himself, 'do you take of your wife's activities?'

Reggie freed himself finally of his wrappings and addressed Napier urgently. 'You should heed her warnings,' he confided. 'She's describing the new temple, the new priestly elect, the new cabalistic language, the new and deadly radiance, the power too great to approach, the new inhuman saviour of the future, the ultimate strength.'

He seemed to have no control of the list gushing out of him.

Napier intervened. 'Aren't you disturbed by the dramatic step she's taken?'

'... the male essence,' concluded Reggie. 'What?' he exclaimed, disconcerted by his own prolixity. Bundle chewed his ear for comfort.

'Don't answer him on that aspect,' ordered Dorothy. Reggie

looked from one to the other at a loss. He felt the turmoil of words rise again in his chest like an involuntary vomit. 'Sacrifice is necessary,' he blurted out, and a catalogue of sacrifices began to spout from him. A glowing smile was beginning to spread over Napier's face. This fellow was repairing all the damage, handsomely.

'Sacrifice of self!' uttered the dybbuk at Reggie's chest.

'And that's all we have time for, folks!'

Irwin Napier had turned away and was addressing Camera One. In the gallery, where the nine other cameras each contained an image different from that received by the nation, the director screwed his eyes up quizzically over the picture relayed by Camera Two. 'That man's a bloody ventriloquist!' he murmured in amazement. 'Or at least . . . it damn well *looked* as if the dog was speaking.'

*　　*　　*

Back in the hospitality room, Napier was being congratulated on conducting a great show. His self-esteem refurbished, he shone at the centre of an adulatory ring. Outside it, Archibald Clegg was angrily demanding top billing on tomorrow's programme, and had to be prevented from assaulting Reggie, who downed a pint glass of white wine while Dorothy threw a dark, hooded length of silk around her head and shoulders.

'I do appreciate,' she murmured in her ghostly voice, 'your coming here.' The pressure of her hand on his arm was very light. Lilac shadows made her eyes enormous.

'Dorothy!' he seized her but she moved quickly away towards the door.

'I must go,' she insisted. 'I have to keep on the move.' She opened the door of the crowded room by reaching behind her back for the handle. 'Gilbert's waiting outside to help me make a quick getaway.'

But immediately outside the door, Stephanie and Anna awaited her.

'Your fee!' Muriel lurched after Dorothy, effectively driving Reggie out into the corridor with the three women.

'My husband will give you Mrs Pike's address.' Dorothy

began to move away, fingertips pressed to her lips. The eyes that she fixed on Reggie were huge with tenderness.

So profoundly startled was he by the sight of the three women together that Reggie was slow to move. He cried out after his wife, and began to run.

'No!' Dorothy's draped arm was upraised. Her palm was curved outward like that of a Thai dancer. 'No! You have done a most important thing, coming here. But you must go home. You will be needed.'

'*You* need me now!'

'You *will* be needed.' She began to recede along the corridor, flanked by the girls.

'Will you let me know? Will you call me?' He was desperate. But she was adamant.

He looked into the retreating faces of each of the women, Dorothy's fire and milk, Stephanie's pale gold, Anna's stern, dark gentleness . . . They regarded him firmly but lovingly.

Be silent!

Be patient!

Be steadfast!

They withdrew and left him leaning against the wall, still clasping both Bundle and an emptied pint mug to his side.

Where the women had stood a pale fire glimmered, then faded.

Part Five

LUGHNASA

23

The call came, but not immediately.

More immediate – far more so than the telegrams, the letters in green ink, furiously cross-referenced, the missives from organizations requesting his membership, his leadership even – more immediate than all these messages that filled the narrow hall of Sunnybank was the note Mrs Pike had jotted down when Garsington rang.

Discerning the look of alarm on Reggie's face, she comforted him. 'You mustn't worry yourself,' she said. 'He was very nice. Said you needed a rest after a hard term. And anyway, there's only a few more days of it to go.'

And she bore Reggie off for a restorative gin fizz, made with fresh lemons. 'Bundle looked so sweet on the television!' she cried as she pressed an ice cube to Reggie's forehead.

*   *   *

Wearing a pair of dark glasses and an old fishing cap of Edmund's, Reggie walked down the glaring, paved street to the camping suppliers, and purchased everything a solitary camper could need.

Later that afternoon the consignment was delivered to the East Tidmouth entrance of the Turtledown ranges where, reloaded on to an Army jeep, it was driven as close to the sea-facing fort as the obliging corporal could manage.

With Bundle at his heels ('You'll be glad of the company,' Mrs Pike had insisted, thrusting the dog and all her medicaments into his arms), Reggie set up his orange tent, unrolled his sleeping-bag, unpacked his books and notes and then, undoing the padlock of the little tool-shed which the Army had thoughtfully erected earlier that summer, he placed his precious water-containers inside, and removed his trowel and wire brush.

He worked without a shirt. The breeze was pleasant on his sunburnt back. The earth was dry and unyielding, but Reggie worked at it grimly, without a care for what Norman Herrington might say when he and his team arrived in a week's time at the beginning of August. The race was on. Reggie knew he needed more material evidence as scaffold.

All day, every day, he worked, crouched beneath the brassy sun. Rather than wash, he swam in the cold, revivifying waters of the cove. He stopped shaving.

Around him the dead grasses and thistles stood yellow and still erect. The sea sang quietly. The gulls mewed. He became accustomed to the blue, twilit appearance of warriors and their menfolk in the cove. One night, they lit a fire on the beach and their bodies rose phosphorescent from the waters.

On other nights, after the bats had ceased their wheeling, he lay beneath stars so bright, so sharp that they seemed to hurt the sky they pierced. His mind played over the progression of peoples who had come to the logic of the male godhead.

From the Near East, from the steppes to the north of it, come the barbarians: the Amorites, the Kassites, the Hurrians, the Armenian peoples of Kizwadana who hold the secret of iron, a secret stolen and nursed by the Aryans of Mitanni, stolen in turn by the Hittites.

Onward the Hittites, on towards Mesopotamia, on and on through that fertile crescent, on towards the dryer lands until they too meet their defeat in the resistant faces of the Mediterranean Sea Peoples, a tiny enclave clustered in Syria, all that remains of these mighty charioteers. And there – oh, blending of nations and notions – there they come alongside of the Israelites who have entered Canaan from Egypt a mere twelve hundred years before the birth of Christ, but already seep northwards bearing their totem with them. The single male.

And now, look northward a little again. Here, in swallowing order, march the matched ranks of the Romans, overlords of Jerusalem. And now, sailing towards the shoreline of Britain where they find the same supple, smeltable legacy of belief long arrived from the northern barbarians of Europe, the Scythians, the charioteers of Galatia, the Gauls, the Celts ... How harmoniously the circle is met! How easily the slain warrior god is incorporated, the inscriptions altered!

*   *   *

Reggie laughs beneath the stars. He laughs to think that he, in his lifetime, believed he had witnessed belief's demise. Believed that man stood alone, naked, foolhardy and brave, sole determiner of his own freedom.

There is no freedom! The comedy is to imagine there must be. Belief in it constitutes the ultimate paradox, since commitment to freedom is a joking negation. Belief is blood to the human being. It is blood and bread, however construed.

*   *   *

And high above the chrysolite sea his thoughts slip inevitably towards bold Dorothy, the emblem of unashamed faith in an era when the Don't Knows have a statistical influence. A beacon in the murk of pragmatism.

And does she call, this clarion creature?

His hearing is pitched above the nocturnal rustle, above the ever-busy sea ... Not yet. But she makes him ponder his costive existence. His ungiving. His small, dry nut of self.

But, he cries aloud, more baying and dog-like beneath the moon than the animal curled beside him, but even the nut is fruitful, the forerunner of blossom and branch.

*   *   *

For nearly a week he scratched at the earth. And reluctantly the dried subsoil ceded its little histories. A bead of faience; a bead of Baltic amber. How wide the world has always been! And though ancient cosmogonies have given way to intergalactic voyage, that reaching after stars has always remained poignantly unchanged.

Beneath his fingers the stubborn earth breaks away. Beneath the stars he sheds his crust. Love and madness, two of life's residual mysteries, are very close. They cannot be expressed mathematically.

High on the yellow configurations of downland, above the

blazing cliffs and olivine sea, Reggie uncovers the golden lunula, precursor of the Celtic torc. Art is the best means we have of honouring the explicable.

Undimmed by the millennia, the gold gleams, a defeat for the alchemists.

It is as clear a signal to go as any more officious call from Dorothy.

Seized with gladness and love, Reggie packed his finds, his tent, his primus stove, stored what he had to, carried the rest, and trudged back across the dying downland. Here and there a solitary blue wild-flowering plant survives.

* * *

Out of love, in his absence, Bella Pike had stuck together the fragments of Samian and other ware that had lain in their trays all year. By means of imaginative reconstruction, she had formed two unshapely pots which stood on the table in his airless sitting-room. Reggie could, at first, have wept. But he did not.

He understands the innocent goodness that lies behind this desecration, and his heart softens.

* * *

The house was empty that Wednesday afternoon, it being the day of Bella Pike's appointment under Piero's flattering hands.

Reggie shaved off his stubble, ignored the enormous post waiting for him and, calling Bundle to heel, walked off down Chandler Street. He had it in mind to visit the music shop in Fossil Lane and buy a brand-new recording of Karl Böhm's *Magic Flute* for Dorothy.

Further down Fossil Lane, emerging from the bookshop, Father Starkey paused as he saw his friend disappear inside the record store. He hesitated for some time. Academic probity obliged him at some juncture to refer Reggie to J. G. MacQueen's study, *The Hittites and their Contemporaries in Asia Minor*. Probably the leading authority on this little-known civilization, MacQueen had several strong points to make. He dismissed 'mistaken ideas' that the Hittites owed their dominance to the secret of iron working; that they formed an Indo-

European-speaking aristocracy; that they emerged from barbarianism. Most awkwardly, he insisted that any temporary prominence given to sky and storm gods was short-lived. The mother-goddess regained supremacy. At the last stronghold of the neo-Hittites, the great temple was dedicated to the goddess Kubaba, Queen of Carcemish.

The priest wavered in the narrow street. The sun hammered on the cobbles. Had Reggie come out of the record shop at that moment, the priest might have walked towards him. But Reggie did not emerge and Father Starkey went instead towards the harbour. It didn't matter.

He had seen his friend's balloon-eyed intervention on television, listened to the lugubrious staffroom diagnosis the following day. But he had held his peace. Something important had been resolved. MacQueen could wait.

Stopping only to buy himself a lemon ice-cream, Ned Starkey sauntered beyond the brine and vinegar scents of the shellfish stall, and proceeded to the beach, where he enjoyed a solitary paddle.

Carrying under one arm a beautiful and carefully wrapped new box containing *Die Zauberflöte*, Bundle tugging adventurously at the other arm, Reggie threaded his way through holidaymakers happily littering the narrow pavements.

Without warning, he felt the most tremendous pull on his right arm as Bundle attempted to dash across the busy road. In that moment Reggie knew he could easily have released his hold on the lead but, perversely, he hung on.

Reggie flew through the air. *Die Zauberflöte* flew too. He was conscious immediately of two things – of a sweet yielding in the bowel and an impact which it was inconceivable the human body should withstand. But he had withstood it, for he found himself on the far pavement looking up at Phoebe.

She reared above him, tall and golden, her hair a flying cape that blew about her waist. Her flower mouth was shaped to form a fond, sad smile. Reggie, attempting to respond in like manner, found he could not. So he transmitted a sense of smiling and saw she understood.

*   *   *

Women fainted on the scorching bloodstained pavement, as they attempted to cover their eyes from the ghastly sight.

Bella Pike, who had been driving from His 'n' Hers Hair Fashions sat paralysed behind the wheel, staring at the familiar, though headless, body trapped between her bonnet and the rear door of a yoghurt lorry in front.

She seemed to sit a long time, but it could not have been long, for helping hands were already reaching towards her as she sprang from the car. Beating them back like staves, screaming that she must get to a phone, she ran into the lobby of the Goat and Compass and dialled hurriedly.

'Ezra?' she said urgently, when the pips stopped. 'Ezra, contact Eddie.' Then she replaced the receiver and dialled 999.

*　　　*　　　*

The ambulance took a long time negotiating the narrow streets densely packed with trippers' cars.

*　　　*　　　*

No unauthorized persons allowed, it said on the door, but Eddie Timmins who had, with Ezra's help, been brought on shift early, was chief mortician at Casterwich coroner's court and pushed through the door unhesitatingly. He struggled into his white coat and looked gloomily at his watch. With the temperatures outside in the eighties, there wasn't a moment to lose. He polished his spectacles and asked Ezra if he'd like a cup of tea while they waited.

He fetched the milk from the big fridge where two Asian gentlemen lay at peace, their still and sallow faces uncovered by sheets.

'Illegal immigrants,' mused Eddie. 'Shame really, having made it this far.' And he closed the heavy door, adding that he'd better remove the crosses from the chapel of rest on their account.

While he did that, Ezra boiled the kettle and poured the water into the teapot. 'Coolest place in Casterwich, this,' he remarked when Eddie returned. He'd known Eddie from years back when his friend had been the best butcher in town. Eddie took a great pride in his newer profession. The slabs sparkled in the dissecting room. His corpses always looked tranquil.

He glanced again at his watch. 'They decompose quicker at this time of year,' he observed.

'Aha!' Ezra heard what he thought was the ambulance, and went over to the window to check. 'Here they come!'

Reggie's decapitated state didn't trouble Eddie, who told Ezra, before his friend left to be outside the station in readiness for the 17.00 hours from Paddington, that he'd make a nice job of the gentleman.

'The pathologist's on his way,' he told the ambulance-men as they trooped into the kitchen for a cup of tea, 'so I'll just get on and slit the customer's waistcoat.' And quietly, in the peace of the dissecting room, the little mortician set about the laying open of Reggie.

But his first task was to drill a circle round the separated skull, quarter it and peel back the sections. Lifting out the brain, he dipped into the cavity with a pair of tweezers and extracted the precious pituitary, the nutty kernel of Reggie. He popped the yellowish bud into a jar of similar buds, sealed the top and marked it ready for despatch. Then, meticulously cleaning up as he went, he opened the remainder of Reggie from chest to groin and had tenderly lifted out the individual organs by the time the pathologist arrived.

The examination took up a mere fifteen minutes. 'I'll leave you to your needlework then, Eddie.' Dr Hooper removed his rubber gloves and stood over the sink, measuring the amount of water that was now permitted.

'He'll look a picture when they come to identify him,' promised Eddie, and he threaded his twine.

All efforts to contact Dorothy for the identification procedure failed as Dorothy, on the very afternoon Reggie found himself sliced between Mrs Pike's bonnet and the yoghurt lorry, was gently tipped from a second-floor window into the basement area below by a man who had shown a close interest in her movements over the past two months. For this reason Anna and Antonia rarely let the sick woman out of their sight, but on that Wednesday, at the moment of the accident's occurrence, Antonia was having a non-specific venereal complaint examined at the hospital where she had probably contracted it and Anna had popped swiftly down the road to the delicatessen, before it closed, for two cartons of cole slaw and a half-pound piece of knackwurst. Baby Basil, lying in his Moses basket, was the sole witness to the incident, and he was found sucking Dorothy's pendant ankh, its broken chain dangling between his podgy fingers.

Eddie's counterpart in Marylebone found a luggage-label round the neck of the deceased demanding that the bearer's pituitary be used in treatment to counteract pituitary dwarfism. There were other features of interest to the resident pathologist, most notably, the severely reduced state of lungs and trachea, damage not consistent with a fall of thirty feet.

*　　　*　　　*

Thus it was that Dis Pater, otherwise known as Teutates the warrior god, alias Dagda, the good god, was propitiated and his orb returned to its rightful possessor.

Thus it was that slowly, over a period of years, Phoebe grew as tall and straight and golden as the corn that flourished in the fields.

The seasons, benignly restored to their proper balance, brought forth great yields of maize, oats, wheat and barley. The river flowed once more through Maidenwell and the old Wellspring ceremony was once again conducted there in its vernacular form, the coarser parodies forgotten. The beasts thrived on their generous pasture and the sun was reconsecrated by the northern barbarians who had once dreamt of constructing tall white temples to Samholdanach, descendant of Lugh, which, being translated, means polytechnician, smith and sorcerer.

As Phoebe grew tall and walked abroad, the folly of this enterprise was so clearly seen, that the barbarians laughed aloud to think they had ever entertained such follies in their minds. Those chief among the perpetrators of the nuclear dream were discredited as false priests, and bound over to dig their gardens in perpetuity.

The beauty of Phoebe Orlebar astounded all who saw her,

not least, Reggie and Dorothy Montis, happily reunited in the Otherworld.

'No, no, no,' explained Dorothy, once Reggie had grasped that it was not she, but Phoebe, who was the resurrected goddess. 'I was just an unwitting agent in the whole business. You mustn't overrate my contribution.'

But this is to hasten some way forward in the story and there are more immediate matters to attend to.

*   *   *

It would be impossible to overrate Dorothy's contribution, despite the alien modesty she acquired in the afterlife for – at the instigation of Antonia and Anna – there was an inquiry into her death that proved to be of signal importance in altering the public to the madness of their leaders.

The dedicated efforts of the two girls were given active support by Stephanie and Gilbert – after their marriage when they could afford to relax their consuming interest in one another just a little.

The ceremony was attended by the Orlebars, who enjoyed themselves tremendously, and by Bella Pike who couldn't help but feel a certain sadness. She left early – not just because of her tears and not because she had to see to Bundle who had, inexplicably, vanished after the accident – but to prepare an evening meal for Mr Herrington.

Though not a man for fantasy, Norman Herrington, from the heights of Turtledown, saw – as Reggie had seen before him – distant figures which made him pause and rub his eyes in disbelief. Not long afterwards, however, the BBC's living archaeology experiment, which had been conducted in utmost secrecy under the tangled trees of Maidenwell, came to an end and the producer went home to his chafing, not entirely sweet-tempered wife. All the same, a certain shift had taken place in Norman Herrington's thinking and when, with Father Starkey's help, he compiled a paper on the Turtledown Dig, he very readily made formal acknowledgement to the late Reginald Montis for his work in this field.

*   *   *

Reggie of course is pleased. He is happy in his new realm. Sometimes he likes despatching Bundle to tease the new and unimaginative occupant of his rooms at Sunnybank. But what he most savours is the opportunity he knows will, in the eternal dimension, arise of chatting to Will and Wolfgang and hearing from their own invisible lips why both, at the end of their lives, felt compelled to write of magic.

THE WORLD'S GREATEST NOVELISTS
NOW AVAILABLE IN GRANADA PAPERBACKS

Iris Murdoch

A Word Child	£1.25 ☐
The Unicorn	£1.00 ☐
An Unofficial Rose	£1.25 ☐
The Bell	£1.25 ☐
The Flight From the Enchanter	£1.25 ☐
The Nice and the Good	£1.25 ☐
Bruno's Dream	£1.25 ☐
The Red and the Green	£1.25 ☐
A Severed Head	£1.25 ☐
The Time of the Angels	95p ☐
Henry & Cato	£1.25 ☐

Doris Lessing

The Golden Notebook	£1.95 ☐
The Black Madonna	95p ☐
Winter in July	£1.25 ☐

All these books are available at your local bookshop or newsagent, or can be ordered direct from the publisher. Just tick the titles you want and fill in the form below.

Name ....

Address..

....

Write to Granada Cash Sales, PO Box 11, Falmouth, Cornwall TR10 9EN.

Please enclose remittance to the value of the cover price plus:

UK: 30p for the first book, 15p for the second book plus 12p per copy for each additional book ordered to a maximum charge of £1.29.

BFPO and EIRE: 30p for the first book, 15p for the second book plus 12p per copy for the next 7 books, thereafter 6p per book.

OVERSEAS: 50p for the first book and 15p for each additional book.

Granada Publishing reserve the right to show new retail prices on covers. which may differ from those previously advertised in the text or elsewhere,